# Kensie's Treasures
## by J.M. Schneider

# Kensie's Treasures

J.M. Schneider

Published by J.M. Schneider, 2024.

# Acknowledgements

I started this book on a cruise I wasn't sure I wanted to go on, in a place I wasn't sure I wanted to go – the Caribbean. Yes, I can see the double takes and eye rolls about that statement from here, but I'm neither a fan of crowds nor tropical heat. And the ship was crowded – people everywhere, especially on the first day. And the islands were hot – like the inside of a furnace kind of hot. So things started off... questionably.

I did manage to have fun, and must admit the completely different vibe down there affected me. Working in Manhattan, I am accustomed to going a thousand miles an hour, and when you see the locals just kind of ambling along, you have to smile. Maybe it's the almost unnaturally blue water. Being familiar with the shore in the mid Atlantic states of Delaware and southern New Jersey, I grew up with salt water that was a dark greenish blue that you couldn't really see through very well. But down in the islands, 15 feet of water hides almost nothing. It's like you get a new dimension of visibility; instead of seeing just the surface of the water, you look through it and it's almost like a second landscape. There's so much more to entertain the eye. That's what led me to the premise of this book – the fascination of discovering a different world that's been there all along.

I wrote almost all of this manuscript during the cursed year of 2020. It was (and still is) a terrible time for a lot of people, and I do not wish to minimize anyone's suffering, but being forced to work from home was a tremendous boon. Instead of commuting four hours a day several days a week, at the end of my work day I simply closed one laptop and opened another. That allowed me to get through the bulk of *Kensie's Treasures* in about five months, which is fairly quick for me. I hope that, when you read it, some of you are able to escape your troubles for a few hours.

But no matter what inspired me to write, there are people that I must recognize for their assistance. These people help me in ways both tangible and intangible, and I probably don't thank them nearly enough.

My wife Vicki-Lynn continues to offer unwavering support and an almost irrational belief that my writing will bring me the success and happiness that I wish for. She is wise enough to know that doesn't necessarily mean I have to make a million dollars doing it; of course, she would love that (and so would I) but she encourages me to keep plugging away regardless of how many books I might sell. I have to admit, sometimes I ask her leading questions to get her to express once more how I'm going to get to where I want to go. I need the inspiration, and she provides it – every time I need it.

I have to thank Gary Cargen, who taught me a great deal about SCUBA diving. Not only do I know next to nothing about the activity, I couldn't even try it out myself because I'm petrified of being underwater and breathing through a little regulator – it gives me the willies to even think about it.

Gary is a man to envy. I know him through my father when they both worked for a very large corporation, and I recall his easygoing disposition, one that you would expect of a man who always had a sailboat and loved being at sea. Many years ago, he took our whole family out for some sailing in the bay, which was a great time, even though my mother nearly got killed by a swinging boom because she didn't know what a shout of "hard-a-lee" meant. Gary's retired now, and he sails pretty much up and down the western side of the Atlantic Ocean and into the Caribbean Sea (and probably other places). I'm jealous.

Gary was gracious enough to accept my expansive list of questions and answer every single one in extreme detail while on one of his many voyages between paradisiacal locations. Even better, he reviewed this book after I finished my first draft and pointed out where I'd misunderstood his information or just made boneheaded mistakes. I think that, for any fiction book to be any good, the factual details have to be spot on, and he helped me a great deal in that aspect. I am grateful for that, and I know my father would be as well. He'd be yelling at both of us for some reason no matter what, but he would appreciate the help.

I must also give thanks to Clive Gale, an underwater explosives expert in England. Like most writers, when I run into a scene that requires technical details that I don't know, I hit the internet and start searching. I came across a company called Alford Technologies, Ltd. that dealt with explosives of all kinds, so I sent an email basically begging for help.

Clive, a former Navy Clearance Diver with over 30 years of experience in underwater explosive ordinance disposal and demolition, responded very quickly despite not knowing me at all. He asked questions that he had to have answered before he could give me advice. Once he understood, he spent a great deal of time and gave me a ton of great information about what would and wouldn't work in the scenario I had envisioned. He politely told me that the way I wrote the scene was not realistic, and he recommended what he would do in similar circumstances, causing me to rework the section and make it much better. I can't imagine that most of my readers are going to have a need to learn about explosives, but if you do, Clive is your man. Thank you for your great help, Clive.

As usual, my awesome beta readers are a huge help. It would be difficult to mention everyone who contributed information about how to improve a section or a plot twist or a character. I don't always take their advice, but I often do, and whether I make a change based on your input or not, they should be aware of just how much I appreciate them investing so much time and focus in an effort to help me publish the best possible book.

Kathy Hummel is always happy to get my manuscript and go through it. Her superpower seems to be the uncanny ability to call bullshit – that this character wouldn't do this, that there's no way things could work out this way, why would he say this instead of that, etc. I almost always shake my head and wonder what the hell I was thinking when I wrote that, and then fix it. While reviewing this book, she sent me an email about halfway through, telling me how much she was enjoying it and how it seemed to flow better than my earlier books. I'll tell you, those kinds of emails make my day, because I'm sure that Kathy would tell me if the book felt labored or boring. Thanks so much for the honest and accurate assessment.

My sister in law Carrie Gerardi is another one who is excited to get the first draft of my books. She is skilled at calling out words and phrases that read awkwardly, and I love when she circles passages and adds notes that are followed by two or three large question marks – essentially, "Are you *sure* you want to phrase this part this way???" Sometimes she even calls to talk to my wife (her sister), and if I walk nearby, my wife hands me the phone, at which time Carrie will mention the latest thing she found. Keep it up, Carrie – it's greatly appreciated.

Dawn Barclay is a fellow writer (and a damn good one at that – I really enjoy her books) and by far my most valuable source of the craft of writing. She is exceptional at noting the little filler words and phrases that I am guilty of including all the time, and she offers new ways to organize sentences or paragraphs so they work better. Once I look at even a small part of her reviews, I start to see all the places where I just couldn't help myself and added a couple of unnecessary words. By the time I get through her suggestions, my book is probably lighter by a thousand words. Since I'm a fan of brevity in my writing, such edits are invaluable, which makes Dawn invaluable as well. I cannot thank her enough.

Special note to all my beta readers: Thank you for pointing out my excessive use of hyphenation in the beginning of the book. I'm not sure why I did it, and when I looked at the many, many places where I screwed this up, I figured I must have taken leave of my senses.

I also must call out some last minute translation help. I kind of foolishly assumed that Google Translate would take the English name I came up with for an important item in the book and turn it into perfect French. Not so much. After discovering that this computerized method was, shall we say, easy to misinterpret, I called out for help from humans who actually spoke French.

I had two people respond. Kathleen Peterson, a French teacher who works with my sister and brother in law, took my original idea and really expanded it. Her thoughts opened up a whole new set of options for me, acting as the seed of the new idea. Then a friend of my cousin's – Muriel Perret – put the finishing touch on the phrase that you will read in this book. The phrase is an improvement on my original idea, translation issues notwithstanding. Both of you were extremely helpful on very short notice, and your efforts improved a key component of this story. *Merci beaucoup.*

So, to everyone else, thanks for picking up *Kensie's Treasures.* I hope it entertains you for a few hours, and I hope to keep writing more and better books in the future.

# Prologue

**Eastern Caribbean Sea, October 1806**

The towering piles of water, topped by frothy foam that reminded him of snow capped mountains, had an impressive beauty challenged only by their sheer force. He could not look at them without feeling a profound sense of awe at such a display of nature.

But he might just meet his maker sailing through them.

Captain Cyrus Buckwell shook the salt water from his eyes and squinted into the raging miasma of spray and rain driven by the 120 mile per hour storm howling around his ship, looking for the next massive wave that threatened him and his crew's safety. Neither he nor the *Aberaeron Fortune* had experienced seas this malevolent, and both had seen a lot. When he dove into the trough between the waves, the water towered as high as his mainmast, and *Fortune* was having trouble getting her bow up and over each crest, taking solid water on her highest decks. The last one had broken the tip of the pulpit right off, sending the jib topsail flapping wildly, and each time the hull crashed down into the valley between two waves, her sturdy boards creaked like they were splitting in half. His men worked the manual pumps and bailed for all they were worth, but he could imagine water entering the hull in a dozen places, making her heavier and less capable of handling the maelstrom.

The only good news was that the naval ships stalking him were no longer in sight, even though visibility had been reduced drastically. They were either dead or had decided that even the cargo he carried was not worth the pursuit, but the second option was decidedly unlikely. Even if they were still trying to follow him, he was sure his latest duplicity had sent them blundering off to the north, forcing them to endure the storm for nothing. Buckwell was always two steps ahead of the Admiralty, and he knew that it frustrated and humiliated the greatest Navy the world had ever seen that it could not catch him, his boat, and the 64 loyal men that crewed her.

Even amidst the berserk waves and the sound of the gale screaming through the rigging, he allowed himself a smile of satisfaction. The weather might take them – no sailor believed himself immune to the power of Neptune – but the laws of tyrant countries never would.

He couldn't be far now. It was entirely too dangerous to step away from the helm to study charts or take a sounding to determine the fathoms of water under *Fortune's* keel, but he had followed the changing course of the wind and used his last accurate position reading to get himself to the leeward islands, and from there he could run southwest to his destination. His *real* destination – not where everyone thought he was going.

Lightning forked through the sky as he cleared the crest of a slightly less violent wave, lighting the area long enough for him to scan the horizon, and that's when he recognized the outline of Petit Cay, a scab of land, about two miles dead ahead.

*Pretty close, Buckwell. Pretty close.*

He steered to starboard and screamed to his crew to adjust the sails to accept the wind so they could proceed on a southerly course. They jumped to action, although the face of more than one showed outright fear at such a brazen, risky move. In this gale, turning broadside to the wind was a fool's bet, almost daring the storm to capsize the boat, even with only minimal sail up. But they had cast their lot with Captain Buckwell years ago, and they were bound to him both by the unique honor code of the sailor/pirate and this latest but risky venture. There was no in between – they would either perish in this endeavor or enjoy the richest of rewards, as even the percentage that Buckwell shared with his crew would make each man wealthy beyond his any dreams of avarice. Plus, Buckwell had pulled them through so many dangerous scenarios that he had earned the right to take risks and have his crew back him. So they pushed at the capstans and the beam swung and the ship listed precipitously to port.

Buckwell timed the waves coming from his starboard side, swinging the wheel to port to coast down the face of each wave and then putting the rudder hard over at the crest to keep the ship as stable as possible and remain roughly on course. Even though things smoothed out to some degree as he passed down the east side of the slightly larger island of Petite Mustique, maintaining control was not easy. Being broadside to the swells was more violent than taking the seas head on, and both men and supplies heaved back and forth, further destabilizing the ship. The crew was lashed to stanchions across the deck to keep them from going overboard, but they were still brutally abused by the intense gyrations of the *Aberaeron Fortune*.

The mountainous terrain of water also made it hard for Buckwell to find his next waypoint, but soon he saw the tiny spit of land. More accurately, he saw the waves breaking fully over the coral and sand that made up Fraunce's Elbow. Nothing more than a half moon-shaped pile of sand that never rose more than 18 inches above sea level on a calm day, it was the gateway to his most secret destination. All he had to do was steer a course of 175 degrees for another 13 miles and he would reach his destination and safety.

Simple. But his compass gyrated wildly between 145 and 205 degrees as the bow twisted this way and that, making it impossible to hold any specific course. Still, he knew he would happen upon his destination if he kept *Fortune* pointed roughly in this direction. He wasn't yet sure that he could get into the narrow and well hidden natural harbor of the island in such conditions, but he was prepared to beach his beloved craft for this latest booty. With what was locked up in his personal quarters, he could have his ship rebuilt 20 times and still have enough to purchase all the rum the islands could provide.

Fraunce's Elbow was about 400 yards ahead and to his right. Buckwell set a course taking them just far enough away from it so the exploding breakers would not affect *Fortune*. He'd taken this track around the shoal many times and knew it to be deep enough that he would not run aground even in these seas. Confident they would pass the landmark safely, the captain turned his attention to the south to get a visual of their final destination.

Buckwell had indeed passed by this tiny island many times, but never in conditions rivaling those he now experienced, and they created a unique and dangerous hydraulic phenomenon. Waves from the west met the rapidly shallowing waters leading up to the island, energized by the fierce winds. Unable to lift all of that water in such a short space, the wave pushed some of the flow around either side of the land, and when the two flows met on the eastern side, they created a violent eddy that drove a vortex, growing larger and stronger with each passing minute.

The hydrodynamic forces of such a swirl of water were beyond comprehension, and they were more than strong enough to pull *Aberaeron Fortune's* bow to starboard, toward the tiny, mostly submerged island. Buckwell sensed the change in direction and, attributing it to a normal wave, adjusted the wheel slightly and continued to look ahead for danger, not realizing it already had him firmly in its grasp. Only when the ship did not snap to the left upon taking the next wave did he become concerned. Even in rough weather, *Fortune* was exceedingly responsive to her helm, but now she was being petulant. He squinted in confusion at the unprecedented actions of his ship, at the same time hearing the shout of one of his men to alert him to the danger.

Ignoring the why, he put the wheel hard over, but he might as well have been trying to knock over Tower Bridge with a slingshot.

*Aberaeron Fortune*, as if deciding that the seas were too tumultuous and that she just wanted out, locked her bow on Fraunce's Elbow in a twisted version of nautical suicide and would not turn no matter what Buckwell did on the bridge.

"Raise the staysail!" Coddington, one of his fastest and most adept sail haulers, moved to do exactly that, but there just wasn't enough time nor any guarantee that doing so would help.

Buckwell saw that he was out of options; he would either meet his end on this normally benign outcropping of coral and sand or providence would intervene and save him, but his actions no longer mattered. He wondered what would become of the magnificent *Couronne Ornée de Joyaux des Anges*, and wished he could be around to see if it would be found someday. *And who will be the next to hold it?*

"Men of the *Aberaeron Fortune*!" he bellowed at the top of his lungs as his ship rode up the crest of a wave just before the island. "I am honored to have been your captain! Save yourselves!" He had no way of knowing how many of his crew might have heard his beatitude or his last order, but he did not wish it to go unsaid.

In the next second, the trough of the wave exposed coral, rocks, and wet sand, and the *Aberaeron Fortune* was turned into a pile of kindling as the ship slid down the wave and exploded into a thousand pieces upon contact.

# Chapter 1 – Chasing the Ghost

**University of Cambridge, Wren Library, present day October**

"Thank you."

All that Paul Downing got in response was a nod and the tiniest hint of a scowl from the excessively wrinkled and chronically aggravated librarian, who pivoted on her heel and walked across the black and white square tiles back to the reference desk without further acknowledging his presence.

At least he had three of the books he needed to start his research. That, he'd been informed, was the maximum that anyone could take from the shelves at any one time. His list of possible source material was long enough that he expected to come back many times.

The paper he was researching was intended to be a foundational study of international relations in maritime matters, back when the British Empire was truly an empire. He wasn't entirely sure what he would learn, but that was part of the fun, wasn't it? His honest expression of intellectual curiosity about the topic and his promise to remain unbiased during his research had impressed Professor Wilkins enough that he had accepted the premise without further inquiry.

Pulling on the protective gloves ("The gloves are to protect the book from you, not you from the book!" the librarian had nearly yelled at him) he lifted the first volume and set it in front of him, throwing up a cloud of dust in the process. When it cleared, he read the title with the reverence that he believed a 194 year old book deserved:

*Researches, Historical and Critical, in Maritime International Law*
*by James Reddie*

He smirked once again at the author's name. He'd nearly spit out his tea upon reading that James Reddie was a 19th-century erotica writer and collector of pornographic works. Only after looking a little deeper did he discover that there were two completely different men with the same name, separated by 34 years and with completely unrelated professions. He'd be sure to specify which Reddie his paper had been based upon in the works cited page.

He opened the book gently, keeping the pages straight as he'd been admonished to do. The text was elegant and ornate, and he felt a sense of reverence at reading something that had been printed during the reign of Queen Victoria and probably not been opened in almost as many years. He knew he had to get started, but he deserved one minute to take a look at a few pages of this history. He ran his fingers along the page edges and turned about 80 of them over gently in one chunk.

*That's odd.*

Sheets of loose paper, tinged with the yellow of age, were folded between pages 86 and 87. Gently, he extracted and opened them. The slightly brighter outline they left behind in the book indicated that they'd likely been there quite a while. He blinked upon seeing that they were not printed but handwritten in the angled and uniform style representative of the times, with the loops and flourishes of every "*f*", "*t*", and "*p*" clearly visible. If that didn't verify the age of the letter, the date at the top – September 27, 1806 – most certainly did. He started reading.

*My most precious Fiona,*

*It has been some time since I have been graced with your beautiful face and pleasant smile. Know that, despite the distance between us, I feel the unbreakable bond that we share, and it sustains my soul as food and water sustain my body.*

*Many days may pass before I can see you again, as I have embarked upon an adventure worthy of our wildest dreams and aspirations. When you receive this letter, I should be well into the most harrowing, dangerous – and rewarding – trip of my life. I know you recall our discussions of certain upcoming activities. I am delighted to say that they are being carried out as I write this, and that they are occurring as we envisioned.*

Paul stopped reading. There were five pages of this, with passages about islands and scenery and something about the smell of the breeze. While he wasn't terribly interested in the flowery prose, he doubted that this letter had found its way between these pages anytime in the previous century, and that meant it could have historical value. For that reason alone he interrupted his barely started research to deliver it properly. He folded the letter and, with the care of a surgeon holding a sharp scalpel, placed it in exactly the same location he'd found it in the old text. Leaving everything behind, he took it directly to the reference desk and the skinny, cross librarian. "Excuse me?"

She turned, making no attempt to mask her contempt for the interruption. "Mr. Downing. What is it *now*?"

"Pardon me, miss, but I do believe you should see this." Setting the tome on the desk, he opened it to the page containing the letter.

"What's this?" she exclaimed, looking up at him and back down at the letter several times. "What did you do?" Paul grimaced. She might have looked older than the book he'd just set down, but Paul had no doubt that she could scold him to within an inch of his life.

"Not me, miss. I opened the book and found it right there, just as you see it now." Pulling on her own set of gloves, she opened the papers and, laying them down on the counter, started skimming them with the speed and ease that a librarian with her probably 200 years of experience possessed. Her forehead, which had been creased with irritation, was now lined with a pattern of curiosity, though it was not easy for Paul to tell the difference. The pages were upside down to him, making it impossible for him to read more than a couple of sentences before she gently moved on to the next sheet.

At the last page, her eyes stopped scanning and locked on the valediction. She blinked, hard, and then shook her head as if dust from the ancient missive had somehow gotten up her nose. Her eyes moved back and forth over the same area several times before she conceded that whatever she was seeing was actually there.

She turned to a graduate student cataloging books at the other end of the long counter. "Get Doctor Wellesley here."

"What? Right now?"

"Yes, right now. And tell him to hurry." The librarian watched the young woman scurry off, allowing Paul to read the closing salutation that had so excited the bibliophile:

*Yours for all time,*
*Cyrus Buckwell*

***

**Climbing Lotus Martial Arts *Dojo*, Lewes, DE – mid-November**
*"Hajime!"*

Black belt Kensie Prescott let fly with a left jab accompanied by a loud *kiai*. The aggressive shout sounded far too deep to have come from her, but the compression of her diaphragm added power to her strike, and it felt good to feel the shield – and the person holding it – rock back.

Her blows were strong and direct, demonstrating a power that was not apparent if one considered nothing more than her trim, 5'5" frame. But, under her gi, her muscles were taut and well developed. Sweat plastered her short, chestnut brown hair to her forehead and dripped into her eyes. She ignored it; Kensie was far too aggravated to let it bother her.

After a few more powerful strikes, she grabbed the shoulders of the person holding the pad and pulled them down while simultaneously driving her knee into what would have been the attacker's groin. It was a good change up and reminded her that, too often, she neglected to train her lower body with as much vigor as her arms and shoulders. She was likely to be smaller – and probably weaker – than any assailant, and her legs were the more powerful limbs on her body.

*"Yame!"*

Kensie paused, holding her ready position for a moment before putting her hands on her hips to help her regain her breath. She looked over at her *sensei*. The son of a bitch wasn't even breathing hard, even though he'd beat the shit out of his partner's pad with strikes that were more plentiful and more powerful than anything she could ever muster.

She heard Catrina let out a sigh of relief as the assault ended. As the person holding the strike shield, she'd been the one absorbing the shock of Kensie's fists, elbows, knees, and feet, and had been knocked around accordingly. The two had known each other since middle school and were the best of friends. Both worked at the Lewes campus of the University of Delaware; Kensie as a marine archeologist, Catrina as a programmer and director of IT projects. They'd gone to different schools for their graduate degrees but remained close, and when the position in the programming department became available four years ago, Kensie pulled a few strings and Catrina got the job. The women were polar opposites, with Catrina more vibrant and self assured while Kensie had a quieter and reserved way about her. Regardless of their different personalities, they had been delighted to be able to hang out regularly once again. Having been friends for 15 years meant Catrina could easily tell when her friend was not herself.

"You, uh, seem to be a little extra – shall we say intense – today," Catrina observed. "Everything all right?"

"Just getting some aggression out," she replied.

"Yeah, no kidding. Can you maybe not do it on me?" Catrina's request was diluted by her smile.

Despite her irritation, Kensie was able to see the humor in her friend's statement. "Whatsa matter? You can't handle getting thumped around a little? You're gonna have one hell of a time at your brown belt test."

Catrina bit off the snarky response that her expression indicated was coming when *Sensei* Wright spoke. *"Nokuri.* Lower belts, do a little technique training with your partner." The instructor pulled one of the newer students aside and started showing him how to improve his stance.

Catrina handed the strike shield over to Kensie. "Can I work on my round kicks? I'm having trouble with my balance lately."

"Sure. Half speed to start." She turned the pad to the side, watching her friend chamber her leg and pop her foot out against the pad correctly, only to wobble slightly when she set it down. "You're not twisting your body enough. You have to pivot on your plant toe when you kick."

"OK." Catrina took her advice and was more successful, so she began a set of kicks to try and replicate the move. "What's got you all bent out of shape anyway?" she asked between repetitions.

"It's official," Kensie responded, not even trying to mask the bitterness and frustration in her tone. "The day after New Year's, a seven day expedition leaves from Woods Hole, and their destination is Bonaire Island in the Caribbean where they will find exactly zilch."

"And you're not on the guest list." Catrina knew better than to make that statement a question.

"After the fuss I put up at the NAS conference, I'm surprised they didn't kick me out of the organization entirely."

"I'm sorry, Kens. I know how important it is to you."

The funny part, Kensie mused as Catrina snapped her leg out to contact the padded strike pad with a bit more force, was that the woman didn't quite know how right she was.

No one fully understood how deeply Kensie was immersed in and enthralled with the famed pirate Cyrus Buckwell, whose myth was larger than life. She'd learned of him in grammar school, and her research into his life and actions had bordered on obsessive. She studied everything she could about him, developing a detailed profile about the man in the process.

In her mind, he'd become a legend about whom no detail could be trivial. Whether by omission or accident, her imagination made his exploits positive, almost playful. He didn't kill men, sink their ships, rape their women, or conscript unwilling crewmen. He was more like a Jack Sparrow kind of guy – hard drinking, crude, and greedy, but honest and trustworthy. Buckwell only stole from the most corrupt merchants, the cruelest governments, and the worst dregs of society. He was a 19th-century Robin Hood. And, oh yeah – so handsome she wanted to bite off his poet shirt.

Through high school and college, she'd come to learn and accept the true nature of Buckwell, the ferocious and callous way he destroyed, killed, swindled, and pillaged. At first, having the reputation of her childhood hero so besmirched had offended her, but she had outgrown such juvenile objections and come to accept the real man. Without a doubt, he was the primary reason she'd gone into marine archeology.

She still loved him in a fantastical, outlandish sort of way. Of course, she understood the gap between reality and desire, but to this day she would sometimes lose herself in a daydream that tossed convention and reality out the window in favor of the illusion.

When she did that, she could imagine them together, standing on the bridge of his brigantine as it rose and dipped majestically in the seas, the reddish glow of the sunset on her face, her low cut bodice exposing cleavage that begged to be touched. The captain would wrap his powerful arms around her, steal a glance at her chest, let the scruff on his jaw rub against her neck, and she would submit to his power and authority.

It wasn't exactly the most politically-correct daydream, but work took up far too much of her time, and it was only natural that this subject – to which she had dedicated too many waking hours over too many years – would bleed into and overtake her personal life.

The recent discovery of her hero's love letter to Lady Jerrams had set a very small segment of the academic community, of which Kensie was a member, aflame with interest. It described, in voluminous detail, his greatest and most notorious crime, the audacious theft of the priceless *Couronne Ornée de Joyaux des Anges* from the Crown Jewels collection in the Tower of London. Kensie knew the story by heart. A gift to Queen Elizabeth from Louis XIIII of France during one of the rare periods of peace between the two adversarial nations, it was a finely-woven platinum mesh worn over the head, and had adorned queens and princesses for almost 150 years. That alone marked it as an object of great historical significance, but the few portraits painted of the Queen wearing it as well as official documents of both governments showed and described the pattern of 156 rubies, emeralds, sapphires, and diamonds totaling over 900 karats set in the mesh. The royal jewelers' assessment had described jewels of the finest quality, which matched King Louis XIIII's reputation for opulence. Conservative estimates put the current day value of the *Couronne* at around $200 million.

Buckwell's audacious crime was the story of the day, solidifying his reputation. He would, however, never live to bask in that notoriety nor recognize a profit from his actions. After a daring solo raid under the cloak of night in which he took the *Couronne* and eschewed many other jewels (Kensie was certain he did that to prove a point), he was already passing the White Cliffs of Dover under full sail before the guards even sounded the alarm. He made a quick stop in the Canary Islands for provisions, where he wrote the newly discovered letter to his love interest in which he bragged of his crime and teased about how – and more importantly, where – he would hide it until it could be sold to anyone willing to pay the price.

The relationship between Buckwell and Lady Jerrams had been secret for obvious reasons. Such a notorious criminal, with a reputation for felonious behavior and debauchery, conversing with a genteel lady of the upper crust of London society was unheard of. But Fiona Jerrams was, in her heart, a rebel who thrived on scandalous behavior. She never caved to familial and parental pressure to attract a "proper" mate, instead content to find ways to meet with her illicit lover when he was in port by taking surreptitious trips to the seashore. Her diary confirmed just how devoted she was to the "Dark Prince of the High Seas." Whether Buckwell truly reciprocated her feelings was highly unlikely based on tales of his sexual exploits from the Americas to Prague, but his letters indicated nothing but passionate love for her and her alone, so perhaps that was all she knew or cared to know.

Lady Jerrams must have been devastated to learn that pieces of her lover's ship, the *Aberaeron Fortune*, had washed up on islands in the southern Caribbean in the days and weeks following a powerful storm that had wreaked havoc upon the islands in that area. Buckwell's body was never found, nor was the *Couronne Ornèe de Joyaux des Anges*, leading to suspicion that he had made yet another miraculous escape from the clutches of nature and justice. Admiralty ships were dispatched and many items stolen by Buckwell were recovered, but the jeweled headdress was never among them.

The harrowing tale had been relegated to history, with no updates, for over two centuries until a student in England discovered a letter inserted in some old maritime law book. That letter, a copy of which Kensie received only days after it was unearthed and authenticated, had initiated a frenetic analysis to see if there were any more clues as to the location of the *Couronne*. And many had been found, or so it was thought.

But Kensie understood something no one else did.

A side effect of her near obsession with the pirate had made the detailed study of his writings and history much less tedious for her. She pored over any tidbit of information she could find about him, going above and beyond any academic standards to the point that she had become quite the expert on him. There were many other experienced and respected scholars who knew just as much as her, but where they saw cold facts, she saw personality and cunning.

Everything that made up Buckwell's life story led her to recognize both his intelligence and duplicity. His diaries and letters to Lady Jerrams and others were filled with long, seemingly pointless diatribes about his life, his desires, his philosophies, and his exploits, but they were considered by most historians as nothing more than the ramblings of an unsophisticated man who delighted in reading his own grandiose riddles.

Kensie saw it differently. Hidden in each of his vainglorious tales were subtle messages with real value, masterpieces of subterfuge. In her eyes, Buckwell was not a self aggrandizing blowhard who wanted to see his own words on parchment. He was more the cocky narcissist who fancied himself such a genius that he could warn people of his intentions and then still pull those feats off without ever getting caught. She theorized that he, knowing how his record of foretold successes was well established, felt he could use these tales as misdirection, to send the law off one way while he made an easy escape.

Kensie was sure this was one of those cases, and that told her exactly where he had been headed when he disappeared.

Even though several of his exploits lined up perfectly with her theories, the letter was the first new information regarding the man in over 170 years, so she had no way to test her suppositions objectively. Even worse, her interpretation of Buckwell was unique; no one shared her views and, as a 28 year old associate professor, she had little chance of bringing them around to her way of thinking. They respected her factual command of Buckwell's history, but otherwise appeared disinterested in her views about his personality and ambition.

Attending a conference of the National Archeological Society in Boston that had been hastily convened specifically to discuss the letter and determine what it meant, she'd listened patiently as scholar after scholar used certain parts of the letter to make their case that the *Couronne Ornèe de Joyaux des Anges* had been lost on the approach to Bonaire Island, just north of present day Venezuela, which he'd noted as his intended hiding spot. Buckwell had used that location to store many of his ill-gotten valuables, and his prose contained many heavy handed clues supporting that location as the best place to find the lost treasure. But no one, Kensie noticed, was even attempting to connect the obvious (to her, at least) dots and draw a different conclusion, the one to which she had come. She waited eagerly for her turn to present her information, and finally got to the lectern at the very end of the second and last day of the conference.

As a mere associate professor, however, she almost immediately realized that the opportunity to speak was little more than a polite overture by the NAS, kind of like putting the backup quarterback in the game after your team was ahead 56-0. And as she presented her reasons for her disagreement with the consensus that had already been formed, she saw shaking heads and sneers of amusement among her older and more experienced colleagues.

"Professor Prescott," the moderator said with his nose firmly in the air as Kensie paused to sip some water after providing her evidence and conclusions on the whereabouts of the treasure, "while we value your input and are, shall we say, intrigued by your unique take on the data available, it is the opinion of this body that your consideration of Buckwell's attempts at misdirection are not concrete and therefore not cogent to this discussion."

"But surely you realize that they have to be considered. They merit at least –"

"I'm sorry, but the meaning that you assign to these documents has been determined to lack validity by some of the more *experienced* members of this body. Based on this development, I think it is time to close the presentation portion of the proceedings. Does anyone wish to hear more from Professor Prescott?" No one did.

Had Kensie been less shocked, she might have voiced her objection to the rebuke and reminded the board that she was entitled to her scheduled time. As it was, she was so off put that she merely stared with a slack jaw as the group voted unanimously to accept the consensus opinion and contract diving and salvage teams to search in the wrong place.

She vented her frustration to her boss the next morning, barging into Wallace Talbot's office as soon as she knew he would be there. It didn't take her long to loudly and passionately explain the basics of her theory and why the entire NAS was a bunch of stodgy and misogynistic jerks with their heads up their collective asses.

"Kensie," the dean had explained with a hint of exasperation in his characteristically calm and sedate voice as he scanned the notes he had taken during her emotional outburst, "you have to realize that you are taking a very controversial position that counters the consensus of a staid and reserved group."

"Big deal!" Kensie had responded angrily. Bouncing between indignation and disbelief at how easily they discounted her theory, she was at full boil. "My theories make sense – a lot of sense – and these geriatric boneheads aren't even listening because they can't grasp that a criminal has no interest in leaving a perfectly factual record of where he hid what he stole!"

Talbot raised his eyebrows, looking off to the corner, something he did when he was digesting new information. Giving him the time he needed, she let her eyes study the wall over his credenza. It was covered with pictures of him shaking hands with exotic and influential persons around the globe; not just leaders of countries, but museum curators, rich collectors (some of questionable ethics), professional treasure hunters, and even leaders of tribes and villages in countries she could barely pronounce. If Wallace Talbot was anything, he was connected, so if she could sell him on her idea, she might have some traction.

After about a minute that seemed like a month, Talbot focused on Kensie once more and drew a breath. "OK, you seem quite certain. Convince me," he challenged.

Kensie launched once more into her hypothesis with great detail, fighting her passion to present her information in what she hoped was a convincing, but stoic, fashion. She went on for 15 minutes, confident that Talbot, despite being her boss, would not even attempt to cut her off. He did not, instead taking even more notes and scanning them intently as she spoke. Just maybe, Kensie hoped, he would see the logic of her approach. She did her best to be clear about when she crossed the line between facts and analysis to pure speculation, hoping that would present her as more reasonable.

When she finished, she once more gave Talbot time to flip through the notebook while he scribbled additional bits of information. She desperately wanted to see what he was writing in the margins of the yellow legal pad, but could only return to her seat and do everything to remain patient.

Finally, he raised his head. "Kensie, I think you might have something worth pursuing further, but not enough to justify an entire expedition. There's too much speculation and not enough hard facts. You don't have it."

"Dammit! I'm not wrong!" she nearly yelled. She felt like she was being minimized, and that did not suit her.

"I'm not saying you're wrong. I'm saying you don't have enough to sell it." His voice remained even and calm, giving Kensie the odd impression that she was the only one engaged in an argument. "Look, take this as a chance to learn a painless lesson. You have good ideas, but you're not there yet. You aren't the first person to get rebuked by the panel, and you won't be the last."

"I should be the last! And it's not painless! They approved spending over $4 million, and they're going to waste that money!"

"Perhaps," he said, maddeningly unperturbed. "But I don't understand what course of action you'd like me to take to mitigate that."

"Give me a few bucks for one of our boats for my own expedition! I'll find the damn thing myself!"

Talbot sighed. "First of all, there's nothing left in our budget for that, and all our research boats have already been committed to other endeavors through July. There's nothing we can do about it, Kensie. It's a done deal. If you are so sure you're right, get something more concrete. A *lot* more concrete, and then you can approach the NAS again – with my backing. Until you get that data, there's nothing more to discuss here." His voice carried the finality of an executive order from the Oval Office, giving her no room to maneuver.

She'd stormed out of his office, frustrated that her dean wouldn't take her side, angry that her years of research and study were being tossed aside because she was young – and probably because she was female. And, after a day catching up on her emails and other administrative tasks, she found herself beating the crap out of a vinyl covered foam pad. At least she could vent her anger more effectively this way.

"Just because they don't believe you doesn't mean you're wrong," Catrina pointed out as they grabbed a sip of water.

"Wrong or right, unless I have proof or at least much better evidence, nothing is going to change." Her mouth was set in the grim line of someone who had ruefully come to an unsatisfactory conclusion.

Catrina shrugged like she'd figured the whole thing out. "So, find it."

"Find what?"

"Proof."

"It's not that easy, Cat. People have been trying to figure this out for 200 years."

The brunette snorted. "So? You know more about this Buckwell guy than maybe anyone on the planet. You've bored me to tears telling me about him when all I wanted to talk about was a cute guy I just met. If they're not seeing what you're seeing, and you know you're right, they must have a bias. Since you still won't come on the cruise with us, you're going to have time over the winter session. The information is out there – somewhere – so quit being pissed off and go find it."

*"Chui!"*

Kensie thought about Catrina's remarks as the class lined up to bow out for the evening. It wouldn't be easy – that was an understatement – but what worthwhile thing was? It deserved one more try.

*Looks like I've got a long day in the library tomorrow.*

***

## University of Delaware College of Marine Studies Library, the following day

Kensie sat at the expansive table in the library, looking through the pile of books, photocopies, and folders for another passage that would support her theory. She had several items set aside for further review, but she was starting to lose faith in them. She was just adding to the mass of supposition and theory that she already had, and that had already been discounted. Having more of it wasn't going to change anyone's mind, certainly not Talbot's. She needed something else.

*But what kind of evidence will make the difference? They're not going to believe anything short of me actually holding up the* Couronne *itself. That would show Talbot and those idiots at the NAS.*

Too bad she couldn't do that.

*Or could she?*

The thought brought Kensie up short. On the surface of it, believing she could find something missing at sea for over two centuries smacked of extreme arrogance. No one had found it; what made her think she could? But part of the reason it was still missing was because no one had ever looked in the right place. And, as she reviewed the details she had gleaned from the letter, her idea started to take on a realistic shape. The water in the area she had pinpointed was almost exclusively less than 100 feet deep, well within her SCUBA certification. Better yet, she had a perfect opportunity to be there in the very near future. Walking over to the entrance so as not to disturb the students and other faculty, she pulled out her phone and placed a call.

"Hey, Kensie," Catrina answered.

"Did you find a fourth for the cruise yet?" she asked without preamble.

"No, not yet. Everyone is crying poor because it's a week after the holidays," came the cautious but anticipatory response. "Why?"

"I had a change of plans. If you still want me, I'm in."

"Absolutely!" Catrina nearly yelled. "Of course I want you! What changed?"

"I'm just spinning my wheels with this research," she half lied. "Nothing I find, at least right now, is going to make a difference. If it's out there, I'm too tired or pissed off to see it. I need a break."

"Yeah, that's what I was thinking at class last night. Drinking Rum Runners under the glare of tropical sunlight is a better way to recharge yourself than beating the shit out of a focus pad, especially when I'm the one holding the pad. Do you still have the cruise itinerary?"

"I'm pretty sure I didn't get rid of it."

"Great! Book your flight as soon as you can. I'll add you to my cabin right now. We'll talk tonight and get the rest worked out. You are going to have the greatest time! We'll wash that moldy book smell off of you and dress you up a little bit and you'll have to beat the guys off with a club!"

Kensie rolled her eyes to herself. Comments like that were at least part of the reason why she had declined the cruise in the first place; the overwhelming belief of her well meaning but misguided friend that her primary goal in life was to find a man, and that Catrina had to be the one to set her up. She had grown tired of hearing it years ago and didn't want to get into it again, but the lure of finding the *Couronne* was enticing enough to make just about anything worth it.

"Look, I promise we'll have a lot of fun, but I am going to spend some time sharpening up my SCUBA skills. It's a perfect place and opportunity to practice."

Catrina was undeterred. "Great. Whatever. All the action on the ship is at night anyway. Just make sure you don't wrinkle your skin digging through the mud and sand, Indiana Jones. We'll take care of the rest."

"Sounds good," Kensie lied. "Diving by day, tramping it up by night. Is that the idea?"

"Kind of," her friend replied. "But there's a topless beach on one of the islands, so there'll be some day tramping too! Bring a two-piece."

Kensie couldn't imagine not wearing a top in front of everybody and their brother. "No way in hell."

"We'll negotiate." When Catrina said that, it meant she planned to go to any length to get her way. "But I gotta run. Talk tonight?"

"You got it. And thanks."

"We are gonna have a *great* time." The line went dead.

Kensie shook her head in exasperation. *If she only knew what I was really going to be doing.* She clicked on the email with the itinerary. It was a fairly short cruise. Departure was from Puerto Rico on the evening of the 3rd, and the 4th would be a full day at sea. The ship would dock at the island of St. Vincent at 6 a.m. on the 5th and not depart until 9 p.m. the next day. The most important part of that destination was that it was only about 45 miles from her pinpointed dive site, giving her two full days to explore. The next destination, Grenada, was more or less the same distance from the site, just south of it instead of north, so she had one more day to search. From there it was another full day cruising back to San Juan, arriving early on the morning of the 9th. She would have three full days to dive and search, and she was sure – pretty sure – kinda sure – hopefully sure – that she would find the *Couronne*.

The next order of business was to let Dean Talbot know she was going to use vacation time. Kensie didn't expect that to be a problem. It would be during the winter recess when there were no students, so no classes to teach. More importantly, she had a reputation among the staff and the dean for being "persistent" (her word – others described her a little differently) when she felt strongly about something, and Talbot would expect her to keep bringing up her ideas about Buckwell, so he would approve the time off without a second thought. She put the books back and walked back to her office to place the call.

"Yes, Kensie?" she heard him sigh. Clearly he expected another round of arguments and complaints and felt ill prepared to deal with them.

"I'm sorry I got so aggravated yesterday," she apologized, doing her best to sound contrite. "You know I get frustrated easily. I didn't mean to take it out on you."

"It's fine. I have noticed your zeal at times. I don't care so much, but it might be a good idea to tone it down sometimes among your colleagues – and especially around the NAS – for your own good." Kensie didn't doubt his sincerity. As the dean, he'd likely gotten wind of her behavior and was growing weary of dealing with the complaints and bruised egos.

"I know. I will learn, I promise." She took a breath. "To that end, a few weeks ago I turned down a chance to go on a cruise because I fully expected to be busy over winter break, but now that isn't happening, so if you're OK, I want to use some of my personal time and go with my friends. Refresh the batteries and come back with a fresh perspective."

A normal person's voice would have perked up, but not Talbot's. "Sounds like a good idea. Where's the cruise?"

She thought about lying but realized that there would be questions to answer if she got found out. Not that she was doing anything unethical or illegal, but it might piss off the wrong person – especially if she didn't return with her prize. "Southern Caribbean."

The pause on the other end of the call told her everything she needed to know about how that news was received. "Kensie, tell me you aren't thinking what I think you're thinking."

"No, it's just a coincidence. Really. Just some time in the sun with some friends and an unlimited liquor package."

"Something tells me I won't be surprised by your answer when I ask you what islands you're going to be visiting."

"We are going near there," she admitted/lied, "but it isn't like I chose this cruise. I'm just a last minute add on because I'm not on the Buckwell expedition."

"OK, that's fine," Talbot said in a tone that suggested it was not fine at all. "But you better not come back here with more unsubstantiated theories and expect my backing. I'm not fond of the idea of rogue academics going off on wild goose chases. We fund certain research for certain reasons. Considering yourself immune to the rules of the situation would be, shall we say," he paused for several seconds, making Kensie look up at the ceiling waiting for him to trot out one of his patented nine dollar sayings, "a rather injudicious course of action."

*He's so damned pompous!* "I understand. That's not what this is about. Honestly, I'm just super frustrated with the whole thing, and this is a chance to get it out of my head for a while. Really, that's it."

Another pause, but this one was shorter. "OK, that's fine. Put the request in and I'll approve it. We'll meet up when you get back and see if there's a new tack you can take with your research."

"Great. I'll put the request in now."

Kensie smiled to herself. Doing this without the sponsorship of the department or the NAS meant she, and not the university, would have the primary salvage rights to the treasure. Not only would her stature in the archeological community grow to the point that she could give the entire NAS board a wedgie and be thanked for doing so, but international salvage law would apply. That meant she could expect to receive the standard 10% finder's fee from the original owner –Queen Elizabeth II of the United Kingdom. It wasn't about the money, but that certainly didn't hurt. She would donate a big chunk of that to a worthy scientific cause, or maybe create an endowment fund to further underwater archeology.

She took a moment to fantasize about meeting the Queen in Buckingham Palace for a formal "thank you" tea, about how she would be able to write her ticket academically anywhere in the world, and how she could fly from interesting site to interesting site first class without a financial care in the world.

Catrina could try and show her off to every guy on the ship, but it wasn't going to matter one bit. She had work to do.

# Chapter 2 – Life at Sea

**San Juan, Puerto Rico, Cruise Ship Pier 11, January 3**

*Enormous.*

That single word summed up Kensie's reaction as the shuttle bus from the airport rounded the corner to expose *Amore of the Seas* sitting placidly in the harbor. She wondered if people had thought the same thing upon seeing the *Titanic* over a century ago. If they did, the historian in her longed to go back in time and tell them that they hadn't seen anything yet. *Amore* was 300 feet longer, 100 feet wider, and *five times* heavier than the legendary ship which had, during her brief and tragic life, been the largest moving object ever built by man.

Kensie and Catrina got off first, followed by Nancy and Liv. The latter were acquaintances of Catrina's, recruited to join her on the cruise when Kensie initially chose not to go. She knew them casually and had become more familiar with them on the flight down. They seemed nice enough, but Kensie was glad she would be sharing her cabin only with Catrina.

"Wow," Catrina said. "That thing is huge!" She smiled at Kensie. "With all the guys they can fit on that ship, one of them is sure to be right for you!"

"I told you," Kensie protested for what seemed like the thousandth time, "I'm not going to spend all my time scoping out horny jerks."

"You won't have to scope them out, honey," Nancy told her. "We're gonna bring them to you! You just throw back the ones you don't like!" Catrina had spent a lot of time on the flight explaining why Kensie was joining them (her version of it), and her friends had bought into the idea.

"Yeah," Liv chimed in. "Remember, I'm in sales. Catrina said we have to make you the hottest commodity on the ship. When we're done, the best ones will be chasing you from the back all the way to the stern."

"Geeze, thanks guys," Kensie responded sarcastically. "I've got my troupe of pimps to tell the entire ship that I'm available. And, Liv," she said with exasperation, "the back *is* the stern. It's either the back to the front, or the stern to the bow."

"Whatever, captain," she responded, not dissuaded it the least. "This is a girl's week, and you're the top girl." They reached the short line that led into the building for processing passengers.

Kensie turned and addressed her companions. "Look. I know you mean well, but I'm not here to meet guys. I've got a few things I have to do."

"And that," Catrina said while looking skyward, "means you're somehow going to make this trip about work instead of fun."

"No, I'm not."

Catrina stared at her with pursed lips and put her hand on her hip. Nancy and Liv watched the unfolding drama.

"Well, not entirely," Kensie hedged after a second.

The piercing glare continued.

"Fine. I have a work angle. But trust me – it's important. It will really help my career." The line she balanced on, the one between bullshit and reality, was so thin Kensie feared she might fall off it.

Catrina looked at her like a parent who knew her kid skipped class while lying to her face. "This isn't about that thing last month in Boston, is it?"

"No," Kensie lied. "There's nothing I can do about that now anyway. The ships are leaving Woods Hole today."

"What d'ya think?" Catrina asked the other two. "Should we leave her nerd professor ass here on the shore?" They looked at each other silently, as if deciding whether they would allow the archeologist to board with them. Finally, Kensie sighed in surrender.

"Fine. I'll let you show me off to all the guys. But only on days when we're at sea. The days we're docked at St. Vincent's and Grenada, that's my time."

Catrina turned back and silently mouthed a kiss to her – which was her way of thanking Kensie for allowing herself to be convinced to do something she didn't want to do. Kensie gave her the wry grin that said there were no hard feelings.

"Now you're talking," Nancy said. "Just spruce you up a bit, and no one is going to believe you're a college professor."

"Oh, they'll know. I'm sure of it."

"Not when I'm done. Your skin is so lovely, just a little bit of pampering is going to make you stand out like a diamond in a coal mine."

"Great." Kensie's voice carried all the enthusiasm of someone who had just agreed to purchase term life insurance.

"It will be," Catrina said with a wink. "I promise. Now, let's get on board."

***

Ninety minutes later, Kensie thanked the steward who delivered their suitcases to her cabin door. She heaved the bags onto their respective beds.

"OK," Catrina said as she clicked to the cruise information channel on their cabin television. "We have a mandatory lifeboat thingy at five, and we depart at six. The restaurant opens then. So what do you say we get all prettied up before the meeting so we're ready for dinner right afterward?"

"It's called muster. But I didn't think we'd have to dress for dinner," Kensie protested. "I thought this was a vacation."

"It is. But that doesn't mean you can't look good – the dress code said 'casual and up'. Let's start the trip with a little *va va voom*, if you know what I mean. Liv and Nancy are going to do it, and so am I."

"Fine. But let's get ready after muster."

"No, before. That way we'll get right in for a table while everyone else goes back to their cabin to change."

"You've got it all worked out, don't you?" Kensie said, impressed with Catrina's well reasoned approach. Her normal procedure was more spur of the moment to the point of low-grade chaos.

She smiled brightly. "You may have signed on three weeks ago, but I've been thinking about this since September. Having the first day planned out is the least I could do, isn't it? Now, either you pick out something sexy to wear or I will – and you know how that'll end up!"

She most certainly did. Catrina was a master of designing outfits that skirted the line between elegantly sexy and revealingly slutty. Unlike Catrina, Kensie lacked the self confidence to pull that off. Not wanting to come anywhere near either side of that border, she held up her hands in surrender.

"OK, OK, I'll do it." She went through the outfits she'd brought – very few, especially compared to Catrina, whose suitcase seemed to contain half of Bergdorf Goodman's fall line. She finally settled on a pale pink sleeveless bandage dress. It barely reached the top of her knees, and a small diamond shaped opening in the front revealed just the right amount of cleavage. She chose a pair of open toe shoes with a two inch heel and ankle straps, completing her look with a small rose gold pendant on a necklace. She stepped into the center of the cabin to model it for Catrina.

"You look really good, Kensie. *Really* good."

Kensie smiled self consciously. "Thanks. Not as good as you, though." She was attired in a dark red sheath dress that hugged her curves like a Porsche hugs the road. Her dark hair hung over her shoulders in loose curls, framing her full lips and big, blue eyes.

"We *both* look good," Catrina said with a sly grin. "We're going to blow the guys away." She frowned. "But I somehow managed to forget to pack deodorant, so I have to go to the ship's store before muster. Why don't you get your makeup finished and meet Liv and Nancy up there? I'll join you as soon as I'm done."

"OK, sure." Catrina breezed out of the room and Kensie sat down at the small desk with her rarely used makeup kit. She took a long look in the mirror. Kensie honestly thought she was of average looks, and felt downright plain next to Catrina and her friends, who not only had the physical features she lacked, but also took the time for eyeliner and lipstick and to work on their hair. It wasn't that she didn't care about her appearance, but she was a scientist whose job was to learn and understand the truth, and somehow spending so much time using makeup to present herself as someone she wasn't seemed counterintuitive.

But was there any harm in cleaning up a little? She applied a touch of color to her eyelids and cheeks, finishing with a pastel lip gloss that she felt suited her light skinned complexion and green eyes. After she brushed out her hair, Kensie paused to take a second look at the entire package and was not unhappy with what she saw. She wasn't on par with her traveling companions, but she *did* present nicely. *Can't ask for much more than that.* Flashing a bright smile to herself, she grabbed her room key, put it in her clutch, and headed to the muster meeting.

Liv and Nancy were waiting outside the meeting room, and Catrina was walking toward them from a different direction. Kensie caught her friend winking at the two women but ignored the gesture, figuring there had been some sort of side wager about Catrina being able to make her look presentable, and she was quietly bragging. She chose not to call her friend out during her moment of celebration.

The muster was predictably boring even though Kensie understood the necessity of it. It reminded her of the safety speech at the beginning of a flight, and people paid about the same amount of attention. She memorized where she had to be in the unlikely event of an emergency while everyone else chatted or played on their phones. *That's fine. I'll be floating away on a lifeboat while you all walk around in circles on the ship as it sinks.* She reasoned they had a much better chance of surviving a sinking ship as opposed to flying into a mountain at 400 miles an hour, making it worth her time. The crew members giving their spiel seemed about as delighted to present the information as the passengers were to receive it, but they dutifully did their job and then encouraged everyone to "get outta here and have some fun!"

As everyone filed out of the room, a man and a woman wearing shirts with **Security** printed across the front in big letters headed in their direction. Kensie didn't give it a thought until they made a beeline for her group and locked their eyes right on her.

"Miss Kensington Prescott?" She grimaced. It was the full name on her birth certificate, but no one called her 'Kensington.' She hated it. It was odd and overly formal and made her feel like she had been groomed from day one for royalty.

"I'm Kensie Prescott."

"Will you come with us, please?"

"Why? What's the problem?"

The woman smiled apologetically. "There was some kind of mix up with your credit card and your booking. The purser's office just needs to ask you some questions to make sure we don't bill you incorrectly. It will only take a minute."

That sounded reasonable to Kensie; she'd paid for her cabin at the last minute, so an issue was possible. "OK, sure." She turned to her friends. "Let me take care of this and I'll meet you at dinner."

Nancy took a defensive posture. "You sure? We can come with you."

Kensie shook her head, but the other security guard answered. "It's going to be super quick. There's no trouble or anything, we just have to make sure we have her booking set up right. It will literally be about two minutes of her time."

"See? No issue. I'll meet you guys at the dinner table."

"OK." The trio nodded in agreement and headed off. Kensie followed the guards in the other direction.

The path to wherever the purser's office was felt awfully roundabout to Kensie. She hadn't had time to scout the ship and learn the layout, but it seemed they walked forward, then down a couple of decks, then to an elevator that took forever to come, and then toward the stern to a set of big double doors.

"Here we are," the guard said. Kensie was about to remark that this was a very odd place for the ship's business offices to be and, when they pulled them open, she saw why she was right.

About 50 or 60 younger men and women were milling about in the room that was far too large to be any kind of office. A banner – "Singles Meet & Greet" – hung from the ceiling, and Catrina, Nancy, and Liv were waiting under it. "Surprise!"

Kensie gave her friends a look. "I should have known." The security guards nodded and headed out while her friends gathered around their victim.

"Did we fool you?" Catrina asked.

"Yeah, you did. This really isn't necessary."

"Come on," Nancy said. "What's the harm in talking to a few guys? Do you have something better to do right now?"

She looked at the faces of her friends. They appeared proud of having pulled off their little scheme and, aside from dinner and maybe exploring the ship, she didn't have any reason to be anywhere else. "OK, I'll hang for a little while."

"That's the spirit!" Nancy said. Catrina grabbed her hand and led her to the line for the finger food buffet, with Liv and Nancy close behind. As the more outgoing duo, they started chatting excitedly about every man that passed in front of them, apparently not caring whether anyone heard them or not. Catrina joined in for a second, making a few fairly vulgar comments of her own, before separating slightly to stand with Kensie.

"You know," she said quietly to Catrina as they shuffled along, "I'm not real good in these situations, right? I feel awkward approaching strange guys."

"You don't have to do anything, sweetie. Just let the guys come to you." They reached the table and collected a couple of the better looking appetizers.

Kensie grimaced. "Guys don't come to me, Cat. You seem to be forgetting our undergraduate days." A brief image of pretty much every college party flashed through her head, where she stood against a wall with a Solo cup in hand, ignored by half drunk guys in favor of prettier girls who knew how to flirt and twirl their hair just right. The only time she got any attention from the opposite sex was when she engaged in the obligatory dialog with the wingman of whoever was interested in Catrina, or toward the end of the party when the pickings were slim. Of course, that meant her pickings were just as slim, which was why she'd never hooked up such situations.

"We are a long way from frat parties, Kensie. You are an accomplished professional and, if I do say so myself, you look very good." Kensie looked away, a bit embarrassed by the compliment. "Someone will come by before long. Just relax and enjoy yourself."

"Fine," Kensie replied, neither convinced nor sharing her friend's optimism. They got their drinks and stepped out of line to wait for Liv and Nancy, but a couple of guys started chatting them up in the buffet line.

"Son of a bitch," Kensie said, shaking her head in amazement. "That didn't take long, did it?"

"That's their gift."

"Yeah, well why didn't Santa ever bring me that gift?" Kensie lamented.

"Because you'd rather find things under the sea than sit on the beach and show yourself off."

Kensie paused while trying to come up with an appropriate retort, but before she could craft a clever response, two men approached. The taller one had intense blue eyes locked right on her, while the other seemed more overwhelmed and intimidated as he sized up Catrina. She felt the tiny burst of mini panic that always flared to life upon the approach of a cute guy and looked down instinctively for a second. When she checked him out again, his gaze had not wavered. He certainly wasn't bad to look at, with close cropped blond hair and an easy grin that showed off strong, high cheekbones. Normally she would be attracted to such a face, but something felt... off about him. *What?*

"Hi," he said confidently. "My name is Van, and this is Brian. How are you?" He switched his drink to the other hand and extended it toward Kensie in a greeting.

She smiled self consciously at the attention of this rather handsome young man before taking his hand. "Hello," she said pleasantly, "I'm Kensie, and this is my friend Catrina."

He looked in Catrina's direction and gave her a perfunctory nod before turning his attention back to Kensie. Brian, however, smiled awkwardly. "Catrina. I like that name."

"Thanks," Catrina replied. Far less intimidated by guys, she frowned at Brian's somewhat hackneyed come on line.

Van ignored their side conversation. "The pleasure is mine," he replied smoothly before gesturing at one of the small pub tables. "Would you like to chat for a moment?"

A little surprised, Kensie hesitated. "Um, OK. Sure." She turned toward Catrina. "Would, uh, you guys excuse us?" Catrina's face indicated that she wasn't exactly thrilled with what appeared to be the lesser of the two, but that she was willing to take one for the team.

"Sure. But don't forget we have to be at dinner shortly," she said, giving Kensie an easy out if she needed one.

"Right. Thanks for reminding me."

Van took note of the veiled escape hatch in stride. "I won't keep her long, I promise." Kensie furrowed her brow a bit at that. Hopefully, he meant it as a joke, as she wasn't his to keep. "It was nice to meet you, Catrina."

"You too, Van," she responded, while Brian kind of half waved, half pointed at Van in a very awkward response. Furrowing her brow slightly at him, Catrina guided Brian in the opposite direction.

"So," Van asked once they had gathered at the small table, "is this your first cruise?"

"Yeah, I've never done one before. You?"

"Oh, yeah... I've done, um... this is my fifth."

"Well," Kensie said, hoping it didn't sound too flirty, "you'll have to give me some pointers on how to have fun on the ship then!"

"I'd be happy to." He flashed a smile that showed very straight and very white teeth. "Do you have any idea of what you'd like to do? What do you enjoy?"

"I'm not sure," Kensie hedged. "I just had the chance to get away, and I took it." She paused, considering the wisdom of sharing her next thought, but determined there was no harm in doing so. "Maybe I'll do some SCUBA diving at one of the islands."

Van nodded. "SCUBA, huh? What are you looking for?"

"Nothing. I just like to see what's down there."

Van nodded. "That sounds interesting. I'd love to tag along if you wouldn't mind some company."

*Whoops.* The one thing Kensie did not want was someone she did not know getting wind of her real goal. If Van was around and she was successful in her attempt to find the *Couronne*, he might not have the same honest intentions with the artifact. She backtracked a bit. "Well, I'm not sure – it's just one idea. I might not have the guts to try it."

"Right, right. But if you do..."

"You'll be first on my list."

"Promise?" Van's tone was casual, but Kensie detected an undertone of interest that went beyond a sincere interest in the activity or even a desire to get into her pants. She wasn't sure what it was about, but she made a note to talk less – even in generalizations – about her plans, especially with Van.

"Absolutely," she said with mock seriousness, fingering her necklace. Van's eyes didn't wander down to eyeball her cleavage like she expected – like any straight man would. *Weird.*

"Kensie, we should get going." It was Catrina, with Brian a few steps behind her, looking overwhelmed.

Kensie didn't mind the interruption, but out of the corner of her eye she saw Van check his watch. "That was quick," he announced.

"I know," Catrina said smoothly. "But I forgot something in the cabin and the steward said that the line, even for set dining times, is super long on the first night."

Kensie felt a little relief. She wasn't totally comfortable with Van, and Catrina appeared uninterested in Brian, so the decision was easy. "No problem, we can go." She turned to Van. "We'll talk another time."

He was obviously disappointed with her decision. "OK. I'll be on the lookout for you. I'm in cabin G114. Let me know if you decide to try diving." He nodded to Brian. "Let's go." The two men headed out of the room, talking quietly to each other.

Catrina grabbed Kensie's arm and guided her in the opposite direction, both women keeping silent until they got back into the passageway. "I hope I didn't cramp your style or anything, but that Brian guy was kind of weird," Catrina told her in a quasi apologetic tone.

"Weird, how?"

"Like he was a middle schooler trying to get me to go behind the gym to make out," Catrina answered, her lips twisting in distaste. "Way too nervous, way too eager. I can't put my finger on it."

Even though Van had not made a good impression, the idea that Kensie might have attracted the better looking of the two men was flattering. She giggled but moved past the thought. "Sounds like the beginning of a bad teen movie," she offered with a slight chuckle. "But it's fine. Van wasn't doing much for me either. And he seemed awfully focused on my plans, to the point that it kind of made me feel like he already knew exactly what he wanted to do with me."

"Or maybe to you," Catrina added, a lecherous smile on her lips.

"Oh, knock it off. Do you really think I'd dive into bed with a guy I just met?"

"Of course not, but he *did* approach you, just like I said," Catrina pointed out. "And maybe he was a little creepy, but Van was pretty cute."

"Yeah, I guess he was."

"Feels good, doesn't it?"

Kensie smiled at her friend. "It does. Thanks. I appreciate the encouragement."

"No problem. You deserve it. Now, let's get a drink before dinner."

# Chapter 3 – Not Quite the Cream of the Crop

Kensie stood on the hard gravel in front of the rickety wood structure that purported to serve as a dock in St. Vincent.

Unlike the other docks that she'd passed in the last hour, which were easily visible right off the road, this one required a short hike down a narrow trail surrounded by thick bushes. Kensie got a little nervous at how secluded it was – she half expected someone to lunge from the brush and grab her – but when she saw the dock itself she realized she feared the wrong thing. It was badly warped and splintered, the victim of harsh tropical sunlight, salt air, and years of neglect. She questioned if she should even consider stepping on it – the badly rusted nails she could see seemed incapable of keeping it together with even her trim frame on it, and Kensie had no desire to be tossed into the drink.

*Stop being dramatic. It's a two foot drop into warm and calm bay water.*

There might not have been much danger, but she was running out of options. And there was a boat – *Julian's Empire II*, the stern proclaimed in faded red letters – tied to the warped pilings, supporting the sign that indicated she was at the right location. The craft was, to put it politely, very well used and matched the dock in appearance, but there was diving equipment visible in the open back of the boat. That was what she needed, and right now this dilapidated option was the only one she had left. With a quiet sigh and a pronounced lack of hope, she stepped as gently as possible onto the gnarled wood.

***

She'd gotten up before six, drawing grumbles and complaints from Catrina even though she tried to dress quietly. From the sound of the uneven steps and the *thuds* from her crashing into the walls in the small cabin late the previous night, Catrina had made liberal use of her drink inclusive package long after Kensie had retired for the evening. She was the only person at the Excursion Desk when an overly peppy woman opened for the morning. "Can I help you?"

"Yes," Kensie said, explaining that she needed information about local divers who would be willing to take a day charter, or perhaps a multi day charter.

"Oh, there's no need for that," the employee explained. "We have several approved companies who take groups of people from the ship out to dive on local wrecks and other features. I can put you on one of their lists from here."

"I'm sure you can, but I'm an experienced diver and I have some specific locations I'd like to explore on my own."

The cruise line employee was undaunted, dismissing Kensie's request and forging ahead about the different locations, pointing out that their dive excursions were for "divers of all skill sets" and that one of the locations even had a shipwreck to explore, her eyes going wide with badly forced excitement. She could talk to the tour director on the embarkation deck and see which one was right for her.

*This is a dead end.* Kensie thanked her politely and exited the ship, figuring she could make more progress once she got on shore, and she was right. The woman at the little chamber of commerce kiosk right at the end of the wharf was much more helpful. She handed Kensie several brochures and pamphlets of local divers and gave her a few tips. Grateful, Kensie grabbed a local cab and, after insisting she didn't want or need to go to a nearby beach, was dropped off without fanfare at Eastern Caribbean Diving, a modest but colorful building a few feet off the bay.

"Oh, hell nah," the suddenly unfriendly man at the counter said, his eyes jerking up from her chest and bulging upon hearing Kensie's desired diving destination. "That's mighty far. It would take over an hour just to get ya there, and it's nothing but a mound of sand. Plus, it's not for rookies." He returned to the newspaper he was reading.

"I'm not a rookie diver, and I'll be happy to compensate you for your gas and any lost time," Kensie said pleasantly.

"I'm sayin' I'm not interested. I don't want to run all the way out there and put the strain on my boat," he told her. She persisted, even going so far as to use her most flattering smile and batting her eyes a little, but it had no effect, and in a minute she was back on the sidewalk trying to figure out which of the remaining divers was closest.

It wasn't a far walk, but the results were the same there, and at the next one. After each visit she shuffled the brochures to determine her next destination, and each time she left frustrated. For whatever reason, no one would even discuss the trip beyond an unconditional refusal and a few excuses about how far it was. It reminded her of bad mafia movies, where the hoods had gotten to the witnesses and scared them so badly they were afraid to talk (*SCUBA diving? Never heard of it.*) Walking out of her sixth stop, she flipped to the last brochure. It was devoid of the exotic images and adventurous language that graced the other documents. It had only block lettering on off-white paper:

**SCUBA Diving – Snorkeling – Site seeing**
**Fully Certified – All Levels of Experience Welcome!**
**Captain J. Burke**
**48 Seraphine Road**

The complete lack of design or color suggested to Kensie that this Captain Burke either didn't have access to anyone with a bit of graphics skill, or he was so good that he didn't need to waste his time and money on fancy advertising.

*What have I got to lose?* She checked the map on her phone and, failing to hail a cab on the busy street, set off on foot.

Twenty minutes later she found herself hot, sweaty, tired, and frustrated, standing at the precipice of a dock that looked like it had been built by three kids with too few nails and no paint, jutting out into a narrow, secluded channel hidden from the rest of the harbor by what looked like tall cocoplum shrubs. With little hope that this encounter would be any different than the others, she stepped on the first wood slat and, finding it to be sturdier than expected, continued down to the boat. No one stirred, and Kensie figured she was out of luck. Still, she had to make the attempt – she was already here.

"Hello? Captain Burke? Are you there?"

No answer.

"He-llo! Anyone in there? Captain?"

Still nothing. Taking a deep breath, she gave it one more try.

"I'M LOOKING FOR CAPTAIN BURKE!" A startled frigate bird took off, but nothing in or around the badly discolored hull moved. She shook her head and turned back to the shore when she heard a hacking cough and grunt come through an open hatch at the bow.

"Yeah, dammit, wait a minute!" He sounded like someone waking up from an epic bender. *Great.* Kensie had already formed extremely low expectations upon seeing the boat, but the crashing and banging from the V-berth suggested that she'd been optimistic. Now that she had his attention, she wished she'd given up after two tries. Kensie would have to waste time talking with him instead of trying to figure out alternatives.

Finally, the boat rocked and shifted slightly, and she heard the heavy *smack* of bare feet plodding on the deck. They were slow and unsteady and the cadence reminded her of a fat old man with a bad hip. She imagined a toothless, tottering wreck of a sailor.

But when the man making the noise came through the hatch, even with his hand shielding his eyes from the sun, she recognized him as an incarnation of Cyrus Buckwell, returned from the dead.

*****

Julian Burke woke with a start at the insistent shriek of a female voice that sounded like it had run out of patience. Women usually roused him more gently, through the artful use of their lips and tongue on certain parts of his anatomy, although it had been quite a while since that had happened. He barked out a response, his voice hoarse and raspy from the dry throat he got when he snored. He only snored after a night of drinking.

Opening his eyes required a Herculean effort, to say nothing of actually getting his feet under him, but he managed to stagger to the head and splash tepid water on his face. He glanced down at his ratty shorts that appeared to have come from a castaway on a deserted island, but they were appropriate in that the holes in the fabric showed nothing inappropriate. His lack of a shirt didn't trouble him; after all, this *was* a tropical island.

He coughed a few times to clear his lungs and took a quick look in the mirror. His hair was nearly to his shoulders and looked like he was allergic to combs. His skin was ruddy from the sun, but it also sagged under his eyes from too much cheap island rum and too many nights thinking of things that needed to stay in the past. Not exactly his best look, but it would have to do.

The boat rocked more than it should have as he headed up to the main deck, which meant that he was probably not quite sober despite the – he glanced at his watch – six hours of sleep he'd gotten. *Not enough.*

The sun was far too bright – the hatch faced the east – so he squinted and shaded his eyes with his hand. Turning toward the dock, he saw a pair of tennis shoes and the bottom of some trim, ghostly white legs. *Fuck. A tourist. Shoulda known.* He wasn't exactly in the mood or physical condition to troll around the island so that entitled college students could dive on the numerous "wrecks" (old barges intentionally sunk in shallow waters to entertain novice explorers) but he could use the cash. He got so few paying customers anymore – he wasn't exactly on the cruise line's list of approved diving instructors, and the few visitors that did make their way here assumed his worn boat would spring a leak any second.

"Yeah, I'm Captain Burke. What can I do for ya?"

"Well, um, yeah – I'm trying to charter – to hire a boat, um, for some diving." Her uneven response sounded a little higher pitched than he expected, like she'd been startled by his appearance. Maybe it was because he was shirtless and she was some kind of religious prude.

"How'd you find me?"

"The lady at the Chamber of Commerce stand at the cruise ship dock gave me your brochure," she said.

"And you picked me first? There must be 10 SCUBA tour places between the dock and here."

"No, not first. But no one else will take the job."

That got Burke's attention. The competition for taking tourists out to the many nearby coral reefs to see the triggerfish was fierce, and he could not imagine anyone turning a young woman down unless she had an enormous number of people with her or was making unreasonable requests. His interest piqued, he lowered his hand and opened his eyes fully, ignoring the slight flash of pain above his nose.

She was pretty – more than pretty. True, she was whiter than Casper the Friendly Ghost in Maine in January, but she had a face that pulled his gaze to it and wouldn't let go. Her chestnut brown hair framed keen, inquisitive green eyes that regarded him with curiosity and... something else. Burke couldn't put his finger on it, but this young lady was checking him out with a mix of admiration and amazement. Her mouth hung open slightly, and she kept turning her head from side to side like she didn't quite believe what she was seeing. It made him uncomfortable.

He shook off the uneasy feeling. "How big is your party?" he asked.

"It's just me."

"And you want to learn how to SCUBA dive?"

"No," she responded in a way that indicated she'd done this dance more than once today. "I've got a master SCUBA rating with a deep diver specialty. I don't need any instruction. I need a boat and gear and someone who knows how to back me up while I explore an area. The right way."

She sounded knowledgeable and determined, and that made her different from other potential clients. *What is this woman about?*

"OK. For a normal party of four, I charge $150 US for four hours. Per person."

"That's fine, but I'd like to get the whole day for starters, and maybe another couple of days depending on how things go."

"That's a lot of money and a lot of diving. How many sites do you want to visit?"

"Just one. Fraunce's Shoal. Do you know it?"

Burke blinked. "Yeah, and that's far. Like 40 miles far, and not exactly an easy run or an easy dive. I don't know too much about it, but I've heard there are a lot of dangerous currents. It's a tricky dive, even if you are highly experienced. I've never actually been there myself."

Her curious look gave way to irritation. "I know. I know all about the area. Even if I didn't, every diver on this damn island has told me about it in glorious detail. That's why I need someone who knows how to get there safely, how to back me up, and how to let me do my job. Can you do it or not?

Burke raised his eyebrows at the slight rebuke. This woman wasn't some bubblehead just interested in recreation; she had a goal and was determined to fulfill it. But whenever people needed his services in a non-recreational manner, they always set things up ahead of time. He'd taken out a bunch of students and academics who wanted to test their theories of sand density and fish migration and feeding patterns, but they'd always given him a check from a university or research center. This was not quite right.

"So this is research? Who are you with and what do you want to find out?"

"I'm working independently for my doctoral thesis. I have a theory about how global warming affects erosion and sediment displacement, and how it interacts with metallic anomalies in the sediment and bedrock. Fraunce's Shoal is the perfect environment for me to learn what I need." Her words came out too fast and too well rehearsed, setting off another yellow flag. Whatever she was after, it had nothing to do with erosion and Burke knew it – her explanation didn't make a bit of sense. He thought about sharing a little piece of his own story with her, one that was very relevant to her fictional task, but chose not to just then. Entertainment is where you find it sometimes.

"Erosion, huh? What school?"

"University of Delaware. School of Marine Science."

"You go to Delaware, and you couldn't hitch a ride on *any* of their research vessels? There's *nowhere* between the shore and the shelf where you couldn't find the conditions you need?"

"If there was and I could," she said with elevating levels of aggravation seeping into her voice, "don't you think I would have done that?" She paused, her big green eyes fixing on him for several seconds, but not in real anger. She was testing him, he felt, seeing how he would react. He didn't know whether she wanted him to snap back at her in defiance or submit to her stern tone, but it didn't really matter; he wasn't about to take the bait no matter what she was looking for.

"People do a lot of – well, questionable things – especially when they get down here," he responded neutrally, taking in the luster of her emerald eyes, so bright they rivaled the pastel blue of the bay. "Just trying to figure you out." He intentionally lowered his voice half an octave for the last sentence, just enough to suggest his interest in her might not be solely as a client.

Kensie's face went from irritated to exasperated as she caught the hidden message. Burke saw the tiniest hint of a twitch in her upper lip before she shook her head dismissively. "There's nothing to figure out. I need to dive at Fraunce's Shoal. I have more than enough cash on me right now and I'm ready to go as long as you have gear that's in good shape for me. Can I hire you or not?"

Burke filed her reaction away for the moment and, turning his mind back to the current topic, raised his hands in surrender. "I wouldn't go around telling strange men that you're carrying that kind of bread, but as long as you have your C-card on you, yeah, I'll take you wherever you want to go and babysit from up top." He noticed the way she pulled a face at his last phrase. "Come on aboard, Miss ...?"

"Prescott. Kensie Prescott." He held out his hand to her, but she eschewed it in favor of hopping adroitly over the gunwale and onto the deck. Pulling off her backpack, she produced a wad of cash, counting out 24 $50 bills, which she handed to Burke. He put the money in his pocket and took the C-card she offered, scrutinizing it closely.

"Kensington?" He raised his eyebrows at her in barely contained amusement.

She sighed. "Yes, Kensington," she snapped back. "For some reason, my parents thought it sounded regal and elegant, so that's my legal first name. But no one," she said, leveling her gaze at him to make sure what she was about to say was clear, "uses it. It's Kensie or Ken."

"Understood. And, since you don't really look much like a 'Ken'" – he swept his eyes up and down her form just obviously enough that she could see him do it – "we'll go with Kensie." He returned the C-card. "Now that we have that settled, seems we're all set. You can pick out your gear – it's at the front of the cabin – while I get things ready, and we'll cast off in a few minutes."

***

Kensie couldn't help but watch Burke's muscles ripple and flex as he worked the lines to free the boat from the dock as she pretended to look over the diving gear. He had the musculature of a man who knew hard work, contained under golden tan skin. A tattoo that she could not decipher decorated his right shoulder. It was a simple tattoo, the uniform greenish gray suggesting it was done by an amateur – or in prison. Either way, it gave him an air of danger and rebellion that made Kensie's stomach twist and her crotch tingle with unbidden and quite graphic thoughts.

But it was his face that had stopped her cold on the dock when he first stepped from the hatch. Of course, there were no photos of Captain Buckwell, but there were paintings and sketches. Kensie had long ago determined (accurately or not she was unsure) what he looked like in her mind, and Burke was definitely his doppelganger, right down to the stubble on his cheeks and chin and the sun bleached streaks in his light brown shock of unruly hair that was just a touch too long to be orderly. The similarity of his appearance to the man whose treasure for which he would be unwittingly hunting had to be nothing more than a coincidence, Kensie was certain, but it assured her that she had ended up at the right boat.

She might have considered his good looks a positive omen, but they did not, however, translate into gallantry or manners. His subtle insults annoyed her, and his snickers and facial expressions suggested he considered himself superior to her, at least in this realm. He displayed an arrogance that seemed unearned, especially based on the boat and where he was docked.

*Whatever. All that matters is that he gets me out and back. You're here for a reason.*

She found the equipment she needed and set it off to the side just as the engine rumbled to life. It had an odd warble to it, sounding old and badly in need of maintenance. Kensie was not a mechanic in any sense of the word, but the uneven rumble and the jarring vibrations coming through the deck reminded her of her first car, a 1983 Chevy Cavalier that rattled her teeth loose at highway speed and spent more time up on jack stands in their driveway – with her father's legs sticking out from under it and a steady stream of creative profanity spewing into the neighborhood – than being driven to and from work and school. And this engine was going to take her out into the Atlantic Ocean?

Forgetting that for the moment, she opened her backpack and pulled out a few additional items, the most important being a small but powerful metal detector. Her plan was to sweep it over the sand, following a grid search pattern and hoping that the slope of the shoal would have kept layers of heavy sand and sediment from building up and burying the treasure forever. She'd never dived in tropical waters, but the heavier mud of the eastern seaboard acted in much the same manner at roughly the same depth, so she had confidence in her plan – well, at least she had a chance.

Making sure everything was secure, she headed back up to the weather deck. Burke was guiding the *Empire* through the wide harbor with practiced indifference, one hand barely on the wheel, the other free to wave at vessels or to people on the docks.

"You're popular around here," she commented nonchalantly.

He grunted. "Yeah, we're a pretty tight community in this bay. Every once in a while someone needs a helping hand. You give help, then you get help." They passed the breakwater and Burke swung the wheel to port. The seas grew a little rougher, not anything to worry about, but enough to make Kensie grab the handhold on the conn. Burke let out a tiny smile.

"I guess you didn't get your sea legs from being on that big cruise ship yet, huh?"

Kensie scoffed. "How could I? That thing barely rocks. I mean, the weather has been downright beautiful, but if you didn't see the water going by, you wouldn't think you were moving at all. There's no chance to get any sea legs."

"I'm sure," he said, a hint of contrition in his response. "You'll get 'em today, though, hon. We got a little chop going on, and it's going to get worse once we get out of the lee of the island." Kensie was about to object to his sexist "hon" remark but was instead taken aback by the increased roar of the laboring engine when he pushed the throttle forward.

It may have been louder, but the increased noise did not translate to much more speed. *Julian's Empire II* accelerated, but only to about 14 knots – pretty slow, considering the distance they had to travel. There were other boats in sight, and they were zipping around at the head of bright, white wakes as if they were showing off.

"Is this top speed?" Kensie asked in a near yell.

"No, but I don't like to push the engines real hard, ya know?"

Kensie rolled her eyes. "It's gonna take two hours to get there!"

Burke nodded. "More like two and a half."

"I'll lose half the day! Can't you get us going a little faster?"

Burke shook his head. "It ain't worth getting there faster if I blow a bearing and we're stranded."

"Yeah, but –"

"But nothing. Getting you out and back safe and sound is my first job. If *Empire* isn't quick enough for you, we can head back right now and I'll refund you." He kept his eyes sighted over the bow, but what Kensie could see of his face told her that, short of a tsunami coming up from behind, the throttle wasn't going forward one additional inch.

*Fucking slow boat to China.*

# Chapter 4 – Unrecognized Dangers

*Finally.* Kensie had agonized for 145 minutes, wondering if they would ever arrive, until Burke took a look at the GPS and cut the engines. Now she sat on the edge of the boat with him, the hot sun almost directly overhead, as he relayed his instructions.

"OK, I know you're experienced, but this is not exactly amateur diving. Right now we're almost at the ebb tide, so it will be good going for a while, but when the tide picks up, you're going to have to be smart. The word is that the flow comes up and over the shoal suddenly, so it can pick up speed quick, and I hear it's dangerous."

"I figured that. I know what to look for."

"Good, but still you have to trust me on this. I'll stay a little above you so I have an overview of the situation. We both have push-to-talk systems as part of our dive masks," he displayed the handheld controller, "so we can communicate pretty easily. Any questions?"

"No," Kensie said, trying hard to keep the exasperation out of her voice. They were wasting time.

"When you're ready..." Burke gestured. Kensie pulled the full face dive mask over her head, tested both the airflow and the communication system and, finding them satisfactory, pitched herself backward out of the boat.

The water was far clearer than anything she'd ever experienced, and she could easily see the sandy bottom of what had once been Fraunce's Elbow. She took a moment to absorb the view while Burke splashed into the water a few feet from her. Being here, firmly believing that Captain Buckwell had almost certainly met his tragic end right here, gave her a thrill that was at once irrational and very satisfying.

A mound rose behind her, stopping only about 15 feet below the surface, showing her where the tiny spit of land had once been, but she was certain that years of current had shifted everything to the east and into deeper water. She got her bearings, signaled that she was headed down and swam toward the deeper part of the slope. Burke gave her the OK signal.

The bottom beckoned, but she forced herself to descend at a safe pace. Everywhere she looked, she could imagine the jeweled headdress resting only a few inches down in the sand. She could not divorce herself from the image of her pulling the immaculately bright metal up and tucking it into her dive bag.

*Calm down.* Fantasies aside, there was a lot of area to cover on this shoal, and it would take a lot of time and effort. She finally reached the bottom and marked her starting point on her GPS before pulling out her metal detector. She turned the discrimination way up and started sweeping it over the bottom.

The detector registered small hits almost immediately. They were far too miniscule to be the *Couronne*, but they might be of interest to her anyway. Pieces of metal, like nails or utensils from Buckwell's ship, would show the direction that the wreckage had drifted after sinking. Despite her plan to fully scan a nine point grid area around her first waypoint before exploring any returns, she gave in to the emotion of the moment, picking the most sizable return and plunging her diving shovel into the dirt. Fortunately the sand was, as expected, loose and easy to displace, although the cloud her digging created muddled the local visibility.

After getting down about 18 inches, she felt something hard *tink* against the curved metal of the shovel. Excited, she put the tool aside and sifted the fine sand through her fingers until they closed around a rough, irregular shape. She knew it wasn't something she wanted before she saw it; just a piece of volcanic rock, one which had a high iron content.

Kensie tossed it aside casually, her ardor cooling. She was letting the excitement get to her and make her act rashly. This wasn't a lark, it was a serious search and she didn't have a lot of time in which to complete it. She had to be more methodical. She was, after all, a scientist. She folded her shovel, put it back in her mesh carry bag, and resumed the search in the next square around her marker.

Thirty five minutes later, Kensie checked her watch, and then her regulator; it was almost time to head up. She hadn't realized how excited she was but, based on the number, she was breathing more heavily than normal and using a lot of air. She looked back at the area she had covered, seeing the eight markers on her hand held GPS screen, and did some quick math. Nine one yard squares for each marker made for 72 square yards she had searched. It was a decent start, but suddenly her task appeared very daunting. This slope alone, at least the part she could search by herself, was about a half mile wide and at least 500 yards long. That made for about 4,500 square yards that she wanted to search, and at this pace she would be lucky to cover half of that in the time she had for diving. It occurred to her that she might have been more than a little optimistic about her chances of success.

*Don't get ahead of yourself.* With a shake of her head, she marked a new spot and started waving the metal detector in a back and forth motion. She had time for one more grid before she had to go up, and couldn't afford to waste a single second.

***

*She's persistent.* It was their fourth and probably last dive of the day, and she had moved like a machine during each one. She was covering ground with gusto, and Burke was impressed with her tenacity, even though he still didn't believe her story about erosion studies.

She was searching for something specific, of that he was certain, and it had nothing to do with the way sediment built up and dissipated. He'd had a lot of clients who believed that piles of gold doubloons were scattered all over the bottom of the Caribbean and had set about searching for them with a $50 metal detector and a conspiratorial air suggesting they expected to discover riches beyond their wildest dreams. They always reminded him of Daffy Duck in the *Ali Baba Bunny* cartoon, where Daffy, having found massive amounts of treasure in a cave, jumped up and down on Bugs Bunny to stuff him back into his hole, all the while screaming, "It's mine! All mine! Mine! Mine! Mine!" Burke knew that wasn't at all accurate; even if someone did find any sort of valuable item, there were volumes of maritime law that dictated exactly to whom it belonged. This far out, the laws might be a bit more vague, but it wasn't like you could just keep whatever you found on the bottom. Depending on what it was and who had owned it last, it usually remained the property of that entity

But that didn't matter because, not surprisingly, no one ever found gold or other treasure in that manner, not while diving with him.

But Kensie was different. Clearly she wasn't some yahoo treasure hunter, but she was searching, and her fairly well thought out lie about what she was doing piqued his curiosity. Normally he had no interest in the ulterior motives of his clients. As long as they paid him and didn't do anything outrageously stupid or illegal, he let them be. Kensie had met both parts of that bargain, but Burke was drawn to find out what she was up to whether it involved him or not.

He saw a shadow pass over him and looked up to see the boat swinging toward the deeper end of the shoal fairly quickly. With two anchors securing the boat, that should not have been an issue, and the movement of the *Empire* suggested a tidal current even stronger than he had anticipated. The safety line he had tied from his tank harness to the stern cleat of the boat went taut for a second before he felt the invisible push of a wall of water moving him in the same direction. This shoal was infamous for the way the tide suddenly increased the flow of water on the "downwind" side, creating powerful and confusing currents that challenged the strongest of divers. He expected that was half the reason why other captains wouldn't agree to take the charter.

"Kensie, can you hear me? Time to come up. The tide is really starting to flow now."

"I just need a few more minutes," she said in the rote, distracted voice of someone fully focused on her primary task. He could see her bubble trail – it still rose almost vertically, indicating that the flow had not yet reached down to her depth. The problem, he knew, was that in the time it would take to reach her level, the force of the water would grow that much worse near the surface and put them both at significant risk. He couldn't allow that.

"No, not a few minutes. We need to go up now."

"Dammit, I'm in the middle of something here," she said in a vexed voice, "and I've still got 20 minutes." Her experience was working against her. Burke knew she felt only the slightest force from the tide, and expected that it would remain at roughly that intensity, giving her time. But she was discounting his warning.

A second, more powerful flow pushed him both forward and down. He expected the lateral movement, but not the vertical. The water was climbing over the shoal and spilling over it from above, just like clouds did over mountains, and it would make their ascent even more challenging. This was, by far, the worst example of this phenomenon he had ever experienced. If they didn't surface soon, they would be in real trouble.

"Kensie, move your ass. Right now!" He saw her pause; he had managed to convey the urgency he felt. She turned over to look at him, jerking her head back at something she saw; likely the odd position of the boat as it strained to move east, the same direction that Burke's bubble stream now trailed in a nearly horizontal path.

The rapidly changing conditions combined with Burke's entreaties made Kensie recognize that something was going wrong.

She touched the screen of her GPS and immediately began her ascent. She only got up a few feet before she started feeling the effects of the steadily growing current. "Whoa! What the hell?" she asked before making her regular ascent pause about six feet below Burke.

"It's the current I warned you about. It's worse than I imagined."

Kensie worked her arms and legs hard to remain in place. "You aren't kidding. I'm getting tired."

Burke was glad the mask hid the face he made. This was a topic he would have to address with her if she wanted to go out again, but for right now she was complying and that was what mattered. "Time. Let's head up." Kicking his feet, he surfaced about 20 feet from the boat and allowed himself to drift to it, with Kensie trailing just behind him.

***

Kensie stowed their diving gear while Burke pulled in the anchor chains and diving flag before firing up the ragged engine. They were already underway by the time she got up to the conn, where Burke stood stoically at the helm as the *Empire* pounded through the growing waves with the sun sinking in the west and bathing everything in a soft, warm orange glow.

She'd heard the irritation in Burke's voice even over the transmitter and felt bad for being the cause. She had acted foolishly today. It wasn't like her to so recklessly endanger herself and someone else. The extra five minutes she would have gained by arguing with Burke was poor compensation for the time she would lose if he decided she wasn't worth the risk and refused to take her out tomorrow.

"Hey," she said casually.

Burke nodded and may have grunted; it was hard to tell with the cacophony of internal combustion and spraying salt water.

"So, it was a good first day. I made a lot of headway." Burke nodded again, keeping his gaze fixed over the paint deficient bow. His silent treatment made Kensie uncomfortable, and the longer he kept it up, the worse the feeling got until she spoke just to fill the void.

"Look, I'm sorry. I got carried away with my work. It won't happen again. You're in charge." She gave her most disarming smile, knowing it was tinged with the regret she felt.

Burke turned to her. "It's not a matter of me being in charge. It's a matter of me recognizing danger because this is my area and not yours, and in this instance I know better." He paused, with a look on his face suggesting he was considering adding something. "You don't take 'no' for an answer very well, do you?"

Kensie's first reaction was irritation, but she quashed that feeling as she recognized the truth in his observation. "Honestly, that's why I'm here. My theory is not really popular with my fellow professors, but I'm pretty sure I'm right, so I'm out to prove it."

He nodded as if approving of her answer. "I have to admire that. Someone that focused on her goals, willing to back up her opinions with evidence and answers – well, that's a trait I can get behind." He flashed a little smile, one that showed just a hint of his teeth, and despite the gravity of the discussion, she felt her knees grow a little weak and the muscles deep in her belly flex.

"Thanks. I meant no disrespect down there. Like I said, it won't happen again."

"Forget it. We're cool."

"So," Kensie said hesitantly, wanting to be sure of her footing, "we can do another dive tomorrow?"

"Sure. I'll be a little better prepared too, with some sandwiches and something more than a few bottles of water. I didn't think I was going out today, so I didn't have anything ready. I'm starving."

Kensie hadn't thought too much about it – she was the kind of person who could ignore basic needs in favor of learning – but the mention of a sandwich made her realize that she was famished. She'd had a quick bite before getting off the ship, but that had been 11 hours earlier, and the exertion of diving had been significant. "Yeah, now that you say it, I need some food when we dock."

"I know a great place nearby. Dinner's on me – it's the least I can do after not offering you so much as a cracker all day. You in?"

Kensie felt she couldn't turn down the offer, especially after seeing Burke's mildly polite side. Now that everything was back on track with their dive tomorrow, she allowed herself to remember just how handsome this rugged islander was and how spending a little more time with him – as long as he wasn't being a dick – outside of the diving environment might be a very positive endeavor.

"Hell yeah I'm in."

# Chapter 5 – Welcome and Unwelcome Company

Burke steered Kensie through the crowd at *Arnhim's*, a tired and run down restaurant just off the harbor about a half mile from where Burke docked. He nodded and smiled at people as he passed them like he was the mayor. As she'd noted when they left the dock earlier that day, Julian Burke was a popular man. She noticed that most of the people he greeted gave her the once over, with reactions ranging from a critical eye narrowing to a more approving grin that she could not decipher.

They took a tiny table near the back, slightly removed from the bustling crowd but still close enough to feel the early evening energy it generated. It was clear that this was not a tourist location – she and Burke had, by far, the palest complexions in the place. Despite that, he was an accepted interloper and she, by virtue of being with him, felt the same way.

A chubby woman in a floral dress and a wide face with a wider smile scurried up to the table. "Burke, man! How you do? Ain't seen ya in a day's year!"

"Hey, Navia," Burke responded, rising to give her a hug. Kensie was surprised to hear Burke grunt as she gripped him in what looked like a crushing bear hug. "This is Kensie. We spent the day diving."

Kensie stood and extended her hand, but was absorbed by the same powerful grasp. "Is so nice to meet yah, Kensie," Navia exclaimed. She was so exuberant that Kensie feared she would be smothered in the taller woman's bosom.

"That's quite a greeting," Kensie responded once she had been released. "I heard this was a friendly island."

"Any friend o' Burke is my friend too." She turned back to Burke as she sat down. "Whatcha needin' tonight?"

"Do you mind if I order for you?" Burke asked, and Kensie gestured in the affirmative. "Two Wadadlis and two jackfish platters."

"Right on yo," Navia said enthusiastically. "I be missin' some people, so you'll be comin' over to get it when it's ready, OK?" Burke nodded and Navia headed away.

"What's a wuh-dod-li?"

"It's one of the best beers on the island," he explained before grimacing in potential embarrassment. "You do like beer, right? I should've asked."

She nodded. "I like beer, and I'm willing to give a new label a try."

Burke wiped his forehead with an exaggerated motion. "Phew. That's good. I'd just *hate* to have to drink both of them." A full smile, the first one she'd seen from him today, creased his face and he winked.

Kensie could not control the deep breath brought on by the full set of gleaming white teeth and dimples that looked as if they'd been drawn on by a fine tip pen. Men who looked like this didn't captain ramshackle boats and hang out in dive restaurants – they were busy being male models or enjoying their equally stunning wives.

Another stirring, stronger than the one this morning, flowed between her legs. To her embarrassment, her nipples hardened under her swim top. She could only hope that the shirt she wore over it was loose enough that they weren't becoming visible to him. Kensie couldn't pass them off to the room temperature – it was already warm outside and the number of bodies inside kept the atmosphere rather sultry.

He was almost *too* attractive – so good looking that women would be afraid to approach him. He was the man that might flash that smile across the bar to a group of women, who would then huddle up like a football team planning the best way to approach this Adonis. He would watch in amusement, enjoying the consternation that his simple act created. They'd hem and haw about who he was smiling at but, if Kensie was part of that group, she wouldn't bother to enter the conversation, knowing full well she was not the object of his attention. She certainly wouldn't go talk to him.

But she was sitting with him – alone – and right now the reason didn't matter. Well, it mattered but, since the dive site was far away and she couldn't do any searching right now, what would it hurt to indulge herself a little? *Maybe I haven't found Buckwell's treasure, but I've got his stunt double right here.*

She realized that far too many seconds had passed since his wisecrack and that she should probably respond. "Sounds like that would be a tragedy."

"Beyond description," he agreed. "Anyway, you're using this research for your doctoral dissertation?"

"Yes," Kensie answered, relieved that Burke either hadn't noticed or possessed the good manners not to mention her reaction. "I have a hypothesis that, with global warming increasing sea levels, tidal flows are going to get stronger as well, and magnetic anomalies are going to exacerbate that. What we experienced today, with that extreme flow when we surfaced for the last time" she continued, ad libbing a bit, "may have demonstrated that and it's one reason I picked this area. I think that this phenomenon is going to radically alter silt and sand distribution in shallow waters, creating numerous problems for ports and waterways with severe economic implications." Approximately three quarters of what she had just explained was total bullshit, with a few buzzwords thrown in for good measure, but she doubted that Burke would question her.

"Wow," he said, leaning away from her little speech. "How long did it take you to memorize that little elevator pitch? That's quite an interesting scenario you just described."

Kensie's grimaced. "Sorry. It's just that I've explained it so many times I've kind of gotten it down to a science. A lot of people don't really understand when I go into the technical detail."

That smile again, but this time it was tinged with... suspicion, like he didn't entirely believe what he was hearing. "Thanks for dumbing it down for me. I appreciate that."

*Did I just insult him?* "I didn't mean that. It's just that what I do is so boring that if I say much more people get kind of disinterested. Honestly, it hurts my feelings when people tune me out and start to drool."

His deep laugh rumbled like the engine on his boat. "I hardly believe that people tune you out when you're speaking, and I doubt it even more when you say it hurts your feelings." If he was trying to flatter her, he was sincere enough about it that she didn't mind one bit.

"You're too kind, Captain Burke." She liked the way that rolled off her tongue – *Captain Burke. Captain Buckwell. Lady Buckwell. Lady Burke. Hmmm...*

*Knock it off.*

"No, you're far too smart and cute for anyone to not focus on every word you say." He trailed off at the end of the sentence, like he had gone just a bit too far.

*Is he flirting with me?* With almost no experience in the matter, she wasn't certain, but that seemed to be the case. She wanted to let him, but it was silly... and impetuous... and ridiculous. It wasn't *her.* She wasn't here for a Caribbean fling, despite the way the heavy, warm air, the soft background music, and the sensual rhythm of the island suggested otherwise. She was here for momentous, serious business, and her intellect told her that Burke could not be staring at her the way she imagined he was. With a face and body like his, not only had he probably nailed most of the women on the island, it wouldn't surprise her to see him waiting as the cruise ships docked so he could pick out his next conquest. That was not what she wanted – at all.

*Then why the hell can't you hide that little grin on your face?*

Their eyes locked together, and there was a moment – Kensie had no idea how long it was – where everyone else faded into the background and they were alone in the crowded restaurant. Her mind started wandering all over his body, from his smooth, tanned chest to the way his shorts hugged his ass, down to the promising bulge at the front of his shorts. In the blink of an eye she imagined her mouth on him, biting, licking, sucking, tasting. It went far beyond seeing him as cute, even surpassing her need to see him as Cyrus Buckwell. It was raw and primal and completely new, both shocking and exciting her. She had no desire for the moment to end – in fact, she forgot their location and the context and everything else. She just *was*.

Burke seemed as happy as Kensie to let the unspoken sexual tension continue for a brief period, but eventually he shook off the spell. "I'm – uh – I'm going to go get our food." He rose but hesitated, as if waiting for a reason not to leave.

"Sure, sure," she replied, blinking as reality intruded into her consciousness once more. With a grin that was half apology and half unfulfilled opportunity, he headed to the crowded counter.

*Shit.* She took a sip of water to calm herself, feeling like she'd had an orgasm at the table. She was soaked in that particular area, and prayed that nothing had seeped through her bottoms and shorts. She took a deep breath and willed her heart – which was suddenly pounding like a *conga* drum – to slow.

"I thought you were going to call me if you went diving?"

Caught off guard by the interruption, Kensie swung to see Van from the previous night standing behind her. "Shit. You startled me!"

"Sorry," he responded in a tone that suggested he cared not a whit for any distress he might have caused. "I thought we had a deal. Why'd you skip out on me without so much as a knock on my door?"

"I got moving early. I didn't think it was appropriate to bug you at six in the morning." He seemed awfully put off.

"It would have been fine," Van said, grabbing Burke's chair and sitting backward on it with his forearms resting on the top. "Where'd you go diving?"

"Just a mile or two offshore," she answered. "Not exactly sure where. Just some cool coral formations and stuff."

Van nodded. "Just corals?"

"Well, yeah, and some fish. Nothing out of the ordinary. Why?"

"Oh, no reason. Just curious."

With her back turned, Kensie wasn't aware of Burke's approach until he spoke right behind her. "Hello."

Kensie turned. Burke stood there with two plates of food and two beers clenched awkwardly to his body. She started to stand so she could help him with the plates but Van spoke before she could grab a thing. "Hi. Something I can do for you?" His tone suggested that Burke was intruding on their conversation and was not welcome.

"Well, for starters you could get out of my seat." Burke must have heard the same thing in Van's reply and was having none of it. If Van sounded less than welcoming, Burke's voice was tinged with outright contempt.

Kensie's peacemaking instincts kicked in immediately. "Burke, this is Van. We met on the ship the other night." She saw Burke's face and was glad she wasn't the target of his intense gaze. It looked like he was waiting for the slightest provocation to turn this into a physical confrontation.

That was something Van, with his skinny and clean cut build, clearly did not want. Unable to counter Burke's determined glare, he rose slowly from the chair and backed away, not taking his eyes off of the larger man. "Sure thing. You guys enjoy your dinner. I'll talk to you soon." He smiled half heartedly at Kensie before disappearing into the crowd.

Burke set the platters down and turned his chair back to face forward before settling in it. "Geez. You talked to that ass hat on the ship?" Burke sounded amazed, almost disappointed in Kensie's taste in men.

"Well, he just kind of came up to me and started a conversation. It wasn't much – only about a five minute chat. Honestly, I hadn't thought about him at all until just now."

"He looked at me like I was moving in on his territory. I hate guys like that."

*I know what you mean.* She didn't voice her agreement; Van was gone and she was unlikely to run into him again tonight or any more on this cruise. Instead, she looked down at her plate. "So what's for dinner?" She picked up a French fry but, upon biting into it, gave it a funny look.

Burke laughed, his mood fully recovered from the minor dust up with Van. "That's not a French fry, it's a fried breadfruit. It's like a potato, but sweeter. Less starchy, too – if that matters."

Kensie took another bite. At least their conversation was back to a semblance of normalcy. "It is very different, but it's good. Kind of crisp. And of course it matters – they make it way too easy to overeat and overdrink on the boat."

Burke's eyes swept up and down her body, and somehow she didn't find his attention unnerving, which would normally be the case. "You've got plenty of calories to spare before it's a problem."

"Thanks." She felt a smile spreading across her cheeks. "But what's this?" she asked, pointing at the flaky white fish.

"That's a jackfish. Popular around here, and it's one of my favorites. Not everyone loves it, but Navia does amazing things with her recipe."

She cut off a piece and tasted it, and her eyes just lit up. "Wow! That's excellent. Most of the food on the ship is kind of cookie cutter stuff. They say it's gourmet, but it's not. It's pretty bland. But this is amazing!"

"Half of the tourists getting off these cruises are afraid of what's on the island. They have preconceived notions, and the cruise lines and taxi drivers guide them to the places that meet their expectations. The real St. Vincent – like most of the islands down here – is far more vibrant and spirited, and most people never see it." He shrugged his shoulders helplessly. "It's sad. They think they're looking for new experiences and adventures, but they're really just looking for a new wrapper on the same old stuff. True adventure isn't scripted or packaged."

*Gorgeous, eloquent, and philosophical too? This is too much – he probably rescues puppies on the side!* "That's very profound, Burke. And I have to admit that I'm like that too. I've never really given it much thought, but I kind of expect everything – including my fun – to happen a certain way. You're right – that's not a new experience at all."

"It doesn't make you a bad person," Burke backtracked. "We all get caught up in certain expectations. In some ways, I've been just as guilty of that as you," he said, and Kensie noticed how his last sentence changed his disposition from thoughtful to downcast.

"Well, then, neither of us are bad people," she pronounced forcefully enough to make the dark cloud disappear from his face.

"I'll drink to that!" He held up his bottle and she clinked it with hers before they both took a healthy sip.

"That's not bad," she commented about the beer.

Their chat moved on to the technical aspects of their dive, delving into the strong current and, as a necessary sidebar, her obstinance about surfacing when Burke told her to. She noticed that he didn't castigate her further for her error, mentioning it only as a matter of course in the conversation. Kensie appreciated it. She would have probably killed someone who did that to her if she were in charge, but he was forgiving.

"Well," Burke said as they finished off their second round of beers and the last of their fries, "I'd better get back to my boat. I've got a lot of prep to do if you want to get moving early, so I need to do it and get some rest. I suspect you're tired too." He pulled himself to his feet.

Kensie *was* dragging ass, but she was reluctant to stop chatting with Burke. Despite her first impressions from earlier in the day, she now found him to be witty, intelligent, and insightful. Combined with the way he looked, there was little reason to walk away. She toyed with the idea of bringing him back on the boat, but that was neither practical nor possible. The policy of the cruise line was very clear; no non passengers were permitted on board.

"I am," she agreed, standing up as well. "It was a long day of diving." She reached for her wallet, but Burke waved her off.

"No, don't worry about it. Like I said, I didn't have anything on the boat to eat, so it's part of the package." He turned and waved to Navia, who returned the gesture. "Ready when you are."

"Thanks, that's very gracious." Heading through the crowd to the doorway, she thought to take a quick look around for Van. She was a little relieved when she didn't see him. If he'd still been hanging around, she'd start to wonder if she had something to fear from him. Right now, he just gave her a creepy vibe. At the sidewalk, Kensie paused to say goodbye, knowing his boat was in the opposite direction of her ship.

"Thanks for taking me out today. I know it was far, but it was very productive."

Burke looked a little disappointed – at least she hoped that's what she saw in his expression. "You don't want me to walk you back to your ship?"

"You don't have to," she told him, not displeased that he asked, but knowing that he likely had more work to do before going to bed. "I'll be perfectly fine."

"OK, no problem. See you at the boat at 6:30?"

"6:30. I'll be there." Kensie had an urge to hug him, but realized that would be rather inappropriate considering their relationship. She settled for offering a handshake. Burke hesitated only a second, and when that massive, strong hand engulfed hers, she felt a slight rush at what that might indicate. His fingers had scars and callouses on them, but between those damaged areas she felt soft skin that she could imagine touching her elsewhere. The touch lingered a second longer than he should have, and Kensie recognized a pronounced sense of disappointment when they broke contact. "See ya."

"See ya."

***

Burke watched her walk away, wishing she'd let him escort her back to the ship. He didn't want to seem overprotective, but that Van guy set off alarms. Whatever he was after, it wasn't Kensie in the sense that he wanted to get her into bed.

*No, that's what you're after.*

Burke smiled to himself. Now that he had a moment to himself, he could consider the idea more fully. Her cute button nose and soft, pursed lips were enticing but, even though it was an over used idea, it was her eyes. Big and green and bursting with the thirst for... *what?* Knowledge? Vindication? Validation? Whatever it was, she was pursuing her passion and would not be denied. As he'd said on the boat, he admired such single minded enthusiasm. It drew him to her like he was parched and she was the cool, crisp drink of water that could slake his thirst.

He'd enjoyed a few relations with some of the tourists that came onto the island to snorkel over a reef, but those interactions were physical only, with no connection and no meaning beyond the taste of lips soaked in rum punch and the feel of a body warmed by the tropical sun and influenced by the hackneyed ideas of what Americans thought life down here was all about.

Kensie was different. She would not be wooed by platitudes and a nice sunset. She could see through appearances and facades. The fact that she had hired him told him all he needed to know in that area. His boat, though appearing run down, slow, and looking as if it was constantly taking on water, was a solid craft – probably the best in the harbor. He'd seen too many tourists stop in their tracks at the site of *Julian's Empire II*, like they thought it would collapse and sink if they set foot on her decks. The locals knew differently, and so did this young woman.

The look they'd shared before the food arrived had been intimate in a way he'd never known. It unnerved him more than a little. She had already found a tiny little spot in his mind and had set up shop. Now that she was entrenched, Burke worried that she wouldn't be so easy to dislodge.

Just like Jessica.

*No! That's different. This is different.* But was it?

Kensie's form grew smaller as she neared the bend in the road that would take her back to the ship. Burke told himself that he was watching her to ensure her safety, but that wasn't it, not entirely. It was his desire to look at her; and, to his amazement, he was not thinking sexually. She was much too far away for him to gape at her ass as it wiggled. He'd already done that on the boat multiple times and liked what he saw. As simple as it sounded, he just enjoyed having her in his line of sight. It made little sense but he was mature enough to recognize what that suggested.

Just before she disappeared around the corner, she looked back. Startled, he realized he'd been staring for over a minute and that it might seem creepy. But if she was put off, Kensie didn't show it.

Instead, she gave him a wave and a smile before she walked out of sight.

Both encouraged and troubled by her reaction, he headed back to *Empire* so he could put a little more thought into tomorrow's dive. No sense in being reckless.

*At least not about the diving part.*

***

The minute she stepped onto the gangway back on the ship, her phone reconnected with the cruise ship's wi-fi and it started exploding. Enough dings, beeps, and clicks emanated from the phone that the crew member checking her sea pass smiled. "Someone's been missing you."

"Oh yeah." She pulled out her phone and saw the last eight texts were from Catrina.

The last one sounded frantic. *Where the hell are you? Do I have to call the St. Vincent police?*

She smiled as she responded. *Just got on board. Sorry long day.*

*Finally! Come up to the Sand Bar.*

Kensie was exhausted and wasn't interested in having a drink with her friend, but figured she owed it to Catrina to spend a little time with her. She was still unfamiliar with the layout of the ship, so she needed an extra minute to find her way.

Catrina sat at a small table, her eyes fixed on the entrance. Kensie smiled and waved, not failing to notice the profile of the handsome young man sitting with her friend. After a word to him, she got up and made a beeline to her.

"Where in the hell have you been?" she demanded.

"I told you – I would be out diving a little, and I want to use all the time I have. Relax. Everything's fine. It's not even 10 o'clock."

"I guess," Catrina said, her consternation apparently mollified at seeing her friend safe and sound. "I was getting a little concerned."

Kensie flashed a cavalier smile. "What? You don't think I can take care of myself?"

"Oh, I know you can. I was more worried about the rest of the island after you got through with it." They laughed, all concerns forgotten. "Now that I know you haven't created an international incident, come over to my table. There's someone I want you to meet."

"I was gonna say... " Kensie allowed herself to be pulled by the hand to the cocktail table, where she could get a better look at Catrina's companion. Unlike their potential suitors the previous evening, he immediately struck her as an honest and personable man. He wore his creamy blond hair short and unkempt, and his smile was sincere and inviting, but his expression was mischievous. The combination gave him just the right amount of mystery – was he a super nice guy or a reprobate? Maybe a bit of both, she reasoned – just the right balance, especially for Catrina.

"Kensie, this is Reid DeMeo. We met coming back on board and we've been hanging out ever since. Reid, this is Kensie Prescott. We've known each other since middle school."

He extended his hand. "Kensie, it's very nice to meet you. Catrina has told me all about you, and she made you sound very impressive. An associate professor at 28 is something special."

Kensie waved him off although she took pleasure in his compliment. "Well, Catrina has a habit of exaggerating, but thank you. I do invest in my work."

"If anything," Catrina interjected, "I've undersold her. I haven't told you half of what she's accomplished."

"Oh, stop it! Reid, don't listen to her."

Reid laughed. "You guys realize you're putting me in a very difficult situation," he said, rolling his eyes for effect. "Support the girl or support her best friend. I can't win, so I'm going to get drinks while you two sort this out. Kensie, what would you like?"

Kensie waved him off. "Oh, no, I'm already exhausted and I've had a few beers."

"Are you sure you won't stay for one drink?" Kensie looked to Catrina, who gave her the half wink that she was welcome – nay, required – to stay. But only for a while.

"OK, you convinced me. How about a Rum Runner?"

"Coming up. And another *Mojito* for you?"

"Of course." He moved toward the bar.

Catrina's smile emitted intense wattage. "What do you think?"

Kensie nodded intently. "He's cute. And he seems nice too."

"Right?" she agreed. "I feel really comfortable with him, but I think there's a dirty side to him that I could have fun with." She ran her tongue over her lips. "I want to bite those fucking lips!"

Kensie shook her head in mild embarrassment. Catrina was rarely shy about expressing her interest in a guy, and was just as comfortable talking about it in detail. Kensie was not a prude, but she had a little trouble verbalizing such desires. She could tell that her friend was smitten.

"Well, do what you have to do, but don't get carried away. You've got a few more nights to bite him wherever you want."

"Of course, mother... I'll ease him in!" The pair giggled as Reid made his way back to the table, his hands wrapped around three glasses, each shaped so differently that he seemed destined to drop them, but he arrived without incident.

"Didn't think I'd make it," he joked, distributing the beverages before perching on his seat once more. He took a sip of his beer before addressing Catrina. "Does your highly educated friend approve of me?"

"So far, yeah." Catrina used a wary tone. "But that could change at any moment, so I'd be on my best behavior if I was you!"

"I promise... at least until I have a few more drinks. After that, all bets are off." He turned to Kensie. "So I've heard all about Catrina's *fascinating* world of software development and project management, but I'm hoping you can steer the conversation in a more – shall we say, stimulating direction."

Catrina slapped his shoulder. "I'll give you stimulating!" They all laughed in unison, and Kensie could see the connection between the new couple. The signs were easy to see in her friend, but Reid's body language suggested that he was both open and receptive to Catrina. The more they conversed, the more she felt comfortable with him. Catrina was not shy around men in which she had an interest, but her choices in them had often been questionable. Maybe this was a shift in the right direction.

She spent a couple of minutes discussing the basics of marine archaeology, answering Reid's very relevant questions, before realizing that in her zeal to describe her passion, she was monopolizing the conversation. "You keep asking me about my work, and that makes me think you're hiding something," she told him playfully. "What do you do?"

Reid didn't miss a beat. "I film, direct, and distribute hardcore fetish porn throughout Eastern Europe."

Caught unawares and a little too tired for her own good, Kensie's gaped at his answer. She was contemplating an appropriate answer until she saw Catrina bring her fist to her mouth in a poor attempt to stifle a giggle and knew that she was being had.

"Excellent," she replied when she recovered. "Maybe I could star in one of your movies someday." Now it was Catrina's turn to gawk at Kensie's response.

Reid lifted his glass. "She's quick. Awesome. I'm actually a police detective in Atlantic City, New Jersey."

"So much for fun. The cops are here." Catrina looked disappointed, although it was obvious she already knew it.

"I told you. I'm off duty and *way* out of my jurisdiction. I have no authority down here."

"Yeah, I know. But I hope," Catrina said with a sly smile that was surely influenced by her latest *mojito*, "that you at least brought your handcuffs in case I get a little... unruly." There was no way any male with a pulse could miss that message, and that meant it was time for Kensie to go.

"On that note..." she stood and knocked back the rest of her Rum Runner. "Reid, it was nice meeting you. Thank you for the drink, and don't let Catrina hurt you too badly."

"I think it's far too late for that," he said with a sidelong glance that was just as salacious as Catrina's had been. "But I appreciate the warning. And it was nice meeting you as well."

She gave Catrina a quick hug. "I'll see you sometime later tonight. My phone is on in case you need me, although I am sure that Reid will take perfect care of you."

"Scout's honor," he said, holding up three fingers in the Boy Scout salute.

"Bye, guys."

Heading forward toward her cabin, she gave an additional moment of thought to Catrina's new beau. Kensie wasn't always great a judge of character – she was more concerned with artifacts deep in the ocean, and they offered little in the way of personality – but she felt good about Reid. At first glance, he appeared to be the complete package: honest, charming, and good looking. *Extremely* good looking – in a way that gave her a fleeting moment of regret that Catrina had seen him first. She had no way of knowing if Catrina might want to see him after the cruise, considering he lived kind of far away, but who knew? Atlantic City was only about an hour and a half away, and there was the ferry to Cape May.

The issue with most of the guys that Catrina went after was that they were all self professed alpha males, convinced that women should be fighting over them. Reid either didn't realize quite how sexy he was, or he was smooth enough to know it and not to flaunt it. That made him doubly appealing.

*Kinda like Burke.*

She paused in mid step as the thought steamrolled into her head. If there was ever a time and place where carnal thoughts needed to be banished completely, this was it. Possibly one of the greatest maritime treasures in history was out there, and she might be the only person who could find it. This was not the time for a fling, or even a passing crush.

*So when is the time? You've always got something to do or study or figure out. When do you get to find your personal treasure?*

It was not the first time she'd heard that internal warning, but this evening it seemed louder than normal. Perhaps it was the possibility of the momentous discovery she felt she was on the brink of. Perhaps it was the romantic vibe of the ship and the alcohol – she wasn't a big drinker and two beers and a mixed drink had her feeling quite happy. But most likely it was those arctic blue eyes, the way the right side of his mouth rose higher than the left when he smiled and exposed his *absolutely perfect* teeth, and the tight muscles that rippled when he walked or heaved an air tank up over the gunwale of his boat.

Whatever it was, she pushed it aside. She had other things to do, like review the charts and other information about the shoal. Now that she had been there in person, she might be able to pick up additional insights as to where to search. She hadn't found so much as a coin today, and if she didn't come up with some leads soon, she would run out of time.

Kensie plopped down on the tiny desk in their cabin and started looking through the papers and notebooks she had brought along with her. She could have started her laptop, but she'd perused every site that might help her and memorized those. She tried to record a few observations, but found that her writing was becoming indecipherable as the fatigue hit her hard.

*Oh, the hell with it. I'll review them on the boat on the way out. It's not like it's a fast boat.*

With that issue resolved, she set the alarm on her phone for a far too early time, turned the small entryway light on for Catrina, and crawled into bed. She was asleep within seconds.

# Chapter 6 – High Seas Exposure

Burke was up long before the sun, and not just to replenish his tanks and stock up on food and supplies. He'd been caught unawares the previous morning and hadn't had the opportunity to get a better understanding of his dive site, and he wasn't about to go out without being properly informed a second time. He rubbed the sleep out of his eyes and hunched his large frame over the laptop in the V-berth of *Empire*.

The topographical and diving specific details were a little different but still predictable to someone with his experience. He could see why the tide was so powerful in this location. Checking the lunar tables, he recognized that the flow would grow stronger each day as the moon exerted greater and greater influence, getting a few minutes later in the evening. Burke made a mental note to keep that in mind; with only his tether connecting him to *Julian's Empire II* as he dove, he had to stay ahead of any problems.

But that wasn't the only reason Burke was surfing the web while stars still shone brightly overhead. He wanted to know what Kensie was after. Of course, he had no reason to care why this young woman wanted to travel all the way out to some hump of sand – he was being properly compensated for his time – but Kensie's story just didn't add up. And for some unknown reason, he was desperate to know more.

She was far too intelligent to be treasure hunting on a whim, and her careful and methodical search pattern was scientific and precise. The geology and topography of the area was interesting, but hardly unique. She could have done her "research" in a hundred other places from Nova Scotia to Florida instead of traveling all the way down here. And her metal detector? She'd claimed it was to locate magnetic anomalies, which made about as much sense as using a divining rod to search for a lost wallet.

He pulled up a listing of shipwrecks and started plotting their locations against Fraunce's Shoal. Not surprisingly, there were many more known wrecks on the western side of St. Vincent than the east. What sane captain would want to take his ship through the rougher, less predictable Atlantic when he could stay in the relatively safe confines of the Caribbean? Even the triangle that could be formed between St. Vincent, Grenada, and Barbados had only a few wrecks marked there. If there was a sunken ship near where they were diving, Kensie appeared to be the only one that knew about it. He should've asked around the island for more details about the location, but there hadn't been time.

He kept running into dead ends with each theory. No matter how he tried to configure a voyage, there was no reason to steer so far offshore toward Fraunce's Shoal, when an inshore track, nearer the lee of the islands, would do. It was far safer, especially if this trip had been before modern electronic communications, and good sailors respected the sea and the power it held. You would only be that far offshore to stay hidden from other ships... or people on the islands... who might see or remember something... if asked in the right way.

*Like if you were a pirate and had just stolen something.*

The idea made Burke smile at first. Was he after real, actual pirate plunder? Buried treasure? That was the stuff of fanciful legend and old books and, although he wanted to dismiss the idea as a delusion of his not totally awake mind, he could not think of anything that would force him to disqualify the possibility.

"Son of a bitch," he mused to the bulkhead. It would explain the white lies Kensie was telling him and everything about her diving habits. He'd have to watch her with a more critical eye today.

A hint of dark blue on the eastern horizon caught his attention, and he looked at his watch. It was time for him to stop playing detective and start being a boat captain. Gathering up yesterday's exhausted tanks, he put them, along with the oversize cooler, on his little pull cart and headed down the dock to get the supplies he needed for the long day ahead.

***

Burke was doing his final gear check when he saw Kensie's lithe figure moving down the dock toward him. He made a show of inspecting the mask that he currently held, appearing to concentrate hard enough to see the molecular structure of the plastic, but the mask could have been made from rock candy for all he saw; he looked past it to home in on the tiny wag of her hips as they propelled her toward him. He found himself nearly mesmerized by the rhythm of her movements and imagined she was doing it for his benefit.

"Morning, Captain," Kensie said in the hushed tone that suggested she hadn't quite shaken off the last vestiges of sleep. Burke dropped any pretenses and gave her his full attention – and nearly dropped the mask he held. Unlike yesterday, the button down shirt she wore was open, exposing her upper body through her bathing suit. Even though it was a one-piece that covered her midriff, the material was both thin and clingy enough that he could make out the bottom curves of her impressive breasts and the outline of her nipples in the dim morning light. He blinked, but it wasn't easy taking his eyes off of her.

Her shorts did little to hide the pronounced curve of her hips, and he somehow found that more enticing than her upper body. He felt powerless to stop the mental movie that played in his head, of him lying on his back in his bunk, his hands grasping those hips (but without those shorts) as Kensie straddled him, those expressive lips parted in a silent moan, her head thrown back, her naked chest heaving as she slid up and down on his rigid –

"Uh, Captain Burke?"

He started back to reality. "Sorry, Kensie. You caught me in the middle of a thought." He glanced at his watch, even though he knew exactly what time it was. "You're early."

Kensie nodded. "I figured I could give you a hand getting ready. I've got a limited amount of time left here, and there's a lot of ground to cover."

"That's true. I'm pretty much all set, so come aboard and we'll shove off." She complied and stowed her pack as Burke fired up the clamorous engines, and momentarily they were out of the privacy of the little cul-de-sac and moving through the main harbor. There was a little activity ashore as people made preparations for another day on the water, but no other boats were moving yet. He expected Kensie to stand by the conn as she had yesterday, but instead she sat at the small table in the main cabin, spreading notes and papers about and making small piles as she skimmed each one. As soon as he cleared the entrance and ensured that there were no boats or other obstacles in their proximity, he put the autopilot on and leaned over.

"Whatcha doin'?"

She gave him a quick glance. "Since we have all this time, I need to record my findings and progress from yesterday and see if I found something I can use."

"Wouldn't you recognize a clue right when you found it?"

"Not necessarily. There's far too much data to analyze in real time," she explained patiently. "When you see trends or things that can't be coincidental, that's what you follow."

"Oh, I see," Burke said neutrally. *Of course, you didn't notate a damn thing yesterday. Why are you lying to me?*

"In fact, I might have to bring up some sand to take back to school for more study."

"You do realize that you can't bring sand or rocks from the island – or any island, for that matter – into the U.S. without the permission of the USDA Plant Protection and Quarantine Permit

Unit?" By the look on her face, he was willing to bet that the issue had not crossed her mind.

"No, I didn't. I guess I'll have to figure that out before I head home," she said kind of lamely.

"Yeah, you might," Burke said, working to contain his amusement. "Maybe you can do your analysis before you get back on the ship."

"Yeah, maybe," she answered. "Maybe I won't have to take stuff home, or maybe just a tiny amount. Do you really think a customs agent is going to be looking for a little baggie of dirt?"

"No. They'll be looking for other stuff in baggies."

She laughed. "If you knew me better, you'd realize how crazy that idea is. I tried pot one time in college – I turned green and almost threw up."

*She's trying to change the subject.* "You do strike me as a little clean cut."

She raised an eyebrow sarcastically, affecting an offended look. "Do I now? What do you use as a measuring stick?"

"Mostly the clientele I take out," he said before turning a little more serious. "You'd be amazed at the number of people who either board the boat shit faced or swig a dozen beers and then think they're all good to go down."

"Really? Do people have that little common sense?"

"I don't think it's a lack of common sense. It's the lowered inhibitions. They're in the tropics, they're on vacation, they want to have a good time, and the rules don't matter for the week they're here. But I don't think I have to worry about that with you. You're working and, like I said, I don't see you as someone who needs to let her hair down so recklessly." He stood up quickly and scanned the horizon to make sure everything was still clear before addressing her once more. "I'll let you get back to work. I've got a boat to drive, and maybe we can get out there a little faster today."

"Thanks."

He returned to the wheel, adjusting course and pushing the throttle forward a bit further than he had yesterday. *I've got a funny feeling this is going to be an interesting day.*

***

Kensie wasn't thrilled with the questions that Burke was asking, even though she would have done exactly the same thing had their roles been reversed. She was shocked when he mentioned the restrictions about taking natural items from an island, because that was the first time she realized that similar rules probably applied to salvage that had a significant monetary value. She didn't really know – and hadn't considered – the legality of doing so. She could try and pass it off as cheesy fake jewelry (who would expect anyone to come back with something worth hundreds of millions of dollars?) but had no idea if that would work. *You might be smart, Kens, but you didn't think this one through.*

Well, she'd have to deal with that issue when and if it presented itself. There was no sense worrying about Step 38 when she was still on Step 5. She looked at the markings she'd made, wondering if she could figure out a way to cover more ground in less time but still be thorough. Her plan, to cover every inch of ground by going back and forth, probably wasn't going to cut it, at least not until she found something that she could use as a new starting point. Maybe she could alternate grid spots? A debris trail would spread out all over the place, so she could double her search speed and still find anything that was there.

She ruminated over her plan, and soon the rocking of the boat and the grinding of the engine faded into the background. Kensie wondered if she could enlist Burke's help beyond having him just stay as top cover. He seemed competent and knowledgeable, and she figured she could request his services with a decent sounding cover story that didn't divulge her true intentions. She'd have to figure out how to get him out of her way if he found something so she could be the one to find the *Couronne* and keep it hidden from him. He seemed nice enough, but there was no telling what he might do if he was next to her when she dug it out of the mud herself. *Good job, Kens. You picked a guy who's six inches taller and a hundred pounds heavier than you, and you're out here alone with him.* She shook her head; sometimes her audacity surprised her.

If she did find the *Couronne*, she'd wondered where her financial obligation to Burke ended. Did she owe him anything more than the agreed upon fee (which she'd already given him for today), or was he entitled to a percentage of the salvage? Right was right, and it would be an affront to her sense of decency to hog all the credit and any reward she might get. She'd have to give him something extra for being willing to take her out here.

*And what kind of 'extra' are you thinking about?*

The thought jumped into her mind unbidden, but she wasn't willing to ignore it. She caught the way his eyes locked onto her chest at the dock, and only belatedly realized that the cool morning breeze off the water had given her nipples a bit of an early wake up call. He'd played it off, but it took no great leap of woman's intuition to know what the male mind was thinking at that moment. Rather than offend or bother her, she felt a little flattered. Kensie wasn't usually the object of a man's attention, so when one as drop dead gorgeous as Burke assessed her body and gave it at least a passing grade, she took it as a compliment, staring at his lips as they'd stumbled through his poor excuse for ogling her.

Truth be told, she had no objection to the thought of having those lips all over her, at least as an abstract idea. In contrast to the chronic scruff on his jaw, they appeared soft and inviting, and she could imagine the way they would feel capturing her neck between them, softly sucking at the skin, moving downward over the top of her breastbone, pulling aside the fabric of her swimsuit to find that her nipples had gone from slightly hard in the chilly air to rock hard from the way he used them on her. And when they closed over the sensitive nub, she could feel her mouth drop open at the exquisite tingling that ran from her chest down through her belly and right to the very center of her –

The engines quieted and the boat began to slow. Shaking her head to get back to reality, she got up and stuck her head out through the hatch. "What's wrong?"

"Nothing," Burke said, giving her a funny look. "We're here."

Kensie glanced at her watch. "Already?" It had only been about an hour and 50 minutes, far less than their travel time the day before.

"Better sea conditions, so we ran a little faster," Burke explained. "Are you OK? You look kinda flushed."

Kensie realized the mini fantasy had gotten the better of her. "Yeah, I'm fine. It's just a little stuffy below and I was kind of focusing on work and not paying attention."

"Cool," Burke replied, shrugging. "I'm going to put us right on the same GPS spot I used yesterday. Does that work for you?"

"Uh, yeah, sure thing."

"OK. I'll drop the anchors. Go ahead and suit up."

***

Kensie waited for the bubbles that accompanied their entry into the water to dissipate before she keyed her mic button. "All set?" she asked Burke, who was treading water a few feet above her.

"You're good to go," he responded.

She used her hand held GPS to return to the area she had already searched, immediately creating a new waypoint and getting down to the tedious but necessary task of waving the detector back and forth like she was weed whacking the bottom. She didn't want to ask Burke to help her search, not yet. She still had time. Today was going to be the day, she kept telling herself. *Today I'm going to find something that confirms that I'm in the right place, that my theory was right, that points me in the right direction.*

Reality disagreed. When Burke called down to remind her to check her air, she hadn't gotten a single hit. She looked back at the underwater slope, surprised at how much she'd covered, but daunted by how much more was waiting. With a little frustration, she kicked her legs to propel herself upward.

"How'd it go," Burke asked once she was back on deck, handing her a bottle of water as she took a few minutes to rest. Diving was hard work.

She drained a third of the bottle with one prolonged gulp. It seemed weird that, after being immersed in water for the better part of an hour, she was always parched after a dive. "Well, I covered a lot of ground. No anomalies, at least nothing I noticed. But that just means I'm eliminating all the wrong spots and getting closer to the right one."

Burke gave her a crooked smile that suggested she was being a bit Pollyanna-ish. "You don't lack confidence."

*If you only knew how much I'm faking that.* "I'm one of those people who thinks a positive attitude helps you get things done."

"Well, then far be it for me to dissuade you. Whenever you want to get back to it, I'm ready."

***

*Keep going. Just keep looking. The more ground you cover, the better chance you have.* Kensie kept repeating the encouragement to herself, almost like a chant. Self doubt was poking around the edge of her consciousness, and letting it in would be like admitting defeat. She couldn't just expect something like this to fall in her lap, she knew. She had to work at it.

Knowing that and believing it, however, were very different things. She was getting angry; at her stupid idea, at the NAS for not listening to her, at the world for not letting her find what she needed to find. So she pressed on. Scan. Mark. Move. At least the monotony kept her from thinking about how she would feel if she – wasn't successful. She almost used the word *wrong* but stopped herself. She knew she was right. She just had to be patient.

*Weeahhhwuhh!*

Kensie was so surprised by the emphatic response coming through her headphones from the detector that she nearly dropped it before regaining her senses. Waving the head back and forth several times, she got a rough fix on whatever she had found and immediately marked a waypoint on her portable GPS. She turned to look surreptitiously at Burke, but he either hadn't noticed her abrupt movement or hadn't cared. With slow, steady movements, she removed her shovel and started to delicately dig, pushing the sand aside and trying to ignore the voice in her head that was telling her to *hurry up!*

She dug deeper and deeper, throwing up a huge cloud of sediment so big that eventually there was no hiding what she was doing. It couldn't be helped, but the less she told Burke, the better. Sure, he was cute (*OK, fucking gorgeous!*) but she still wasn't comfortable giving him any more information than necessary.

She heard Burke key his transmitter. "You find something, Kensie?"

*Shit.* "Maybe. There's quite a shift in the magnetic field right here. It's worth checking out."

Burke merely grunted. He seemed to vacillate between insightful questions and casual disinterest without rhyme or reason, but this wasn't the time to care. She had to concentrate on her work. If there was something of value right below her, she couldn't lose it or damage it by being careless or hasty.

*Clink.*

It was the softest of reports, barely enough to feel through the handle of the shovel, but it was unmistakable, unlike the natural metal deposit she'd struck the day before. It felt *different.* Carefully, she reached into the sand, pushing down slowly to get under the return so as to not further displace whatever it was. Her index finger hit something solid and straight, and she knew from experience that straight lines rarely existed in nature.

Leaving her hand in place, she retrieved her seine net and started working it into place a couple of inches behind the object so she could scoop it up. She refused to break contact with whatever it is; it would be far too easy to lose it despite it being so close, so she pushed the net along her hand until she was sure it was directly underneath the item. Then, with agonizing slowness that belied her urgency, she pulled it up and guided the artifact until she felt the mesh give way to the unyielding presence of an item far larger – and heavier – than sand.

*Gotcha!*

Of course, pulling it out released another storm cloud of sand and sediment, so she had no choice but to wait one more interminable minute until the water cleared and she could get a good look at it.

It was a nail, but not a nail that one would buy in bulk from Home Depot. The head was rounded, but unevenly, and the first centimeter or so of the shaft was round as well, while the remainder of it was four sided, tapering down to a dull point. Even in the water, Kensie could feel the substantial weight, making the nail wrought iron. She felt almost light headed. This was a lead, a real lead.

More. She needed more. One nail could be a random occurrence, but several established a pattern. Not only would it help her search, it would be *real* evidence – even if she didn't find the *Couronne,* it would be enough to convince her colleagues that she'd been right. That would be almost – but not quite – as satisfying as pulling the jeweled headdress itself up from the bottom.

Carefully, like it was alive and might swim away if she allowed it, she transferred the nail from the net to the pouch on her belt, making sure that the drawstring was secured tightly before resuming her search with renewed enthusiasm and gusto.

***

*She's onto something.*

Burke watched from his vantage point about 15 feet over Kensie as the brown cloud spread out under her. He waited as long as he could stand, but when he asked what she was doing, her answer was such an obvious lie that he felt insulted and considered calling her out right then and there. His irritation, however, morphed into curiosity as she pulled her net and fished something from the sand, placed it in her bag with care, and started waving the detector around once more.

"What'd you pick up?"

The excitement in her voice was unmistakable. "A nail. It looks pretty old, like early 19$^{th}$-century. One of my colleagues will go ape shit when I tell him I found this here."

*At least that lie was a little more plausible.* "That's interesting. I can't wait to see it."

"I'll be glad to –" With her finger on the transmit button, her voice was drowned out in favor of the sound of the metal detector indicating it had come across more items. Kensie must not have realized that, as she continued her sentence unabated when the noise ended. " – looks like I found some more." She grabbed her shovel and resumed digging.

Burke thought about going down to join her, but his job was to watch her back, and he had to take that role seriously no matter how curious he was. She moved a little faster, digging a little more aggressively, every few seconds depositing another item in her dive bag before waving the detector around again. She settled into a pattern: dig, collect, move, scan with the detector. He listened as she worked; either by accident or design, she'd left her mike open. She had a habit of mumbling to herself when she was concentrating, and her current running commentary was sprinkled with excitement. "OK... right there! Careful... got it! Nope. OK, wait. What was?... oh, nothing. This looks... what the?... wait. Oh wow!" Burke felt like he was listening to a football game on the radio with the worst announcer in the world.

Kensie worked in a meandering line down the underwater slope, going deeper with every item she retrieved. He watched carefully, trusting her smarts but thinking she might follow the trail to the abyssal ocean bottom if left to her own devices. She was getting close to 60 feet when he checked his watch.

"Kensie, check your air. You've got to be getting a little low."

"Already?" She checked her regulator. "Shit. OK. Do I have time to get this last thing I'm reading?"

*At least she's asking.* "Yeah, you've got a couple of minutes, but make it quick."

"Fast as I can, I promise." She resumed digging. "All right, let me mark my final spot." She pressed a few controls on her GPS and started her ascent, pausing near Burke. He could tell she was trying to control her breathing, which was still forceful. He doubted it was from the exertion of digging down 24 inches in soft mud.

"Looks like you hit some kind of motherlode," he said to pass the time.

"Yeah, I did. The things I found are pretty cool!"

"Does this play into your magnetic distortion theories?" He watched her face through her mask intently as he asked the question, and his hypothesis was confirmed by her reaction and momentary blank stare.

"My what?

"The magnetic distortion issues. The reason you told me we were diving."

"Oh. Actually, no. This is just kind of a surprise, but a good one." Her eyes reminded him of his little nephew's on Christmas morning looking at all the gifts that he was about to open.

"You seem pretty enthused about it though," he remarked.

"It's a discovery," she said. "Some of this stuff is 200 years old, and I'm the first person to see it since then. That's kinda cool, don't you think?"

"Yeah, I suppose." He glanced at his watch. "Let's head up." *I need to find out what you're really doing here.*

# Chapter 7 – Man-Bun and Hat-Head

Back on the deck, Kensie, in her excitement, dropped her diving gear all over the place in her rush to open her dive bag. Her hands shook with the emotion of the moment; if she was right, Cyrus Buckwell might have actually touched some of the items in it, and for her that was the equivalent of getting backstage passes to a *Rolling Stones* concert and having a drink with Mick. She fumbled with the drawstrings for several seconds before finally getting the bag open.

Burke moved more casually, putting his diving equipment back in the appropriate places and shaking his head at his passenger's scattered mess before sitting next to Kensie at the table in the cabin where she was setting her booty out. Even in her haste, she noticed that he hadn't bothered to put on a shirt, and a wave of heat moved through her lower body. *Like I'm not already excited.* Of course, they were two very different kinds of excitement, but she found them to be cumulative to the point that she was nearly hyperventilating.

Burke set a plastic container on the table and filled it with fresh water. "How'd you know I'd need that?"

"Kensie, this is not my first day diving. I've found things underwater before, and I know how to take care of them. Especially metal objects. At the very least, they need a freshwater bath."

"Oh. Right." Kensie felt a little foolish; Burke was smarter than he had first appeared, and she was thinking of him like some sort of lackey. A very enticing lackey, to be sure, but that was rude. "Thanks very much."

"Welcome."

"OK," she began, taking a second to get her breathing to settle down. "Here, obviously, we have about 25 nails. These are Type A nails, which means they were used in the late 18$^{th}$ and early 19$^{th}$ century. Obviously, from where they were found, they were used in a ship – probably a brigantine because they were constructed almost exclusively with this type of nail. You can see how the thin edges of the head are bent slightly out, which was common with ship nails because of the constant stress put on the timbers of the hull." She saw Burke grin in uncontained amusement. "What?"

"I've never seen anyone get so excited or know so much about 200 year old nails, that's all."

"This stuff doesn't exactly change too much, so it's not hard to memorize it." She picked up the other nails in groups of five or six and immersed them in the tray. "Now here," she said, grabbing the first of several coins in the pile, "this is even more interesting. This is a halfpenny provincial token from Middlesex County in London. These are actually fairly common as collector's items now, but they were minted at about the same time as the nails.

"This one is what's called Maundy Money. We find it all the time in shipwrecks. It's not really money – it was given out the day before Good Friday by the church to elderly or poor people, and they would trade it with friendly merchants for food, who kind of accepted the coins as charity. Now," she said, flipping it over, "the date says 1800, but that date was used on any Maundy coin minted between 1800 and 1815." She placed it, along with the other coins, in the water with the nails.

Kensie picked up the last item, which definitely wasn't a coin. It looked more like an ornate magnifying glass with the glass broken out of it. The gold handle was meticulously crafted and badly bent but otherwise intact, with a small jewel that looked like a ruby in the middle and a smaller ring at the bottom. "I don't know what this is. It looks like a magnifying glass, but it seems awfully –"

"It's a quizzing glass," Burke interrupted.

"A what?"

"A quizzing glass," he repeated. "It's the early version of a monocle. Men of status and privilege who liked to look fancy – they were called 'dandies' then, kind of like metrosexuals today – would wear one around their necks by a chain from the small ring at the bottom, and pick it up to read things. It was a fashion choice."

Kensie gawked. "How do you know that?"

"I do have an education, Kensie. I know what I'm talking about."

He sure sounded like he did, but his description confused her. If Burke was right, there was no way such a man would have ever been on *Aberaeron Fortune*. Not only would he never be invited on board, he wouldn't last 10 minutes with the lot on that ship.

"But that doesn't fit," she mumbled, furrowing her brow and looking down and away.

"Doesn't fit what?"

Kensie kind of heard him, but she was so deeply lost in her own set of questions that she barely registered that a question had been asked. When it finally came to her, she answered reflexively. "The crew. There were no fancy gentlemen in the crew."

"The crew of what? A ship?"

She nodded, still pondering. "Yeah, the *Aberaeron For –*" Realizing she had just exposed her lies, she turned to face him once again. She felt the color drain from her face when she saw Burke's arrogant grin that told her he has just learned something very interesting.

"You're not here to analyze sediment deposits and magnetic fields, but that is about the most impressive load of bullshit I've heard in a long time. If you went to all the trouble to craft that kind of lie, there has to be a really good reason to do it. So, since I've sailed all the way out here – twice – how 'bout you tell me what you're really doing?"

Kensie was busted and she knew it. For a couple of seconds, her mind raced as she tried to come up with another lie to explain her way out of this, but nothing came to mind. She let out her breath in surrender. "You're right. Sorry, but I thought a cover story was a good idea. Guess it wasn't good enough.

"I'm here because I suspect a ship called the *Aberaeron Fortune* sunk on this spot in 1806, but no one in my scientific community believes me. I think it carried something valuable so, when I had a chance to come here and look for myself, I jumped at it. You were the only one willing to drive to this spot, so here we are."

Burke's eyes narrowed, like an idea was forming and he was sorting it out. "Who was on this ship?"

She felt a little foolish telling him the name of her dead love interest, even though he couldn't know about the romantic aspect. "A pirate named Cyrus Buckwell."

He smirked in satisfaction, like he'd just confirmed a theory. "And this Buckwell stole something valuable, and you think it went down with the ship in this spot?"

"That's my theory. Or at least it was until I found that thing," she said, gesturing toward the quizzing glass. "Buckwell was a ruffian of a man. There's no way in hell a guy who considered himself a hard as nails pirate would ever have something like that. It's like a biker riding his Harley in a tuxedo. It makes zero sense." But it also made zero sense for ancient ship building nails to be in the same place as a toy for dainty gentleman. Was she on a wild goose chase, wasting her time in pursuit of a ridiculous fantasy? Maybe she'd have been better off staying on the *Amore of the Seas*, sucking down Rum Runners and bleeding off stress and having fun, instead of searching the ocean floor on nothing more than a hunch. She looked at the deck, troubled. She was sure her theories had merit, but the evidence suggested otherwise.

Burke put his hand under her chin and lifted until she met his gaze. She figured he'd take the chance to give her a polite piece of advice about how reality worked. Who turns a cruise vacation into a search for lost treasure?

But when Burke spoke, his tone was one of a teacher trying to help a slow student make an elementary connection. "So you think that this pirate stole a valuable treasure but don't think it's possible that this same man swiped a little jeweled monocle – made of gold, with a ruby embedded in it – from some high society sissy?" He looked amused and waited patiently for Kensie to process the possibility of the scenario he presented.

Kensie's somber eyes widened once more as she realize his idea made perfect sense. There were numerous accounts of Buckwell seeing something he wanted and taking it on a whim, and with the almost non existent risk that a cultured wimp presented, he would almost be begging to have it taken. Buckwell probably wouldn't have even bothered to beat him up.

Coins of the time period, the right kind of nails, the right place, and now something that Buckwell or one of his crew could have easily "liberated" from a delicate gentleman – it did make perfect sense. "This could really be the *Aberaeron Fortune*!" In her overwhelming excitement, she reached over and wrapped her arms around the taller man's shoulders, pulling his upper body down to her in an enthusiastic and aggressive hug. "Holy shit!"

Burke started but didn't back away, and as Kensie went to disengage, she caught sight of how his eyes rivaled the color of the water and how the muscles around them softened as his gaze bored into hers. Her wide, intense smile slowly faded and she felt no desire to look away. Without consciously deciding to do so, she closed her eyes and moved her head forward just enough to press her slightly parted lips to his.

His mouth was soft and tender, and she nibbled just a bit on the delicate flesh, letting the tip of her tongue peek out and slide across his lower lip. He seemed shocked and wooden at first, evidently not expecting such an assault, but in short order she felt him respond with a firm, soft movement of his own. She felt his hands grip her back and shoulders with a light caress and inhaled deeply. Burke's skin, infused with salt water, made for a bouquet both musky and fresh like the sea. It was *manly* in a way she'd never known nor imagined, and it made her nipples go hard under her swimsuit. She didn't care if he felt them or not.

Finally, she leaned her head back and let her eyes peek open, and only then did she fully take stock of what she had done. "Oh! Geez, I'm sorry. I just kinda got caught up in the moment, that's all. I didn't mean to – well, you know." Neither she nor Burke let go of the other person.

Burke seemed a bit flushed and breathless but otherwise unconcerned. "Kensie, I didn't exactly pull away, did I?"

"No," Kensie replied. Replaying the last few seconds, she felt as if he'd restrained himself from going further with her.

"You're a big girl. I'm sure you understand."

Kensie felt a silly grin spread over her features at Burke's acknowledgment of the chemistry between them.

"But, for right now, I think we have other work to do. Don't you agree?"

Kensie, with her body doing all sorts of fascinating things in all the right places, had no idea what he was talking about for a second. Burke darted his eyes to the side, at the plastic tray containing the remnants of the *Aberaeron Fortune* as if to remind her of the other reason she was so excited.

"Yeah, you're right," she agreed, releasing her grip on his shoulders and settling back into her seat. She loved the way his fingers brushed along her arms as she withdrew them.

"Good. We will revisit this topic at a better time," he said, his eyes flashing with deviltry, "and in the right place, but we have a lot more diving ahead of us. So let's get to it."

"Right." She followed his lead and stood, going back on deck to get a fresh tank from the rack when a flash demanded her attention. "What was that?"

"What was what?"

"I saw a flash – like off a window or something. Northeast." She pointed, and he quickly spotted the tiny white dot of a boat running at high speed and almost right at them. It was about a mile away.

"Who the hell would be coming over here?" Burke mumbled, half to himself.

"I'm sure they're just passing by," Kensie said hopefully.

Burke shook his head. "They should have seen us by now. Either they're not looking where they're going, or they have a reason to come right to us. Either way, I don't like it."

Kensie had the presence of mind to re-enter the cabin, remove the artifacts from the tub of water, and put them back into her dive bag for safekeeping. She stashed it just inside the door to the cabin, ensuring it was well hidden. She had just as much idea about what was going on – zilch – as Burke did, but he seemed worried, and his concern was contagious.

*No good's gonna come from this.* "Get behind me," Burke said quickly to Kensie, using his massive arm as a guide to ensure she followed his direction. She didn't argue or even resist; at the moment being behind this massive man sounded like a good idea. "Stay close." He took a few short steps to the conn and moved his right hand along the edge until he found a long leather sack secured to the side of the pedestal. She saw him unsnap the top flap and grip something inside it.

***

Burke heard Kensie gasp in surprise when she saw the metal and dark wood of the butt of his venerable pump action shotgun. He neither had the time nor the inclination to remind her that this wasn't the waters off the coast of Hilton Head or Montauk, with Coasties every mile. There were things far more dangerous than reckless boaters, especially this far out. Unlike the dead pirate they had just discussed, there were still real, living pirates, and boaters who went out without some sort of defense did so at their own peril.

In Burke's experience, people approaching a boat at full power that had a diving flag out were either idiots who didn't know the proper way to handle their craft or people with nefarious intentions. And this boat was coming in way too fast. People who knew boats understood that they didn't just stop like a car on a paved road and planned accordingly, but these chuckle heads didn't have a clue. He started his engines and nudged the boat forward so he had a little bit of play with his anchor chains in case he needed to move, keeping his eyes locked on the speeding vessel. He was just about to slam the throttle in reverse when they cut the engines all at once, slowing and turning slightly until they were about 20 yards off the port quarter. They were still drifting closer, but at least they weren't careening at *Empire* at breakneck speed.

The boat was a 30 foot Grady White cabin cruiser, and two men were visible. The one on the wheel was sporting a brand new sunhat that looked like it had been bought yesterday at one of the tourist traps on the island. The other had his long, brown hair pulled up into one of those ridiculous man buns that were not part of the local culture. If that didn't mark them as non islanders, the sunburned shade of their skin surely did. Most discomforting of all, both of them were staring right at him and Kensie. They stared hard. Hard in a way that made him nervous, like they had something already in mind. Hard like dangerous men.

The man not on the helm suddenly and spastically waved, as if he had just become aware that he might be coming across as less than friendly. Burke took a quick glance at Kensie, who looked as concerned as he felt.

"Something I can help you with?" he yelled out, deliberately putting an edge on his voice.

"Hi," Man-Bun said. "How's it going?" He and his shipmate smiled like the proverbial Cheshire Cat, but one that was hopped up on speed.

"You roared over here at full throttle and got inside my diver flag radius to ask me how it's going?" Burke said, putting his anger on full display. Whether they had dishonorable intentions or not, their stupidity had already pissed him off.

"Oh," the helmsman said. "Sorry about that," he said perfunctorily. *Sorry about maybe killing someone with my props.* "I didn't see it."

"It's all right." It wasn't, but there was more to this situation. "What do you want?"

"We were over there a little ways and we noticed that you might have hauled something aboard. We were wondering what it was and hoped we could maybe see it."

*A little ways?* There was no way anyone that far away would have seen any part of what had happened without high powered binoculars pointed right at his boat. Burke didn't know what these men were about, but he surely wasn't going to invite them on board to view the artifacts that Kensie had brought up. He was about to make sure they understood that what he did on his boat was none of their fucking business when Kensie spoke up.

"They're rock formations – greenschist laced with dolomite crystals that looked like they've condensed into basanite. Very, very rare. In fact, so rare that we might have just made a major scientific discovery. See, we're marine geologists." Burke tried hard to keep the amazement off his face. Nothing she had said made a bit of sense or was even vaguely scientifically sound, and of course she wasn't a geologist. She'd just lied her ass off, something she was proving to be pretty good at and, in this case, quite beneficial. *Good move, Kensie.*

The smiles faded, as if the two men had been forced to take a path they didn't know. "That sounds interesting," Hat-Head responded after a second's pause. "Can we see it?"

Kensie shook her head. "I can't take it out of the fresh water tank. Being exposed to the air might alter the strata formations in the rock, and I can't risk that. It would make the piece unacceptable for scientific study." More lies, but while these two idiots appeared to believe the gibberish, her explanations didn't seem to dissuade them.

"Sure, that makes sense. Maybe we could hop on board and just look in the tank. It sounds really cool, and it would be awesome to say we saw something for the first time." Hat-Head turned the wheel while Man-Bun moved to the gunwale, ostensibly to grab onto *Julian's Empire II.*

"No," Burke said firmly. "We don't have time to be showing things. We've got to prep for additional dives and she's got a lot of observations and stuff to write down."

Hat-Head goosed the throttle slightly, and the other boat moved a bit more quickly toward his vessel. "C'mon," he said, flashing his toothy grin once more. "We won't be any trouble. We just want to look in the tank, that's all."

Burke squinted. They were definitely up to something – the way they spoke and their forced Disney theme park happiness reminded him of the street gangs he encountered in his youth when he was dumb enough to venture off the Air Force base his father was stationed at, the way they grinned to keep you off balance just long enough to get within attack range. These guys wanted to get on his boat – badly – and the only reasons they would want to do that had to be devious.

His voice rose a few decibels and grew deeper in the human equivalent of a dog baring his teeth. "No, I need you to heave off. I said we're busy and we do not have time for visitors." He moved his hand further into the pouch until he could feel the trigger guard of the shotgun. This time, he made his move more obvious.

The prospective boarders must have noticed his move based on the shift in their body language. "OK, man. Sorry, no worries. Not trying to be unfriendly. We don't want any trouble." The words were what Burke wanted to hear, but he noticed that Hat-Head had neither cut his throttle nor turned the wheel. His platitudes continued, but each word allowed the boats to get a few inches closer. In about 10 seconds, Man-Bun would be able to grasp *Empire's* railing. He was already leaning over as if to do that but kept his head up to watch Burke.

Burke's concern turned to full fledged alarm, and he yanked the Mossberg from the pouch and pointed it in the general direction of the other boat, being sure to aim slightly above their heads. "I said heave off! Now! I'll blow a hole in that fuckin' boat if you get any closer." His voice sounded like rolling thunder.

That got the desired result. Hat-Head moved the throttle to reverse to counter his forward motion but, somewhat to his surprise, they didn't duck down or try to avoid the weapon like any normal person would. These men were neither intimidated by nor unaccustomed to being on the wrong end of a 12-gauge shotgun. They just stared at him, like they were trying to assess just how serious Burke might be. *Who the hell are these guys?*

The boat came to a stop about 10 feet from *Empire*. Man-Bun glanced over at Hat-Head, his face a question, and Burke saw his shipmate shake his head discreetly. Man-Bun turned back with a twisted smile that carried no good wishes. Burke recognized that grin. It was the kind a punk used to indicate he wasn't afraid.

"You really shouldn't have done that," Man-Bun said, his voice far more confident than it should have been given his exposure to such danger.

"You really shouldn't have tried to board my boat, asshole," Burke responded. "Get the fuck out of here." He lowered the gun another couple of inches toward their heads to try and convince these men he was serious.

"We'll see you soon," he replied, and the stern swung and dipped as Hat-Head turned the wheel and applied power. In a few seconds Burke was looking at the name of the boat on the stern – *Seas The Day* – and that it was registered in Kingstown in St. Vincent as it motored off. That made it something they'd rented on the island, telling him a little more about them. Once it was clear they weren't coming back immediately, he lowered the gun and blew out a breath.

"Jesus!" Kensie exclaimed, feeling as winded as he sounded. "What was that about?"

"Hell if I know," Burke responded, putting the weapon back in the pouch. Now that the immediate danger was passed, Burke felt a surge of fear pass through him. The gun hadn't even been loaded, and it would have taken far too long to get to the shells.

He picked up binoculars and trained them on the departing vessel. The men spoke animatedly to each other, looking back at *Empire* every few seconds. They turned on a course that would lead them back to St. Vincent. He watched them as they grew smaller until they disappeared over the horizon. If he couldn't see them, he didn't know if they stayed on course, and that meant they could be planning to come back from another direction. He decided that staying here, at anchor and exposed, was not a good plan. "Stow your gear and get everything else shipshape. We're leaving."

"But we have to go back down!" Kensie protested forcefully.

"Bad idea, Kensie. Those guys gave me the creeps. How about you?"

"Yeah," she admitted. "Something was up with them."

Burke started picking up the items scattered about the deck. "So you want to be 50 feet down, with me in the water covering you if they come back and board us?"

"No, I guess not. But I need to do more searching!"

"Look, you have valid artifacts that point to your shipwreck, and you have the GPS coordinates locked in. I believe you found something. Your colleagues will believe it too."

Kensie squeezed her lips together in frustration before turning away. Burke was exasperated; being persistent was one thing, but she seemed unnecessarily obsessed. She had real evidence and a precise position, and there was now a potential danger. "You don't really need much more," he declared, trying to get her to understand.

When she faced him once more, Kensie had an earnest, almost pleading expression. "We need something else."

***

Kensie wondered if she had a chance in hell of convincing Burke to stay. He struck her as one of those men who, once he'd made a decision, wouldn't be swayed. And he *was* the captain, which would only reinforce his decision. "It's worth the risk."

Burke glared. "What aren't you telling me?"

"Nothing. I just told you the whole deal."

"No you didn't, not entirely. I'm not used to having sketchy men try to board my boat, and I have a funny feeling that I'm not the reason."

"Are you saying I am?" Kensie asked with a hint of indignance, although she suspected he was right.

"Yup, at least whatever you're up to. That whopper of a lie about those rocks wasn't your first."

"I just said we found rocks to throw them off the trail," she explained. "What did you expect me to do?"

"No, I get that. But greenschist and dolomite turning into basanite? That's a nonsensical line of crap and you know it. You're pretty good at lying, Kensie, and that means you're probably pretty good at omitting the truth too. What kind of 'valuables' are you talking about on that ship?" His eyes were hard and determined, and they told her that he would not be dissuaded.

"Hang on." She disappeared into the V-berth for a second and emerged with a photograph that she handed to him. It showed a painting of a woman in late 18$^{th}$-century clothing wearing some kind of silver mesh headdress with dollops of brilliant blues, greens, and reds scattered about it.

"What's this?"

"That," she said in a clipped, formal tone, "is the *Couronne Ornée de Joyaux des Anges*, and this is one of very few paintings of it. It's one of the Crown Jewels. In the most daring theft of his life, not to mention one of the boldest in history, the pirate Cyrus Buckwell stole this from the Tower of London and was making his getaway in the *Aberaeron Fortune* when he smashed the ship to pieces in a hurricane on what was then the tiny island of Fraunce's Elbow. It was about two feet above sea level and a couple thousand square feet at the most. That island disappeared, either in that storm or another one, and it is now Fraunce's Shoal. Based on what I just found, I'm confident that the ship – what's left of it, anyway – and the *Couronne* are right below us this very second, and I wouldn't be surprised if those men were hired by someone who thinks the same thing."

Burke took a few minutes, alternately studying the photograph and then Kensie's face, as if to see how truthful she was being. "That explains a lot, Kensie. At first, I thought they were just punks looking for an easy mark, but then I keyed in. Those guys are pros, and they had a very specific task."

*Shit.* Burke's confirmation of her worst fears drove home the idea that they might be in real danger. "I made a pretty big stink at a conference in November where they ignored my ideas, big enough that I made an impression on more than a few people that day. When you're talking about an artifact – a treasure – like this, people can get funny."

Burke twisted his head as he caught the full import of Kensie's words. "Tell me about it."

"There are 195 gems on that headdress – diamonds, sapphires, rubies, emeralds, you name it. Almost a thousand karats total, gems of the highest quality. And the mesh is platinum. The metal alone weighed about 4 pounds, so you do the math." Burke's eyes moved back and forth rapidly as he tried to do exactly that, and when he finished he stared at her agape.

"That's gotta be worth like $10 million," he almost whispered.

"That's probably conservative. The jewels alone are worth ten times that, and if you include the historical value, estimates are more like $200 million."

"Jesus H. Christ on a stick," he mumbled before his voice became firmer. "But, if they think you know where it is, why would they send those shifty fuckers to take it? Why wouldn't they just set up an expedition of their own?"

Kensie smiled, much in the way Burke had smiled at her when she had failed to make the leap that Buckwell might have stolen the quizzing glass. "Expeditions are expensive, and they take time to set up. Contrary to what you see in the movies, salvagers don't fall for the 'I'll pay you when I find the treasure' line. Hell, the expedition that was agreed to at the conference was a rush, and it still took seven weeks to get set up, and that was only because the National Archeological Society put their weight behind it." She shrugged. "And, let's be honest, scientists can be greedy too. We aren't all super ethical old men in bow ties doing everything for the benefit of society."

"But they're not going to be able to sell it at the corner pawn store. Are you trying to tell me this is two professors having a slap fight to get their name in a textbook and maybe get some recognition from their colleagues, so they sent hired goons 2,000 miles to steal it from us? That's hard to buy, to say the least."

"No, I think someone at that conference thought I might be right and now they think they can have it all to themselves, so they hired the dirtbag brothers to do their dirty work. Then maybe they'll charge an exorbitant ransom to sell it back to the Royal Family or auction it off to some *uber*-rich jerkoff and disappear with an absolute shitload of money."

Burke paused. Clearly he hadn't considered that angle. *Well, it shows that he's got an honest streak.* At least he did, but now that she'd introduced the concept of wealth beyond anyone's wildest dreams...

"I suppose. But, if you're right, I don't see what we can do about it right this second."

Kensie pursed her lips indignantly. "What do you mean? We go back down for it! Now!"

Burke shook his head and let out a sigh. "I know you're an experienced diver, but have you ever really searched for something underwater?"

"Kind of. I volunteered for a team that searched off the Florida coast for satellite parts that spilled off a barge during a storm."

"Sounds interesting," Burke allowed. "How many divers? How long did you search? And how deep were you?"

"Eight divers for five days, in about 50 feet."

"Big pieces?"

"Some as small as a frying pan, some as big as a desk."

"And how did that work out?" Burke asked, sounding like he knew the answer.

"We found 12 out of 73," she responded sullenly.

"So, you spent 300-plus man hours looking for things 20 times the size of this headgear that had been in the water for a couple weeks, and you had, what, a 15 or so percent success rate? But somehow, now you think you'll find something smaller with one more dive after it's been laying in shifting sand and tides for 200 years? I'd call that wildly optimistic."

Kensie realized Burke was right, and that his earlier statements about having valid evidence were also true. "It is optimistic. But are you willing to risk that, as soon as we leave because they scared us away, they won't be back here sniffing around?"

"There's no way we can really stop them."

"Sure there is. We don't leave!"

Burke looked at her like she was crazy. "You mean just sit here? For how long?"

"No, not just sit here. We keep diving. Even if we don't find it, we can get more artifacts. The more things we find, the more data we have, and the stronger my case will be."

"Number one, I'm not at all set up for night diving, so we won't be able to search once we lose the light. Also, you realize we will run out of air pretty soon, right? Like by sundown. Sooner or later, we either have to go back in for more tanks – unless you are *really* good at holding your breath – or we just sit here until we starve to death. I don't have any fishing rods on board." He retrieved the shotgun and a box of shells and started putting them in the tube magazine of the gun. "And that's assuming that they don't come back with guns of their own." He worked the pump action and made sure the safety was on.

"Well, yeah. I know the odds are long, and it's dangerous, and we need supplies, but we have to try!" Kensie felt her frustration growing. Burke just didn't get it. Now that she was this close to the *Couronne*, to the *Aberaeron Fortune*, and to whatever remained of

Buckwell himself – his bones might be around here somewhere – she wasn't going to just give up. She *couldn't*. There had to be a way.

She turned away from him, staring over the stern. "I'm too close to just walk away and give those two assholes – or anyone else – a chance to take this thing," she said to the open expanse of blue ocean, her voice subdued but still loud enough to be heard. "I've been dreaming about something like this for half my life, and now I have a chance to be the person that discovers not only a priceless and famous artifact, but my personal holy grail. Do you understand what that means? I'd be like Howard Carter or Domenico Fontana or Kangmin. It's the chance of a lifetime."

Burke didn't give an inch. "If this is all true, and this thing is worth all that money, and someone went to the trouble of hiring those guys to take it from us, do you want to put yourself in that kind of danger?" he asked.

"It's *history*," she said, her voice impassioned in a way that surprised even her. "That may sound silly to you, but it's important to me. Things like this need to be preserved so they can be seen and studied and enjoyed. It's like the *Mona Lisa* or Michelangelo's *David*. They have to be shared. It's bigger than any one person."

"That's noble... almost too noble. How do I know you're not in this for the money and you're playing me right now? Why should I believe you won't do exactly what you think these guys might do, sell it off to whoever for a nine figure account in the Cayman Islands?"

Kensie whirled back to face her accuser. "Cause I couldn't live with myself if I did something like that!" she nearly yelled. Burke pulled back at her outburst and his face changed. He seemed to be assessing Kensie for the first time. His eyes locked on hers. She didn't know exactly what he was looking for, but it felt like a challenge, and she wasn't about to back down from it. Neither blinked.

Kensie folded her hands behind her head and took a deep breath. He had put his safety on the line a few minutes ago for her, and had earned the right to know what drove her. When she spoke again, her voice overflowed with emotion. "Haven't you ever had a dream, one that you rolled around in your mind over and over until you knew exactly how you wanted it to turn out?" Her eyes burned with determination. "Haven't you ever known that kind of passion, Burke?"

His look softened, and she saw his mind go somewhere else, seeing something to which she was not privy, something private that touched him deeply. It clouded his face, making him look endlessly sad, forcing Kensie to wonder exactly what she'd said to evoke such a reaction. He was gone but a second, and when he returned he kind of shrugged to himself.

"OK, look," Burke said in the manner of someone who had made a decision that he was not entirely comfortable with. "There's time and air for one more dive – I'm not risking the last tank because we're out here all by ourselves, so I'll need it if I have to go in to help you. Instead of being in the water, I'll stay on deck to watch you and keep an eye out for those guys, and I'll keep the shotgun loaded and handy. But you have to agree to listen to me when I tell you stuff – without any question. And then, no matter what we find or don't find, we have to go in for more air and supplies after that dive. Period. Got it?"

Kensie felt a little bad, like she had pushed him into a corner. She *was* putting him and his livelihood at risk, and that wasn't entirely fair to ask so much of him. *I'll have to make it up to him.* Their kiss came back to her, and she realized she might have a perfect opportunity to do exactly that later. "Yes, I promise. Thanks. Thanks a lot."

Burke nodded, throwing off the gloomy disposition that settled over him. "So gear up. You've got a treasure to find."

# Chapter 8 – Stress or Adrenaline?

Kensie pitched herself backward over the gunwale and into the water. Burke watched her get her bearings, give him a thumbs up, and head down. The water was clear enough that he could make out her form at 45 feet, at least well enough to see that she got right to work.

He turned in a full circle, his eyes locked on the horizon for any signs of Tweedle Dum and Tweedle Dee coming back for another round. It amazed him that avarice and greed existed in what should be a purely scientific community, but he knew that was naïve. He'd seen first hand just how easily money could corrupt even the most pure of heart person and understood that it applied here too.

Kensie was different. At least she seemed different. He hoped that he was right about her. He thought he was, but he'd also thought that he knew Jessica. That mistake came back to him in full Technicolor, with lovely slow motion instant replays that were fresh enough to make him think it had all just happened yesterday. He shook his head, wondering for the millionth time how he'd been so blind to have not seen it coming. That he'd avoided jail time was the closest thing to a miracle he'd ever known.

At least he'd learned not to trust anyone, a lesson he was suddenly ignoring. *Dumbass.* It was that fucking kiss. It had to be. He'd never had such a fairly innocuous act turn his insides and his head to jelly the way Kensie's lips had. Just before she closed her eyes, they'd revealed her passion for him, and the taste of her as she ran her tongue around the perimeter of his open mouth just doubled down on the heat level. For a few seconds, he could think of nothing except the passion that hit him like the mountainous breakers that crashed on the cliffs of the eastern shore. He thanked his lucky stars that he'd been sitting during the kiss – it would have been mortifying if she'd felt him get hard in about five seconds.

*So are you doing this because you want to fuck her or because you believe her?* It was a question he couldn't answer right now, at least not honestly, even though he knew how important it was. He realized it didn't matter; he'd been sucked in by her quest and now he wanted to be part of the effort to recover the treasure. He'd have to hope his instincts were better the second time around.

Then a new thought occurred to him, one that caused him to laugh out loud. *Shit. I really AM a treasure hunter!*

***

Kensie was as good as her word. Within 30 seconds of Burke telling her it was time to come up, she had closed her dive bag and was ascending. Five minutes later she was climbing onto the dive deck on the stern with Burke's help. "How'd you do? Looked like you found a lot more stuff."

"You could say that!" She felt like her eyes were going to pop from their sockets with all the times in the last 45 minutes that she'd gaped at her latest discovery. She was even more excited than before, but she tempered it long enough to sweep the horizon with her eyes. "Any issues up here? Any more visitors?"

"We're clear," Burke assured her. "Haven't seen a single boat since you went in."

"Good." She smiled sheepishly. "I appreciate you helping and looking out for me."

"Hey, it's not all about you," he chided before using a more earnest tone. "My ass is on the line too."

"True. But thanks anyway." When Burke dropped his guard and that softer side surfaced for a second, she could imagine herself just fading into him. She remembered his smell and his strength and his rough stubble against her face, and judging by the way the corner of his mouth twitched upward, she was willing to bet he was doing the same.

Burke broke the mood first. "So, what did you find?"

"Right... right." She took the towel he offered and rubbed it quickly over her head before pulling her dive bag from her belt and opening it. "So, I went toward the upstream end of the trail first, and I found this." She laid an ornate brass piece on the table. It was heavy, with an oval base and a jointed handle that still swung freely.

"A dresser pull," Burke asked.

"Probably," Kensie told him. "This is representative of the right time period. And right next to it," she continued as she reached into the bag, "I found this." She laid down a solid brass candle holder. "And look at the bottom!" She turned it over, and it was easy to see the letters on the bottom: A.F.

Burke nodded. "*Aberaeron Fortune*," he mumbled reverently.

Kensie nodded. "Probably. Well, possibly." She proceeded to show him what looked like the top half of a small oil lamp, a pocket watch casing, and the handle of a cane. She stared at each item as she pulled it out, thinking it was the first time they'd been out of the water in two centuries, and that Buckwell might have been the person to last touch it. She knew that most people would laugh at her geeky excitement, but she didn't care.

"I figure," she said when she finally emptied the bag, "that the *Couronne* is at the lighter end of the trail because it would get caught in the current and sail further, and get buried last. We're close, Burke. Really close."

He raised his hand and cocked an eyebrow as if to reign in her enthusiasm. "Yeah, that sounds likely, but until it's on board, you can't get too carried away. The sea doesn't give it up just because you think you're in the ballpark."

"I know, I know," she said, her words tinged with breathless excitement. "And I'm not one to think like this – ever – but I *feel* it. It's almost like something is guiding me to it." She caught herself. "Yeah, I get it. You think I'm nuts."

Burke chuckled. "No, I don't think that. It's like you said before – you're passionate about this. There's nothing wrong with that." He looked down at the items she'd laid out. "Shit, I'm excited too, and yesterday I didn't know this stuff existed, so I'll give you a little leeway." He picked the watch casing up, turning the silver over in his hands. "So what time do you have to be back on board?"

Burke's question caught her off guard. She'd gotten so carried away with her task (*and him*) that she'd forgotten that she was due back on the cruise ship. She supposed she *could* just not board, but Catrina would have a fit. It wouldn't be right to just abandon her, especially because she hadn't been truthful about what she was doing out here.

"I'm supposed to be on board by eight for departure by nine. I figure there's a little leeway in the boarding time."

"Yeah, they do that on purpose." He checked his watch. "It's just after four. We have time to get back in, grab a quick bite, and then I'll escort you back to the wharf so you're there before it's a problem."

Kensie nodded, feeling disappointment run through her veins. That sounded like a prelude to a goodbye, and that didn't appeal to her. She didn't want to waste more time getting another dive boat in Grenada. It would take far too long, something that she could not tolerate now. Time spent traipsing around that island like she had yesterday morning was time not in the water, time not digging in the sand, time not spent fulfilling this unreal fantasy. And it was time that she would spend without Burke, without seeing his rugged muscles and soft eyes, eliminating the chance of anything further happening.

At the moment, she wasn't sure which of those issues bothered her more. Combined, they were intolerable. She certainly wasn't going to just accept it.

"So you're just gonna drop me off at the ship?"

"They won't let me on board. You know that," he answered.

"Not what I meant. There's more work to be done down there, and I'm not about to give up on this," she told him.

"I'm sure."

"So, what are you going to do about it?" Kensie tried to sound nonchalant but, at least to her ears, she came across as too eager, almost desperate. *Maybe that's not a bad thing.*

"Do about it?" he asked.

Kensie wasn't sure if he was giving her a hard time or if she wasn't sending the right signals his way. She didn't have much experience with flirting. Not wanting to miss this opportunity, she pulled out her ace in the hole and shot him her best coquettish look.

"I don't want to go searching for another dive boat, and Grenada is actually closer to Fraunce's Shoal than St. Vincent. Is there any reason you can't follow my ship there tonight so you and I can go out tomorrow?"

***

Burke managed to keep his face stoic despite the way those soft and expressive seafoam green eyes pierced into him. Not only would he get to see more of her, she wanted him to follow her, and she wasn't being very subtle about it. In any other context he would have scoffed at the notion that he should chase a woman for any reason. But here, with this delightfully sexy woman mastering him with nothing more than her expression, he realized he was hooked.

But that didn't mean he would just knuckle under. He had a little pride left. "So you expect me to sail 50 miles of open sea at night just to chauffeur your butt back out to this pile of sand? With criminals all over the place?"

She didn't buy his false protest. "I do, and I think you don't mind so much." Her eyes went from teasing to coy. "For more than one reason."

When she put it that way, there was only one suitable response. "You got it."

He started the engine, both because they were ready to go and because it gave him something to do rather than ponder the possibilities their discussion had just raised. There were many – all of them good – and he suspected she had already set her mind on one course of action, but now wasn't the time to explore them. Instead, he pushed the throttle forward and put *Julian's Empire II* on a course for home.

The grinding and pounding of the engine made it easier for him to avoid any conversation for a minute. He didn't understand why, but he was sure that words would only lessen the import of the moment, so he stared over the bow. Kensie went down into the cabin, and he could see the back of her head and shoulders as she hunched over a notebook, scribbling something while clicking through the GPS she'd brought down with her. He wondered how her hair, still stringy and wet, could look so damn good.

After about 15 minutes, she came back to the wheel. Burke gave her a polite, appropriate grin, but he noticed she had a question on her face. It didn't take her long to get to it.

"So, now that I've told you everything and we have a minute, can I ask you something?"

Burke wasn't sure if he should be wary or not. "Sure."

"I'm just wondering... you didn't even look at me funny when I mentioned Howard Carter, Domenico Fontana, or Zhao Kangmin. You knew who they are, and that's pretty rare. Maybe you remember Carter from reading about the discovery of King Tut's tomb, but not too many people know Fontana or Kangmin."

"So? Maybe I like to read."

Kensie blinked skeptically. "The only books about Pompei and the Terracotta Warriors that mention those guys are hardcore – mostly textbooks. It's just not the kind of thing everyone knows. But, giving you the benefit of the doubt on that topic, you also knew that my rock compositions were bullshit. Again, that's not common knowledge."

He tried to come up with another answer, but realized he would be stretching it. By now, he realized, coming clean wasn't a big deal, and he couldn't suppress a smile at being found out. "I have a master's degree in Ocean Engineering from the University of New Hampshire and a BA in Geological Oceanography."

Kensie nodded, as if confirming a theory. "That explains a lot," she said "I thought I saw your mouth twitch when I first explained why I wanted you to take me out diving."

He laughed. "Yeah, metals in sediment and bedrock having a magnetic effect on erosion because of global warming? That was some Grade A bullshit, just as bad as those rocks. I was going to call you out right there, but I figured there was something pretty interesting behind that lie." He rolled his eyes. "That was an overly conservative guess if there ever was one."

"I *am* sorry about that," she said earnestly. "I never expected that kind of problem to come up."

He waved her off. "I know. Forget about it."

"I appreciate it. But," she stated hesitantly, as if trying to phrase something delicately, "how did you go from such a technical and specialized field to running an island dive boat?"

"You don't think that piloting the *Empire* a half mile offshore of St. Vincent to take amateur divers to sunken barges in 18 feet of water with a floating rum bar nearby requires two scientific degrees?"

Kensie laughed. "Not exactly."

"Well, I'm just lucky, I guess. I decided that the stress of working on billion dollar projects wasn't worth it. I don't have reports and clients and deadlines, and I'm a lot happier for it. It's not always about the money, you know. And the weather's a lot better down here." He looked over to see Kensie with pursed lips and crossed arms. "You buyin' any of this?"

"Nope."

He paused. He'd not told this story in years, not to anyone. *Is this the right time? Is she the right person?* There was only one way to find out.

"I was quite the go getter after college. I put a down payment on a 28 foot Parker – the first *Julian's Empire* – bought the best diving gear, and started offering my services doing underwater surveys, designing offshore platforms for drilling and research and such. I had a fairly unique skill set and found out I was really in demand, and then the idea of offshore wind turbines took off, and I had more work than I could handle, up and down the coast and even in the northern Caribbean.

"I met Jessica in the Bahamas during one of my jobs about eight years ago. She was this beautiful redhead, witty, smart, sexy – everything I ever wanted. It seemed like we had instant chemistry. I would work and stay there for a week, and then go back to Port St. Lucie where I had another job, and stay there for a week. I was raking in the cash. It seemed too good to be true.

"She had an import/export business and was planning on opening a second office in Fort Lauderdale, so she asked if I wouldn't mind taking small stuff back to Florida and putting it in storage for her. Being young and dumb and having a beautiful woman ask for such a small favor while playing with my dick, I said no problem. She rented a storage unit in Port St. Lucie and gave me the key. Each trip, she'd give me one or two suitcases to drop off in the unit, telling me that she was having an associate pick them up each week and deliver them to her new location. I did it five times in total.

"The last time I arrived, I'm tying the boat up in Port St. Lucie and like 20 cop cars come roaring up and point every gun in the world at me as I'm standing on the stern. I figure it's a big mistake, but then they show me a warrant, pull Jessica's suitcase out and open it, and it's full of cocaine. Apparently I'd been a drug mule for a couple of months.

"I ratted her out about as fast as I could, of course, but when the police asked the Bahamian authorities to arrest her, turns out they had no idea who she was. They tracked her down through the house she was renting, but she used a fake identity. I never even asked what her real name is. And, of course, she disappeared completely. To this day I have no idea where she is – but she left me holding the bag. My boat, my diving equipment, most of my stuff – it was all seized by the DEA. I managed to convince them that I was an innocent idiot, so they decided not to charge me, but that didn't mean I got my boat back. Plus my reputation was in the shitter. Everyone canceled their contracts and suddenly I couldn't get hired to dive in a kiddy pool.

"So I came down here, scraped up enough cash to buy *Julian's Empire II*, and I do what I do to pay off a loan for a boat that I no longer own." He stared ahead bitterly. It surprised him just how angry he still was at that bitch, and how stupid he felt that he'd been so blind.

"I'm sorry about that, Burke. That must have been a tough pill to swallow."

He couldn't keep his voice from cracking. "Yeah, it was." He shook his head and cleared his throat. "But it's ancient history."

"You're still angry about it, though."

He wanted to yell at her for being obtuse, but taking his irritation out on her wasn't fair. "Damn right I am," he said. "Eight years ago, and it still really gets to me." To his surprise, he chuckled. "And now I'm after something that's perfectly legal and worth 100 times all the drugs she moved through me. Maybe she bailed out too early."

"Seems to me she made a lot of bad decisions," Kensie said. "And not just related to money."

Burke looked over to see her grinning at him – not in the come hither way she did a few minutes ago, but with comfort and reassurance. It felt good having someone show him a little empathy, and it made him happy he had opened up to Kensie. She was like a breath of fresh air for his soul, and it made him feel even better about whatever this relationship with this smart, sexy, and tender young woman was turning into. He smiled back – easily and comfortably, with a light, happy sensation he hadn't felt around anyone in a long, long time.

*Am I getting carried away with all this?*

He knew he couldn't answer that question about himself, at least right now. More importantly, he wasn't sure he cared.

***

Kensie looped the rope around the stern cleat and made it fast with a hitch, making sure it was tight enough that the boat wouldn't bounce hard against the bumper she'd hung between the gunwale and the dock. Burke secured the bow line before coming back to check her work. Satisfied that the boat wasn't going anywhere, he set about the task of collecting everything that needed to be hosed down with fresh water and laid them on the dock. Kensie sorted the items she had brought to the surface. The bigger items – the doorknob, the spyglass, and the shoe buckle – each went in their own baggie, while the nails, coins, and buttons were grouped into others based on category. She crammed them into her backpack as Burke finished with the hose and started returning the equipment to the boat.

She could barely contain her enthusiasm. She was *this close* to the *Couronne* – she could feel it. She didn't believe in ghosts or spirits, never seen any reason to, but somehow Buckwell was talking to her, telling her not to give up. She *knew* it was there. Kensie wondered how close she'd come to uncovering it this afternoon. Maybe she'd come within mere inches of it. It was easy to imagine the feeling of her finger snagging part of the platinum mesh, the way the valuable metal would gleam in the water as she pulled it free.

As exciting as that was, it wasn't everything that occupied her mind. Burke and her growing desire for him were setting up shop in her head right next to the *Couronne*. It wasn't like her at all to feel so hedonistic, especially with a discovery of such importance right in her face, but she couldn't help it. He was just so damned sexy. The way he smiled, the way he moved, the physical power she'd felt from him when they'd kissed... but, more than anything, it was that deep rumbling voice that did very interesting things to her. Despite the danger when he'd threatened the two men in the other boat, she felt an excitement rush through her body. It was truly erotic and sexual, but it was also more than that.

"I'm going to guess you're taking the artifacts with you." She snapped out of her reverie.

"Absolutely. These things aren't leaving my side unless they're locked safe and secure somewhere." If she wasn't fortunate enough to find the *Couronne*, these would become even more valuable to her and to the archeological community at large.

"Tell you what. Let's grab a beer at *Arnhim's* and then I'll take you back to the ship."

"Do you ever go anywhere else?" she kidded.

"No," he responded. "Why would I? They know me and they always have cold Wadadlis ready."

"Fair enough." She would suffer through a Pabst Blue Ribbon right now if it meant she could spend another hour or two with him.

They walked off the dock and onto the trail between the bushes. Despite the somewhat historical nature of their quest and the dangers that the day had presented, she felt lighthearted, almost giddy. Burke seemed more than happy to join in the mood, his eyes animated as he talked about the following day and how their search efforts would play out. Kensie found herself looking up at him instead of paying attention to the path ahead, content to watch his full lips undulate and the deep dimples that formed when his mouth made long vowel sounds. She wasn't sure she would make it to *Arnhim's* without pulling that mouth down and doing unspeakable things to it. Kensie was planning her move when she saw Burke's smile disappear in an instant. She turned to see what had upset him so and released a tiny gasp of fear and surprise.

*The men from the boat they encountered earlier stood about 15 feet in front of them.*

They were wearing different shorts and T-shirts than before. The helmsman had lost his hat, but the other still had his hair pulled up on top of his head, and both retained their greasy grins. "I thought you'd remember us," Man-Bun remarked. "I told you we'd see you again soon." He unsheathed a Bowie knife and turned it deftly in his hand, making it clear he had skill and experience using it. "You look a little more scared without that shotgun, big man." His partner clicked open a switchblade that, while smaller than the Bowie knife, was big enough to do plenty of damage.

Burke's massive right arm slid in front of Kensie's body as he firmly pushed her behind him. Stunned and frightened, she allowed herself to be moved backward. "Look, we don't want any trouble," Burke told them.

"Neither do we. So, if you give us whatever you found at the dive site, we'll be on our way." The former Hat-Head looked at Kensie. "Something tells me that you wouldn't have left anything you found out there back on the boat, so I suppose you could just give me that backpack."

"Not gonna happen," Burke said menacingly. Kensie was having difficulty following the conversation due to the sound of rushing water in her ears.

Man-Bun twirled the Bowie knife again so the blade extended from the pinky side of his hand. "Oh, it's gonna happen. The only thing we don't know yet is what's gonna happen to you." He took a step forward, trying to learn what kind of reaction he would get.

Burke backed up a step. Kensie did too. She wanted to look behind her to see if it was clear to run, but she couldn't take her eyes off the knives. To her, they looked 10 feet long, and it seemed that either man was close enough to just reach out and stab her at any moment. She was on the edge of panic. Her mouth was suddenly as dry as a desert.

"C'mon, sweetheart," Hat-Head said, his voice oozing false charm, "we all know what's in the backpack. Just give it up and we won't hurt you."

Suddenly, the entirety of the situation rushed into her mind. They thought she had the *Couronne* and, when they found out she didn't, they would probably kill her and Burke and go back out to the site tomorrow to recover it themselves. She was still frightened, but the cold calculus of the moment told her to fight back or die.

She stepped around Burke's still outstretched arm and forward until she was even with him, and raised her arms in her best fighting stance. "He just said that's not going to happen. So why don't you get lost?" She hoped they couldn't see the way her hands trembled as she prayed that her four years of martial arts training would be sufficient to save her ass.

Both men grinned in genuine amusement at her words and her pose. "Darling," Hat-Head said, "it's not like you have a choice here. Don't make this any worse than it has to be." He took a couple of steps toward Kensie.

Burke moved to intercept him, but was forced to stop when Man-Bun advanced, commanding his attention. Kensie understood their strategy immediately. One man would engage Burke to keep him from helping Kensie as the other took the backpack from her. And that meant she was on her own. She glanced at Burke and then back at her attacker.

"I'm not going to ask again, honey," he said in anything but a friendly voice. His face, however, remained rather serene.

She heard her *sensei's* voice in her head; *Make him make the first move.* "Good," she replied, "'cause I'm tired of hearing you." With a shrug, he resumed his approach. She wanted to stand her ground, but every instinct in her body made her back away, still hoping that she could avoid this fight.

In her peripheral vision, she watched Man-Bun charge, his knife raised. Burke blocked the first strike, and they locked arms and began to struggle back and forth. A second later, Hat-Head attacked as well, leading not with the knife but with his free hand.

Kensie chopped down aggressively, making contact solidly just above the wrist and stepping outside of his attack path. Thrown off balance by her strike, Hat-Head stumbled a bit before regaining his balance and turning back to face Kensie. Now he looked angry. Flexing his fingers and rotating his wrist, he came at her again, leading with and slicing the air with the glistening weapon. She recognized that his movements were too dramatic. The wide, arcing path of the blade suggested an intention to scare, not to cut.

She timed his movements and, with a step that was faster than even she expected, moved inside the arc of his swipes and delivered a crisp blow to the sensitive inside of his elbow with her right hand, blocking down with her left to make sure the blade didn't find its way back into her body. Her attacker yelped with pain but didn't, as she had hoped, drop the knife. Her strikes simply weren't strong enough to have that kind of effect. She started backing away to get out of his range, but before she could he landed a clumsy blow with his non knife hand on her right shoulder. It was powerful enough to knock her sideways and send a dull ache through her entire arm. Fortunately, she did not lose her footing, and she immediately snapped back into a ready stance.

Hat-Head scowled at his elbow before glaring at Kensie. "Now I'm gonna kill you, bitch." He sounded determined, but this time he approached more cautiously. *A couple of good, hard strikes would teach anyone that lesson.* Feinting and weaving, he looked for an opening.

A roar of pain sounded off to her left; she could spare neither the effort nor the attention to look that way, but it sounded like Burke. If he had been hurt or incapacitated, she knew she was done for; Kensie could hold her own against this one guy, at least for a while, but it would be all over if a second opponent came at her. A second later she heard the *smack* of a solid strike, a fist or a foot contacting muscle and bone violently.

Seeing an opening, Hat-Head closed the distance briskly. She snapped out a low kick in defense. He stopped just in time, causing her strike to miss, but it would give her attacker something else to think about. *You don't need to kill him, Kens. You just need to get away or make him leave.* As long as he was willing to stand there and shadow box, she would comply until he grew either frustrated or tired.

"Hey, asshole!"

Both Kensie and Hat-Head turned their heads toward the sound, but Kensie doubted her opponent got a good look at Burke as the captain blasted the knife from his hand with a savage blow to his wrist. The blade tumbled toward Kensie, but she was able to duck and have it fall harmlessly behind her. The force of the first strike spun Burke's victim nearly 90 degrees, giving him no chance to block or avoid his follow up punch, which landed cleanly on his cheek at the corner of his mouth and sent him to the ground.

His chest heaving, Burke looked down at the man to make sure he was not moving before looking to Kensie. She saw Man-Bun lying on the ground about 10 feet away. His legs were kicking slowly, but he appeared no more likely to get up than Hat-Head. It was only then that she noticed blood streaming from a good size cut on the top of Burke's forearm about halfway between his elbow and wrist.

"You're bleeding," she stated unnecessarily, panting heavily.

"I'll be fine," he said. "Are you OK?"

"I think so," she said. Right now every fiber of her body tingled and her vision tunneled, reminding her of the time she'd gotten a shot of a powerful painkiller in the emergency room as a child. Even though this time was likely from adrenalin instead of drugs, just like then, a wave of nausea passed through her body. "I'm… oh, shit. I'm –" She took a couple of steps, leaned her head into the bush as she dropped to her knees, and released the contents of her stomach onto the white sand.

She coughed a few times, spit in a very un-ladylike manner, and then stood back up, wiping the sweat from her brow. "Sorry about that," she said, feeling the color come back to her face. "Too much excitement." She tried to smile at her lame joke, but it felt more like a very unnatural grimace.

"It's fine. Just so long as you're OK," Burke reiterated.

"Yeah, I'm a little shaken up, but I'm not hurt."

Burke gave her a quick once over and, obviously agreeing with her diagnosis, retrieved both weapons from the ground. He quickly folded the switchblade and put it in his pocket, but the Bowie knife was far too long to conceal that easily. "Turn around," he told Kensie, and when she complied he opened the flap and slid the blade carefully between two notebooks.

"There's a rag in the side compartment," she said. "Get it." Burke followed her directions and gave it to Kensie, who wrapped it twice around his injury. It became saturated with a red stain almost immediately.

"OK, let's get out of here."

"Where?" Kensie asked, and only after she saw Burke nod in the direction of one of their combatants did she realize it might not be a good idea to broadcast where they could be found in a few minutes. She nodded and let him lead her away, both of them walking quickly. Kensie kept looking behind her, half expecting to see one or both of their attackers coming for them, but they did not materialize and in a minute they were back in the open on Seraphine Street. The minimal foot traffic here was comforting, but she could not stop her eyes from darting every which way. She was sweating, but her blistering pulse and her bone dry mouth told her that it wasn't entirely from the heat or the fight. Burke turned with a purpose, leading her down the uneven sidewalk and crossing the street until they arrived in front of *Arnhim's*. A few locals were sitting outside on the porch, but they didn't seem to notice or care about their arrival.

Kensie raised her eyes in some surprise. "I know I made a joke about you always coming here, but now I'm serious. We have to find a hospital. That cut needs stitches."

"I know," Burke said. He leaned in and spoke quietly. "You remember Navia, right?" Kensie nodded. "Go in, tell her I said I need a room and the kit, and go with her. Got it?"

"You aren't coming in with me?"

Burke held up his arm and several drops of blood fell to the pavement. "Not sure it's a good idea for me to walk in the front door while I'm bleeding like a stuck pig. Might frighten the dinner crowd," he joked.

"So what are you going to do?" Kensie realized she was looking at Burke as her protector, and the idea of him not being next to her scared her deeply.

"It's all good. Just tell Navia exactly what I told you. I'll see you in a second." He pointed, and she proceeded toward the entrance, while Burke turned and headed between *Arnhim's* and the building next to it.

She watched him trot away, suddenly more uncertain of the immediate future than she'd been in quite a while.

# Chapter 9 – Surgical Precision

*Arnhim's* main room wasn't as crowded as the previous night, but there was still activity, enough that it took Kensie a minute of frenzied scanning to find Navia. She waved urgently, and the woman flashed her giant smile and came over to her. "Kensie darlin'! Good on ya to be comin' back." She paused for a beat, taking in Kensie's wide eyes and clenched jaw. "My goodness! Are ya seein' the ghost o' St. Christopher hisself standin' behin' me? What's da trouble? And where's Burke?"

"He said that we need a room and that he needs the kit," she said. Her voice shook and she felt silly making the clearly codified request.

Kensie may have felt silly, but the phrase garnered a quick response from the restaurant owner. "Burke, dat man ees' just full a' dah' chupid." She turned her head and yelled to the bartender. "Get Burke from out dey back an' bring 'em 'ere." The man nodded, put down the glass he was washing, and immediately headed back into the kitchen. Navia intertwined her arm with Kensie's, directing her up the stairs. "Ya come wit' me, darlin'. Everythin' jus' fine now – ya in a safe spot now. Burke'll be along in a secon'. Are ya hurtin' dear?"

"No, I'm fine," Kensie said, "but Burke has a cut on his arm that's bleeding a lot."

Navia smiled, reminding Kensie of a housemother at an all boys school upon learning that one of her residents had skinned his knee. "Ya don' nee be worryin' 'bout that, my swee' Kensie. I got wha'll fix him up jus' a' good a' new." She escorted Kensie into the first room on the right. It contained a bed with a nightstand, a dresser, and a straight back chair at a table. The single window was open, but the room was an oven, even compared to the already excessive temperature downstairs. "I'll be comin' right back, so ya jus' relass yaself," she said before exiting.

Kensie turned in a circle, unable to relax a bit. She felt like events were flying by her at the speed of light, passing before she had a chance to think or react at all. A hint of dizziness flashed, and she knew she had to slow her breathing before she hyperventilated. She sat on the edge of the bed and bent forward, trying to will her body to stop sucking so much air.

She was making progress when Navia returned with Burke, carrying a worn fabric bag. He held a fresh towel over his arm, but a red stain was already seeping through the cotton, and his hand was still smeared with his own blood as it dripped from the cut to his fingers and onto the floor. For all that, he was making small talk with Navia as if nothing untoward was going on. When he entered he turned his attention to Kensie and smiled at her. "Hi."

"Hi. How are you doing?"

"I told you, I'll be fine," he said, sitting at the table on which Navia set her case while grabbing the other chair. Kensie was sure he was acting for her benefit; no one with a bleeding gash in his arm could be so calm as he laid the limb on the table. Navia adjusted herself so she could access his injury and pulled the towel away.

Kensie hadn't really looked at his arm yet – there was more blood than she'd remembered seeing from any wound – but she was curious how badly he might be hurt, so she leaned in. The cut was about three inches long but it had clean edges and, to Kensie's untrained eye, didn't appear too deep. Still, her stomach rumbled to remind her that it still wasn't quite ready to see such things.

She figured that Navia was going to sterilize and wrap it before taking him to the hospital or a clinic, so she was more than a little shocked to see her pull some curved needles, thread, and gauze from the bag and lay them out on the table.

"Wait. You're going to stitch him up right here and now?

"Don't worry," Burke told her. "Navia and I have a long history with medical procedures. Plus," he dug into the bag and came out with an unmarked bottle of clear liquid. "She has the *best* anesthesia."

"What is that?" Kensie asked, eyeing it like it might be poison.

"Darlin', dis here is my special feelin' no pain medicine," Navia said, her smile exploding in all its glory once more as Burke tipped the bottle back for a healthy sip. She took it from him and poured a bit on the cut itself, causing Burke to make a fist and grimace in pain as more blood flowed. "It soothes da' mind and heals da' body," Navia added as she held the bottle out to Kensie. "Sup a little, darlin' – ya lookin' as if ya had a rough time o' things."

Kensie took it and sniffed at the bottle, but was stymied. There was no odor. Unsure if that was a good thing or not, she put her lips to the opening and took in about a teaspoon of the stuff – and immediately learned that was far too much. The taste of rubbing alcohol mixed with kerosene assaulted her senses and created a burning sensation in her mouth and throat that she likened to swallowing sulfuric acid.

She sucked in a great breath, wondering how Burke could have possibly taken a slug of it, and coughed several times before she felt she wasn't going to die. "What the hell was that?" she asked them as they chuckled.

"Grain alcohol. 190 proof."

"190 proof?! Are you trying to kill me?"

"Nah, darlin', but seems all we all could use a taste o' the giggles, am I right?"

Kensie nodded. "The giggles!? Geez, if the last few minutes didn't kill me, that stuff sure will!"

Navia looked squarely at Burke. "And sumtin' tellin' ol' Navia dat you don' wanna be talkin' 'bout dem las' few minutes none."

Burke took the bottle back from Kensie. "I knew I could count on you, Navia." His face contorted again as he poured another liberal dose of the astringent liquid into the cut.

After laughing at his discomfort, Navia went back into her bag and came out with another bottle containing a dark brown liquid sporting a Mt. Gay label. "Here," she said, giving it to Kensie. "Dis more t'be be agreein' witcha' tummy, darlin'. But ya na be stingy wit it, no?"

"Certainly not." She pulled the cork and took a sip. Compared to the grain alcohol, this was like iced tea.

Navia had pulled the thread through the curved needle and held it up. "Ya ready for dis?"

Burke held his hand out for the rum bottle, which Kensie gave to him and watched as he gulped another mouthful. *Christ, I'd be on the floor if I drank that much!* "Ready when you are," he told his surgeon before glancing Kensie's way. "Are you gonna be able to handle this?" he asked her.

She glowered at him. "I know I'm not knocking back rum and moonshine like you are, but I'm not exactly a softie."

"No? You yakked when you saw my arm, remember?" Burke reminded her as Navia positioned the point against one of the flaps of skin.

"That was because of the stress, not the blood." Even though she'd tried to sound like it was no big deal, Kensie felt her eyes widen as Navia pressed the needle thru his skin. Unwilling to look away, she grabbed the bottle and took another, heftier swig of the rum, but her gums started watering in a telltale sign of impending nausea as the gleaming metal pierced his flesh. Muscles in her belly contracted and twisted, forcing her to clench her mouth shut to avoid retching.

Burke bit his lip while smiling in amusement at the effort she displayed. "Well, pardon me, Miss Tough Guy." They passed the bottle back and forth, with Kensie taking tiny sips and Burke doing what he had to do to alleviate the pain until six stitches closed the cut.

He raised his arm and studied the repairs, flexing his fingers and moving his wrist in a complete circle. "That's good work as usual, Navia. How many does that make?"

She grabbed his arm and started wrapping it in gauze. "Dat's 48, ya' hooligan! Don' be givin' me need ta stick anymore in ya, ya hear?"

"Forty eight what?" Kensie inquired as she regained control of herself.

"Stitches," Burke told her with a rueful smile. "Navia is my unofficial emergency doctor."

"Fool ah talk, but nah fool ah listen," she said seriously, and then they both laughed. It must have been an inside joke, because it made no sense to Kensie. Navia put everything back in the bag, except the now half full bottle of rum, and stood. "Now, I got me a place downstairs that be needin' me, unless I wan' the money to up and walk itself right out tha door. You stay here long as ya need, hear?"

"Thanks, honey," Burke said. "I appreciate it and, as usual, I owe you one."

"Yes," Kensie agreed. "Thank you for your hospitality."

She squeezed Kensie's cheek with her fingers like an Italian grandmother. "I like ya, Miss Kensie. Ya got spunk and ya got brains, an' some a' us be needin' dem brains," she pronounced, looking squarely at Burke. Then she leaned forward like she was imparting some crucial secret that was meant only for Kensie's ears, but she barely lowered her voice, ensuring that Burke would hear every word. "Burke's gotta fancy for ya, darlin'. And don' let that broken down, full a stitches body fool ya – what's inside is da stuff ya be wantin'. He's a right man in evra way."

"I'll keep that in mind," Kensie replied with a self conscious grin, and even the heat of the room could not disguise the rise in temperature of her skin as a blush spread over her face and neck. Navia headed for the door, but turned back to Burke.

"And I suppose you'll wan' me ta be a lookin' out for ya too, makin' sure I ain't heard o' ya nor seen dat ugly face?" She tried to sound like he was burdening her, but even Kensie could tell she was playing with him.

"Thank you, beautiful," Burke replied in a sing song voice. Navia shook her head and exited the room, shutting the door behind her.

Kensie sat down on the bed, exhausted. She'd gotten up early, and diving was not a restful endeavor. Add in the excitement of her discoveries, the outrageous stress from the fight that was finally starting to bleed off of her, a little (*a lot*) too much alcohol, and being a spectator to impromptu surgery, and she knew it would not be long before she collapsed.

"You handled yourself pretty well today," Burke observed, walking over to her. "On the boat, on the dock, and up here."

She rolled her eyes, not sure she agreed with him. "Maybe. I have to admit, I came closer to barfing right now than you think."

"I saw the color run out of your face. I know exactly how close you came."

She had to laugh at that. "Guess I wasn't quite as slick as I thought."

"You weren't, but you held it together. That says something." He paused. "And you really did well in that fight."

"I don't know what would have happened if I had to deal with him much longer," she admitted.

"I think you could have taken him," Burke said, and Kensie appreciated the lie. "What style are you trained in?"

She looked up in surprise. "*Isshin Ryu.* How did you know?"

"I could see it in the way you moved. Tight strikes, good stance. Plus, I learned a lot of *GoJu Ryu*, and that's –"

" – the Okinawan equivalent of *Isshin Ryu*," she completed. "Sorry, I was a little too busy not getting my ass kicked to see what you were doing."

"I saw the end of it, before I slugged him, and I know two things: one, he couldn't get inside to hurt you, and two, he was absolutely trying to take you out. That guy was not fucking around."

Now that they were no longer in imminent danger and Burke's injury was under control, his complement caused her to more fully consider what could have happened, and it hit her all at once. "Jesus! I could've been killed!" Her pulse suddenly tripled, her breathing increased, and her throat closed around a sob that she choked out before the real tears started. "Oh my god!"

Burke sat down next to her and put his uninjured arm around her shoulder. "It's OK, Kens, really. You did great." She believed him – or, more accurately, wanted to believe him – but the crying released so much tension that she let it come out until there was no more.

"Thanks," she said, wiping her eyes with her shirt. "That wasn't exactly the most distinguished reaction I could have had. I'm sorry."

"Don't be sorry. I'm betting this was the first time you were ever in real danger, right?"

"Yeah," she nodded before releasing a bark of a laugh. "I've led a very sheltered and safe life until today."

"It's natural to have to release that tension. Some people talk non-stop for hours because they are so amped up. Some people get drunk or high. Some people cry." Burke looked around furtively, like he was about to impart a secret, even though they were alone. "I cried for 10 minutes after my first no shit fight," he admitted with a crooked smile that Kensie found irresistible. "And I won it – easily. There's no shame in being human, at least after the fact. You showed more than enough strength – and I don't just mean physical strength – dealing with a guy who was armed and bigger and stronger than you. I'm impressed."

Recognizing the sincerity in his words, she looked right at him. The exterior was tough and battle scarred, but his eyes were tender, and they matched what she was hearing from him as he expressed admiration and compassion... and longing. He'd yet to show it outright, and maybe didn't even realize it, but there was something missing in his life, and he was reaching out for someone to help him. *Could I be the one to fill that void?* She mentally snickered at the juvenile double entendre, but beyond that was the certainty that she was that person.

Everything he presented – those eloquent eyes, that rugged jawline, the injury that he'd sustained defending her – overwhelmed Kensie. She wanted Burke. Badly. In a way that she'd never known, never even dreamed possible. It made her little crush on Buckwell seem like a delicate and childish spell from a nursery rhyme. The slight pressure of his arm on her back sent shivers down her spine, and she marveled that such an innocent touch could be so laden with sexual import.

Burke's slight smile of reassurance faded as he read the signals that Kensie was putting out, but he still looked... uncertain. His reluctance to assume that she was offering herself to him was adorable, and it provided even more proof to her of the type of man he was. *Perhaps one more nudge.*

She reached for his injured arm, the one not wrapped around her. Grasping the wrist, she turned it gently. "Does your arm still hurt?" she asked quietly, not able to tear her gaze from his.

He blinked, surprised by her question, what with more pressing matters at hand. "A little, but it's no big deal," he responded.

"Good." With a steady, firm movement, she brought his hand to her chest just above her bathing suit so his fingertips brushed against her skin where it glistened with sweat. She glanced down, enthralled with the look of his big, powerful hand touching and caressing her. It was electric, causing Kensie to draw a deep breath as her arousal grew.

She knew where that hand belonged, so she slid it over and pressed it down on her right breast, looking up at him with parted lips and beseeching eyes that made it clear there were no barriers in Burke's path, that she was his if he wanted her.

He did. Flexing his fingers, he moved his hand to fully cup her breast and leaned into her. Feeling the urgency of the moment and expecting Burke to overpower her with an aggressive kiss, she was surprised to feel a whisper soft sensation on her lips as he explored, tasted, and claimed her mouth with his own. His light yet insistent technique made her entire body tingle. She wanted more, but was perfectly happy to accept his teasing.

She moved her left hand down to his leg, feeling his muscles quiver and ripple under her touch, and started sliding upward. Her fingertips slid over the faded denim of his shorts, drawing little designs on his upper thighs until she felt the slight loose fabric grow taut where it accommodated the bulge between his legs. She laid her hand over it, both excited and intimidated by how big it felt.

Burke moaned into her mouth, and his kiss became more intense and forceful. She loved his control and authority, the way he demonstrated his power just by using it sparingly. Not normally a submissive woman in any part of her real life, she had an intoxicating desire to be taken by him as he wished, to be used as an instrument for his passion and pleasure, to be *his*. The harder he pushed into her and the more vigorously he massaged her breast, the more she "fought" against him, challenging him to be the rogue that her desires wanted and needed him to be. Kensie moaned back at him several times, and when his other hand slid up to grasp the back of her head and hold it in place while he drove his tongue into her mouth like he owned it, everything melted away and she knew only that her body was his and his alone.

She was unsure exactly what extra signal she gave Burke, but it was direct enough to cause him to roughly pull her shirt off, and when he tossed it aside he wasted no time in freeing her upper body from the confining top of her swimsuit. His hand returned immediately to where Kensie had put it, and this time he took her nipple between his thumb and forefinger and pinched it with just the right amount of force to send fiery impulses down to her clit. She squealed into his kiss, pressing her tongue against his in a desperate attempt to dissipate the sexual energy that was steadily consuming her. Her left hand fumbled over his crotch as she tried to find a button or a zipper or something that would get her closer to that very desirable part of his anatomy.

He laughed softly at her difficulty, and a flash of irritation – not real anger, but the kind that led to a more spirited reaction – coursed through her. She growled, both at him and the recalcitrant pants, until he opened his lips wide and smothered her mouth with his to silence her for a second. When Burke applied pressure with his left hand to twist Kensie's head to a more advantageous position, she felt her eyelids flutter with the raw passion of the moment.

Burke dropped his right hand down to his own crotch, pushing hers away briefly, and when she reached in once more she found that most of the buttons making up the fly of his shorts had been undone. From there, it was a simple matter of her finding the top of his underwear and plunging her hand in the right direction.

*Oh my god.* It felt big through his shorts, but now that she had confirmation of its size, his penis felt like a fantasy come to life. She'd had little exposure to erotica or any other sort of pornography, and could never understand how women "hungered for his manhood", but now she did. Her response was instinctual, and it made her desire to get him inside of her as much of a need as air was to live.

He broke his kiss to hiss in pleasure as she wrapped her fingers around him, and she opened her eyes fully to see the flush of his skin. It pleased her that her simple touch aroused him so, and she was committed to making good on her unspoken promise of more. With a burst of strength, she pulled her head away and pushed him down so he leaned on his elbows. With him now so vulnerable, she pulled her knees under her, leaned over, and wrapped her lips over the very tip of his member.

"Fuuhhh... ohhh!" The nonsense spurting from Burke's mouth told her that he was as eager to receive as she was to give, so without hesitation Kensie slid her lips the rest of the way over the shaft and took it into her mouth. He felt so good, the way the hardness filled her mouth in a manner only a man with such power could. He might not have been a villainous criminal pirate, but he was damn sexy in every sense of the word, and she could not get enough of him.

Kensie ran her hands over his hips while pressing her chest into his thighs, enjoying his warmth even in the broiling room. She could not imagine taking such pleasure from the act of pleasing a man, but her arousal told her it was so. Burke thrashed his head this way and that, heaving his midsection upward every time she wiggled her tongue on a very specific spot.

Kensie loved the feeling of Burke in her mouth, but her body screamed for the feel of a man's hands – this man's hands – on it. She was far more excited than she'd ever been, and moaned around Burke's cock upon thinking that, as good as this felt right now, it was going to get even better.

Almost too fast for her to realize it, Burke grabbed her arm and, using his thick legs for leverage, rolled her on her back, ending her oral ministrations. Whether by design or by happy accident, he ended up kneeling between her spread legs, and the only thing separating them from consummating the moment was her willingness and his intentions. She had no doubt about how willing she was, and she was pretty sure she knew Burke's intentions. Still, his abrupt assumption of control demanded at least a token response.

"Hey!"

Burke did not have the look of a man interested in the *faux* protests of the half naked woman below him. He smiled like a predator about to feast on his prey, and it took him very little time and less effort to grab both of her petite wrists in one hand and press them into the bed over her head. He used his other hand to pull her suit down to her knees, exposing every part of her to the air which, even though it was sultry and still, felt like a cool breeze compared to the heat being put out by her arousal. He moved a bit so she could kick the garment to the floor and wedged his legs in between hers to open her thighs with ease.

"I'm gonna fuck you, Kensie," he said, his voice a low and menacing growl that triggered a primal response in her, and she closed her eyes to let the rumble wash over her like waves on one of the island's tropical beaches. "I'm gonna fuck you hard, like I've been thinking about doing since you stepped on my boat yesterday morning, and that's all there is to it." Kensie moaned and tried to provide some sort of protest, just to play the part, but whatever came out was not any language she recognized. It was a jumble of fantastical role play, willing submission to a far stronger man, and a need to be fulfilled – and *filled*. She tugged at her wrists, both knowing and enjoying that she lacked a fraction of the strength to pull them free, all the while arching her hips in a desperate attempt to get him inside of her.

After a few seconds, she realized he had hardly moved, and she opened her eyes fully to see if there was something wrong. He stared down at her, his face an odd combination of desire and amusement, making her think he wasn't sure about his next move. She thought to ask him, but he spoke first. "Beg me for it."

*Oh shit.* Her entire body did a loop, like she was on a roller coaster with an endless series of steep plummets that excited her more and more each time. She was *not* the kind of woman who took orders from anyone, and would *never* beg, but being told to do so now to get him inside of her body sounded like a good idea. Still, her lust fogged mind told her it was "wrong" to just obey. *Where's the fun in that?*

"Go to hell," she moaned.

"I'm not going anywhere, and neither are you. Try again."

Kensie pulled harder at her wrists, but he seemed to barely notice the increased effort. *Wow, he is strong!* "Let me go." The words, which came out in a breathy, dulcet tone, were not at all convincing.

"I don't think so. You know what you have to do."

She wanted to give him a harder time, but her body wouldn't permit it. "Burke, goddammit," she moaned. "Please!"

"Please what?" he said with a teasing lilt in his voice. He slid his hips down until the head just touched her outer lips, rising away quickly as she tried to absorb him. "You have to say it."

To Kensie, Burke sounded like he could wait all day and all night to give her what she had to have, meaning any resistance was a losing battle. The idea that this was truly forced, that she was a captive being used without regard to her well being, safety, or pleasure, flashed through her mind, bringing with it a blast of carnal animalism that wrecked her body and forced the words from her.

"Burke, fuck me! Fuck me now! I'm yours – do whatever you want! Please!"

That must have been enough, because the way he slid into her, smoothly but forcefully, almost made her pass out. She had a moment of concern that he might be too big for her to handle, but she was so far past the point of normal arousal that he was fully inside of her in one massive stroke. Through the body encompassing tingle, she recognized his balls pressing against her, and the very fact that she had been impaled on such a substantial piece of anatomy gave her a deeply erotic feeling, one of being a beautiful, desirable, sensual woman.

Kensie felt him pause for a moment, and she silently thanked whoever might be listening that he was still considerate and in enough control to make sure she was comfortable. It wasn't necessary – she was more than ready to take whatever he could give her – but it spoke to his gentlemanly side, which lurked just below the surface of his savagely hedonistic actions.

Burke started fucking her with powerful, rhythmic strokes that sent waves of delirium to all the different areas of her body. Kensie felt pleasure that curled her toes, made her bite the air, made her nipples so hard they hurt, and those were just the side effects. It was far more than she could handle, entirely too powerful to fight were she of a mind to try. As much as she wanted this divine meeting of two bodies to go on forever, it was only a few minutes before she felt the familiar stirrings that told her she was reaching the point of no return.

"Oh god, Burke! I'm – oh shit, it's – son of a... oh no!" Spreading her legs wider than Burke had already forced them, she wrapped them around his ass and interlocked her ankles, using the power of her breaking orgasm to pull as much of him as possible into her and give her even more pleasure. She was strong, but Burke was even stronger, and the approach of his own orgasm made him pull back and slam into her that much harder each time. Just as her desire crested and her orgasm flooded her body, and she opened her mouth in a silent scream.

Almost simultaneously, she felt Burke flex every muscle in his body and explode inside of her. His hips worked like a piston in a 400 horsepower engine, driving into her and generating the perfect friction that only added to his frenzied movements. Barely able to form a coherent thought, Kensie fell back on her instincts, which told her to move her body. She tried, but with her lower half being mastered and controlled by Burke's power and passion, she was little more than a rag doll. A very happy rag doll, but one without much say in what happened to her.

Finally, Burke slowed and rolled his glistening body off of hers, and they both lay on the bed panting like they'd just sprinted to the end of a marathon. For several seconds, there were no words passed, no meaning laden looks. It was both too difficult and unnecessary; even the most obtuse person would understand just how much the other had enjoyed the last few minutes.

Once Kensie felt that she had recovered sufficiently, she glanced over at the man who had just obliterated and redefined her quaint ideas of sexual intimacy. He was already staring at her, his eyelids heavy, his expression relaxed nearly to the point of unconsciousness, but for all that she felt as if he had just thrown a heavy weight from his shoulders. She wanted to learn more, to talk with her lover and hear his thoughts after their wonderfully deep intimacy, but she was as tired as Burke looked. The alcohol was hitting her hard; she would have to settle for some brief, superficial conversation.

"How are you?" he asked, his words slightly slurred, and Kensie remembered how much high proof booze he'd consumed in the last hour.

"Wonderful," she answered, watching his eyes slowly close. "Amazing. Wrecked. That was... there are no words. How about you?"

"Do I look anything less than happy?"

"Not to me," she smiled, her energy fading fast. "You look about perfect."

"Good. That's what I was going for," he mumbled. "Why don't we catch... a... quick... nap?"

"Just a quick one," Kensie agreed. "Like 10 minutes, OK? Burke?"

He was already asleep, and a few seconds later Kensie joined him, a smile on her face.

# Chapter 10 – Moonlit Cruise

Burke was dreaming, reliving every aspect of Kensie's body and the way it moved and felt when touched just right, when an odd, high pitched tone intruded. He tried to shut it out, but it persisted until he was conscious enough to open his eyes and look around the room. He saw Kensie's phone on the table next to the bed, jumping about as it vibrated and rang.

"Kensie," he nudged her. "Your phone."

She opened her eyes and looked at him, uncomprehending much of anything until she heard the next ring. She turned and grabbed it, propping herself up on one elbow. "Hullo?"

The voice of a woman who was nearly yelling was audible to Burke, making Kensie pull the phone from her ear. "Where the hell are you, Kensie? The cruise people just asked me if I knew why you weren't on board!"

"Catrina? What do you mean?"

"I mean it's 8:30 and they asked us all to be on board half an hour ago! And you aren't!"

Kensie's eyes widened, struggling to focus as she turned her arm to look at her watch. "Shit. OK, I lost track of time. I'll be there in a few minutes, I promise."

"You better be. They said they pull up the gangway at nine no matter what." She hung up.

Kensie sagged back onto the pillow. "Oh man," she groaned. "I've got to get moving, but I think I'm still drunk."

Burke understood what she meant. He was still fairly toasted, enough so that he would refuse to drive if given the opportunity. He looked out the window, seeing an inky black sky. Just before they'd drifted off to sleep, only the slightest hint of dusk had been visible. "Can you walk?"

Kensie took several deep breaths. "Yeah, I think so."

"OK, let's go then." He rolled out of bed to his feet, looking around for his shorts and shirt.

Kensie smiled at seeing him standing there in all his glory. "As much as I hate to do this..." She leaned over, grabbing his clothes from the floor next to her side of the bed, and tossed them to him.

"Thanks." Burke pulled his shirt and shorts on and then, spotting his shoes, grabbed them as well.

Kensie pulled herself up and dressed rapidly, and he could tell she wanted him to ogle her just a little bit. Burke gave her a sidelong glance, but kept his gaze up around her face and head. "Don't think I don't want to watch the show, but if you want to get out of here, that's not in your best interest." She bit her lip and tried to suppress a smile, but she wasn't successful. That look was sexy/cute and he was glad that the mental image would not be leaving him anytime soon.

She grabbed her backpack and they went downstairs. *Arnhim's* was jumping, with Soca music pumping from the speakers. It was one of the more authentic night spots on the island, far better than the generic steel drum garbage that most Americans and Europeans expected at the tourist traps, and the pump of the bass and the just-right tempo had most of the patrons slithering and grinding against each other in a most salacious manner. It fit the moment and the place, and most importantly it was a reminder of the passion he had just experienced. It was sexy, it was sweet, it was dirty, and it was just right. He wished her long shirt didn't camouflage her ass as he walked behind her. He wanted to see that perfect shape one more time.

They hit the main floor and Burke paused to wave to Navia behind the bar. She shook her head as she responded; he had no doubt that she knew – in far better detail than he cared to imagine – what had happened upstairs. Navia always knew everything she needed to know, and it would not have surprised him one bit to discover that she had the entire place wired for sound and probably video. Either that, or she was some sort of fucking witch, and he would not give odds either way.

They made it to the street. Like the previous night, Kensie turned to him as if to say goodbye for the evening, but both the stakes and the mood had changed radically in the past 24 hours.

"Don't even think I'm letting you walk back to the ship alone," he said in his no bullshit tone.

Kensie grabbed his hand. "What makes you think I was going to try and do that?" If she kept giving him those captivating, inviting grins, he wasn't sure he would be able to keep himself from throwing her over his shoulder and taking her back to *Julian's Empire II.* But right now he had to set that yearning aside for practical matters. *That sucks.*

"Well, then. Let's go." Not letting go of her hand, he assumed a rapid pace that his sexually satiated and still drunken body had no interest in maintaining. Forcing himself to concentrate, he managed to walk a fairly direct line down the sidewalk to the massive white hull that grew steadily larger as they approached.

He was nearly exhausted when they passed through the mostly closed duty free stores and stopped at the entrance to the wharf, where a big sign proclaimed that only passengers could proceed beyond this point. Kensie looked at her watch. "8:53. Plenty of time to spare."

"Seven minutes." He was a little surprised that his alcohol impaired mind was able to do the math so quickly. "Got any ideas about how we could spend that much time?"

Kensie slid her body so her legs straddled his massive left thigh, and she moved her hips with such skill that he grew hard almost immediately. He did not try to hide it from her, and she clearly took it as a compliment, because her hands slid around his lower back. "Seven minutes is *way* too short for what I want to do to you," she told him in a low voice.

"As much as I want to ask what that is right now, I don't know if I can handle the answer."

She grabbed his ass with both hands and squeezed his cheeks. "Too bad. Maybe not right this second, but sooner or later I'm going to tell you. In (*kiss*) – very (*kiss*) – specific (*kiss*) – detail (*kiss*). So make sure you're ready. I'll see you tomorrow morning in Grenada."

His head swam. He'd never wanted anyone like this. Burke longed to wrap himself up in her, dive deeper into that sensual body and that brilliant, passionate mind, and never leave. A little, nagging voice managed to make itself heard, just for a second: *Don't do this! Don't fall for another one!* That voice may have given good advice, but it was far too late and far too faint to have any effect. He wrapped his arms around her and kissed her deeply, and his only coherent concept was to wonder how many hours it would be until he could see her again.

***

Catrina was waiting for her right inside the arrival portal as Kensie stepped from the gangway to the deck. "Nice of you to make it," she said in a biting tone.

"I'm sorry. I lost track of time," Kensie said, pushing the elevator button to head back to the cabin. She figured Catrina wouldn't stay, but she still had a pretty serious buzz on and needed to get some sleep if she was going to be ready when the ship docked in Grenada. It was only a matter of time before her friend noticed the silly grin that she couldn't seem to hide; hopefully she'd be in her room before then. If not, Catrina would demand to know more.

"I get it – I know how you are when you're working – but it's been dark for a few hours, and I know you don't dive at night."

"Yeah," Kensie agreed as the elevator arrived and they stepped inside. "I was working, but then some other things happened."

That caught Catrina's attention. "'Other things'? What are you even talking – oh, my god. You were with someone, weren't you?"

Kensie had demonstrated her ability to lie very well recently, but not about this topic. She was dying to tell her tale and Catrina was the perfect audience. She still had the wherewithal to be a little mysterious about it, so she arched her eyebrows quickly in response.

Catrina grabbed Kensie's arm. "I thought you were doing some research or something!" She immediately pushed another button. "We are going to have a drink and you're going to tell all about him!"

"No, Catrina – I'm already kind of buzzed. I need to get some sleep."

Her protest was as effective as trying to drain a lake with a teaspoon. "Yeah, I can tell, and getting drunk and fucking some cute island guy is gonna make an even better story! And you know I'll just talk your ear off all night if you don't tell me, so you're coming up to the bar for a drink and to share your naughty little adventure."

Kensie knew she was overmatched. Catrina could be very persistent, and Kensie *had* dangled a very enticing appetizer right in front of her. It would be cruel not to give her the basics, at least about most of the night, and it would be wonderful to finally be the object of another woman's envious stare as she told of her exploits. "OK, you got me."

Catrina clapped her hands excitedly as the elevator opened and shut at their deck before proceeding to the upper decks, where most of the bars were. She headed directly for the Tidal Wave, one of the smaller watering holes, but it was quiet with subdued lighting and that meant they could talk without shouting to each other. It also didn't get busy until later in the evening.

As hoped, they found it less than half full, and after grabbing two Rum Punches, they found a booth out of the way with high sides that would give them some privacy. "OK, you slut," Catrina said as her eyes danced, "let's hear it."

"It's not like that," Kensie objected, taking a sip of her drink. Compared to the Mt. Gay rum she'd been sipping straight from the bottle a few hours ago, this beverage was a pale and bland substitute overloaded with sugars and other crap that somehow diminished the purity of her recent experiences. Kensie craved the sensuality of plain, good rum, just as she'd craved that muscular body in the tiny room above *Arnhim's*. She wasn't just some tourist anymore, willing to accept being told how to have a good time by a corporate cruise line and a commercial. Burke had awakened something carnal in her, and although it might go back into hibernation once the booze wore off, right now it was a part of her and she would embrace it.

A member of the wait staff was passing by. "Excuse me," she said to catch his attention, "could I have a Mt. Gay on the rocks?"

Catrina gawked at her friend.

"Certainly. Anything else?"

"No, that's it. Thank you." The man turned to leave, but Kensie had another inspiration. "Can you make it a double, please?" He smiled and headed back to the bar.

"And now you're drinking straight rum?" Catrina asked incredulously.

"I acquired a taste for it today," she said slyly. "It was a medicinal necessity."

"Oh my god!" Catrina squealed like a five year old. "This story is going to be fucking epic! Don't leave out a thing!"

Kensie started recounting her story, about finding Burke far off the beaten path and how they'd been diving on a fascinating area, and how she'd come across some very cool artifacts that were still in her backpack, but soon realized she'd trapped herself. In order to explain her sudden love of the sweet liquor, she realized it would be almost impossible to leave out the fight with the scumbags after they'd docked and Burke's resulting injury. Thinking quickly, Kensie decided to play it off as an attempted random robbery. If she thought for a second that Kensie was in danger from any sort of organized effort against her, Catrina would latch herself to her friend's leg to prevent her from getting off the boat. Or, even worse – she'd insist on coming along to "protect" her. For that reason as well, she completely skipped over the first encounter with those men in the boat. She hoped she was sober enough (or drunk enough) to make her story believable.

She was. Kensie relayed the details of the fight honestly, watching Catrina's eyes threaten to pop from their sockets as she recalled how she held off her attacker until Burke had finished him off, and how they'd gone to *Arnhim's* for Navia's special brand of medical treatment.

"Holy shit," Catrina responded. "Did you go to the police?"

"No," Kensie replied, pausing to come up with a good reason for that course of action.

"Why the hell not?! You could have been killed!"

"Burke said it wasn't worth it, that the local cops only worried about the places where the tourists went. Plus, they might have tried to confiscate my artifacts, and these have real scientific value. I'm not giving them up."

To their surprise, a blond head popped up from the other side of the booth. "I thought that was you. Thank god you're safe!" It was Van.

The ladies shared a look, and Kensie had very little trouble conveying her exasperation. *This guy keeps turning up at the wrong time!* She was about to ask him what he was doing there when he disappeared and came around to their side of the table. "Hey, Catrina," he said perfunctorily. "That's a totally amazing story! What do you think they wanted?"

Catrina opened her mouth, obviously ready to read him the riot act, but Kensie's newly discovered boldness overtook her. "Van, we were having a private conversation, and I'm not sure I like you eavesdropping. Do you think you could give us a little space?"

The chiseled face blinked. "Sorry. I just was amazed when I heard that story and then realized it was your voice."

"Well, thank you for your concern. Now, if you don't mind, I'd like to talk with Catrina. I'm not much in the mood for entertaining right now."

Van gave her a hard look, much as he had at *Arnhim's* the night before, and then he smiled, like he was turning on the charm. "Hey, sure. I'm sorry to have butted in. I'm just glad you're OK." Met with icy silence, he waited a beat before nodding. "So I'll see you around, OK?"

"Sounds great." Kensie coated each syllable with a healthy dose of bitter sarcasm.

"OK. Bye." He paused for one more awkward beat before turning and heading out of the bar.

Kensie rolled her eyes. "That fucking guy is like my shadow. It feels like every time I turn around, there he is."

Catrina replicated the look she'd given her friend upon hearing her revised drink order. "What the hell has gotten into you? Besides your dive instructor, I mean? I've never seen you so aggressive."

"Maybe I developed a taste for danger," she said, surprised at how unaffected she felt by the low grade confrontation with Van. Normally, she would have stewed over hurting his feelings, but now there was nothing but a feeling of power at having stood her ground.

"Yeah, I guess you did," Catrina responded. "So, back to the story. What happened next?"

Catrina became quickly caught up once more while Kensie explained about Burke's "surgery" and how she developed her sudden affinity for hard liquor. She felt like she was bragging a little as she described how well Burke reacted to her touch, but Catrina seemed mesmerized by the story, not interrupting as Kensie provided details that were just intimate enough to cross the line.

By the time she got to the point in the story where Catrina called her, Kensie was well into her second drink. Her head was swimming, but she likened it to thinking about what had just transpired, and that meant she wasn't drunk – she was *alive.*

"So you got bombed on 100-proof rum and then fucked your captain, stitches and all, in a little room over a local bar? That is so hot *I'm* sweating right now." She raised her glass and clinked it with Kensie's. "I always knew you had it in you, girl. You just needed the right man to pull it out of you – or, more accurately, put it in you." They giggled like schoolgirls. "Too bad it was only one night."

"Oh, it wasn't. He's going to meet the ship in Grenada tomorrow and we're going to see what else we can find."

Catrina rolled her eyes at her friend. "Really? I know it was an amazing experience for you, and it probably was for him, but do you really think this guy is going to chase you hundreds of miles just to dive with you tomorrow on the chance you'll fuck his brains out again?"

Kensie shook her head, far more certain of her position than she probably should be. "I told you, he's not like that. Plus, it's only about 50 miles, not hundreds. This was something special." She could see the way her friend smiled patiently at her, like a mother trying to explain to her daughter how boys could say and do the meanest things.

"I'm sure it was, probably almost as much for him as it was for you. But look at it from his point of view. You're from the States, and you'll be gone after tomorrow. Even if you were that good, there's nowhere for this to go, right?"

"I don't know," Kensie answered honestly. "We didn't think that far ahead. But he didn't kiss me like he was saying goodbye. He kissed me like tomorrow was a promise, one that he wants to fulfill. I can't explain it, but I can feel it."

"You can put it off, but it's only going to be harder to handle if you lose yourself in fantasy land."

Kensie tried not to feel defensive. Catrina meant well, but Kensie Version 2.0 was seeing things differently. Now she wanted to embrace the unknown, take a chance, roll the dice, believe the impossible – all the *clichés*. "I'm not living in a fantasy, but I am going to play this hand for all it's worth. If I'm wrong, I'll deal with it. But I don't think I am."

A beep sounded on Catrina's phone, indicating someone was contacting her via the ship's texting app. She looked at it quickly, and Kensie saw the way her eyes flashed and her mouth twitched. "It's Reid. He wants to know if I can meet him at the stern. Do you mind?"

"Of course not. You go ahead. I need to get some rest anyway. Busy day tomorrow."

Catrina took her friend's hand. "I hope you have a busy – and wonderful – day. I really do. I didn't mean to bring you down. I just don't want you to get hurt, that's all. If you're certain he'll be there tomorrow, then I know he will be. Just be careful, OK?"

Kensie accepted the unnecessary apology gracefully. "I appreciate your concern. Isn't it funny how our roles have reversed?"

Catrina blinked at that one. "You've got me there. I blew off your good advice about a guy more times than I want to remember."

"So it's my turn now. Maybe you can meet him tomorrow, and maybe you'll see what I see. And I'm sorry – we talked about me and Burke this whole time, and nothing about you and Reid. It must be going good with him, right?"

Catrina stood up. "Tonight was about you. But yeah, it's going real good, and you're damn right you'll hear more about him soon." She leaned down and kissed her friend on the cheek. "Good night."

Kensie watched her head out, noting the extra spring in Catrina's step. She took a minute to finish her drink and then stood, surprised by how badly the ship seemed to be rocking. It hadn't seemed that severe before. She made her way to the bulkhead and looked out a window to see what epic storm had descended upon them, only to find the moonlight reflected in a glass calm sea. It was then that she realized that it was she and not the boat that was rocking. *Overdid the rum, didn't you?* She managed to make it to the door and out on the deck, clinging to the railing for dear life. She wanted to try and see the island one more time. Her metamorphosis on this tiny lump of rock and sand had been complete, and it seemed like something she should reflect upon.

She could still see the lights on the southern tip of St. Vincent fading into the distance off the port side of the stern, and she was fairly sure she could make out where the *Amore* had been docked. When she'd boarded, a quick backward glance showed Burke still standing by the Passengers Only gate, looking at her, and she imagined he was still there, staring at the fading lights of the boat as it headed over the horizon.

*Please be there tomorrow morning, Burke.*

***

Once Kensie disappeared through the hatch and was safely back on board Burke, despite still being fairly drunk, could finally think more with the big head rather than with the little one. He knew he wouldn't be following the ship in the sense that Kensie probably thought he would; that is, 100 feet behind it all the way to Grenada. The captain would surely not be pleased to have a small craft right up his ass, and he was in no condition to pilot a rowboat across the harbor right now, let alone take a night trip over 50 or so miles of ocean. He'd sleep till about three, and that would refresh him enough that he could make the voyage safely and still be there in plenty of time. He even knew a marina right next to the cruise ship berths where he could tie up the *Empire.*

*Shit! The boat.* It was his home, his livelihood and, as odd as it sounded, his friend, but he'd not thought of it since he got Kensie to *Arnhim's,* and then he'd gotten rather... distracted.

He headed back at a double time pace, hoping that she had not been ransacked or worse – stolen. The remains of his life were on it, and he had to force himself not to think about running to the end of the dock to see *Empire* sitting on the bottom of the harbor or not there at all.

His worry increased the closer he got, and he broke into a jog as he got near his dock. When he broke through the brush to see the harbor, he was relieved to see the outline of *Empire* floating serenely at her moorings. He slowed to a walk and, panting heavily, approached her.

Even in the dim light, Burke could see that interior of the ship had been tossed about. Air tanks and swim fins and other assorted items were lying haphazardly on the deck. He jumped over the gunwale and started going through the loose items, and was happy to realize whoever had done this (probably those fucks they'd fought with, but he couldn't be sure) had been more about looking for stuff and less about breaking things, so there was little damage. He just had to clean up.

It didn't take long to put things back in their proper place. Once finished, he took a minute to stand at the bow so he could see out the harbor entrance where it opened to the Caribbean. A small mass of lights was moving ever so slowly away from the island under a bright moon off his left shoulder. He knew it had to be the *Amore of the Seas,* and that meant Kensie was on it. He couldn't help but stare at it for a little while, and he wondered if (*hoped that*) Kensie was standing on one of her weather decks, looking back at the island

and thinking about him the way he was thinking about her, until it disappeared completely from view. *Good night, Kensie.*

Setting his alarm, he checked his dressing to make sure it wasn't bleeding before settling down in his bunk. He had a lot of booze to burn off in the next few hours.

***

Man-Bun leaned back in the chair, an ice pack on his forehead, just above the two black eyes that were still forming. He avoided touching his nose; never having had it broken before, he was amazed at how the slightest pressure shot white hot pain through his sinuses.

His partner came in with his own ice and sat on the army cot against the wall. The cool compress wasn't doing much to help the ache in his jaw, and he wiped his chin with a paper towel. The holes where three teeth had recently been refused to stop bleeding, and his lip was so swollen that he couldn't keep the reddened saliva from running over it.

They shared a glance but no words. Man-Bun could barely speak without feeling like someone was driving a railroad spike between his eyes, and Hat-Head wasn't sure he could form words. Their look said it all; *how the fuck did we get beat to hell by a boat captain and a girl when we had the knives?* Even more worrisome to them was that they would have to explain themselves to their employer.

As if on cue, the cell phone on the nightstand rattled and chirped. Hat-Head looked at it and nodded, picking it up like it might explode as Man-Bun came over and sat down beside his partner. He punched the Speaker button and held the phone up.

"I thought you gentlemen were the best around," said the irritated voice on the other end.

"We are," Man-Bun responded with a questioning look at his partner. "What makes you think we aren't?"

"A colleague of mine reported to me that two of you were bested in a physical confrontation by our adventurous explorer and some broken down boat captain." The voice went up a few decibels. "What the fuck is going on?"

"We took them a little too lightly," Hat-Head said. "It won't happen again."

The speaker crackled as the next words were loud enough to overload it. "You're goddamned right you won't! I thought I explained to you what was at stake here! I thought I told you how serious this was! And I thought I offered you the right amount of money to get the fucking job done! But I guess I wasn't clear, so let me rephrase – if I have to find someone else to deal with this situation, I'll make sure that my new employees deal with you too! You understand me, you fucking morons?"

Eyes bulging, both men nodded at the phone. "Yeah, yeah, we understand," Man-Bun said, his voice jumpy.

"Good," the man said, the voice once more calm and even. "I'm glad we cleared up that misunderstanding before something else went awry. The good news is that they didn't find the prize. Now, I want you to get your asses to Grenada and handle this situation appropriately."

"We're on it," Man-Bun told him, his voice earnest yet submissive.

"I sincerely hope so. I won't be pleased if I have to make another call like this one." The line went dead.

***

Burke's eyes popped open. At first he thought he'd heard something, but he remained perfectly still and the noise did not return. That was the beauty of living on a boat; it was almost impossible for someone to board it and walk anywhere on it without the occupants knowing. After about a minute of listening, he sat up quickly.

And regretted it. He immediately became dizzy and disoriented in the darkness, gripping the sides of his bunk tightly to make sure he didn't fall forward onto the deck. His arm burned, and he touched the bandages to feel the warm wetness of blood. *Is that a problem?* Despite his extensive experience with stitches, he wasn't sure. He wondered if he should go back to Navia, or even to a real clinic when he remembered he was supposed to be somewhere.

*What time was it?* He grabbed the digital clock from his dresser and checked it out. The alarm was set for 3:00, and he felt a surge of anger at the broken device, wanting to hurl it at the bulkhead in frustration before he realized that, in his well soused condition, he'd set it to 3:00 PM, not AM. It was now 5:33 in the morning, putting him well behind schedule.

*** 

Kensie woke with a pretty decent headache and a mouth that was so dry her tongue felt like sandpaper. Dim light came through the sliding glass door to the balcony, meaning that she'd been sleeping solidly since she fell onto her bunk. She looked at her phone: 6:15. Sunrise was imminent, and that meant she had to get moving.

That was easier said than done. Her stomach rumbled, and the trifecta of symptoms made for the worst hangover she'd ever had, making it difficult to perform tasks rapidly. She took slow, deep breaths as she pulled herself to a sitting position. Kensie gave herself a minute before rising to her feet, pleased that the ship wasn't gyrating like a raft in Class 5 rapids beneath her as it had last night. *At least I'm not still drunk.*

She was alone in the room. No surprise there; even bombed out of her mind, she could tell how excited Catrina had been at seeing Reid's text, and she was not prone to patience regarding her amorous intentions. Kensie hoped her friend had picked a winner.

*Like Burke.* She smiled despite her physical condition thinking of yesterday, of her wanton disregard for decorum and Burke's enthusiastic responses. He made her feel beautiful and desired, something that had never been part of her self-image.

Anticipation crackled through her body. *I'm going to see him in a little while, and I'm going to find the* Couronne. Kensie could not figure out which event excited her more, but it was enough to get her to rush through her preparations despite her self-induced maladies.

She wanted a shower but settled for brushing her teeth and hair quickly. Grabbing her backpack, she made her way to the departure portal and hustled into the warmth and humidity of the tropical morning well before 7 a.m. Her throbbing headache and churning stomach faded into the background as she anticipated what this day could bring.

She exited the wharf and looked around for Burke. He was not to be seen, but no worry. He could be in a lot of places. She walked down the broad sidewalk, tersely refusing the taxi drivers looking to score an early fare to the nearest beach or tourist trap. Kensie knew they couldn't begin to guess what she was really going to do today or who she was going to meet, but she still felt mild irritation that they were distracting her from getting to the one person she *had* to be with.

At the end of the gauntlet, she saw a small marina about a quarter mile away. *Easy peasy.* Burke would know where she would end up upon leaving the ship, and he would be docked there waiting for her. She headed forward at a rapid pace, glad that they would get moving fairly early but disappointed that they would have to shove off immediately. There were so many other ways they could spend time in the golden glow of the early morning sun, and most of them were so inviting that she considered delaying their departure.

She looked down the first dock, but all the boats were crisp and clean and perfect, the complete opposite of *Julian's Empire II*. No worries. She walked to the next wooden platform, find more boats that looked like they'd just returned from a photo shoot for the cover of *Yachting* magazine. She kept going, certain that she would find the decrepit little craft tucked among one of the floating palaces.

But she was wrong. When she got to the end with no success, she back tracked, certain she'd missed Burke or his boat, but a more careful inspection proved that her handsome sailor was not here, and she didn't know where else to look.

*Well, now what?*

It was a question both heartfelt and practical. She longed to see him again, to kiss those lips and touch those muscles, but she needed him as well to find the *Couronne*. It would take too long and require too much work for her to find and convince another captain to run her all the way out to Fraunce's Shoal. She was far too tired for that right now, and not just from a lack of sleep.

She turned in a circle, knowing that she looked every bit the tourist who was completely lost and confused, even though the situation was completely different.

***

The verdant hills of Grenada rose over the blue horizon as Burke pushed his boat far harder than he had in years. The engines were sucking fuel to the point he hoped he had enough to get to the island. The RPMs were much too high and had been that way for too long, but he kept the throttle as far forward as he dared, driven by an urgency that he barely understood. As he monitored the wind and the waves, the rest of his consciousness could not escape the idea that Kensie, having not found him, was at this very moment agreeing to go out with another captain in a cleaner, newer boat. He would take the job because the money was good and because he saw the curve of her body through that swimsuit and could imagine exactly what those lips might do. And he might not be as honorable of a man as Kensie deserved.

*You had the same "dishonorable" thoughts the first time you saw her.*

But that was before he learned who she was. Things were different now. He owed it to her to keep his promise, but it would have been a lie to deny his desire to see that teasing smile, those soft lips, those big eyes, and the way she moved when she walked, like the air itself was a fluid that she could glide through. And he'd be damned if some other jerkoff was going to get to see them before he did again. *Jesus, you sound jealous.*

Of course the berth for the cruise ships had to be on the southwest corner of the island, about as far away as it could be. He looked at his watch – 7:14. The second hand raced around the face of the worn Omega like it had something to prove, while *Empire* seemed perfectly content to plod along as if enjoying the view and having nowhere special to be. He resisted the urge to pound on the wheel – it wouldn't do a bit of good and he felt angry enough to break the thing right off the conn. Then where would he be?

Finally, he saw a white point edge over the horizon and realized he was seeing the top of a cruise ship – if it wasn't the *Amore of the Seas*, it was another ship next to it. He pushed the throttle forward another inch, wincing at the high pitched whine of the pistons as they threatened to throw a ring and turn the engine block into a lump of shredded metal. *Hold together, dammit.* She would – she *had* to.

Fifteen minutes later he was looping around the stern of *Amore* and another giant ship whose name he didn't bother to read. He knew where he would dock, in the marina just south of the large quay where *Amore* rested, but he wasn't sure if Kensie would still be there, or if she'd figured out to go there at all. He shouldn't have been so casual about things. It was all fine and wonderful to romantically tell her that he would find her, but it was hardly practical, and for all he knew she had walked halfway around the island to explore every dock on the south end looking for him or for another charter.

Well, he told himself, he'd find her. He'd walk or sail or hire a helicopter and scour the damn island to find her. Whatever it took. He was running through his options when he turned his bow into one of the guest berths, one that you could rent for the day, and backed the engines down hard to glide to a stop at just the right time. It was actually a very fine piece of seamanship, but he was far too preoccupied to congratulate himself on his boat handling skills. He grabbed a line with the boat hook and was tying it hastily around a cleat when he saw a very familiar figure in profile at the end of the quay, hunched over and sitting on a bench.

***

Kensie couldn't summon the energy to raise her head, let alone stand. He wasn't coming. She didn't know what was worse; the humiliation of being used as a fuck toy, her child-like crush on a handsome islander, not being able to look for the *Couronne*, or how Catrina had been right despite her drunken insistence to the contrary. She'd been casually betrayed, acting like a foolish teenager who'd fallen for a handsome but married man, someone she could never have. At the moment, she could give a shit about finding some centuries-old gaudy museum ornament no matter what it was worth academically or monetarily. She just wanted to go home.

"So, you want to go diving, or what?"

Kensie spun around at the baritone sound of Burke's voice, both angry and joyful. The angry side came through more intensely. "Where the hell have you been? I thought you bailed on me!"

He appeared to take the tongue lashing in stride. "I guess I can't handle my liquor the way I used to. I set my alarm wrong and didn't wake up. I'm sorry."

Kensie wanted to yell more, primarily out of relief, and she wondered if this was what a parent felt after finding her kid who had wandered off in a crowd – the desire to strangle and hug the child at the very same time. The moment passed, and she was left needing only the hugging part. She felt her smile overpower the scowl. "You better be sorry, jerk!" Standing, she took a step forward and jabbed a finger into that rock hard chest. "I'll kick that fine ass later."

"I guess I deserve it," Burke responded with mock gravity, taking her hands in his. "I didn't mean to make you worry. I was hoping that you still be around. The idea of you on someone else's nice, clean boat on the way out to Fraunce's Shoal kind of annoyed me."

Kensie didn't want to be mushy, but she read the meaning under his playful words and wanted to respond in kind. "There are an awful lot of really beautiful boats here," she pointed out, "but I doubt that those captains could give me the – extra attention – that you've provided."

She knew she struck the right tone by the way his mouth twitched. "Happy to be of service, Ma'am." He leaned down to give her a kiss that wasn't quite quick but wasn't too carnal either.

"I'm happy to get that service. So let's go!" She looked around for the boat.

"Whoa! We gotta do a couple things first."

"Like what?" Kensie was impatient; now that her man was here, she felt a renewed sense of purpose to accomplish her other goal.

"Well, the boat is running on fumes, so I have to get some gas. And I didn't have a chance to get any food, so one of us should pick something up."

Kensie pulled a face at the mention of food. "Ugh, no thank you. I'm surprised that you can't tell that I'm severely hung over. I probably look as bad as I feel."

"Now that you mention it..." Burke said and received a smack on the arm for his trouble. "We don't have to eat it right now, but we'll definitely need something. There's a food truck just past that traffic circle – can you grab a few things and meet me back here in 15 minutes?"

"Is that a direct order, captain?"

"It can be. Your choice."

"What would happen if I disobeyed you?" *I can't believe the way I'm talking!*

"I have very special ways of dealing with insubordinate crew members," Burke responded. "You might not want to discover those. Or you might. But, for now, on your way."

"Aye aye, Sir!" She gave him another kiss and headed toward the circle.

Twelve minutes later she was hopping on board the *Empire* with a bag of sandwiches, bottles of water, and two cups of coffee. Burke wasted no time in getting underway, turning north along the coast until it disappeared behind them before adjusting his course to the northeast. She watched the cliffs of smaller islands pass them on both sides as they headed out. The sea was a little rough, with two to three foot ground swells giving *Empire* an active ride.

Kensie stood on the open deck behind the cabin, letting the cool sea air wash over her. Breathing it deeply seemed to help minimize her hangover. She sipped at her coffee, pleased that her stomach no longer wanted to reject it out of hand. She knew she probably shouldn't be diving today; being hungover meant she was severely dehydrated, and it was pretty much a rule that you didn't go down in that condition. But this was a very special event, and the regular rules no longer applied. She'd finish her coffee (yeah, the caffeine would make her more dehydrated, but she needed it) and after that it was water all the way. She did have two hours.

The blue sky, warm sun, and verdant hills of the island around her were beautiful, but Kensie found her gaze wandering to the open hatch to stare at Burke's shoulders and the side of his face. Maybe it was her imagination, but from her vantage point he looked more... peaceful than he had before last night. *Gee, I wonder what might have happened!* It filled her with pride that she could do that to a man. She had to admit that he'd had a similar effect on her. The heady bravado she'd experienced last night was, as she'd anticipated, tempered by her sobriety, but it was not gone, and she couldn't stop being amazed and impressed with the new Kensie. And at least part of that was because of the handsome man in the tank top and ragged denim shorts at the wheel.

*What the hell am I doing way over here then?* With nothing but time on her hands until they got to the dive site, she stepped over to Burke. He didn't seem to notice her approach, but he was slick, raising his arm to put it around her and grasp her left shoulder with his massive hand as she sidled up against him. His body was solid, powerful, enticing. It felt like home. And she wanted to go home.

She rested her cheek against his bicep, feeling the muscle quiver with the rumble of the engine. She turned her head to it, letting the aroma of his skin, the rhythm of the waves as they plowed through them, and the salt air take over, relaxing her body and soothing her mind. The events of yesterday and the potential dangers of today faded into the background as she leaned on her captain. Right here and right now, she knew to her core that he would keep her safe and sound.

He was her hero.

# Chapter 11 – Where's Your Watch?

Burke cut the power about 40 yards from Kensie's GPS waypoint, remaining far enough away from the site of the artifacts so that a heavy anchor was unlikely to land on anything important. Once she'd gotten at least her temporary fill of the sight, feel, and smell of her man, Kensie had spent the last hour going over tides and charts in the cabin until she came up with a plan that she felt would maximize their chances of success.

"So, what I'm going to do," she told Burke as he set up on the anchors, "is work east, in the direction where the artifacts got lighter, but I'm not gonna dig them up one by one – we don't have the time. I'm going to find the edge of the debris field and then start investigating the most likely returns."

Burke nodded. "Still sounds like a lot of ground to cover. It might not be possible."

"It might not be, but if you've got a better plan, I'm all ears."

Burke shrugged; obviously, he did not. "I'm more worried about having additional visitors today. I doubt I'll be able to scare them off with an unloaded shotgun this time." He looked grim.

"Well, maybe you should load it," Kensie responded, trying to lighten the mood a bit. He was far sexier as the devil may care swashbuckler than the brooding worrier.

"It already is," he told her, exasperation creeping into his voice. "You know what I mean."

"Yeah, I do. What's your plan?"

Burke killed the engine and watched the anchor chains while he spoke. "I think the same as yesterday. Unless they have radar, no one followed us out here, but that doesn't mean much since they know where we'll be. If someone comes roaring up, you'll have a little over five minutes at best, depending on how fast the other boat is. I've already got a quick release on the anchor, so I can be moving long before you get to the surface. So be ready to come up if I see something."

"Five minutes," Kensie mused. That didn't give her much time for her safety stop during her ascension.

"I know. I don't like it but I can't leave you down there and *Empire*, as you've observed, ain't exactly the fastest boat around."

"All right," she responded. Like Burke said, it wasn't a very graceful solution, but she would do her best to minimize the ascent time. "Let's get to it."

A few minutes later Kensie was in her diving equipment and ready to go. Burke stopped her just as she was pulling the dive mask down, giving her a quick but intimate kiss. "For luck," he explained.

"Thanks. I'll take all the help I can get." *Haven't I been lucky enough on this trip?* Maybe she had, but right now she was being greedy. She pulled her mask in place and splashed into the sea.

Kensie got her bearings rapidly and swam to the furthest contact she'd found before moving forward once again. The detector chirped dutifully upon every hit, and with each sound she marked another waypoint. She proceeded down the slope as the contacts continued to pile up. There seemed to be a drop off, or at least a steepening gradient about 30 yards ahead, and she decided that would be a good place to take stock of her situation.

Burke apparently felt differently. She heard the familiar crackle of communication, followed by his voice. "How deep are you, Kensie?"

She rolled her eyes but took care to keep any irritation out of her voice. She didn't think he sounded overprotective or condescending, but it was the first thing that entered her mind. Still, he was right to ask. "85 feet."

"What's your deepest dive?" he asked.

"110."

She was pleasantly surprised at his next remark. "OK, I'd appreciate it if you'd stay in constant voice comm if you go below that depth, just to be safe." She'd expected him to try and order her to stay above it, and appreciated his respect for her intelligence and abilities.

"I can do that," she replied, marking another hit. The screen was becoming covered with tiny plus signs.

About 20 feet from the ledge, the returns stopped abruptly. She kept moving forward to be as sure as possible that she'd reached the end of the debris field, but when she got to the lip of the increased slope, she had no more contacts. Kensie checked her depth. 105 feet. That worked out well. "OK, I'm at the edge of the drop off and I've had no contact for a few yards, so I'm going to work back to get the borders of the field. I won't be going below 110."

"Copy that." Even through the altered sounds of the electronic communication, Burke sounded relieved, making her smile. It was nice to have someone worry about her, even if it wasn't necessary. She turned back, her sweeping motion with the detector becoming a part of her swimming stroke.

She hit the edge of the debris field exactly where she expected it, and the returns were about the same. Kensie knew she had no basis for what kind of return something like the *Couronne* might generate, but these felt just like everything else. Coins and buttons and nails and buckles. In any other context she would be celebrating such a find and would be eagerly digging up every single one of these things, but right now there were bigger fish to catch.

But the bigger fish weren't biting. She continued to sweep the area until she had a fairly defined debris field. Probably 60 or 70 returns, Kensie estimated, and none distinctive. She was just about ready to surface, and decided that her best course of action was to come back down and dig up the biggest targets. The strategy felt wrong, but she didn't have a better plan, so, after surfacing and getting Burke's tacit agreement with her approach, she was back at it, digging to recover the first object. She was not surprised when she pulled a group of six coins from the sand.

Kensie could feel the tension in her jaw as she gritted her teeth with frustration, digging up one unremarkable artifact after another. As she'd expected, the field was littered with buttons, pocket watch chains, eyeglass rims, and a few rings. She even found a tiny lump of gold that confused her until she realized it was probably a filling for a tooth, which creeped her out a great deal.

But these were all small items, suggesting that an item as substantial as the *Couronne* was not among them. *Had it broken apart in the sinking?* Kensie had not considered that possibility, but it fit the scenario. Would bringing a piece of it back to the States be enough? It would, but she would be lying if she tried to convince herself that it would be the same as finding it intact.

Forty five minutes and 37 very uninspiring artifacts later, Kensie headed to the surface, wondering if her third or fourth dives of the day would be any more successful than this morning had been.

*****

Burke could feel Kensie's frustration as she stared at the deck, absent mindedly chomping on one of the bacon, egg, and cheese sandwiches that she'd picked up before leaving Grenada. His was cold and soggy, and he suspected that she wasn't even tasting hers. In all honesty, he was at just as much of a loss as she was. They had to be looking at something the wrong way, considering something incorrectly.

Kensie was thinking along those lines too. "This isn't making any sense. I'm doing something wrong, missing some data." She was half talking to herself, but then she raised her head and stared pointedly at Burke. "Are you sure the currents are always west to east here?"

"Yeah, pretty much. The tidal flow is so strong over the shoal that any back currents would be minimal, especially over the time frame we're talking about."

Kensie affirmed his statement with a clenched lip expression that would have been a curse had she decided to enunciate. Her eyes moved back and forth; she was considering what she knew about the situation, but every few seconds she shook her head as she dismissed another idea.

"OK, we're stuck," Burke said. "Maybe you're too close to this whole thing. Why don't you just give me a brain dump about the situation and I'll try to provide some distance analysis. Start with him taking the *Couronne*."

Kensie nodded and recited the story as she knew it, clarifying what was historically accurate and what was conjecture. After the theft, he'd made two stops, one in the Azores and one at the eastern tip of Puerto Rico, staying only long enough in each port to get some supplies. Those were the last places to which he could be definitively traced. After that, only the artifacts they'd recovered lent credence to her theory that they were searching in the right place.

Burke frowned. There was nothing in Kensie's tale that might explain why the *Couronne* might not be here. "Tell me about Buckwell's crew," he said.

"Not too much is known about them," Kensie said glumly, thinking this was a dead end, but she persisted. "We know he had a very small core of senior crew members that he seemed to trust with his life, but his writings only ever mentioned two of them – one named Daniel and one named Erasmus. They were the ones he trusted to keep the ship on course and keep the crew in line when he was sleeping or doing something else. There were probably others, but he never wrote anything about them."

A thought started forming in his head. "OK, so they were his trusted lieutenants and probably got the biggest share of whatever he stole."

"Most likely, yes."

"So how would the rest of the crew get paid?"

"Normally, the entire crew got an equal share, but it wasn't at all unheard for very liberal forms of accounting to go on. A crew member might be the first one to find something, and he might come back to the captain saying he found 30 gold coins when he really found 40. But if they got caught, they'd be lucky to be stranded somewhere. A lot of them got keelhauled." Burke grimaced; he could not imagine anything worse than being dragged under a boat as punishment.

"Buckwell was reputed to take a little more than his fair share because he was so damn good at stealing, and because he was becoming a legend before he died. A few letters mentioned how he, along with Daniel and Erasmus, would split half of everything among themselves and divide the other half up to the crew. Because he was so successful, the idea is that his crew accepted this because they still did better than on other ships. That, and because Buckwell was not a man to be fucked with."

"So how would they have planned to divvy up a single thing, like this headdress?"

"No one is certain. This kind of unique treasure would be more complicated. If he cut it up, it would be worth far less than the whole but easier to sell. He probably would have kept it in one piece, but that meant he would need to find someone who could afford such a thing, and that wouldn't have been easy. One guess is that he promised his crew a much higher percentage on later journeys and planned to split the proceeds from the *Couronne* among his senior men. But that would mean holding onto it for possibly a very long time, and he'd know that Admiralty ships were out looking for him."

Burke felt a vague notion forming in his head. *It's about keeping the treasure safe until he could sell it.* "And would that delayed payment maybe have made some of the crew angry?"

"Yeah, maybe," Kensie said as she tilted her head to consider what appeared to be new information. "Buckwell was reputed to have, shall we say, liberal morals. If that was the deal, they might have thought Buckwell would sell it and disappear, and then where would those men get their fortune from? A higher percentage of zero is still zero."

"So maybe one or some of them, or the whole crew even, might have wanted to take it. And that means that he had to protect it from them, right?" Burke asked. The wheels were spinning, but the idea wasn't quite taking shape just yet. "And he only had a few other men he would trust?"

"Yeah." Kensie appeared enthused by his line of questioning; she thought something was there too.

"How many crew on a ship like Buckwell's?"

"Probably at least 60. Maybe more. *Aberaeron Fortune* was a brigantine, and they normally had about a 100 crew."

"So not too many guys to hold out against 60 to 100 pissed off crew?" Just as he finished the sentence, the answer they were looking for slapped him across the face. "Does that sound like a good plan to you?"

"No, not even a little bit." She squinted at him, probably alerted by the way his face changed.

He took her left wrist in his hand. "That's a nice watch, Kensie. Citizen. Good, solid dive watch. What did it cost you?"

"About $200," she answered, her face a question. "Why?"

"Is that the only watch you brought on the cruise?"

"No. I brought a Tag Heuer for dinners and going out and things."

"Pretty fancy. What's that one worth?" he asked. He was enjoying drawing this out, even if Kensie appeared to be growing impatient.

"Like $2,500 or so. What does that matter?"

"You're not wearing it. Where is it now?"

She gave him a cross look, like he was wasting her time with such silly questions. "Of course I'm not wearing it. It's valuable and it's not for diving. It's in my cabin, in the..." The irritation disappeared and her entire face went slack. "Holy shit. It's in the cabin safe."

"That's where I'd have it, just like where I'd keep a super treasure on my ship when I'm surrounded by men I don't completely trust. It'd be in the strongest safe I could afford, bolted down to the deck, and only me and my trusted cronies would have the combination."

"Yeah, of course. And a safe would fall straight to the bottom when the ship sank. It sure wouldn't drift – not in a hundred feet of water." She licked her lips as her brain went into overdrive. "Where's my GPS?" Burke was already handing it to her.

Kensie powered it up and scrolled until she reached the opposite end of the field. "OK, this mark is for the candlestick I brought up," she said, turning so Burke could see the screen and stabbing her finger at the furthest mark. "And that was the heaviest and densest thing I found. So it's a good bet that any safe is west of this point."

"That fits," Burke agreed. "How deep was the candlestick?"

"Um... 36 feet. Why?"

"Think of the shoal as an underwater island that just dropped down below the surface. The top of the mound would be where the island would have poked out of the water, and a sailing ship like that would have only drawn seven or eight feet, I'm guessing, so it wouldn't have hit the island until it was pretty shallow. So it's probably up near the top of the slope."

"Yup. Up this way," she ran her fingers over the GPS screen, indicating the shallower part of the shoal.

"So, if I were you, I'd follow the exact same strategy as you did this morning, just in the opposite direction. Find the border of the debris field this way. I'll bet dollars to doughnuts that the safe is at the exact point where the *Aberaeron Fortune* hit the island." He grew strangely excited at his deduction; while still nothing more than conjecture, Burke felt like it was the right track. It was like a hunt, and he was the hunter that had just figured out how to corner his prey.

He noticed that Kensie was getting even more excited, but that wouldn't do, not right now. He could afford it – he wasn't going to dive – but she would be, and excited people used their air far too quickly. Kensie needed to spend every second she could in the water.

"You look a little flushed, Kensie. You need to calm down."

"I am calm!" she snapped in a voice that was anything but.

"I'm excited too. But if you use up all your air or – worse – hyperventilate down there, you're not going to be able to stay down for 15 minutes, so settle yourself. There'll be time for freaking out later. Right now, you need to be a professor, not a fan girl."

Kensie scrunched her nose at him in mostly feigned irritation, but nodded. "Yeah, I know. Give me a second, but then I'm going in. And I'll find it." Burke wondered where this attractive, almost delicate looking woman hid the steel of resolve that now flashed in her eyes.

***

Kensie gave Burke a quick thumbs-up before setting out in the opposite direction of the day's earlier dives. The white sand, with little spots of coral sticking out here and there, beckoned to her. The sunlight filtering through the water looked like a spotlight to her, guiding her inexorably to her moment of destiny.

*You're being a little dramatic, aren't you?* She admonished herself for losing focus. Burke had been right; this was like being a surgeon operating on the President of the United States. No matter who your patient was, you stayed calm and did your job. And she would do her job the same way, no matter what she thought she was about to find.

Passing over the westernmost mark on her GPS, she started sweeping the floor, much as she had this morning. The detector squawked loudly with the heavier marks it picked up, and did so with great regularity. The sheer number of returns were worrisome. That was a lot of things to dig up, and she simply didn't have the time. Kensie knew that she had more than enough evidence by now to justify a new expedition – hell, she could make them call it "The Kensie Prescott Expedition" at this point – but she wanted to bring the *Couronne* to the surface herself so badly it almost hurt. She wanted to show it to Dean Talbot, to have him force another meeting of the NAS, and to walk in with the headdress raised over her head like she was skating around the rink having just won the Stanley Cup. Being ignored and ridiculed by a bunch of septuagenarians still stung, and there was only one thing that would act as the appropriate salve.

These thoughts rumbled about Kensie's brain as she continued over the buried debris field. The screen on her GPS was coated with so many marks it looked like a solid color, just like the eastern field had on the earlier dives. She was going to have to pick one of them, dig it up, and use that information as a baseline to pick the most attractive target. This was still going to be damn hard.

Then the returns completely stopped.

At 21 feet, the detector went instantly silent, like the batteries had failed, but the screen remained lit. Slightly confused, she turned back to the last mark and heard the dutiful wail of the device as the electromagnetic field proved it was still working. "Burke?"

"Yeah, Kensie?"

"I was getting a ton of returns, and then they just stopped dead. It's like I crossed a border or something. What d'ya think?"

She got no response, and in a few seconds Kensie wondered if she'd transmitted at all. "Did you copy my last?"

"Yeah. Hang on." He must have been considering this new evidence, so while she waited Kensie took the opportunity to scan forward a little further. Still nothing.

"Kensie, I think you should keep scanning the dead area for a while."

"And ignore all the juicy hits I just got? Isn't that a waste of time?"

"No, it's not. You said he sunk in a storm, so that means even heavy stuff would move with the current, but a safe is still going to go straight down. So just search higher up the slope."

"OK." She headed up toward the apex of the shoal, making quick, broad sweeps. If she heard anything at all she planned to stop, but nary a peep came from the device. She reached the peak of the underwater hill, pivoted, and started back down the same side but on another path, ensuring that she did not overlap any part of the sand twice. The silence was frustrating.

*This is stupid! I'm out of the hot zone. I'm not going to find dick all the way up – "*

***BEEEEEEEEEEP!!!***

The return hurt her ears, so much so she had to pull the device away to prevent blowing out her eardrum. She lowered the sensitivity and ran it over the same place. Another hit. Although not as loud, it was intense enough to indicate a very big return.

*I'm getting a Very Big Return. Oh my god.*

She didn't bother to mark the GPS even as she realized that ignoring that step was reckless. Dropping the detector to let it hang from her belt, she pulled out her shovel and plunged it into the sand. She dug in a controlled frenzy, going too fast and obscuring the visibility, but she expected to feel the target before she saw it.

Kensie dug deeper, getting into more tightly packed sediment. It didn't stop her, but it was a little harder to pull each scoop out, and it slowed her down. She grew tired, so she took a quick break, which would also allow the cloudy water to clear.

When it did, Kensie was surprised by how deep she'd dug. She should have found something by now. Grabbing the detector, she waved it over the area and was rewarded with the same response that told her she was in the right place, but just not deep enough. *So keep going.*

She returned to her task, trying to quell her building enthusiasm. She was breathing so hard she was starting to worry about CO2 poisoning. Kensie started repeating a simple phrase, almost like a mantra: *keep calm, keep calm, keep calm...*

*Clank.*

Kensie froze in place, allowing the particulate to settle, and when she cleared the last vestiges of sediment, she saw the unmistakable straight, almost black edge of something that could only be man made. She touched it, finding it cool against her fingers in the warm tropical water, like metal would be. Her mouth was suddenly bone dry.

"Buh- Burke?"

"Yeah."

"I, uh, I think I have something here."

The edge on his voice was unmistakable. "Something what?"

"Big. Metal. With a straight edge." She tried to move the exposed portion, but it didn't even think about budging. "And heavy." Kensie didn't dare say what she thought it was, like that would jinx it.

Burke had no such concerns. "Sounds like a safe to me. Try to dig around the edges to get a feel for the dimensions."

Kensie moved to obey, scraping away the mud until she had a rectangle, about two feet by three, with a mound of sand in the center. She brushed it away until two features became easily visible; a handle and a dial. "Oh yeah, it's a safe all right."

"How big?"

"Maybe six square feet. Not sure how deep."

"Damn it. That's pretty big. Can you dig under it?"

Kensie stuck her shovel into the sand as far as she could, but the metal ran down further than she could reach. "I don't think so, not without a lot of effort and half a day."

"Hang on." The mike went silent for a minute, and Kensie cleared more sand off the front. There appeared to be remnants of a couple of words there, but she could not read them. She started digging a little deeper around it, but made only miniscule progress. They would need several dives – at least – to clear the sand and silt from it.

Burke's voice entered her ears once again. "I'm coming down."

"What? Why? I thought you said it was too dangerous with those guys maybe around somewhere."

"We've only got one fresh tank left, Kensie. You want to leave this thing sitting there so any idiot can see it? Hell, I think I can see it from here." And he was at least 30 yards away and on the surface.

That was a good point. It would take no great exploratory skill to see a big black rectangle in the nearly white sand and clear water, and someone with the right equipment or the right number of people would have this out of the sea before Burke and Kensie could run back to Grenada, get more air, and get back here.

"I don't know if it'll matter whether you come down or not. This thing seems pretty big. I don't think even you and I can dig it out, let alone lift it up to the boat."

"I have a winch I can mount on the stern, and plenty of heavy chain. But we can't attach a line to it unless we can dig out under it, and yeah – that's gonna take time." It would take far too long, and Burke sounded like he'd figured that out as well.

"We can attach the chain to the safe handle," she suggested.

"Might break it off," Burke commented.

"Shit. Can we cut it open with a torch?"

"No, I don't have one anymore. I have a pneumatic jackhammer, but the hose isn't nearly long enough."

"Dammit, Burke!" Kensie said, growing frustrated with him shooting down her ideas even though she knew he wasn't the problem. "Do we have any other options?"

"I don't know. Let me think. You keep clearing it as best you can – maybe you'll find something."

*Like what?* Unsure that it would do any good, she returned to the annoyingly slow task of scooping more mud and residue from the sides of the metal box. She forced herself to reconsider the problem as she moved around it with the shovel. *Think. There's GOT to be a way.* Could she use a bar as a lever to tip it up so she could wrap the chain around it? Did Burke have something that could float this to the surface? She didn't know, but with his experience he would be the one to tell her if any of her fantastical ideas were valid.

She started digging down along the side, discarding the shovel in favor of her hands. She could scrape more sand that way, and it wasn't necessary to be delicate. The safe certainly wasn't fragile, and the more she could expose it, the more options they would have.

*Ow!*

She pulled her hand back at the pain of cracking her thumb on something sturdy near the corner. Kensie rubbed her digit for a second and, after confirming that she'd not broken any bones, excavated the immediate area until she exposed a piece of metal extending from the bottom of the safe. It was an inch or two thick in the middle and flared out to a wide base. It was a claw foot, like on a tub.

And a chain could be attached to it pretty easily.

"Burke." No answer. He must have laid the dive mask down on the deck to do something. "Burke!" Still nothing. She couldn't spare the time to surface, tell him, and then dive again, but what other option did she have? *Goddamn waste of time!* She was about to push away when she heard his voice.

"Did you call me, Kensie?"

"Yeah. Jesus! It's got claws!"

***

Burke wondered if he'd heard Kensie correctly. She'd nearly screamed her last words, but it sounded like she said the safe had claws. Either he misunderstood her, or she was having a hypoxic delusion. "I'm sorry, you broke up. Did you say 'claws', like an animal?"

"Yeah, but no! Claws, like a claw foot tub!"

He got it then. He could use them as an anchor point for the winch chain. "Oh, OK! Can you find more than one?"

"Hang on." He didn't have to wait long. "Yeah, one on each front corner. I'm guessing there's two more at the back, but I can't get to those because the safe is sitting face up."

"That's OK. Two should be enough, as long as the suction isn't too severe. How much bottom time do you have left?"

"About 20 minutes."

"OK. Make sure you have two good hook points that are totally clear. I'm going to rig up the winch and send it down. When you get it connected, I want you to come up. We'll save the last tank and hope like hell we don't need it."

"Got it."

Burke nearly dove into the cabin to get the winch and the snap hooks he needed. His hands were trembling, not only at the momentous possibilities, but because they were very short on time. Normally, lifting a three- or four-hundred pound safe from 20 feet deep was child's play; the winch could handle that weight without even straining.

But the suction that might have built up after 200 years screwed everything up. There was no way anyone could know how powerfully it had settled into the ooze. Their only option was to proceed and do so with all possible haste.

He backed the boat down toward Kensie and the safe, not caring that the anchor clip released to drop the buoy. He could get it later. Burke inserted the winch in the mount near the stern, attached two of his sturdiest snap hooks to the chain and, arresting the motion of the boat with the throttle, released the brake to send the terminal end of the rig down to the bottom.

"Did you get it, Kensie?"

"Yup."

"Good. Hook the clips to the legs and surface."

"Maybe I should wait down here unless something goes wrong."

Burke shook his head, belatedly realizing the uselessness of the gesture. "No. I don't know how badly that safe is stuck in the mud, so I don't know how long it might take to get it up, and you're getting low on air. We have one more tank if we need to go back down to fix something."

"OK." Burke looked over the edge to watch Kensie work. It took only a moment to get it secured. "All set. The hooks are in place, and they look like they have a pretty good hold. I'm coming up." Burke waited, his urgency building every second until Kensie came to the surface and got on deck. Just like the previous day, she dumped her equipment on the deck where she stood in her rush to help.

Burke was already at the winch handle, taking up the remaining slack, but he only got through a few cranks of the handle when it stopped dead. He put a little pressure on it, but there wasn't a hint of give.

"What's the matter?" Kensie asked.

"The suction. It's significant. The safe is dense and heavy, and it's been sitting there forever. It's gonna be a bitch getting this up."

Kensie frowned. "Anything I can do?"

"Yeah," Burke chuckled grimly. "Expose yourself to some gamma rays."

"What?"

"You know," he prompted, "Bruce Banner. Gamma rays are what made him transform into the Hulk." He stopped upon seeing her cocked eyebrow and disgusted face. "Not a comic book fan?"

She shook her head brusquely. "Maybe it's the tension of the moment, but can we discuss real ideas?"

"Sorry. Get on the winch with me and, when I say, give it everything you've got." He allowed her to position her body inside of his and wrapped his massive mitts on the handle outside of her more petite hands. He wondered if her extra strength would make much of a difference, but they needed every Joule of energy for the task, and she had proven herself skilled in the martial arts, so she was probably stronger than she looked. He leaned back right behind her, positioning himself as the big spoon. "Ready... ready... NOW!"

They flexed their arms simultaneously and threw their weight backward, grunting with the exertion. Burke's injury from the previous day demanded recognition with a fresh shock of pain, but he ignored it and continued. He felt a tiny bit of movement, giving him hope that they were having some success, but it occurred to him that they were probably just pulling the boat backward slightly. He took his efforts to the next level while pressing one foot on the gunwale. He heard Kensie tugging for all she was worth too, but after about 30 seconds of concerted effort, he was growing exhausted and they weren't doing a damn thing. He let go and stepped away, flexing his hands.

Kensie plopped right down on the deck next to him. "What now?"

"Now we use the engines and hope internal combustion does the job."

Kensie gaped at him. "Then why the hell did I just dislocate my spine trying to crank that handle?"

Burke went to the conn. "Because if this thing doesn't want to give, we might rip the transom out. We could sink the boat, that's why."

"The safe can't be that heavy, can it?"

He turned the key and Kensie heard the unique rumble of the engine as it woke. "Not the safe, no. But there's a lot of suction going on – we just felt that – and we don't know if it's attached to half a ship under the sand. Waterlogged wood can be stubbornly strong – especially when you don't want it to be, and I don't know whether the chain or the back of the boat will give way first."

"Oh, right," Kensie said. "I hope you at least have life jackets."

"Well, one for me. You're kinda screwed," Burke kidded. "Now get to one side. If the chain does break, it could cut you in half." He watched her move to the corner and goosed the throttle forward. A burst of bluish white water shot from the stern and the boat moved forward a few feet, but the chain went taut and forward progress halted with a jerk.

"Nothing," Kensie said unnecessarily.

Burke nudged the throttle forward another inch. *Empire* wiggled back and forth slightly, like a dog straining against a leash, but didn't gain any ground. He looked back to confirm that water was still flowing from the engine cooling ports. The chain ran from the tip of the lift and angled into the sea like a frozen rope, quivering with the strain he was putting on it.

Burke looked down at the gauges indicating temperature and oil pressure; still good. He wasn't pushing the engine too hard yet, but he also wasn't accomplishing much. The engine was due for an overhaul, something he'd been putting off for weeks because funds were tight. Better, he figured, to push it up hard and go for it rather than inch up and strain things longer.

"Hang on!" He moved the throttle up to the cruise setting, and a blast of foam shot from the stern. The hull quivered in a way it never had, forcing Burke to eye the corners closely to ensure things weren't starting to come apart. If anything was breaking off, he couldn't tell, so he kept his power setting.

But the boat still showed no forward movement despite the churning propeller. If he kept his eyes forward and shut out the noise, he could imagine the *Empire* bobbing in a calm sea. But when he looked astern, the bubbling white cauldron suggested otherwise.

Burke started swinging the wheel left and right, trying to swing the chain back and forth and apply pressure from different angles. It was the right idea, but he didn't have the setup or the equipment to do it correctly, and despite Kensie's assurances he could not guarantee that the hookups to the safe were totally secure. Breaking off would set them back drastically.

*This is getting us nowhere.* They should be at least inching forward or seeing some sort of movement, but it was like he was hooked to the bottom of the ocean itself. The Cummins marine diesel engine continued to hold together, giving him confidence that it had a little bit of fight still in it, so he wasn't about to give up yet. He scanned the instruments again, finding the temperature, oil pressure, coolant, and the other gauges all in the green.

Burke knew he had a decision to make. The status quo was not doing a thing, so he could shut down and try another approach, or he could floor it. The first option was the sane and sober course of action, but it was unlikely to garner results. Option two was the bolder way, but it could blow the engine or sink the boat and kill them both.

*Fuck it. Go big or go home.* He pushed the throttle all the way up and looked astern.

Kensie jumped back in surprise at the increased roar and the explosion of water.

"It moved!"

He turned back to Kensie. "What? Are you sure?"

"Yeah! About six links of chain came up!" Just then the boat surged forward far enough that they both felt the movement. The entire lift was quivering. He saw Kensie lean over the stern, but the froth from the engines would obscure the view below them.

The bouncing of the boat became rougher. Burke realized he should have trimmed the engine better before he applied power, but now the bow was lifting and the entire vessel was becoming more unstable as the stern settled down further in the water, to the point that the roiling foam was starting to splash onto the deck. He needed all this power, but using it was threatening to swamp the boat.

He glanced down at his instruments and saw what he feared more than anything; the engine temperature going up. At full throttle, *Empire* should be cutting through the ocean at about 24 knots, and cool sea water would be forced into the engine by the combination of the forward motion and the impeller. By itself, however, the impeller wasn't pumping enough water around the engine, so the heat was rising steadily. He figured he had 45 seconds or so before he had to power down.

*C'mon! C'mon, dammit!* He caught Kensie's eye; if he looked as intensely worried as she did, he painted a bleak picture indeed. "Anything?!"

"Maybe," she shouted back. "Tough to tell with all the foam and shit!"

"I can't keep the engines like this for long!" He stole another glance at the gauge; 250 degrees was marked in red, and the needle was just passing 200.

"Just a little longer! Please!" Her voice was heartrending in its desperation. As bad as he wanted to pull this safe up, it had to be 10 times worse for her. He nodded and decided he would not back off the power until it was absolutely necessary.

Once more, he tried to wiggle the boat back and forth, though not so drastically as he had under lesser power. Like rocking a car back and forth to get it out of the snow, he hoped the motion would help break the suction – at this point, he counted on it.

225. He stopped turning the wheel. He couldn't risk getting a bad reading on the gauge right now because the boat was bouncing.

240. "Anything, Kens?"

"I don't think so!" She looked like she was about to jump out of the boat and start pulling on the chain with her bare hands.

245. Only a sliver of black remained between the needle and the red line. It wasn't going to come loose. Maybe he could let the engine cool and give it another try in a few minutes. "I gotta shut it down!"

"NO! Just another minute!"

"Kensie, I'll blow the engine! I have to!" He reached for the throttle... and was immediately thrown backward as *Empire* surged forward like a sprinter out of the blocks. He was able to hold onto the wheel, but he heard a splash behind him as he pulled the throttle back to neutral. The boat slowed almost as quickly as it started. Turning, he saw that Kensie was nowhere to be found.

Burke rushed to the back of the boat and was relieved to see Kensie's head pop up about 10 yards behind him. She gave him a thumbs up and started swimming back to the boat. As the water cleared, he looked down to see a big, black rectangle trailing behind and below the ship at the end of the chain like some giant square metal fish dangling on a hook.

They had it.

He opened the dive door and knelt to help Kensie up on the platform. As she indicated, she seemed none the worse for wear, so he went back to release the catch on the winch and start winding. Now that he was only dealing with the weight of the safe and not the suction, it turned easily. He was excited, but made sure to crank with a steady movement. It wouldn't do to have gone through all this trouble only to have the connections come loose and drop the damn thing back down to the bottom.

The safe from the *Aberaeron Fortune* broke through the surface of the water for the first time in 214 years about five feet behind the stern of *Julian's Empire II*. He locked the winch in place while Kensie grabbed the boat hook and tried to catch the chain. Burke rotated the lift to the starboard side as far as it would go, and Kensie was able to catch one of the links. In a moment she had it pinned against the hull.

"Switch with me. When I tell you, start winching." Kensie handed off the boat hook and jumped back to the lift.

"Am I gonna be strong enough to do this?" she asked, gripping the winch handle with one hand. The other hovered over the release.

"Yeah, I'll probably only need a little help, just enough to get it over the lip and drag it on the deck." Grasping the chain, he braced himself and bent his knees, hoping he would be able to keep his footing on the wet surface. *Jesus, don't drop it.* He took a deep breath. "Go!"

Kensie clicked the release and immediately started winding. It turned, just a little at first, and then more easily as Burke flexed every muscle in his body to pull it up the ledge of the dive platform. It didn't look like it should be as heavy as it felt, especially once about half of it was out of the water. He wished the seas were rougher, as it might allow him to use the momentum of the sea to get it up the last few inches he needed.

"A little more!" Burke shouted, half at himself, half at Kensie. "Come on, we're almost there!" He heard Kensie grunting with exertion, and knew she was putting everything she had – and then some – into the cause. The safe leaned against the platform at a

30-degree angle, not quite high enough for him to tip it up and onto the deck, but oh so close.

Kensie had cranked the winch handle far enough so it was at the bottom half of its arc of motion, allowing her to adjust herself so that, rather than pulling, she could push down on it. The added weight of her body and the assistance of gravity was just enough to drag it up the remaining inches until about half of it was above the ledge. With one final tug, Burke tipped it back and it thudded onto the dive platform. Wasting no time, he dragged it back through the dive door until it was safely inside the gunwale and used his foot to push the door shut, ensuring it would not be returning to the sea anytime soon.

Burke looked at Kensie. Both of them were panting like landed fish, and he was far too tired to feel any sort of satisfaction. His first considered action was to stagger to his feet and confirm that the temperature of the now idling engine was almost back in the normal range and that nothing appeared to have broken off of his boat. With that good news, he turned his attention back to the safe once more.

Kensie was staring at the safe with wide, mesmerized eyes that blinked away the salt water as it dripped from her hair. "Got something for ya," he said, trying to sound overly casual.

"Yeah you do," she agreed, and the first hint of a wide smile started to spread over her features. She stopped ogling the safe long enough to look at Burke. "I can't believe it. I didn't think it was coming up."

"For a minute, I didn't think so either. That's how strong suction can be."

"I've never seen it that strong." She stood up next to Burke. "Let's crack this thing open!"

"Yeah, after all that trouble, I guess we should." He turned to get his equipment from the cabin, but stopped when Kensie grabbed the front of his T-shirt.

"First, though, you deserve a big thank you." She tugged the fabric and pressed her lips to his in a kiss that was surprisingly tender considering all the heavy lifting she'd done in the past couple of minutes. Even soaking wet with salt water, to Burke she tasted like the sweetest wine as he accepted her gratitude.

"You're quite welcome."

She ran a finger over his chest. "There's more where that came from, I promise, especially if that safe holds what I think it does."

Burke assumed a hurt expression. "What? I don't get the good stuff unless there's a priceless treasure in there? That's a little superficial, don't you think?"

"Oh, you'll get the good stuff no matter what," she said.

"I think I already have."

"Good, so you know what's at stake," she kidded before snapping her head to the right. Her eyes went wide. "Oh, shit," she said. "Here comes someone."

# Chapter 12 – This Ain't a Speedboat

The bouncing white dot was just clearing the horizon, but to Kensie it looked exactly like the approach of yesterday's visitors. Burke twisted his head in the same direction and reached the same conclusion. "Not good. Let's go." He leaped to the conn and pushed the throttle forward. "Tie that thing off good to the cleat so it doesn't slide around the deck," he ordered.

Kensie grabbed some stout rope from a deck locker and wound it around the nearest cleat and to two of the legs, making sure it was as tight as possible. When she finished and checked the position of the other boat, she was shocked to see that it wasn't there. Spinning her head around, she saw that they were headed right toward the oncoming craft. "Burke, what the hell are you doing?"

"This is the way back to Grenada. Going away from them takes us out to sea – we'll run out of gas eventually."

"But you're going right at them!" she protested.

"Yup. I've got a plan. So hang on!"

*What kind of a plan involves running headlong at a boat carrying people who want to kill you?* She kept her peace; Burke had already gotten them out of two tight spots, and Kensie fervently hoped his winning streak would extend. But the two boats continued to close the distance. To her eye they appeared to be on a collision course, and things only got worse when Burke corrected his course slightly to *ensure* there was going to be a crash. "Are you trying to joust with them?!"

Burke didn't respond. His attention appeared riveted on the other boat. With *Empire* going about 24 knots and the other boat moving even faster, the range closed far too quickly. In seconds she could tell it was either the same boat as yesterday or an identical one. It really didn't matter. There were more important things to worry about besides identification.

With maybe 40 yards separating the two craft, Burke yelled, "Down!" and twisted the wheel hard to the right. Kensie crouched down behind the cabin bulkhead and saw the other boat heeling violently away from the *Empire* in a hard turn of its own as they passed. They couldn't have missed by more than a foot.

The bigger and heavier *Empire* generated quite a wake at high speed, and the other boat caught one of the waves awkwardly, flopping up several feet in the air and coming back down on its port side perpendicular to the way it had been going. Water gushed over the side before it mostly righted itself, but it had slowed to a crawl and rode much deeper in the water. White smoke indicated that the engine had stalled. Burke made no effort to stop or even slow his boat, but he did look back with grim satisfaction on his face.

"That was close!" Kensie yelled.

"It had to be," Burke answered. "I was betting that they wouldn't want to hit us because they might lose the safe. And I'm pretty sure it's those same assholes as yesterday, so they don't know shit about conning a boat."

"Well, good guess then!" The boat was getting farther away, but she thought she saw a stream of water shoot out one of the sides. "Will they sink?"

"No. A boat like that has strong pumps. They'll be moving again in a couple minutes, and they'll be coming back."

"So what are we going to do?"

"Right now, we're going to put as much distance as we can between them and us."

"But they're faster than us!"

"That's why," he stated, pausing to reach over and pull his shotgun from the case, "I'm going to make sure they don't get too close."

"You aren't going to shoot at them, are you?" She feared getting caught in an escalating gun battle, as it was foolish to assume the other guys didn't have weapons of their own.

He pulled a box of shotgun shells from under the wheel. "I'm not going to wave the gun at them like Harry Potter's wand," he answered sarcastically. "Do you know anything about handling a boat?"

"A little, I guess," she said. Realistically, beyond turning the wheel the way you wanted the boat to go and knowing the throttle was like a gas pedal in a car, Kensie didn't know what more there was to know.

"Well you better learn fast, 'cause it's your job now." He gestured for her enter the cabin and grabbed her hands, putting them on the wheel before jabbing his index finger at the compass. "The course back to Grenada is 225, but do what you can to keep our stern to them. Get it?"

"What do you mean?"

"I mean turn however you have to turn to make sure our stern is pointed at that boat no matter what, but always try to come back to 225."

Kensie kind of understood, but wondered how she was going to do that. With the other boat so much faster than *Empire*, she didn't think Burke's request was realistic. She also knew this was no time to argue. "OK."

"And keep your head down as best as you can, especially when they're behind us."

"How will I see where I'm going?" she demanded.

"There's nothing to hit out here, Kensie." Burke looked at her with fear contorting the flesh around his eyes. "I don't want you to get shot."

*This is turning into a nightmare.* "I don't want to get shot either!"

"Well, it's unanimous, at least on this boat." He pulled out binoculars and trained them on the other boat. "Looks like they got their engine started."

"That's just great," Kensie said, half to herself. Burke went to crouch behind the transom, and she scanned ahead. Burke was right – nothing but flat horizon as far as she could see. She turned the wheel a couple of times to get a feel for how the boat handled, and found it wasn't too different than what she expected.

She chanced another look back, but was not pleased with what she saw. The boat was moving again, and it was getting noticeably closer every few seconds. At this rate, it would be on them in maybe five minutes. Maybe less.

"Burke, they're gaining! Can't this fucking thing go any faster?!" she yelled, pushing on the throttle even though it was already all the way forward.

"I know, but this ain't a speedboat, Kensie!" he yelled back. "Just keep going and remember what I said about keeping them on the stern!" He checked the shotgun to ensure there was a round in the chamber but kept it out of sight.

She turned so the needle on the compass pointed at 225 and straightened the wheel, figuring that any more turns would just slow them down. The light swells were already making the bow bounce up and down, hurting their speed. *Well, I can't control that, so just drive.*

She chanced another look back at their pursuers, who were now only about 200 yards astern. It had to be the same boat as yesterday, but she couldn't be sure if it was manned by the same men. Their faces were obscured with bandanas, which would have looked silly if it hadn't been such a portent of the danger they faced. The other boat, with a 10- or 12-knot advantage, came up on *Empire's* port side. Kensie stared at it with absolutely no idea what to do next.

"Don't let him get so close!" Recalling Burke's instructions, she swung the wheel to the right, pointing the back end of *Empire* at the other boat and forcing it to take a wider turn, and also making the boat slow as it went through *Empire's* wake once again. The distance widened once more. *Maybe Burke knows what he's talking about.*

"Just like that, Kensie!" he screamed. "Just turn a lot sooner next time!" Only his eyes and nose were above the gunwale, but he still held the shotgun low as the other craft roared up once again, this time trying to overtake them on the starboard side. Kensie rolled the wheel the other way, pulling the same maneuver and achieving the same result. Burke's plan was clear now; the other boat could be faster and could chase *Empire* from now until next Tuesday, but if they couldn't block her path or make her stop, they couldn't get on board.

Kensie continued with the tried and true evasive turn each time the other boat approached, and it continued to be effective. More importantly, they got several miles closer to the islands, to other boats and safety. Their pursuers couldn't keep this up with other eyes all over the place, so they would be in a hurry. Kensie just had to keep them at arm's length a little longer. *Shit, we might just get out of this.*

Her joy was short lived. The next time she looked back at the other boat to see what it was doing, Kensie saw the glint of sunlight reflecting off a long, dark metal tube that one of the men held up. A gun.

***

Burke was starting to wonder how long it would take, but his stomach still tightened up at seeing one of the men on the other boat raise the weapon. He wasn't sure if it was a shotgun or a rifle, but desperately hoped for the former. He didn't know if the 40-year-old fiberglass of *Empire's* hull would stop a rifle bullet, and had no desire to find out right now.

He trained his own gun out and over the side, making sure they understood what would happen if they shot. He sighted on the white hull, finding that he could draw a pretty good bead on them if they held course. But that made the reverse true, which was unacceptable. Burke was about to yell to Kensie to start twisting and turning, but she must have read his mind, as he nearly fell over when she sent *Empire* heeling off to starboard.

"Good! Keep it up! They've got a gun!" he yelled by way of encouragement.

"Kinda picked up on that!" She sounded angry, but he couldn't blame her. It did cross Burke's mind that she might be taking out her frustrations on him when she swung the wheel harshly in the other direction and nearly sent him tumbling overboard.

He heard the loud report of a shot fired, followed by the rattle of tiny fragments against the hull. *Shotgun, but they're using it too far away to do any good.* He peeked back up to see them at least 60 yards out. He had a tight choke on his gun, which would make his shots more effective at a longer range, but he'd save his ammo for when they got close. With what he had loaded in the gun and the shells remaining in the box, he only had about 15 rounds total and couldn't afford to waste them.

*Boom!* Another shot, this one from closer in, but he heard no impact at all. He had to back them off. He trained the gun on the shooter but couldn't bring himself to pull the trigger even though he knew a fatal shot was unlikely. With a curse at his perceived cowardice, he sighted on the bow and pulled the trigger.

He took satisfaction in seeing the men duck down, and even more in seeing the small, ragged hole that appeared about six inches above the waterline. It would be nice if he could make that hole a little bigger and swamp or slow the boat, so he worked the pump action and aimed for the same spot.

And missed entirely. *Dammit.* It wasn't much of a surprise – it would be a tough shot standing still on dry land with nothing riding on it, but those were luxuries he did not have. They took another shot, and this time he heard one of the cabin windows toward the bow shatter, followed by a scream from Kensie. Fortunately, she didn't appear to be anything more than startled.

*This is bad and getting worse.* It would only take one lucky or good shot to get one of them very hurt. He pulled the trigger on the shotgun in quick succession until it was empty, but didn't score any additional hits that he could see.

The shotgun wasn't going to do it. He needed something else, like a bomb or a torpedo. *Or an explosive.* He double checked that the gun was empty before setting it down on the deck and army crawling forward into the cabin. Kensie looked down at him in surprise. "What are you doing?" she screamed. Her voice sounded high pitched and frantic.

"Getting something. Keep us off them another minute." He went to the forward locker and removed a sturdy case. Opening it, he quickly found the C-4 plastic explosive, tubing, initiator, and blasting caps he needed. They had been one of the few things he'd kept from the first *Julian's Empire*, but he never expected to need them the way he intended right now. He made his way back toward the stern, still staying low and grabbing 100 feet of rope and a roll of duct tape on the way.

Kensie took her eyes off the pursuing boat as Burke passed by in a severe crouch with his arms full. "What are those?"

"Explosives."

"*What?*"

"Don't worry about it. Just keep doing what you're doing."

"Don't blow us up!"

"No promises." Burke made his way back to the stern, taking another peek at his pursuers. They seemed either unable or unwilling to get closer than about 30 yards, meaning he'd have to bring them in a little closer. This was going to be dicey, to say the least.

*You mean suicidal.*

"Kensie!"

"What?"

"When I tell you, cut the throttle to about half and get down. Then, when I yell a second time, go back to full power in a straight line!"

"Why? Are you nuts?"

"Just do it, dammit!" *She was too smart for her own good.*

"OK!"

Working as fast as he could, Burke cut the paper covering from the C-4 and stuck it on the man overboard ring at the stern using the adhesive on one side. The white explosive blended in nicely with the white stripes on the life saving device; with any luck, their pursuers would think the ring had just broken free of *Empire* and was nothing to worry about.

He tied the line around the life ring securely and taped the shock tubing to it, leaving enough slack to insert the detonator at that end into the explosive. Ensuring he had the other end of the line and the initiator firmly in his grasp, he took a deep breath and pushed the detonator into the malleable material. He'd worked far too quickly and broken far too many safety protocols to be anything other than petrified, but he had no other option.

He slid the life ring over the back of the boat and simultaneously yelled to Kensie. "Half speed now!" She did as directed, pulling the throttle back hard enough to toss Burke forward with the loss of momentum. He regained his position and popped his head up to see them charging at *Empire*, closing rapidly on the life ring as it drifted backward.

One of the men had climbed up on the bow, aiming the shotgun right at Burke, or so it seemed; all he could see were the twin black circles at the end of the double barrels. "Both of you, stand on the back deck, hands up!" Burke did not immediately move to obey. He couldn't stand up too soon; his only advantage was surprise, and if they saw the rope or the initiator in his hand, they might figure it out. He had but one chance at this, and it *had* to work. And he had to make sure the other boat didn't get too close, lest he disobey Kensie's wishes and blow them both up.

The ring drifted to his left a little. He moved to the other corner of the stern, hoping to position it so the other boat would run right over it, but it barely turned. *Shit.*

The voice roared again. "Now goddammit!" It looked like they were going to miss the preserver by four or five feet; Burke could only hope that the explosive would be powerful enough to have an effect from that distance. Oddly enough, he'd never detonated one of these above the surface of the water and wasn't sure what might happen.

But Poseidon or Neptune or the little triggerfish that darted in and out of the coral reefs had his back. The other boat was closing too quickly, so the man on the helm cut the wheel – *to starboard* – and it was immediately clear that it would run right over the explosive.

Burke checked the rope in his hand – about 15 feet left. He'd have to time it just right. Ducking his head back down and dropping the rope while holding the detonator, he screamed for all he was worth. "FLOOR IT AND GET DOWN!"

*Empire* surged forward once more. Burke paused for a heartbeat before mashing the button of the initiator down and simultaneously tossing it over the side.

Even with the vibrations of the engine and the acceleration, he felt a heavy thud through the hull a second before what sounded like a waterfall materialized behind him. He gave it another second before he raised his head – and got doused with seawater.

The other boat was awash at the stern, with shredded fiberglass and plastic sticking from the water and black smoke pouring from the outboard engines. He didn't see any movement from any of the occupants, but at this point he was beyond caring. Somehow it wasn't quite as gut wrenching to have possibly blown them up as opposed to shooting them. *Maybe it's because I can't see them.* He dismissed the irrelevancy to check on Kensie.

She was crouching behind the wheel, barely able to see over the top of the conn in front of her. The fingers of her left hand were white on the wheel, and her right hand pushed the throttle so hard against the firewall he feared she might break it off.

"Are you OK?" he asked as calmly as he could while still being heard over the diesel roar.

Kensie jerked her head up and down, not bothering to look back. She was sweating profusely, her lips a solid, thin line on her face, her skin pale. She seemed uninjured, but appeared to be in some sort of shock. Burke couldn't blame her.

"Let me get in there." Kensie didn't answer, but she did allow him to nudge her aside so he could reduce the power to the cruising speed and set the autopilot before helping Kensie over to the seat opposite the conn. He plopped down the captain's chair behind the wheel, blowing out his breath. Kensie appeared near panic, her eyes darting around frantically.

"It's OK, Kens. We took care of them. That boat isn't going anywhere." She didn't react, so he repeated the message.

She looked at him after he repeated the all clear a third time, looking unconvinced. She remained silent.

"Are you with me? Relax. We're past everything, I promise."

Finally, she took a gasping breath. "I can't handle this!"

He smiled, doing his best to appear reassuring. "You can handle this. You just did. You were amazing."

"They almost shot me!"

"I know. Me too. And it was scary as shit. But you kept your head and did what you had to do. Just like yesterday." *Jesus, did that big fight just happen yesterday? It feels like a week ago.* "I'm really glad I had you on my side both times."

"Well, yeah, but –" Even though she seemed to be calming down, she was still unable to complete her sentence.

"And, unless you forgot, we have a safe to crack open and a treasure to recover." He gestured back to where the safe remained tied to the cleat.

Kensie looked at it, blinked hard like she might have forgotten about it, and let a hint of a smile show. Her eyes lost the wild, prey being pursued look of pure terror. "Yeah. I guess we do."

"You feel better now?" Burke asked, knowing the answer.

"Getting there. Thanks. And thanks back there too. You sure as hell got rid of them. I'll bet that boat sinks now." She sounded fairly pleased at that thought.

"No," Burke disagreed. "It will swamp down, but it probably won't sink."

"Too bad," she responded, and a glint of anger flashed in those big green eyes. "Maybe we should go back and finish them off."

Burke looked at her in surprise, even though he suspected she didn't really mean it. "I didn't know you had such a vindictive streak in you."

"Everyone has their limits," she said darkly. "When you try to kill me twice in two days, I get a little pissed off." She paused again, resetting her demeanor to something less vicious. "I really am sorry to have brought all this trouble down on you. I never expected something like this to happen, not in a million years."

He smiled. "Well, I wouldn't do this for most of my clients, but you're pretty as hell. Kinda makes everything worth it." Burke said with a tired smile that belied how much stress he'd just dealt with.

"I'm not sure I'm worth it in any case, but I still appreciate the compliment." Even with everything going on for both of them, she was still able to give him butterflies by pursing her lips and letting the corners tick upward unevenly. *If she knew what that little grin did to my insides, she'd own my ass.*

They said nothing for a moment as they came down off the high of having survived yet another attempt on their lives, but eventually Kensie returned to the elephant in the room – or, more accurately, on the boat. "Should we try to open it now, before we get back?"

"Absolutely," Burke answered. "The jackhammer will make a shitload of noise, and people will come by if we're docked in Grenada cutting this open, and your secret will be out. So you keep watch and I'll get my equipment."

She agreed and continued to scan the horizon as Burke lugged a compressor, hose, and a very heavy jackhammer out to the stern. He handed Kensie a pair of headphones and goggles. She pulled the eyewear into place but laid the headphones to the side with a look of disdain as Burke switched out the bit and connected the hose from the compressor to the hammer. He pulled his headphones on, motioned at Kensie to do the same and, without checking to see if she complied, flipped the switch on the compressor. It made an unholy racket; realizing the headphones were a good idea, she grabbed them and covered her ears.

*You'd think she'd learn to trust me by now.* Suppressing a grin, Burke slid his goggles over his head and lifted the heavy tool, wedging the bit in the miniscule gap between the door and the frame of the safe. The fissure was maybe three millimeters wide, concerning Burke; he might not be able to get a good entry point. He motioned for Kensie to stand back and pulled the trigger.

The jackhammer exploded into life, instantly jumping out of position and skittering across the front of the safe like a drug fueled kangaroo. He let off the trigger and arrested its movement before it got to the fiberglass deck, guiding it back to the desired area, feeling his face turn red with the effort. *You ain't so young anymore, are you?* He wasn't, but he tried to tell himself that the previous night with Kensie and the copious amount of alcohol he'd consumed had sapped his strength. *Right.*

Calling on his reserves of energy, he made a second attempt, and was more successful at holding the tool in place. The bit of the hammer pounded into the fissure but didn't appear to be doing much more than rattling the entire boat to pieces. The safe seemed impervious to the force and sat there placidly, as if scoffing at the modern tool. Burke was surprised; steel from that long ago was full of imperfections, and it should have given way fairly easily. Sweat poured from his forehead in the blistering tropical sun. The constant undulations of the boat demanded all of his strength and focus to keep the hammer properly positioned.

Ignoring the noise, Kensie leaned in to see whatever she could see. Burke noticed her expression in his peripheral vision. If ever a glare could split steel, Kensie possessed it. Her eyes burned with a fire suggesting a preternatural belief that she *could* and *would* force that door open one way or another. It was almost comical, but Burke was both too tired and too intimidated by her intensity to laugh.

He wondered if that glare was her special superpower when small cracks started appearing around the frame. Kensie smacked him in the arm and pointed; Burke nodded but, unwilling to break his concentration, did not lift his head. Metal started separating, allowing him to push the bit deeper and apply more force. The wall of the safe started giving way, and things were proceeding well until he hit what had to be the bolt keeping the door shut, as the rhythm and noise from the jackhammer changed dramatically.

*This might take a while.* Kensie poked her head down far too close to the clattering bit for safety. He stopped the hammer, glad for the excuse to rest his arms for a second, and motioned for her to lift her headphones. "Stand back," he said. "Something flies off of this thing, it could do some serious damage. And you're supposed to be looking out for boat traffic anyway."

She stood, pulled the goggles to her forehead, and did a 360-degree scan of the horizon. "We're fine," she said, replacing her eye and ear protection before kneeling back down, almost in the exact same place.

Burke reached over and lifted her headphones. "Sit over there," he ordered, pointing to the opposite side of the stern. She gave him a cross look, but he returned it until she saluted – poorly and with a pithy look – and did as her captain directed. "Stay there. I'm not going to jump overboard with the safe, and nothing is going to escape." She nodded, looking a little embarrassed at her eagerness. He jimmied the bit into the crevice at a different angle and started hammering again.

It took another 15 minutes of concerted effort before the bolt finally gave way. Not surprisingly, the door was still sealed shut, so he worked up and down the edge until the entire side separated just a bit. He removed his goggles and headphones, glad that he was free of them. They made him sweat even worse.

"Go get two crowbars from the forward compartment on the starboard side, and then grab the WD-40 from under the wheel."

Kensie fairly flew into the boat and returned a moment later with the items. Burke sprayed the lubricating oil liberally over both hinges, slid one crowbar in place, and applied pressure. The safe groaned and creaked, but the damn door didn't move one bit. He alternated between a steady pressure and a rocking motion, hoping the combination would break the seal.

"Give me a hand," he grunted. Kensie came around to his side, worked the other crowbar into the narrow gap, and threw her weight against it. It continued to make odd noises, so Burke knew they were doing something, but it was still aggravating to be working so hard with nothing to show for it.

"Son of a bitch!" Kensie yelled, releasing the bar for a second and flexing her hands. "This thing is impossible! You got another one of those bombs?"

Burke straightened up to participate in the impromptu break, grabbing the WD-40 to spray a little more on the hinges and around the edges. "Yeah, that's a great plan – blow up the treasure," he replied. He knew she wasn't serious – it was the exhaustion and frustration talking.

"Well, I can't lug a safe up the walkway to get back on board the ship," she pointed out, and Burke realized she thought there was a time element involved. To his mind, it wasn't exactly a show stopper if she missed her departure.

"Kensie, considering what you think is in here, would you actually leave it behind to get on a cruise ship?"

Kensie blinked. "No, I guess not."

"So stop worrying about the damned time. We have hours – we'll figure something out. And if we don't, I'll take you home on this boat myself."

"This morning you thought I had an impossible task ahead of me – now you're an optimist?" she teased. "What happened to you?"

Burke's light hearted retort dissipated as he looked into her eyes. Despite his objections to her search plan this morning, he'd had this weird belief that she'd succeed. It was totally unlike him – at least it had been for a long time. He'd known nothing but failure and monotony for so long that he had come to expect it. But Kensie had shifted his world so profoundly that he just *knew* that he – no, her – no, they – would accomplish whatever they set out to do.

"I think you happened to me," he said.

Kensie drew in a breath and her face, already red and sweaty from her exertion in the heat and sun, fairly glowed as the deep scarlet of a blush filled her cheeks. She looked surprised, but it was clear that Kensie didn't mind his words. "I... well, I don't know what to say," she finally blurted.

"Don't say anything," he answered. "At least not right now. Keep it in mind for later. Right now, we've got a safe to open. You think you got enough left in you to get it done?"

She smiled grimly, and the set of her jaw demonstrated her eagerness to accept his challenge. "Try and stop me." She walked back to her crowbar, re-inserted it in the gap, and resumed her efforts. Burke followed suit.

Their bravado was still not enough to convince the recalcitrant door to give, and in a few moments they were both grunting and struggling once more. Burke was not about to give up, but he also realized he would run out of energy sooner or later. Even as he continued with everything he had, he started racking his brain for other ways to get into this bastard once they were back in Grenada.

***EEEEEERRRRPPP!***

Kensie fell to the deck, her crowbar flying out of the gap and clattering to the deck. Burke nearly dropped right on top of her as the door opened about one inch. For a second, they both stared into the tiny dark opening as if they expected aliens to come crawling out.

"Told ya we'd get it," Kensie said between breaths.

"Never in doubt," he replied. "C'mon." The progress energized them, and they repositioned the crowbars and started again. It took another minute, but the hinges lacked the endurance and determination of the two treasure hunters, and the metal screamed with what sounded like agony as it submitted to this forced entry, opening another five or six inches.

Burke repositioned himself to get more leverage, blocking Kensie but knowing that he could have more impact by himself than with her in the way. She went around to the side and started trying to insert the crowbar elsewhere, but she didn't need to; Burke could feel the very slight vibrations that suggested the hinge was ever so slowly releasing its grip.

The obstinate safe finally gave up the fight and allowed Burke to open it halfway, more than enough to see inside the compartment. Kensie nearly crawled over his back in her urgency to see, but when the light penetrated the 200-plus years of darkness, they gasped in unison.

It was completely empty.

***

Kensie looked around the confines of the compartment like she could have missed something, even though every inch of it was clearly visible. She couldn't wrap her mind around the idea that, after everything they'd been through, after following all the right leads and making sense of the disparate clues, after the strain of getting the safe on board and their dangerous getaway, it didn't contain Buckwell's stolen treasure. Her treasure. Their treasure.

"What the hell?" Kensie asked the world. "There's nothing here!" Her mouth hung open.

Burke sagged back, his arms shaking from his recent efforts. He looked utterly defeated and stared blankly at her, either unwilling or unable to add anything of substance to her observation.

"Where the hell is it?" she nearly screamed at him.

Burke shook his head slowly, bewilderment etched into his features. "I really thought it would be in there," he finally responded. She stared at him for a second, then back into the empty chamber again, like the *Couronne* was somehow concealed behind something, but there was no nook or cranny that it might be hidden behind, just a wide open box. *It's not going to appear out of thin air.*

"I... I can't. I can't believe this. This isn't possible." Kensie walked to the other corner of the stern and just stood there, her fingers folded behind her head in resignation as she stared out at the horizon. *You were fooling yourself. This is a giant ocean. How did you expect to find one thing in all this?*

"Look," she heard Burke's voice over her shoulder. "I know you're disappointed, but you've done so much work and accomplished so much. You've got proof of a major archeological site, and you alone were smart enough to find it. You're going to be down here in a couple of months with a real expedition team, better equipment, more help, and you're going to find it."

Kensie shook her head. The tiny part of her brain that still worked intellectually told her that Burke was right, that she had done something quite extraordinary, but right now it just didn't seem to matter. She didn't have the words to explain the despair that filled her like lead, and she plopped down on the deck, legs splayed out, too emotionally exhausted to move. Tears welled up in her eyes and ran silently over her cheeks, but she couldn't be bothered to wipe them away. She'd hated crying in front of anyone – it reinforced the weak and emotional female stereotype – and she'd done it far too many times in front of Burke recently. Problem was, she couldn't stop.

She heard Burke take a couple of steps toward her, but the idea of anyone touching her right now in any way made her skin crawl. "Don't," she croaked out, and the footsteps stopped. "I need my space right now, OK?"

"Sure thing," he answered. "I'm here if you want to talk." She felt him move away, and she leaned forward and folded her legs so as not to fall over. *Not gonna be enough rum on that ship tonight.*

# Chapter 13 – Magic

Burke felt atrocious. Sure, he was disappointed too, but he recognized how important this was to Kensie. He hoped that, after the shock of the setback passed, she would recognize everything she had accomplished.

He sat on the railing and idly kicked at the safe. So much effort for nothing more than a gallon of sweat wasted and the promise of very sore muscles tomorrow. It didn't seem right that they had almost gotten killed for an empty metal box.

He was suddenly very angry at this Buckwell asshole. *What kind of idiot has a super heavy safe and doesn't put his prized treasure inside of it?* It just made no sense. Did he have a second safe, one that was somehow hidden? Maybe, but that didn't sound right to him. This one seemed awfully substantial to be a decoy.

Was it the wrong ship? What were the odds that another ship, with artifacts matching the time period of Kensie's pirate, had sunk here instead of or in addition to *Aberaeron Fortune*? Almost zero. In the war books he'd read, soldiers being shelled during bombardments slept in existing craters because the chances of a second shell landing in it were too low to consider. This had to be the ship, and this had to be the safe.

Burke fell back on the approach he'd suggested earlier, when he instructed Kensie to tell him everything she knew about the theft and the crew of the ship. The data led him to one conclusion – that it all came down to keeping the treasure safe from less than upstanding men who wanted it. It was logical to put that treasure in a safe. You'd lock something away so that no one could get to it. But Buckwell had eschewed this idea in favor of another method. How else do you protect something from falling into the hands of the wrong person? How would he keep something so priceless away from others? Depending on the situation, he'd fight them, or make sure they knew the risk associated with fighting him, or he'd lock it away. If they couldn't get to it, they couldn't take it.

*Or he could hide it.*

Buckwell was a pirate at heart. Even though it was a cliché, history was replete with examples of pirates burying their treasure. But Buckwell probably wouldn't risk leaving something this valuable behind, so he had to have hidden it somewhere on the ship itself. A safe, while secure, could be broken into with enough time and effort (he'd just proven that), and it kind of screamed, "come look inside me!" so it would be the first target of thieves. Maybe Buckwell wanted his crew to think it was in the safe, perhaps even going so far as to tell them that to throw them off the trail.

*But where could you hide something on a ship that was more secure than a safe?* The only idea that made sense was perhaps under the deck planking or inside a bulkhead. But it would take time to hide something that way, and more time to recover it. Buckwell would have been far too concerned with making his getaway to spend time prying up timber, and he would likely have considered the possibility that he'd have to get off the ship in a hurry. No matter how he thought of it, a safe remained the best option.

Burke tilted his head, studying the thickness of the steel box as it lay on its back, the door hanging open like it was mocking him. Was it his imagination, or was the compartment not as deep as the body of the safe? One way to find out. He went to the conn to get a tape measure to ascertain the outer depth of the safe: 30 inches. Then he put the tape measure inside the compartment: 16 inches.

*Interesting.*

Dropping to his knees, he started running his hands along the back wall of the compartment. It was completely smooth to the touch, with no panels that could easily be removed or opened. Grabbing the screwdriver, he banged the business end against the outer walls of the empty chamber, listening to the pitch and timbre of the noise. Then he hit the back wall.

*Clank.*

It was definitely a different sound. Tinnier, and the note had more of a vibration. He pressed his hand on it and pushed hard, but it didn't want to move. Or did it? Perhaps it was his imagination, but maybe it shifted just a tiny bit, just a quarter of a millimeter, just enough to tell him it might not be completely solid.

He ran his fingers around the edge of the back wall, but there was nothing to grab, so he started running them along every inch of the inside, being more thorough in areas he could not see, like behind the lip of the opening, which was about an inch deep. An irregularity passed under his index finger.

*Hello. What's this?* It was a small indentation, maybe half an inch square, and it felt like there were two seams running perpendicular from it, suggesting that it could be pulled like a lever. He carefully inserted the tip of the screwdriver into the tab and worked it for a few seconds until the lever moved.

And the back wall popped up about a half inch.

***

Kensie's mood had not improved even though some time had passed. She now had a tremendous headache, making her wonder if she was having some kind of stroke or embolism. At the moment, she wasn't sure that such an affliction would be the worst thing in the world. She closed her eyes and put her fingers on either side of the bridge of her nose, squeezing in the hope of relieving the pressure or at least redirecting the pain. She heard Burke walking around and banging on things, and she hoped he was attempting to throw that fucking safe back over the side so she could be done with this whole mess.

"Kensie?"

"Burke, not now. I feel like shit."

"I really think you should look at this," he said quietly. With his voice devoid of fear or alarm, she knew there was no immediate danger, and beyond that she didn't want to hear it.

"Jesus, Burke, leave me the hell alone!" She felt a little bad for snapping at him, but she had said that she didn't want to be bothered, and Burke was ignoring that request. He deserved the rebuke.

Burke's next words rumbled like an edict from the gods. "Kensington Prescott, you get your ass over here right now."

*That son of a bitch called me Kensington!* Needing to release her anger and seeing the perfect opportunity to do so, she stood and whirled to face him, ready to settle his hash in no uncertain terms, but came up short. The look on his face, the way she could see white around every part of his lovely blue irises, and the way he'd gone pale tempered any thoughts of vengeance. "What is it?"

"Come here. Give me your hand." When she did, Burke ran it under the rim of the opening, making sure she felt the irregularity.

"What is that?"

"It's a lever of some sort. Pretty damn well hidden, I'd say. And it gets better." He'd not released her hand, so he pressed it down on the back compartment and moved it around so she could feel the surface wobble.

An overwhelming wave of hope, fear, and outright panic exploded in her belly. "A hidden compartment!?"

"You said he was smart," Burke replied. "Someone breaks into the safe, doesn't see the treasure, he figures it's somewhere else."

"I never would have thought of that in a million years! What do we do?"

Burke handed her the screwdriver. "'We' don't do anything. You are going to open this compartment and see what's hidden in it." He retreated to a position where he could watch her but from which he wouldn't be able to see exactly what she was doing.

"You don't want to help me?"

"This is your discovery, your treasure, your dream, Kensie. Not mine. You should be the first one to see it."

*What a gesture.* "I owe you one, Burke. No, maybe a thousand, or a million."

He licked his lips in a manner that appeared both anticipatory and lascivious. "And I will collect. But, right now, you should get to work." He jutted his chin toward the safe.

Kensie nodded, gripping the screwdriver tightly to control the shakes that were overtaking her body. *What if this part is empty too?* The thought terrified her and shot yet another unhealthy dose of adrenaline through her system. She was a young woman, but didn't know exactly how much more stress she could put on her heart before it decided to up and quit on her, and she'd overloaded it far too many times in the last 24 hours. Right now it was palpitating so hard and so fast she could feel her pulse in her ears, in her gums, and even in the tips of her fingers. She took a second and closed her eyes, drawing a breath to calm herself, and when she opened them she was better able to control her hands.

She found that pressing on the bottom of the false back caused the top to push forward enough for her to insert the tip of the screwdriver just the tiniest bit. It was a tight fit, and all she could do was work the tip of the tool back and forth to slowly get it a little further and deeper. Eventually, she was able to get some leverage and, with a screech that made her think she was opening a mummy's crypt, the metal came away faster and faster until she could get her slender fingertips around the edge and pull it completely away. It was heavy, requiring both of her hands to lift it completely out and set it to the side before she could peer in.

On a pedestal that was roughly the shape of a human head, she saw the *Couronne Ornèe de Joyaux des Anges* resting as if it were still sitting on display in the Tower of London, albeit on its side.

The compartment exploded in glittering light as the sunlight struck the precious metal and perfect jewels, which seemed determined to shine with an intensity that would make up for the frustration of being locked away in darkness for 214 years.

Kensie's vision tunneled, and she found herself unable to draw a breath. She had to put her hands on the opening to avoid falling forward and conking her head on the safe.

"What is it, Kensie?" Burke's voice brought her back to reality, and she regained both her breathing and the coordination needed to reach in and touch the jeweled prize. When her finger made contact with the platinum, her skin tingled with a sensation she likened to some magic of the *Couronne* thanking her for liberating such beauty. Silly, she knew, but her emotions were running away with her, and she had no control over such thoughts. She pulled it out and held it up in front of her. It was even more beautiful in the direct sunlight, and she turned toward Burke so she could look at it and him in the same glorious gaze.

"Found it." More tears, these of awe and triumph, sprung from her eyes. Like those that signaled her utter despair only a few minutes before, she neither tried nor cared to brush them away as they streamed unabated down her cheeks. She started laughing and sobbing at the same time, amazed by the pure elegance of the finding, overwhelmed by the power of the moment, and awed by how triumphant she felt. "Look at it," she managed to say in hushed tones.

Burke leaned his head forward but did not get near to it, as if the artistry held a power he feared getting close to. "It's amazing, Kensie," he said softly. "I can see why Buckwell stole it." His voice returned to a regular tone. "How's it feel to be vindicated?"

Suddenly, Kensie couldn't answer; her throat was tightening with a joy that threatened to burst from her cataclysmically. She could do little more than shrug, but Burke seemed to get it. Through the blur of tears, she saw his wide, earnest smile and knew that he understood what was going on inside her. The noise of the engine and the ride on the waves faded away and Kensie knew only that all was right with every part of her world. She felt a strong connection to the man who had probably been the last person to touch it. Whoever and whatever he had been, she now had a bond with the dead man that no other living human could ever claim, and that made her feel special.

Eventually, though, reality told her that she couldn't just stand there like the Statue of Liberty with something worth more than the GDP of some small countries in her grasp. She pulled the *Couronne* back to her body, cradling it in her arms like an infant while taking a surreptitious look around the horizon. She felt like a criminal for doing so, but was nonetheless relieved that there were no other boats to be seen in any direction.

"What do I do with this thing?" she asked as her mind returned to its normal working speed and considered practical matters. "I mean, I can't just walk back through duty free in Grenada with this thing in my fist like a water bottle."

"I've got some ideas about how to do that," Burke said to Kensie's relief. At least he was thinking ahead. She'd been so obsessed with finding the *Couronne* that she'd given nary a thought to how she would get it back to the States and to the proper authorities so it could be returned to the Queen of England. She wanted to hear his plan, but right now imagining presenting this sublimely elegant headdress to the head of the British monarchy made her laugh. "The goddamned Queen," she mumbled.

"What?" Burke asked.

"It's just amazing," she responded. "I have something in my hands that is the property of Queen Elizabeth the Second."

"I thought the government of England owned the Crown Jewels," Burke protested.

"No," Kensie corrected. "The current king or queen is the actual legal owner of all the Crown Jewels as per English law. The Crown Jeweler looks after them, but they are the property of the Queen."

"I'll bet she'll be keen to get this back then, huh? Wonder what she'll pay for it?"

"I don't know that she has to pay anything. Legally, though, I think I'm entitled to salvage fees, which are 10% of the appraised value."

"Yeah, that's the norm," Burke responded automatically before he did the simple calculation in his head, and his eyes nearly bulged out of his head. "That means, if you're right about the value, Buckingham Palace has to cut you a check for $20 million!"

"That's how I see it," Kensie responded with the confidence of someone who'd already considered most of this. "I wasn't after this for the money, but I'm not so philanthropic that I'm going to turn it down!"

"And that makes you my new best friend," Burke said with *uber*-sincerity.

"Burke, however this all works out, I'm going to make sure you are taken care of. I couldn't have done this without you, your ideas, your expertise, and your muscles," she answered, making a show of letting her eyes wander over his upper body.

She expected Burke to be thrilled, but he seemed almost saddened by her words. "*However this all works out,*" he repeated. "That sounds an awful lot like 'when I dump you for someone better, I'll make sure I give you a nice payday.'"

Kensie would have imagined that nothing could tamper the high of her success, but Burke's tone brought her right down with him, and she felt bad that he'd misinterpreted her words so completely. "Burke, no, not at all. First of all, I doubt I could find anyone better, but that's not even close to what I meant."

"You sure?"

"Yes, completely sure. When I came down here I had one goal – find the *Couronne*. Yeah, I'm human, so I figured I would make some money from finding it, but that wasn't really my main motivation. I would become a success professionally. Show those assholes at the NAS that I was right and rub it in their faces. Get recognition from my peers. Write my own ticket for the rest of my career.

"Then I met you. And, at first, I wasn't too impressed. Yeah, you were hot as hell, but you weren't my type. You were rough, kind of rude, and a little gross," she ended with a smile. "But then you showed me who you really are, and that man is someone I like – a lot."

"Or maybe you just liked me enough to have a good time with me while drinking good rum upstairs at *Arnhim's*."

Kensie shook her head; he just didn't get it. "Burke, I'm sorry you've been hurt after trusting someone." She saw him look away at the mention of his past. "I'm not Jessica. I don't have an ulterior motive and I'm not using you. Money doesn't matter to me – not that much anyway. What matters to me is that you stood up for me and believed in what I was doing. Even more than that, you made me feel *wanted*. I'm not the girl that men lust after, that men think about, that gets hit on at parties. I'm the nerd, the last one left alone at the end of the night, the friend. The smart one. You make me feel special, desirable – and *sexy*. I've never known a man that could make me feel that way about myself, Burke, and I like it. I'm not ready to give that up. So, I can't be sure how things are going to end up because this is such a unique situation, but that's separate. Whatever happens with the *Couronne* doesn't matter to me. If I get money, you get money. If I don't, you don't. I'm not the same person that walked onto your dock in St. Vincent anymore. I'm changed. I'm a new me, and I need you to make an 'us'. That's what matters."

She lowered her gaze, slightly embarrassed by her sincere and emotionally raw discourse. *Did I go too far?* "Anyway, that's what

I meant. I got the *Couronne*, but I want to be with you too." She peeked back up, unsure of what expression she might see on his face. "Is... is that maybe what you want too?"

Burke said nothing for a moment. His eyes searched her face, but she had no idea what he was looking for. She studied him in return. His expression was fearful... but hopeful. After a minute that lasted about 100 years, he spoke.

"Eight years ago I lost everything because I thought I was in love and trusted that person. It kind of felt like life was teaching me a lesson because, since then, luck has skipped right by my door every single time. Nothing good happened for me. I was just getting by, surviving, not caring anymore. And then, quite recently, this aggressive, ridiculously adorable, brilliant, fascinating woman screamed my name one morning from the dock, waking me from a hungover sleep, and everything changed. It's been scary and it's been rewarding and everything in between, but I've loved every second of it. Maybe I'm desperate or crazy, but I know that the idea of you tossing me aside like some island fling would destroy my soul. I just want to be with you."

Burke's words turned Kensie's insides to jelly. Right then, she need to be with him; not in a sexual sense – although that percolated just below the surface. She wanted to become one with him, to wrap herself in those eyes and that smile and his desire for her and just *be*. The idea was so liberating that she stood and moved to him, to her man, to her lover.

She went to wrap her arms around him so she could see those cerulean eyes up close and get lost in them, but Burke intercepted her right hand. She felt him removing something from it and realized she was still holding the *Couronne*. "Let's put this somewhere," he said softly.

Kensie was so overwhelmed by Burke's sincere declaration of his feelings for her that she'd completely forgotten that she held one of the greatest treasures in history in her right hand. *Good lord, I'm being swept away!* He was right, and she'd have done the same thing if she was in her right mind. She let him take it, watching him place the *Couronne* in a clean, soft rag before placing the whole thing in a drawer, which he then shut and secured with a turn of the knob.

"Now, where were we?" he asked. Kensie had no doubt that he knew exactly where they were and was prepared to pick up right from that point. They wrapped their arms around each other but, as if by some unspoken agreement, they did not press themselves together frantically. Instead, they paused and shared a look. Kensie loved how Burke's face was framed by the tiny reflections of sunlight as they glinted off the waves in the background, like a thousand *Couronnes* were behind him, their beauty framing his face with an effect that both surpassed and diminished by her lover's countenance. His big, intense eyes possessed her, and in that moment she knew, without a doubt, that she was his. He had taken her, yes, but she had also taken him.

"Burke..." she moaned, allowing her lips to fall toward his until they met in a soft, impassioned dance. Kensie drank in every bit of him: his emotion, his passion, his body that was the envy of women everywhere. She loved saying his name. He was the fortune that she didn't know she had been searching for, and now that she had discovered him, she would not let him go. She'd come looking for an amazing treasure and somehow found two of them – and she had no idea which she valued more, as if she could assign some kind of rank to either. Kensie's kiss was an open invitation and a declaration that this man was hers and she would not give him up without a fight. Her kiss and her touch became more aggressive as her desire grew.

Burke allowed her to take what she wanted from him while staking his own claim to her body and spirit. She gave him the control he silently demanded, neither wondering nor caring that she was both vanquishing and acquiescing to him, acting as both conqueror and victim, dominant and submissive, master and slave, lover and loved.

Kensie pulled the thin strip of fabric of his tank top from his shoulder, baring his nipple, which she slid her fingers over to caress and squeeze. It was, like his lips, an impossible combination of strength and tenderness, and there was nothing to do but bite it. She did exactly that, breaking the kiss and moving her mouth down to it, using just the right mixture of tenderness, intensity, and fervor. Her tongue slid out, tasting the flesh further. Doing so was making her crazy; she couldn't imagine what Burke was feeling.

She got a clue as she heard the intake of air suggesting he needed oxygen elsewhere, and confirmed it by sliding her other hand down over those holy shorts to discover that he was already at full attention. If she could do this to him so quickly, and he could return the favor, there seemed to be no limit to the depths their shared passion could reach.

"God, Kensie, stop," Burke begged. *Why would I do that?* Kensie heard the begging, but knew damn well what he was really begging for. With fingers far more adept than the previous night, she worked his button fly herself to expose his manhood, gripping it firmly. Her hand felt tiny doing so, but that was just fine with her.

"Dammit, Kensie, I'm... I'm... " She started stroking him, slowly and steadily, using her tongue and lips to capture the soft bud of flesh on his chest, sending him gyrating in pretty much every direction. She felt him push at her but she knew that, if he truly didn't want her touching him, he would have applied his power and done the job properly. He couldn't, he wouldn't, and his little games were more arousing than any touch or any tender words ever could be.

"Having a problem?" she teased. She loved pushing and taunting him, knowing that whether he acquiesced or resisted didn't matter. The authority and power they shared in their sexual forum were like a blisteringly powerful aphrodisiac that she responded to as much as he did, and right now it overwhelmed her until she didn't care about much else. There was little danger to either of them as the boat cut through the waves on its programmed course to Grenada, but it wouldn't have mattered if they had been driving a Ferrari at 150 miles an hour on the freeway. The risk, the concerns, the problems, all faded away under the torrent of pleasure.

"Goddamn you, Kensie, you're such a…" He could not complete the sentence. *What am I, Burke? A bitch? A tease? A slut?* It didn't matter what she was to him, as long as she was his, and right now those titles seemed more like labels of honor than insults. She started stroking faster and harder, feeling him grow and swell even further under her grip. His hips bucked in rhythm trying to make each stroke longer and harder and that much more satisfying.

Finally, as if he could stand no more, Burke caught her with a look that was hungry and menacing. He cut his eyes at her as if to scold, but she knew it was passion disguised as a threat, so she showed no fear. She also didn't stop stroking him, pursing her lips in unspoken defiance.

Burke rose to meet that challenge. "Oh, you wanna tease? Lemme show you something." With a move worthy of a *ninja* in a bad '80s movie, he turned his body and used his arm as leverage to guide her quickly down to the deck, using his other hand to arrest their fall just before a violent impact.

Kensie *oofed!* but was not injured. Well, if she had hurt herself, any pain was being subsumed by the glow of passion emanating from her legs, so she did not resist when Burke more or less tore her Tommy Bahama shorts from her body, pushed her bathing suit aside, and slid his head between her legs to attack her most sensitive area.

The sudden pressure hit her far more powerfully than she expected, and for a moment she could neither think nor draw her breath. When her body forced her to take in oxygen, she was barely able to let loose a curse of approval. "Ohh. Fuck!"

The oral assault was sublime, destructive, and addictive, and Kensie feared it would be her end. This wasn't normal. There was no way she should be feeling this good. He was taking her with an assault disguised as pleasure, and the feeling was driving the needle right off the scale. She grabbed the back of his head and pulled him into her more, not believing that his tongue could somehow drive her to greater heights of bliss, but it did.

"What are...? What the hell...? Oh, fuck, I can't..." Confused by the overload of her nervous system, she thought to push him away but kept tugging him into her, like a schizophrenic unsure of what defined her reality anymore. Her vision tunneled. *Am I dying?* She didn't think so, but if her life ended under this avalanche of felicity, she would go to her grave with a smile on her face.

Burke was only busy for a few seconds before Kensie felt her body pass the point of no return. She heard (or maybe felt) him grunt as she dug her fingernails into the bronze skin of his upper back, but he did not stop, leading her to arch her hips upward in a desperate attempt to get more pleasure from him. Part of her regretted the increased intensity, but another part of her craved it, and she exploded with an orgasm that surpassed the one from the previous night by an order of magnitude.

Kensie lifted her head and strained her neck, not to see anything specific, but because her release was generating so much energy that her muscles seemed to be her ignoring conscious control. A high pitched noise reached her ears; a tiny part of her mind told her that something might be wrong, but then she realized she was wailing like a banshee. Even after she stopped, her mouth remained open as Burke continued making exactly the right moves. His stamina and vigor belied an urgency that told Kensie exactly how much he strove to please her, and that was almost as fucking sexy as what he was doing to her.

Finally, like a curtain coming down, the blissful orgasm ended all at once, but the afterglow was a different kind of pleasure she felt just as intently. She could do little more than collapse back down on the deck, panting frantically and trying to gather herself after the most intense physical reaction of her life.

***

Burke loved how fiercely he'd made her come, but was not yet ready to rest. He was still rock hard and needed his own release. More accurately, he needed that release with Kensie, and Kensie only. Without a second's hesitation, he repositioned himself in order to enter her, rubbing himself against her so she would know what was coming. The message was received, and her languid smile told him she welcomed it. He wasn't surprised. *After all, she started it.*

With a steady, powerful move, he slid into Kensie. She was wet and ready, and her body offered no resistance as he felt the soft folds of her flesh envelop him. It occurred to him to wait, to give her a second to grow accustomed to his girth, but she showed no discomfort, so it didn't seem necessary. He started pumping into her, and found that he instinctively matched his rhythm to that of the boat pounding through the waves, hitting a crest every fourth thrust. It felt natural, like their sex was in perfect harmony with the world.

He wasn't sure if Kensie felt it the same way, but she appeared happy with what Burke and the sea were doing to her. Even completely spent, she smiled wantonly and cracked open her eyes to look at him as he fucked her.

He couldn't help but smile back. She hadn't lied before; there *was* a difference in her now. She acted like she'd been awakened. Burke was skeptical that a sexual experience, even one as powerful as they'd enjoyed the night before, could be so transformative, but it must have played a part in making her the woman she'd become. She'd been attractive, intelligent, and interesting to him before her metamorphosis, but now she put out a siren song that pulled him inexorably to her, and to his amazement, it had very little to do with sex. To be able to touch her, smell her, and taste her – these were just bonuses.

Kensie ran her tongue over her lips as she reveled in the moment, calling to Burke, so he adjusted his body to kiss them deeply while continuing to slice into her. It wasn't easy – they bumped their mouths together more than once, leading to a few silly giggles, but no harm was done. Burke felt powerful but passionate, being able to please his woman with forceful strokes while getting – and giving, he was sure – such a transcendent tingle from the kiss. The different feelings combined into a multi layered experience that wasn't comparable with anything he'd ever known.

He was frustrated that he felt his body nearing climax so soon. All he could think of was enjoying this sensation and this moment for as long as possible, maybe forever, but no man could hold out against something so magical. He cried out into Kensie's mouth and his body went into overdrive. Kensie laughed into his wail and, with a laugh, pushed her body up against each hammer blow to make them that much more vivid and extraordinary. He had no choice but to break the kiss or risk one of them losing a tooth.

"Dammit, Kensie!" As good as the previous night had been, this was better, and that was unbelievable.

"What's the matter, Burke," Kensie said, sounding both breathless but exhausted, telling him she was nearing a second orgasm. "Can't handle me?"

Burke wanted to protest her implication, but he lacked the energy to speak at the moment, so he decided to show her how very misplaced her question was. Like a marathoner at the end of the race, he summoned all of his will and drove into her even more urgently.

"Ohhh... yes, Burke. Yes!" The words were barely more than a moan, but her cries carried an erotic pitch that acted as the last straw, and he exploded violently. He closed his eyes, seeing oddly shaped designs on the backs of his eyelids. In the next second, he heard Kensie grunt and realized she was coming as well. She threw her arms around his shoulders and squeezed until they moved as one entity, one being, one creature.

The couple rocked together, doing their very best to wring every ounce of rapture from this enchanted moment, wishing it wouldn't end but knowing that it must. Finally, Burke collapsed down, using his last vestige of strength to roll to the side in the cramped cabin to avoid crushing or smothering Kensie. They looked at each other's sweaty, satiated faces and grinned. It was all Burke could muster at the moment.

"Are you OK?" Kensie asked, taking his hand in hers. She held it for a second, and Burke had the feeling that it fit perfectly.

"OK doesn't begin to describe it," he answered. "I don't understand what you do to me, but I'm addicted."

She looked away, embarrassed, and Burke saw a tear form in her eye. "What's wrong?"

Kensie swallowed hard and faced Burke once more. "Nothing. Nothing at all."

# Chapter 14 – Come Sail Away

Kensie tied the stern line to the cleat, just like she'd done yesterday, but far more quickly. *I'm becoming quite the sailor – driving the boat too!* She slapped her hand to the front of her right hip for what seemed like the thousandth time, but the fanny pack was still secured to the leather belt Burke had put around her waist.

After they'd recovered from their extracurricular activities, and after Burke belatedly looked around to ensure they weren't in any boat traffic, he retrieved an ugly and dirty canvas satchel about eight inches long, with sturdy leather loops at each end near the top. Pulling the *Couronne* from the drawer still wrapped in the cloth, he'd put it in the bag. Then he'd taken his belt, passed it through the loops of the satchel, cut the end off, and used an awl to punch a new hole in it so it would fit around Kensie's waist. He stuffed a shirt and some socks on top of it to help hide it and made sure the satchel was at the front of her right hip when he secured it in place so she could not be easily pick pocketed.

"There," he commented as he secured it. "No one can pull it off you, and I'm sure that no one will suspect what's in it because it's so ratty, so they probably won't even try."

Kensie knew he was right, but paranoid concern flowed through her at the thought of walking around in public with such riches right out in the open. Burke's words didn't help. Basic human nature made her worry, and she realized she'd probably stay worried until she had the headdress back in the United States in... well, where the hell was she even going to put it? She realized her first order of business upon her return would be to purchase a safety deposit box.

They jumped onto the dock. "So you'll keep the safe and all those artifacts – well, keep them safe – until I can arrange to have them shipped back to the university?" It was the fourth time she'd asked the question in one way or another since they entered the harbor.

"Yes, Kensie, relax. This is a very safe marina. I mean, look at *Empire* compared to the other boats here. People wouldn't even want to use it for target practice, let alone think there was something in it to steal."

"I'm sorry. I'm being paranoid."

"Yeah, but it's been an interesting couple of days," he responded charitably. "You're entitled."

"Thanks." She smiled at him and took his hand as they reached the entrance and moved out into the street. Kensie felt like she had a flashing neon sign over her head, inviting any and all unsavory characters to ask her if anything interesting had happened today and to tear the satchel from her person.

But she also had protection next to her in the form of Burke, whose posture and demeanor suggested to everyone that he would oversee any such questions. Ask the wrong one, and he would make that person regret their query. Despite her earlier fears of walking around, she felt incredibly secure near her man, and there wasn't much better than having your own personal bodyguard, especially one who'd demonstrated how far he'd be willing to go to protect her.

As nice as it was being escorted, she dreaded the moment that was coming up so quickly, when she'd have to, at least temporarily, part with Burke. She stalled, stopping to look in the windows of the duty free shops that lined the path to the boarding gate, asking Burke what he thought of that necklace or that watch or that scarf. Burke's answers were what she expected – slightly bored and filled with generic adjectives, just like a regular man who was shopping with his girlfriend would sound. Even that thrilled her. *I'm just like everyone else!*

Finally, though, Burke stopped and tugged Kensie's hand to face him. "It's time to get on the ship, Kensie." His voice and face were resigned.

"We still have 25 minutes," she protested like a child who didn't want to go to bed yet.

"I know," he said, sounding for all the world like the father that admired his child for trying to stay up even while he had to remain firm. "But it's still dangerous out here. On the ship, you're safer."

"Look," she said in a sharp tone, "I didn't ask you to start using logic and good sense, did I?"

"Someone has to."

Kensie tried a new tack. "I'm not ready to say goodbye," she told him with a raised eyebrow and a coquettish pout.

"This isn't goodbye," he responded. "I don't know how you can think it might be when you look at me like that. It's just a..." he paused to come up with the right term, "a temporary separation brought on by extraordinary circumstances."

"Oh, big words. Do you promise?" Even though she'd been convinced of his sincerity when they'd talked on the boat, now that the moment of truth was at hand, insecurity and fear gripped Kensie. This man was far too sexy, too desirable, too *perfect* for her to believe he might want to see her again.

"Yes, I promise. I'll cross my heart, hope to die, stick a needle in my eye, whatever other forms of self mutilation you might require."

"Those eyes are too beautiful to stick anything in them," Kensie said, "and you better not die anytime soon."

"Geez, you're making it kind of hard for a guy to keep his promise."

"I won't ask you to hurt yourself as long as you meant what you said," she answered.

"I've never meant anything more in my entire life." The way his face went from playful to sincere was so enthralling that it nearly made her melt.

"You can't say things like that, not right now," she protested, feeling the beginning of tears, wondering how this man could pull such raw emotions from the depth of her soul so easily. She tugged his head down and kissed him tenderly, and suddenly she was desperate to spend the night with him, to wake up with this Adonis in her bed after another round of epic passion. "Come on board with me. Stay with me. Leave it all behind."

Burke giggled. "As much as I like the idea, you know they won't let me get on that ship. And as much as I want to take you back to *Empire* and do things to you that might scare the fish in the harbor," he grinned with lecherous intent that made Kensie wet on the spot, "like I said, that's not safe. Remember what you have in that satchel. You have to get on board, and when you dock in Puerto Rico, you go right to the airport and go to your gate. They followed you pretty far, and the cruise itinerary is available to anyone at all."

"And we're back to the logic. Whatever happened to romance?"

"It's on hiatus until a certain something is in the hands of a certain someone from London." Grasping her shoulders firmly, he turned her in the direction of the boarding gate. "Now march, young lady."

With an exaggerated pout, she allowed him to guide her forward. She walked with the heavy footfalls and exaggerated pout of a child being forced to get on the bus for the first day of school. Burke was being safe and he was right, but she hated leaving him again. At the gate, she turned to her captain once again. "Do I at least have time to give you a proper send off?" she asked.

"Right here?" Burke acted surprised, but Kensie knew he was merely playing along. "I know this is a hedonist's paradise and all, but there are still laws against that sort of thing in public."

"Oh, well. I guess you'll have to settle for this." She took his face in her hands and, arching up on her toes, planted her softest kiss on that mouth. However long she would be apart from Burke, she wanted to be able to recall his taste, his smell, the texture of his scruffy cheeks – everything until they could be together again.

Kensie handled her man aggressively, just as he had done to her the previous night and earlier today, and he let her do so, moving his head to comply with whichever way her hand yanked his hair. The kiss was too short, but when she pulled away, she was thrilled at the way he leaned in to follow her mouth as it retreated and nearly pitched forward.

"Easy, captain. Wouldn't want you to fall overboard."

Burke grinned in minor embarrassment. "Oh, I fell sometime yesterday," he replied as he gently guided her to the boarding gate. "But I'll get you for doing that to me," he quasi-threatened.

Kensie took a couple of steps but turned her head back to Burke as they checked her passenger ID. "Don't make promises you can't keep."

"Never."

"See you soon." It was almost physically painful to look away from him so she could walk without stumbling, but she did. At least Burke could not see her expression, one of unmitigated joy. She was unable to describe the energy that flowed through her body. It was like being carried away on a cloud of pure bliss, and it plastered a silly grin on her face that threatened to become a permanent fixture. *Shit, Catrina's gonna take one look at me and I'm going to get the third degree.*

Kensie climbed the gangway and, as the crewman checked her badge against his system, she took one last glance back. Burke stood at the fence, hands clinging to the chain link fence, looking at her like he wanted to run right through it because she'd been out of his company for too many seconds. Even from 100 yards away, she could feel his fiery blue eyes cutting a hole straight through to her heart.

That thought alone brought a new set of tingles with it, and she had to fight to suppress a shiver in the tropical air. The crewman either didn't notice her actions or didn't care as he handed her pass back to her with a perfunctory grin. She took it from him and, hanging the lanyard around her neck once more, stepped forward to the metal detector.

She tried not to pause, but a wave of concern flooded through her. Despite her plan to deal with having the *Couronne* detected upon entering the ship, she was again convinced they would see right through her lie, seize the treasure, and have her arrested for some obscure island law about stealing something they never knew was there anyway.

Kensie approached the archway, trying to feign a look of indifference as she put her gym bag containing her diving equipment on the table next to the detector, ostensibly forgetting the smaller satchel at her waist. She stepped through and, even though it was expected, she still cursed to herself as the device beeped.

"Pardon me, Ma'am," said the snappily dressed crewman as he stepped in front of her.

"Was that me?" she asked stupidly.

"Yes," the crewman said with more boredom than concern. "Are you carrying anything metallic on your person?"

"Oh, jeez," Kensie replied as she rolled her eyes like the forgetful idiot she hoped they thought she was. "I bought this thing at some gift shop in St. Georges this morning for like ten dollars and completely forgot about it." She unzipped the satchel and fished out the headdress from below the clothes Burke had pushed in on top of it. With an indifference that required quite the acting job, she held it up for the man to see.

He raised his eyebrows in mild interest. Kensie wondered if he would try to confiscate it, and what she would do in that case, deciding that grabbing it and running back off the ship was her best play. She'd have to move decisively; there was no telling what the two other men at the door might do, and if she got caught trying to run there would be many, many questions, and she'd never see the

*Couronne* again. It would be better to be back on the island (with Burke!) and have her treasure. Catrina would certainly understand.

After a quick second, the crewman ran the wand over her body and, receiving no other alerts as to more hidden metals, nodded. "Thank you. You're all set." He returned to his chair against the wall while Kensie went to get her dive bag and stuff the *Couronne* back into the deepest recesses of the satchel, cursing herself for the raging case of paranoia that had overtaken her. She was the only person on this entire ship that had any inkling of what she carried and, if she would just relax and go on about her business, there was no reason for anyone to give her a second glance. Her only chance of screwing this up would be if she overreacted. The *Couronne* was as secure as it could possibly be, and she was just as safe.

*Just play it cool, Kensie, and you're in the clear.* She left the small compartment to head to the bank of elevators, completely failing to notice the security camera with the blinking red light that had witnessed the entire event.

***

Burke waited until Kensie's trim figure disappeared through the hatch before he turned to go back to the *Empire*. The emptiness surprised him, even though he was already calculating exactly how he would get back to the United States. He shook his head. *Am I really going to uproot my entire life for a woman again?*

All it took was one mental glance at her shapely body, that saucy little grin, and those big green eyes that exposed that wonderfully intelligent and independent mind, and the answer was obvious.

He was sure he wanted to do it. He just wasn't sure how.

*Sell the boat and hop a flight? Keep the boat and sail it to Florida?* He trusted Kensie implicitly but, like she said, neither of them knew exactly how things would play out, and it would be reckless to just abandon everything and fly off on a whim. For all he knew, he might be back here in two weeks. He'd just counseled her to do the smart thing; could he be any less responsible? Of course not.

But...

It wouldn't be too irresponsible to follow Kensie's ship to Puerto Rico, would it? Considering all that had happened to them in the past couple of days, he couldn't discount the danger that she might be in, even on the relative safety of the ship. She was carrying something of immeasurable value, and he was one of two people that knew it. It was probably worth as much as the massive ship on which she rode, and a couple people (it bugged him that neither Kensie nor he knew who those people were) had demonstrated a willingness to do whatever it took to get their hands on it. When he looked at it that way, it would be irresponsible *not* to follow her; how else could he keep an eye on things and ensure both his girl and her treasure remained safe? All things considered, he had no choice.

*Geez, you can talk yourself into anything, can't you?* He smiled at the mental gymnastics that determined his course of action. But now he had to make sure he could do it.

Arriving back at the *Empire*, he pulled out his charts and started scratching some numbers on a pad. According to the itinerary Kensie had shared with him, *Amore of the Seas* would spend tonight and all of tomorrow at sea, putting in at San Juan early the following morning. He did some quick math. That worked out to an average speed of about 15 knots, which meant he'd be able to keep her ship in sight during the voyage. Better yet, at that speed he'd get about 350 miles on a full tank, maybe 400 if he had smooth seas. With San Juan some 520 miles away, that meant a fuel stop, but it wouldn't be terribly difficult to find and catch back up to the cruise ship.

Once he was in San Juan, he'd make sure she got on the plane safely and with her cargo intact, and then he'd undertake the trip to Florida. A longer and tiring voyage, but still very doable; he would be passing through the many islands of the Bahamas and would have safe refuge if anything were to happen, or if he needed to bed down for a couple of hours.

He'd already committed to going, but now that he had decided upon his course of action and had a plan, the finality of his decision hit him hard. It made him a little sad to be leaving his home of eight years so suddenly when he'd not given a thought to anything like this even a day before, but it felt right in every other way. He just couldn't envision a future that didn't include Kensie, or – if he was being totally honest with himself – at least the attempt to make one together.

He went to his bunk and opened the drawer in which he kept his cash. He had fuel and stores to purchase, and neither was cheap down here, but Kensie had been as good as her word and paid him for every second of his diving services, so he had more than enough to cover such expenses. After that, there was nothing left to do but start the engines.

*I'll see you soon, Kensie.*

***

Kensie headed directly to her cabin. She needed a shower and to close her eyes for a few minutes before getting some dinner. She'd started the morning tired and hungover, and a day filled with diving, heavy lifting, the extremes of disappointment and triumph, the stress of mortal peril, and blisteringly hot sex had exhausted her. *Geez, this was one for the books!*

Her phone chimed with a text from Catrina. *U on board?*

*Yeah. Gonna take a shower.*

*Cool. We'll be down soon to get u for chow.*

That was a relief. "We" almost certainly meant that she was with Reid and, as much as she was bursting at the seams about her accomplishment, the distraction he would provide meant Kensie would be more able to avoid pointed questions from Catrina.

Sharing her secret right now could only put her friend at risk as well – if there was any risk now that she was on board. Of course, that didn't mean that she couldn't share more details about Burke with them, something she intended to do regardless.

She undressed and stepped into the small shower, being sure to hang the satchel on the towel hook and leave the curtain back just enough so that she could see it. Letting it out of her sight was not an option, so much so that she rushed each time she had to close her eyes to rinse shampoo from her hair. Kensie knew how silly it looked, but her peace of mind was more important than appearances, especially in private. *If a person does crazy things and no one is around to see them, is she really crazy?*

She exited the shower and grabbed some clothes, placing the satchel on the desk right in front of her. Kensie pulled on a polo shirt and shorts, tightening the belt after passing it thru the loops of the satchel to reattach it to herself. Unable to resist, she dug into the canvas bag, moving Burke's (hopefully clean) T-shirts and socks out of the way until she felt metal and pulled the *Couronne* out one more time, staring at it, picking a couple of the colorful jewels to examine very closely. If there were any imperfections in the stones, she lacked the visual acuity to see them.

*BOOM! BOOM! BOOM!*

Kensie nearly jumped out of her skin at the incredibly loud report on the cabin door. Her first thought was to stuff the headdress back in the satchel as far down as she possibly could get it, yanking the clothing over it as quietly as possible. *Had someone followed her on board? That shouldn't be possible!* She retreated from the door until her back pressed against the far wall of the cabin, her head swiveling about looking for something she could use to defend herself, but came up empty. Most things in the cabin were secured to a surface to prevent them from sliding about in the event of rough weather. The best she could do was one of Catrina's Birkenstocks.

"Come on, Kensie!" a very male and completely unfamiliar voice demanded. "We know you're in there!"

*They know my name! How the fuck do they know my name?!* That didn't bode well, but she sure as shit wasn't going to open the door. Sooner or later Catrina would come down to meet her. They had to know she could call security. She could wait them out.

That plan died a quick death when she heard the *buzz* of a key card being inserted into the lock. They had a way in. Her mind froze for the interminable second the door took to swing open, and then she was facing a younger-looking man with a shock of brown hair and a deep tan. Kensie's first impression was that he looked neither threatening nor dangerous in the least.

She knew why when she saw Catrina and Reid standing behind him, with Liv and Nancy peeking their heads in the opening as well, wide grins on their faces. All five broke into clearly-drunken laughter upon seeing Kensie in a defensive posture, holding the colorful shoe like she was about to throw out the first pitch at a Phillies game.

It took Kensie a full second to comprehend the situation, and another for her body to abandon its fight or flight pose. The unknown man grinned sheepishly and stumbled forward as everyone else pushed their way into the cabin.

With the danger now passed, and with it any outlet for the built up stress, Kensie felt a surge of anger flow through her. "What the hell?! You guys scared the shit out of me! What were you thinking?!"

The laughter faded like someone had flipped a light switch, and for several seconds Kensie and the others faced each other mutely, one with an expression of unrivaled fury, the others with looks of stunned confusion. It took several seconds for Catrina to break the silence. "Kensie, we're sorry. We just thought it would be a little funny to surprise you, that's all. We were going to grab you and take you up to the bar for drinks, that's all."

Kensie's outrage deflated like a balloon that someone had stuck a pin into. "Yeah, I'm sorry for yelling. You guys just scared me."

Catrina's eyes went wide. "I forgot about yesterday!" she exclaimed. "Oh, this is all my fault! I should have said something!"

"What happened yesterday?" Nancy asked.

"Kensie was attacked on St. Vincent," Catrina explained. She went on to give a brief recount of the event, leading to apologies all around. Kensie felt bad about snapping at them, realizing that she was unnaturally tense and defensive, and that her friends were far enough along in their consumption of alcohol that their judgment was seriously clouded.

"And who's this?" Kensie asked, pointing to the boyish looking man who had first entered the room.

"That's Corey," Liv said. "We met at the beach. He's pretty cool."

Kensie shook his hand. "Nice to meet you," she said, "and I'm sorry I was about to attack you."

"It was a dumb thing for me to do. I don't even know you," he answered, giving Liv a wry look. Kensie silently agreed with his assessment. It *was* a dumb thing, even if he said it like he didn't believe it.

With everything sorted out, the group headed to the upper decks for whatever bar they had in mind. Kensie hung back and wasn't surprised when Catrina slowed to walk next to her. "I hope you're not still mad. That was stupid of us, but it was my idea."

"It's OK, really. I guess I am still a little on edge from yesterday, so it was just bad all around." Calling herself "a little on edge" didn't begin to describe her mental state at the moment, but she was determined to avoid giving even a hint of what was really going on.

Catrina nodded in appreciation. "Thanks. Let's make the best of the rest of this cruise. You're stuck on this ship like the rest of us until San Juan, so you're going to have fun whether you like it or not." She paused, her eyes glinting. "Speaking of all day excursions, did your diver boy toy show up this morning?"

Now *that* she could talk about, and she relaxed at the change in topic. Her smile exploded all over her face. "Oh yeah, he showed up. And then some!"

Catrina did a double take. "Are you serious? I have to be honest, I really didn't think he would! What I wouldn't give to have some sailor chase me around the ocean! I wish I could have met him! Was there any more fun before you got back on board?"

Kensie hesitated, considering how much she could share, and decided that a little disclosure was OK. Even more than that, it would be fun. "It was out of this world. And I have a funny feeling you might get the opportunity to meet him," she said with a coy look as they entered the Rum and Fun Bar, a new one to her. *Where do they get the names for these bars?*

The group grabbed a table but, holding up her finger to them, Catrina grabbed Kensie's hand and pulled her aside. "What's that supposed to mean?"

The lovestruck woman just nodded like she owned the keys to the kingdom. "Just what I said. Don't be surprised if we're on a double date with you and Reid when we get home."

Catrina rolled her eyes. "Kensie, now you're being crazy. OK, I was wrong to think he wouldn't come to Grenada to see you one more time, but you really think he's gonna follow you to *Delaware?* That's a little nuts."

Kensie, who was even more sure of Burke's commitment to follow through on his word than she had been last night, just maintained her confident disposition. Being the one with the juicy story laden with romance was new to her, but she was having fun in the unique role. "Yeah, it's a lot nuts. But you're going to see."

Shaking her head, Catrina appeared ready to object when her eyes tracked to the satchel on Kensie's waist. "What the hell is that disgusting thing?"

*OK, fun is fun, but I've got to stop this before she asks the wrong question.* Kensie took Catrina's hands in hers and stared into her eyes. "Cat, we've been friends for what, 16 years?"

"Yeah, something like that. Why?"

Kensie took a deep breath. "We've kept secrets for each other from parents, teachers, guys, whoever, right? And more than once."

"Of course."

"That's because I always trusted you completely. Do you trust me?"

"You know I do. What are you talking about?" Catrina looked like she was going to jump out of her skin.

"If I ever needed you to trust me, I need it now. I will see Burke again, for sure. I don't just wish it, I *know* it. And, as big as that is, there's something else going on, something bigger – *way* bigger. So, whatever you do, don't ask any more questions about the satchel. Don't mention it – at all. Don't draw attention to it – at all. In fact, just pretend it doesn't exist – even if we're alone. Everything will make sense in a day or two, but right now I have to keep something from you, and I need you to be cool with that."

Catrina tilted her head, recognizing that Kensie was both serious and, all indications to the contrary, sane. After a second or two, she shrugged her shoulder. "OK, but it better be a damn good payoff."

"Thank you. And, believe me, you will not be disappointed. You'll understand soon."

Her friend nodded. "So, can I still talk to you about this Burke guy?"

Kensie giggled and felt herself growing emotional with the joy of knowing that they would be together again soon. "If you don't, I'm going to be that pain in the ass that won't shut up about her new boyfriend."

"You really think that he's going to relocate for you and you're going to be a couple and everything? Really?" Her disbelief was obvious.

Kensie was still holding her friend's hands, and she squeezed them with an unintentional intensity that made Catrina wince. She backed the strength down but could do nothing to control the passionate certainty that drove her next statement. "Cat, I love him." The surge of emotion at actually saying those words out loud caused a tear to form in each eye. One broke loose and ran down her cheek.

Catrina's expression softened with hope for her friend. "Are you sure? Does he love you?"

"I didn't say it to him and he didn't say it to me, but I feel it in my bones, in my heart, in every part of me." She wiped away the tear, but more threatened to follow. "If he's not, or if he doesn't feel like I do, well... I'm willing to play the fool to find out."

"Then I guess I do have to meet him," Catrina said before she hugged her friend. "I'm so happy for you. Let's get back to the group before they start asking questions." Kensie nodded and they returned to the stares of their party. They gave the group vague excuses for their side chat that revealed nothing, and the mood, as well as the drinks, made it easy to steer the conversation in a new direction.

Kensie sat with her back against the wall, mostly because it meant she could keep the satchel protected on her hip, but also so she could scan the room. It seemed like something she should do – what was the term? *Cover your back? Cover your ass? Back to the wall?* It didn't matter what it was called as long as she did it.

She sipped at her Coke and observed everything quietly, smiling when everyone else laughed, affirming statements that she wasn't listening to with nods, and noticing the group's sobriety was falling by the minute. That didn't thrill her, but it was more important to be in a group – even a drunk one – than to be alone.

Catrina started cracking atrocious jokes, telling Kensie she had crossed the threshold from buzzed to very buzzed. Everyone groaned at her earliest one liners but, as glasses were tipped further and further to the vertical, they amazingly found her wisecracks funnier and funnier. They were comical in a slapstick *ba bum dum* kind of way, but they played well to this particular crowd.

Nancy and Liv and, by extension, Corey, were terribly concerned that Kensie wasn't consuming alcohol, and seemed determined to make it their mission to get her to imbibe. With the insistence of someone who was drunk enough to be overly pushy without realizing it, all three of them questioned, cajoled, and teased her into "just one drink!" Kensie did nothing more than smile and politely decline over and over, to the point that Liv went to the bar and came back with a tray carrying one *Pina Colada* for everyone. "Now you can't turn it down or it will go to waste!" she stated as if proclaiming victory.

Kensie rolled her eyes, not unfamiliar with such shenanigans. She'd spent most of the parties she'd attended as an undergraduate student interacting with – and enjoying the exploits of – people who thought they were sober, although very few of the drunk frat boys had been concerned with how much she drank. She was about to put a little more force behind her denial when, to her surprise, Catrina grabbed the drink from in front of her and sucked a large portion of it down through the straw while winking at her friend.

Kensie smiled back, more than a little happy that Catrina had her back, even though she was far from sober. She alternated between Kensie's drink and her own rapidly, and then sat back with her fingers pressed against her forehead just above her nose. "Wow! Either I've got the brain freeze from hell, or there was a lot of booze in those drinks. Maybe both!"

Everyone at the table laughed at Catrina's antics, and eventually Catrina's friends lost interest in force feeding her spirits. Kensie settled back once more, her right hand resting on her the worn canvas. She caught Reid giving her a curious look, so she flashed her most disarming smile at him. He just nodded in reply. Kensie didn't know him well enough to read him, but he seemed to recognize that she was acting oddly.

"Shit!" Catrina jumped up as Corey, in a fit of amorous intentions, tried to grab and kiss Liv but instead knocked over Catrina's drink, shooting the milky liquid all over her bright red shirt. She jumped up, making most of the people in the room turn and look for a second.

"Oh, I'm really sorry!" Corey was slurring his words badly, and his attempts to brush the drink off Catrina's shirt looked for all the world like he was trying to cop a feel. Liv punched him as she saw him do it, and Catrina laughed at Corey's poor attempt to rectify the situation.

"I better change," she told the group. "I'll be right back, but then we should go to dinner while we can still find the dining room and use utensils."

"Want me to come with you?" Reid volunteered.

"Why?" Catrina responded with a flash of mischievousness in her eyes. "You think you might catch a little peep of me changing my top?" She pushed her chest out to show exactly how terrible she considered that idea.

"No!" Reid said with what had to be feigned forcefulness. "Well, maybe." He seemed much more sober than Catrina.

"Thought so! But that's all right. I'm OK to make it to the cabin and back." She brushed a little more of the dampness from her shirt. "Plus, if you play your cards right, you might get to take it off me yourself!" Everyone at the table *wooh hoo ed* like 5<sup>th</sup>-graders at the lascivious suggestion.

Reid just arched his eyebrows in anticipation. "Can't wait."

"Damn right you can't. I'm *that* good." Blowing a kiss in the air, she managed to make her way out of the bar and toward the elevators with only a slight wobble. *Maybe I should go with her.* But Kensie figured her friend would be OK, and right now staying in a crowded public place was her best bet outside of her cabin.

Reid shook his head. "She's funny when she gets drunk," he commented to Kensie, who nodded.

"Yeah, she thinks she's a regular comedienne after a few drinks."

"I like that. She doesn't take herself too seriously all the time."

"No, the only thing she gets worried about is her career and her job. Most everything else, she figures it will all work out." Kensie sighed. "And it usually does. It amazes me, but no matter what she steps in, she comes out smelling like a rose." Kensie felt the jealousy that made itself known whenever she wondered how her friend pulled it off, but that was immediately replaced by indifference as she remembered her own sudden good fortune. She'd taken a tremendous chance – two, really – and it looked like she was going to be rewarded for her boldness.

"I could use a little of that in my life," Reid remarked, his eyes burrowing in on hers. "Do you think she might be interested in spending time with me after the cruise is all done?"

Seeing how Catrina had been responding to Reid, Kensie was convinced there was something there, but it was not her place to over- or under- encourage him. She did feel it was all right to plant a little seed. "I'll say that she seems interested in you beyond a shipboard fling. I don't know for sure, and I wouldn't come on too strong, but I think you'd be OK if you tossed out a few openings."

Reid nodded. "Thanks. I didn't mean to put you in an uncomfortable spot."

"It's fine. I'm glad you asked. I don't want her used."

"You don't have to worry about that," he answered.

"I didn't think so," Kensie answered.

"So," he said, his disposition changing instantly. "What's the matter with you?"

She started slightly. "What makes you think there's anything the matter?"

"You're a completely different person tonight. It's like you're very worried about something."

Kensie furrowed her brow, wondering how he could tell. He didn't know her that well, but his judgment was spot on. *He is a cop. It's his job to pick up on things.* "A little, and I appreciate you asking, but it's not something I really want to talk about."

He narrowed his eyes as if he suspected there was something more behind her words, but the look lasted only a second. "OK, no problem. Sorry to pry." Without another word, Reid turned his attention back to the others.

Kensie had to act more naturally to keep Reid's instincts from going off. It wasn't easy for her to control her emotions, but she was doing her best, so she could probably keep him at bay for a little while longer. She leaned back in the seat, happy that she might have helped her friend into a decent relationship – for once. She revisited her comment to Catrina about a double date, and allowed herself to get lost in the little fantasy. Two handsome men – Reid wasn't as drop dead gorgeous as Burke, but he was no slouch – and two beautiful women (*holy shit, did I just think of myself as beautiful?*) at a high end restaurant with a ridiculously overpriced bottle of wine, or maybe on the boardwalk in Rehoboth, playing arcade games and getting dirty water hot dogs from one of those carts. She had to suppress the giddy smile that threatened to turn into full blown laughter.

After indulging in her fantasy for a few minutes, it occurred to Kensie that Catrina had been gone much longer than it should have taken her to change her shirt. Worry tickled at the very outside of her consciousness, which she immediately attributed to her overdeveloped sense of unease. *She's fine. She's an adult. Settle down.*

Still, she had been kind of drunk when she left the room, and Kensie wondered if she'd been right to allow Catrina to proceed by herself. The *Couronne* had overruled every other consideration, but now she was rethinking that decision. Normally, she would have escorted Catrina regardless of any protests, but her actions had been selfish. She had to fix that, but she should still act cautiously.

"Reid, you wanna come with me and check on Catrina? I have a funny feeling she's passed out face first on her bed with her shirt half on."

"Now that's something I have to see!" They both stood up, and Reid addressed the group. "We're going to check on Catrina. Why don't you guys go to the dining room and we'll meet you there."

Nancy nodded. "OK, that *shounds* – sounds – like a good idea." Kensie had doubts about their ability to find the dining room, let alone actually get a table, but Catrina was her priority. Without waiting to see the girls and Corey try to stand, Reid and Kensie headed out and down the hall. They chatted lightly, with Reid asking about what Kensie had been doing during the days on shore. She told him about the diving but avoided specifics and Reid, to her relief, did not revisit his suspicions.

They neither rushed nor dawdled down the passageway. Kensie knew that Catrina could take care of herself, and suspected that Reid was thinking the same thing. Still, she kept her wits about her and one hand on her hip package at all times, tensing slightly as others passed by. She saw Reid glance at it once, but he didn't bring it up. He might not be asking about things anymore, but he was still taking notice of her actions. She resolved to try and act more naturally.

That resolution went out the window in an instant as the entire passageway went totally dark.

***

Burke used his experience to glean the course and speed of *Amore* pretty much by sight, setting the autopilot and throttle so that he would maintain a steady distance of just over a mile from her. He wasn't necessarily concerned about losing track of it – the enormous ship was lit up like a Christmas tree – but his recent exertions, both good and bad, had worn him out, and if he drifted off to sleep it would be a pain in the ass to re-acquire her, especially if that happened after the sun rose.

About an hour after the last vestiges of the sunset faded from the western sky, he noticed the glow of St. Vincent coming over the horizon ahead and off to the right. It pleased Burke to have a chance to bid farewell to the island that he had called home for the past eight years, at least from a distance. He wished he could stop in and thank Navia for all her hospitality and friendship – as well as all the nights drinking and laughing with her, but that wasn't possible right now. Well, there was no rule that he couldn't visit her in the future.

An odd trilling sound reached his ears, and it took him a few seconds to realize it was his satellite phone. He'd had one since he'd started going out of sight of land in the first *Julian's Empire* and felt it was a justifiable expense to maintain when he got down here despite his regular marine radio. But he never gave out the number – incoming calls got costly quickly – and he'd been lucky enough to not have needed it in years. He looked at the number. Not surprisingly, he did not recognize it. "Hello?"

"Captain Julian Burke?"

"Yes. Who's this?"

"Let's not worry about that right now. Let's worry about why you're following that enormous cruise ship as we speak."

Burke's eyes bulged, and the first thing he did was step out from the wheelhouse and turn a complete circle to see if anyone had snuck close to him. There were no lights close except for the *Amore*.

He quickly decided to play it stupid to see what else he could learn. "What? I'm not following some ship."

"This will go a lot easier if you dispense with the bullshit, Captain Burke. Right now, you are about 2,100 yards astern of the *Amore of the Seas* and have been in that position since you departed Grenada. The lights of St. Vincent are just becoming visible on your starboard bow." Burke grabbed his handheld rangefinder and pointed it at the ship. The Distance To Target on the display held steady at 1.22 miles. *Shit.*

"So I enjoy big ships at night. What's it to you?"

"You and I both know what your lady friend has in the canvas satchel she carried aboard a couple of hours ago. I'm wondering what kind of cut she had to promise you that would make you follow a ship all the way to Puerto Rico."

Now his face ran pale. Whoever this was knew exactly what was going on and was crafty enough not to use names or mention specific details. If this guy knew his location and what Kensie had with her, there was no sense in being evasive. "That's not why I'm following her, not that it's any of your business."

"Right. Lemme guess – she fucked you a couple times better than a thousand dollar a night whore, did all those things you love, and batted those big green eyes at you so you'd chauffeur that cute ass all over place. Then she promised you a piece of the action."

"Look," Burke interrupted. "Fuck you. I'm hanging up."

"But," the other voice continued as if Burke hadn't said a word, "you aren't *really* sure that you can trust her, so you're going to sail to San Juan and hope you can get a ticket on that plane. Then you hope that she gets more than a token reward for giving the prize back to the crown, and then you hope that she gives you a fair cut, even though you did all the heavy lifting. That's an awful lot of hoping, and you aren't comfortable with that. Tell me I'm wrong."

"You're wrong," he responded firmly, "but, for the sake of argument, what if everything you said is true?"

"It is true, and if you want to lose that garbage scow and buy a real boat and proper gear, and have money to spare, you'll be smart and listen to me instead of following a piece of ass for the chance of getting some table scraps."

"Sounds like you have it all figured out. So why do you need me?"

The voice chuckled deviously. "We don't really need you. In fact, we wouldn't even be having this discussion with you at all if you hadn't been John Fucking Rambo – twice. But enlisting your assistance will make things easier. We need a boat. You know these waters and these islands better than a lot of people, or so we've heard. We need you to help us disappear."

"Not interested."

"You say that, but you haven't hung up yet, have you?"

Burke glared at the phone like it was the reason he had yet to terminate the call and then put it back to his ear. "Call me curious. But why should I believe you any more than her? How come you think you can get your hands on it?"

"Smart man – wants proof. Keep your eye on the ship now, Captain Burke, and give me a few seconds." Burke did as requested, watching the blobs of light that illuminated the decks, the portholes, and the rigging while a heavy lead ball formed in the pit of his stomach. Something bad was coming – the man on the phone had been far too confident to be bluffing. His patience, never his strong suit in any situation, was already greatly reduced by worry and evaporated steadily as five seconds turned to 10 and then more as 10 turned to 20. He opened his mouth to protest into the phone, but the words never came out.

Every glowing point of light, from the top of the smokestack to the waterline, went out at the same second. Burke gaped. All he could think of was the time that David Copperfield made the Statue of Liberty disappear as he watched on live TV, and that he was even more amazed right now.

"I hope I have your attention now, Captain Burke?"

"Yeah. Yeah."

"Good. Now here's what you're going to do…"

# Chapter 15 – The Heart of Darkness

"What the hell just happened?" Kensie asked in the perfect darkness of the passageway. Instinctively, she reached out to touch the wall while smacking her hand down on the satchel to make sure she'd feel it if someone tried to pull at it.

"I guess the power went out," Reid narrated unnecessarily.

"Does that happen? Does power just go out on a cruise ship?"

"I think it just did," he responded. Kensie felt a hand bump lightly into her chin. "Sorry. Just trying to get my bearings. It's so disorienting."

Kensie knew what he meant. It wasn't just the darkness. It was like they had entered some weird void where there was nothing at all, and then she realized why. All the subtle white noise of the machinery on the ship that she'd gotten used to over the last few days was completely gone, just like the light.

*And that means the engines have stopped.* There was no way this was a coincidence.

Fear replaced confusion in an instant. "Reid?" Her voice was tinged with concern that bordered on panic.

"It's OK, Kensie. I'm sure it's just a generator failure or something like that. It'll be back up in a minute."

Kensie reached out until she felt his body and grabbed his shoulders firmly, turning him so they were facing each other, even if there was no visual evidence to confirm this. "No, I don't think it is. You're a cop, and I need you to listen to me like a cop for a second. It would take too long for me to explain and you probably wouldn't believe me anyway, but this is happening because of me."

"Because of you? What are you talking about? Was your soda spiked?"

"Look," Kensie implored. "I know I sound crazy, but you have to trust me. This is almost certainly part of something bigger, and I'm probably in danger. I can't explain why, but it's the truth, and I need you to help me."

He didn't respond for a moment, and Kensie wished she could see his face to get an understanding of his thought process, but all she could do was wait for those interminable seconds. She half expected him to abandon her in the hallway, but when he spoke, his voice carried the all business tone of an officer of the law. "OK. I understand. What do you need?"

*I owe you one, Reid.* "Thank you. Right now, I need to get somewhere away from everyone else. Back to my cabin."

"OK. Let's go." He grabbed her arm firmly, activated the flashlight feature on his phone, and started making his way unsteadily along the passageway. Just then the PA system crackled to life.

"Attention all passengers. Attention all passengers. We have suffered an electrical systems failure at this time, and it is affecting most areas and onboard processes. There is no immediate danger to the ship, so for the moment please remain wherever you are. The emergency passageway lights should come on momentarily. When they do, please proceed to your muster stations safely and quickly. There is no cause for alarm, so do not run." The message repeated over and over.

"Still want to go to your cabin?" Reid asked.

"Yes. I'm sure that's the standard response, and whoever did this knows it, so I'll be a sitting duck in a group of people at the muster point."

"You think someone is going to just attack you with everyone around?"

Kensie realized Reid was taking the approach that violence was her primary concern. It was, but not in the way he was considering it. "It's not like that. They're not going to beat me up. I just have to stay away from everyone."

"It's like you're afraid of catching a disease." Frustration came through in his tone. "Shouldn't we get ship security involved? There's more of them and they can protect you."

"No. I don't know how we'd find them right now anyway."

"True. But, still –"

"Please, Reid, I can't stress how important it is that we just keep this quiet."

"Kensie, you sound like you're trying to hide something. I have to ask, did you do something illegal?"

"No! I see how you could think that, but I'm doing the right thing for the right reasons. It's legal and ethical, I promise." She could almost *hear* his eyes roll at her answers.

"This doesn't make sense."

"I know it doesn't. When this is over, it will. I promise. But, for now, we can only trust Catrina, Nancy, and Liv, and we probably shouldn't trust Nancy or Liv too much." It briefly occurred to her that she hadn't known Reid that long either, but if he wanted to do something to harm her, he would be doing it by now. "Just think of everyone else as potentially dangerous to me, OK?"

"I already am."

"Cool." She continued to stumble forward, hoping they would be able to navigate the stairwell down to her cabin – if they ever found the stairs, that is.

Even with the tiny halo of light from Reid's phone, which seemed to be eaten up by the complete blackness, the trip took far longer than normal. Despite the orders from the PA system, a few groups of people were trying to make their way about below decks just like Kensie and Reid. During each encounter, Kensie just clamped her hand down on the satchel and prayed that no one would touch it, inadvertently or otherwise. She was irritated with them for not following the stay in place order, even though she was ignoring it as well. *I'm sure their situations are nothing like mine right now.*

It took at least four or five minutes of very tentative steps just to reach what they hoped was the opening to the correct stairwell. When they confirmed it, it took even longer to trek down the two flights to the correct deck – Kensie was amazed at how treacherous simple stairs seemed with such limited illumination. Just as they finished the second flight of stairs and moved back into the passageway to Kensie's cabin, the emergency lights flared to life.

"Great timing," Reid said, the stress in his voice evident. The light was definitely dimmer than usual, but it was more than enough to get around by, allowing them to quickly get to her cabin – where they stopped when they saw the door was ajar.

They looked at each other for a second with alarm in their eyes before Kensie surged toward the entrance, only to be stopped as Reid grabbed her shoulder. "Let me." Kensie almost snapped at him for such a misogynistic act until she realized he was doing exactly what she asked him to do – act like a cop. She allowed him to step past her.

He pushed the door open tentatively, moving forward until he disappeared from view. She waited apprehensively, looking left and right to ensure the corridor remained empty, until Reid called out to her. "It's clear."

She entered her cabin and was immediately struck by the mess. The drawers were all open, with the contents spilled on the floor or shoved to one side. Both mattresses were stripped of bedding and askew on the bedframes, and both suitcases were wide open.

Reid went to the wardrobe, with Kensie peering over his shoulder. The door of the safe inside it was slightly ajar, and he pulled it open, reaching in and coming out with Kensie's watch, as well as earrings and necklaces that belonged to Catrina. "What kind of thief takes the time to break into a safe and doesn't take things worth a couple thousand dollars?" He looked absolutely perplexed.

"The kind that's looking for something a lot more valuable," Kensie answered, half to herself.

"Are all these things yours?"

"Just the watch. The other stuff is Catrina's."

Reid shook his head, perplexed. "Your watch is worth a couple grand. And, based on what I know of Catrina, she probably doesn't buy cheap jewelry."

Despite the gravity of the situation, a slight, quick grin twisted one side of Kensie's mouth. *If you only knew...* "No, she doesn't. But trust me, she could shop at Tiffany's and it wouldn't matter."

Reid's brow furrowed more in irritation than confusion and he opened his mouth, but before he could voice a protest or a demand for more information, Kensie's phone chimed with a call. She looked at the number, but the screen read **UNKNOWN**. "Yes?"

"Good evening, Kensie. I'm sorry about your cabin, but you really shouldn't be surprised." The voice was familiar, but she was unable to place it.

"Who are you? What the hell is going on?" Reid looked at her, a puzzled expression on his face.

"I'm sure you realize what is going on. You have something. We want it. That's the whole picture."

"What makes you think I'm going to give it to you or anyone else?"

"You're going to turn it over to me because you value the safety of your friend."

An icy chill ran down Kensie's spine. "Where is she?"

"I really can't tell you, but I assure you that she is completely safe right now. I don't claim that she is happy, but that's to be expected. At this point, she is my best assurance that you'll play nice and make this go as easily as possible."

Reid mouthed the words *what the fuck?* but Kensie waved him off, much more concerned with Catrina's welfare. "I don't believe you."

"You guys are so skeptical," he answered. "Hang on." His wording struck her as odd. *Who are 'you guys'?*

She had little time to ponder the question before she heard her friend's voice. "Kensie?!"

"Cat! Are you OK?"

"Yeah, I'm fine." Catrina sounded scared to death but Kensie could tell she was trying to hold it together. "What do these assholes want?"

The voice faded away and was replaced by the caller. "I'm sure you believe me now."

"Yes, I do," she responded. Her instinct, with Catrina in peril, was to follow whatever directions she was given. "What do you want me to do?"

"Go up to your muster station just like you're a regular passenger. Don't say anything about this to anyone. The ship will be towed into port, the auxiliary power will be hooked up, and then they'll release everyone from muster. Go back to your cabin and wait there until we contact you again. Oh yeah – make sure you have that satchel on you the whole time. If someone other than I or my associates gets their hands on what's in it, it will be bad for you, and worse for someone else." The line clicked off.

Kensie looked at the screen like it would give her some kind of clue of the whereabouts of her friend, but the electronic device was not forthcoming with anything of value. She slid it back into her pocket, feeling a killing rage overcome her fear. Her friend was in danger – real danger – because she had to be so fucking smart and clever, *and* because she'd valued the safety and security of the treasure over escorting her. This was completely and totally her fault, and at the moment she had no idea how to fix things. She was sure of only one thing – both her life and Catrina's were on the line.

Reid interrupted her train of thought with a very serious tone. "What was that about? Where's Catrina?"

Kensie tried to focus on the problem at hand. Self recrimination would not help, at least not right now. "Catrina's been kidnapped," she said. "That was the person that took her."

Reid blinked, trying to come to grips with reality. "Who would kidnap her? Why? Especially on a ship? What do they want?"

"I don't know for sure, but he said to go up to my muster station and, when the ship docks and they hook up shore power, they'll dismiss us so I should come back here and wait for another call."

"So this is what you were talking about when you said the blackout was aimed at you?" Reid stated, more as an accusation than a question.

"I guess," Kensie shrugged, "but I never imagined anyone would do something like this."

"You have to tell me what the hell is going on now, dammit! This is getting out of hand."

"And it's going to get worse if more people know."

Reid tried a new tack. "I could just go to security right now, you know."

"You could. I can't stop you. But all I can tell you is, if you do that, you're going to screw things up more than you can possibly realize, and I'm saying that knowing full well how much danger Catrina is in."

Reid stared at her – hard. She held firm and did not blink until he turned away. "I don't like this. Not one bit."

"I know. I don't either. But my explanations aren't going to help Catrina. You deserve an explanation, and you'll get one, but right now it just won't matter one bit."

Reid's turned away to stare out at the blackness outside the glass door that led to their balcony. "It's just that I'm a little personally involved here, and that's new to me."

"Well, that's two of us," she admitted. "But let's put that aside and figure out what we should do, OK?"

"I think you're wrong for not telling me, but I'm not going to beat it out of you. So, for the moment, we should probably follow his directions."

*Thank god.* "So, I guess we go to our muster station?"

"Yeah. We don't have any other moves."

"That's not encouraging," she remarked.

"Neither is you keeping secrets. But that's where we are. Come on." They headed out of the cabin and back to the location they were assigned on the first day. For those too forgetful or worried to remember where that was, the loudspeaker continued to broadcast where each collection of cabins was supposed to go. At the end of each dry read through, another pre-recorded message asked everyone to move quickly but not panic, that this move was more of a precaution than anything, that there was no real emergency and no reason to worry.

Kensie disagreed.

***

Burke tied up quickly at his regular mooring in St. Vincent, looking off to the west to see if the tugs that were tasked with bringing the *Amore of the Seas* back to port were visible yet. He didn't see them, meaning he had enough time to comply with the instructions he'd received via his phone after the ship had blacked out.

But he had another stop to make first.

He trotted along the path to Seraphine Street, making sure that no one was watching or following him. He didn't know how many people were involved in this situation, but he had to assume they had enough manpower to cover all their bases. For that reason, he turned left instead of right on the sidewalk, going about 100 yards before he slipped between two trees and spent a minute looking for anyone that might have been following him. Seeing no one, he reversed course and headed rapidly to *Arnhim's.*

It was starting to hop as usual, and the noise and crowd made it easy for him to slip in without being noticed. He chose a dim corner and surveilled the room from that vantage point, trying to pick out anyone who – hell, he didn't know. Someone who looked "suspicious?" He was totally out of his element, so all he could do was trust his instincts.

No one stood out, so after another minute he drifted toward the bar, where he found Navia yelling orders to the kitchen staff, pouring drinks, and chatting up customers at the same time. Her energy level always amazed him.

He waited until she made eye contact, and was relieved that she read his body language and facial expression well enough to realize this was not a social call. She tilted her head toward her small office just off the kitchen, and Burke followed, shutting the door behind him.

"Wha' ya go an' done now, Burke?" she asked without preamble. "I see dem eyes tellin' me you runnin' wit' da troubles. And where's me Kensie? Ya don' wan' be sayin' ya got her in a spot. I like 'er, and she gotta real fondness for your ugly hide as well."

"I didn't get her into trouble, but I've got to do something to make sure she gets out of trouble," he explained. "I'm sure you know about the cruise ship being brought in for repairs?"

"Ya," she answered, looking none too happy about it. "Two ah my guys got called for the work detail by Grimm's, so I'm shorthanded and scramblin' round' like a salamander wit' na front legs," she finished, referring to the only repair shop on the island with the equipment that might possibly be able to fix something the size of the *Amore of the Seas*. She changed her tone. "Wha' cha be needin' from Navia, hon?"

Burke winced as he wasn't sure how she would take his request. "I need a piece."

Navia turned her head and looked at him askance. "Is dat bad, is it?"

"Probably not, but I can't be sure. Better safe than sorry."

"I don' think ya be unnerstanin' da meanin' o' either of dem words, mah boy. But turn yasself 'round – no one gets to see Navia's secret spot." Burke dutifully followed orders, ignoring the sounds of Navia moving whatever hid the opening to wherever she kept her valuable and not quite legal items until she was finished. She handed him a cloth with a solid object encased within it. "Ya' knowin' da rules, right?"

"I found this on the dock last year. No idea where it came from."

"Good boy. Now go an' do wha' cha gotta' do and be safe 'bout it. Keep mah Kensie safe as well."

Burke hesitated. He was deeply upset at this turn of events, but one silver lining was that it gave him the opportunity to see his good friend one more time. He didn't want to worry her, but he did want to thank her. He slid the cloth bundle into his pocket and took both her hands in his. "Navia, thank you so much for always being there for me. I wish I could tell you more, but it's better that I don't. I might not be around for quite a while after tonight, but all I can say right now is 'thank you.'"

Navia looked a bit stunned. "Ya makin' me worry more now. Evrathin' gonna work out, ya say?"

"It will. But I have to go. Love you, darlin.'" He hugged her quickly, but with a fierce intensity, and finished with a kiss on her forehead. "Bye for now."

"Bye." In a second, he was out the door.

***

Kensie found Nancy and Liv sitting in one of the booths, looking around in mild irritation and sweating in the thick atmosphere. Emergency power ran the lights but not the air conditioning, and with a couple hundred people in the enclosed space in the tropical atmosphere, the heat was getting worse by the second. They slid over to allow her and Reid a seat.

"Where's Catrina?" Liv asked. Unsurprisingly, the group seemed more sober.

"I don't know," Kensie lied as smoothly as possible, and Reid shrugged. "We kind of assumed she'd come back up here because she wasn't in the room when we got there." She tried to change the subject. "Where's that Corey guy?"

"He has a different muster station, so he went there." Liv shrugged. Clearly, she didn't have a very strong attachment to the young man beyond his good cheekbones and unkempt hair, and she returned to her original topic. "Maybe I should call her."

Kensie and Reid shared a look, hoping the kidnappers would not pick up her phone. They had to be smart enough to realize that the more people that got involved, the harder it would be for them to accomplish their goal of getting away clean with the *Couronne*. Kensie tried not to appear worried as Liv held the phone up to her ear, only to pull it away suddenly. She could hear the loud beeping on the other end before she killed the call. "Didn't go through."

"Yeah," Nancy chimed in. "With the power off, there's zero cell service until we get closer to the island."

"Oh, right."

Kensie leaned over to Reid. "Then how did they call me?" she whispered.

"Probably a satellite phone. It doesn't need cell service to connect." Kensie nodded. She didn't know if that was true or not, but Reid's explanation made sense.

Liv was still very concerned. Kensie understood why, but her persistence wasn't helping matters. "We have to tell someone she's missing." She raised her hand and a crew member walked over.

"Yes?"

"Hi. Our friend Catrina Andersen isn't here and this is her muster station." She nodded in Kensie's direction. "That's her roommate. She just came from their cabin, and she's not there either."

The man tapped on his tablet. "Yeah, she hasn't checked in yet."

"Is someone looking for her?" Liv snapped.

"We have about a dozen crew checking every passenger-accessible place, including staterooms. There are a few people unaccounted for, but we always find them."

"We can help!" Nancy said while standing explosively. Liv nodded to signal her willingness to participate.

"No, please," the crew member said. "Captain's standing orders when sending passengers to muster is that they can't leave for any reason. Otherwise it would be impossible to keep track of where people were if we needed to evacuate the ship."

"But the message over the loudspeaker keeps saying there's no danger, that this is just a precaution," Liv protested.

"Yes, I doubt there is much real danger, but the Captain doesn't issue orders like this for no reason. I'm sure we'll find her soon. Every so often someone manages to slip by the check in, but they always turn up." He flashed a charming smile. "We haven't lost one yet."

*First time for everything,* Kensie thought pessimistically.

Nancy frowned but sat down, understanding the reasoning behind the order even if she didn't like it. The crewman nodded and headed away.

Kensie cursed silently to herself. She wanted to scream at the two of them, to tell them to just sit down and shut up, but that would lead to a million questions and might put everyone in more danger. She didn't know Nancy or Liv that well, but they both seemed impulsive and likely to fly off the handle if they knew what was really going on.

"Look," she said. "Cat's a big girl, and I'm sure she just went to the wrong muster station. She was a little drunk and probably just followed the crowd. There's no reason to get worked up, OK?" She sat back in her seat, doing her best to appear calm but realizing she was getting quite the headache from the worry lines etched into her forehead.

***

Burke knocked on the open door of Grimm's Marine Repair loudly enough to overcome the bustle of activity before stepping inside. As Navia had indicated, pretty much every person with experience working on boats of any type was collected in the main building, scurrying this way and that, grabbing tools and parts and instruments and placing them on carts. He knew a couple of them and nodded in their direction during the pause brought about by his loud pounding. Even though he was not a mechanic, his familiarity with boats and connections with the group would make his presence seem reasonable.

"I'm looking for Samuel," he called out, and to his relief a man broke free from the chaos and headed to him. He pulled Burke aside as the noise and activity resumed.

"You're Burke?"

"Yeah. You talked to Mr. Jones?" Burke rolled his eyes at the obviously fake name the man had given him over the satellite phone.

"I sure did," he answered. Mr. Jones had been a young man with a rather fat lip who had stopped in the shop a little while ago and recommended Burke as a highly skilled mechanic who should be part of the repair party. However, once on board, he stated that Burke should be left alone to do his own thing. The pile of money that the gentleman had pushed into his fist convinced Samuel of Burke's qualifications. "You can get a shirt and hat over there, and I'll make you a temporary ID."

"Great."

Samuel made to step away but paused, and when he turned back Burke felt a tinge of concern at the way his dark eyes burned. "I don't know what's going on and I don't care, but if you fuck up this repair or screw up the reputation of this company, I'll drown you right on the wharf with my bare hands. You get me?"

Burke closed his eyes. The warnings and threats he'd received in the past hour were starting to wear on him, and he wanted to tell this guy that if he was so worried, he shouldn't have taken whatever bribe had been offered to put him on the team. But that would help nothing. "I get you. This has nothing to do with the ship or your company."

Samuel gave him a once over before nodding and getting back to work. Burke headed over to get his company apparel, absent mindedly thumbing through the red shirts on the rack until he found a 2XL and held it up, regarding it with all the joy of a man choosing the clothes in which he would be executed.

He was not a religious man, but he reasoned that a general request to the universe couldn't hurt, could it? *Please give me the strength to do what I have to do.*

***

Finally, mercifully, the main power came back on a few minutes after a *thud* more felt than heard indicated that they had docked, powering the normal lights and sending a burst of cool air from the vents over the sweaty, tired, and aggravated passengers. A spontaneous ovation exploded from the crowd, and as it faded they heard it repeated in other parts of the ship.

Kensie wiped the sweat from her forehead, not as relieved as everyone else to have power back. It meant that soon she would be getting instructions that would put her and her friend – and maybe Reid – in serious danger. While they'd waited and perspired in the dim light, Kensie had mulled over what had transpired and speculated about what might come to pass, and could only fixate on the fact that this was entirely her fault. The guilt was already killing her; if anything worse happened to Catrina, she had no idea what she would do. She felt nauseated.

The loudspeaker crackled to life once more, and this time it was a live voice instead of the repeating canned message. "Ladies and gentlemen, we thank you very much for your patience. As you can tell, we have been connected to an electric umbilical from the island and power has been restored throughout the ship, so you are released from your muster stations and are free to move about the *Amore of the Seas* without restriction. We will remain docked until propulsion has been restored and tested. Due to this being an unscheduled arrival, we will not be permitting anyone to leave the ship, but we encourage you to take advantage of our numerous shipboard activities."

People started rising, eager to head out to anywhere that promised a bit more fun. "OK," Nancy said. "Let's make a plan to search for Catrina."

Kensie jumped in, knowing she had to control this part of the narrative. "Good idea. Someone should search and someone should wait in the cabin in case she comes back before we find her."

"Yup," Liv agreed. "But I don't want to sit around anymore."

"Fine. You guys have spent more time on the ship anyway. I barely know the layout, so you two search while I wait in the cabin."

"OK, but what about you?" Nancy asked, looking at Reid.

He looked indecisive for a second, but that passed. "I can start at the lowest deck and work my way up, and you guys start up high and work your way down. One of us is bound to spot her."

"Cool. Let's go." Nancy and Liz went in one direction, with Kensie and Reid heading down to the cabin. She noticed how he stood very close to her side, his left hand nearly touching her hip, while his head tracked back and forth, reminding her of a German

Shepherd guard dog on full alert. The trip was infinitely easier now that the passageway was properly lit, and in a minute they were sitting on the beds. Kensie felt helpless and stupid waiting around, like a sheep waiting to be led into the slaughtering room, and kept looking at her phone reflexively.

Reid seemed a great deal more composed, and while Kensie figured he was a little more used to things like this, it still pissed her off that she appeared to be the only one having a nervous breakdown. With nothing better to do and her nervous energy threatening to overwhelm her, she started straightening up the cabin.

"Kensie, don't. You might contaminate some evidence."

She shot him a look. "You think that's gonna matter?"

"It might," he responded, but his voice lacked conviction, making it easy for Kensie to return to her task. She was happy for anything to do. Her senses were raw, as if someone had rubbed sandpaper across all five of them, and not only could she not just sit still, she was in no mood for an argument or a discussion, even an irrelevant one. She started scooping clothes off the floor.

But Reid wasn't done. "It'll be OK, Kensie." His insistence on talking infuriated her and gave her an easy outlet to vent. She stood and stormed the three steps to where he sat on the bed and jabbed a finger in his face.

"How is it going to be OK? How? My best friend is in serious trouble and so am I, and now maybe you too! And it's mainly because I'm selfish and stupid!" The anger left her as quickly as it came, and she turned away from him. The remorse of everything she'd done tonight, capped off by lying to Reid even though he was trying to help, weighed her down like Jacob Marley's chains. "How the hell will this be OK?" she asked in a plaintive, almost helpless voice.

Reid came up to her and took her hand in his. She half expected him to twist it behind her back to force the truth out of her, but instead he held it and waited until she turned back to face him.

"It will be. It has to be," he said in a low monotone. "I like her. A lot." He plopped down inelegantly, leaving Kensie standing next to him, stunned and silent, at a complete loss for his sudden change.

"I'm not real good with women, but being with Cat just feels right, you know? It's easy. It's fun. I never felt like I had to be cool or act important." His eyes filled with tears. "I know how much she means to you, but I don't want to lose her either."

Kensie swallowed the last of her anger. *I'm being selfish. I'm not the only one who's scared.* She sat down next to him. "I'm sorry, Reid. I've been so wrapped up in me and Catrina that I didn't stop to think of anyone else – like you."

Reid nodded, giving her a weak smile that was in no way reassuring. "I know. And I know I don't have any right to bitch compared to what you've got to be going through, but I can tell how worried you are, and that makes me worried."

"Well, we're a couple of worriers," she said, hoping she could lighten the mood just a bit. However much he might need reassurance from her, Kensie needed him back on his game.

***

The second the power was restored from the umbilical cord on the wharf, the security guard at the front of the gangway moved aside and allowed Samuel and his team to start boarding. Burke made sure he was last in line; he had no idea where he should be going and didn't want to advertise his presence by turning the wrong way or looking lost. *Plus it'll make it easier for me to disappear.*

The metal detector they passed through yelped constantly, picking up the numerous tools that they were bringing on board. To Burke's relief, the security guards manning the station ignored the alerts and waved everyone through quickly. When he got to the entrance, Burke mimicked the actions of those in front of him, holding up his ID and proceeding after one of the guards looked at it for a microsecond. Clearly they had orders to get the work crew in position as quickly as possible so they could solve the problem and get the *Amore* back at sea. Every additional minute spent at this unscheduled stop had to be costing the cruise line a fortune.

The line of men snaked toward the middle of the ship and entered a non descript door that led to a markedly less elegant portion of the ship, where passengers did not transit. They headed down several flights of bare metal stairs, and toward the bottom he saw a man dressed in the uniform of a waiter nod to him. He stepped out of line at the landing.

"Come." Without waiting for a response, he turned and led Burke through a series of twists and turns. Unfamiliar with ships so large, he became thoroughly lost and followed his guide closely. After what seemed like a mile of walking, the man stopped and picked up a small wrench, using it to rap three times on a pipe.

A man unknown to Burke stepped out of the shadows, perpetuating the cloak and dagger bullshit. He pressed a bill into the hand of the escort, who smiled, bowed his head slightly, and headed on his way quickly. Burke watched him go before turning his attention back to the man he was supposed to meet.

"How do you do, Captain Burke? Thank you for complying with my instructions."

Burke just glared.

"Come now. This will end up better for everyone involved if we just take the animosity out of it."

Burke nodded. "Fine. What should I call you?"

The man thought for a moment. "You can call me 'Dean.'"

"OK, Dean. But know this – if you hurt Kensie or her friend, all bets are off. You got me?"

The man nodded, giving Burke the distinct impression that he was being patronized. "Yes, absolutely. As long as she plays ball, no harm will come to anyone. This is nothing more than a business transaction."

"Bullshit. You tried to kill us – twice! – and now you've kidnapped someone. If you're a businessman, I'm a ballerina."

"It is unsavory, but necessary. Now, come with me so we can go over the plan."

"What plan? I'm your getaway driver, that's it. I'm not even sure why I'm here instead of waiting for you on *Empire*."

"There is a bit more to your role than just driving a boat, Mr. Burke."

Burke closed his eyes. He had been afraid of this. "What are you talking about?"

"You seem like an intelligent and thoughtful man, so I'm sure you can understand that I don't want Miss Prescott to see – and be able to identify – me. Actually, there's more to it, but that's all you need to worry about." The man smiled like he was imparting some wonderful news. "Since she already knows you, you're going to be the one who takes the item from Miss Prescott."

Even though he knew how unlikely it would be, he'd hoped to do all of this without Kensie seeing him. "So I end up as the only one that she can identify as being involved."

The gentleman smiled without mirth. "As I said, I knew you were intelligent."

"I didn't sign on for that."

The dark haired gentleman nodded as if he expected the protest. "I'm aware of that. But you're going to do it anyway."

Burke didn't bother to mask his irritation, feeling the heat in his face as his muscles tensed in preparation for battle. "I don't take orders."

"You'll take this one. As I indicated on the phone, my associate is keeping Kensie's friend as an insurance policy. The problem with my associate, you see, is that he's a little... disturbed. If I'm not in a certain place at a certain time, he won't have a problem disposing of the young lady. So, if you're balled up fists are indicative of a predilection toward violence on my person, you'll wish to reconsider."

*Fuck.* This was getting worse by the second. "But why me? Why not have one of your other 'associates' make the exchange?"

"This is a very small operation with few assets. My main associate has to keep Miss Prescott's friend under control, and no one else has the connection – or the understanding of the gravitas involved – that I do. That leaves you. So you are going to accept the item from her and turn it over to me in order to secure your payment and the release of Miss Prescott's friend. End of discussion."

Burke felt sick. He was getting in deeper by the second, but he didn't see an escape route at this point.

"I know you aren't fond of the way this is working out," the man continued, "but it's going to be better for everyone involved. Especially you. Your compensation for this task will be more than adequate." He turned and headed back where he'd come from, gesturing for Burke to follow. Burke did so, not so sure that things would be better for anyone after this – least of all him.

# Chapter 16 – Opportunity Cost

Reid walked slightly in front of Kensie as they approached the mid-ship elevators. Just before the open waiting area, a tall figure with dark skin in the white jacket and bow tie of a shipboard waiter leaned against the wall. Upon hearing footsteps, he turned and nodded to confirm that he was the man they were looking for, but then frowned. Kensie wasn't sure why he seemed displeased, but they had no choice but to proceed, albeit with great caution.

The waiter waved them forward eagerly as if he had a schedule to keep, but Kensie felt like she was walking in thick mud and dared not try to speed up lest she trip over her own feet. She felt the tremendous tension in her neck and jaw and saw spots. Stress – it was a bitch. She focused on a single thought. *Keep your cool.*

When they reached the waiter, he looked her and then Reid up and down as if confused. "You," he said, pointing at Kensie, "OK. But you," moving his finger toward Reid, "no."

"Why not?" Kensie protested.

He shook his head. "You. Not man."

"I need him with me," she insisted. Her voice remained quiet but increased in urgency.

The man stubbornly stood his ground. "One person. Woman. Not man."

"Look," Reid said, grabbing his wallet and pulling out $20. "We're a team. I go where she goes." He offered the bill.

The man looked at it and appeared tempted, but then shook his head even harder, gesturing toward Kensie first. "You come." Then at Reid. "You go. Or no."

Kensie sighed in frustration. This standoff wasn't getting them anywhere and every second that they argued with this man was another second that Catrina remained in danger. She turned to Reid.

"I'll be OK. Just wait for us back in the cabin."

"No!" He kept his voice down but there was no mistaking his urgency. "I have no idea what's going on, and neither do you! You can't go alone!"

Reid didn't like it. She didn't either, but their escort apparently had very specific instructions, and either the size of whatever bribe he'd gotten or fear of the person that had given it to him meant that he wasn't going to deviate from them. "We don't know where to go. If he won't take you, he won't take me, and then we have no chance of helping Catrina."

Reid looked at her for several seconds and then nodded before he addressed the waiter. "If anything happens to her," he said very slowly while pointing at Kensie, "I'll find you. You got that?" While he probably didn't understand the words, the waiter picked up on the tone of the statement and nodded, his eyes wide and a sheen of sweat coating his forehead.

He turned back to Kensie and squeezed her upper arm. "Be careful." He took a step back, but that was not far enough for the man, who made shooing motions until Reid moved about six paces back.

Without taking his eyes off Reid, the waiter turned and fished keys out of his pocket to unlock the door, holding it for Kensie while speaking a single word. "Come." Once she entered, he locked the door behind her and led her down a series of staircases. Kensie noted the stark difference between the opulence of the main hallway and the utilitarian nature of the service area.

Kensie had the distinct feeling she was being led to the 7$^{th}$ level of hell and her demise. Or was it the 8$^{th}$ level? She couldn't remember the crimes specified in each level of *Dante's Inferno*, but reasoned that she surely belonged in one of them for the mess she'd created. Maybe hubris?

At the bottom of the last flight of stairs, they stepped out onto a grated metal floor. Her escort led her around a corner, through a narrow passageway, and then halted near a small open area, surrounded by large tanks and other machines behind which anyone could be hiding. Kensie felt terribly exposed and wished Reid or Burke was with her.

"Stay." He looked at her to ensure that his instructions were being followed before leaving the area.

*Now what?* Should she call out to tell whomever that she was here, or just wait? She turned in a complete circle, hoping that she would discover some clue as to what to do next, but the dingy gray pipes, vents, and complex contraptions revealed nothing.

She didn't have to ponder the problem very long. Footsteps approached, and she instinctively put her back to one of the tanks. Bravery came easily standing in a well lit, well traveled hallway filled with passengers and with a cop by her side, but down in the dingy and hot bowels of the ship that smelled vaguely of fuel oil and grease, with the ominous approach of god knew who, she was merely an unarmed individual facing off against people who had proven their willingness to kill her for what she carried.

*What was that about hubris?*

Just as she was able to make out a spectral form approaching her, the footsteps stopped, leaving the figure almost entirely in the shadows. "Thank you for coming, Miss Prescott." The voice struck her as familiar once more, but in the stress of the moment, recognition escaped her.

"Oh yeah, no problem. Where's Catrina?"

"She's nearby and unharmed. We can worry about her later."

"No. I see her right now." She thought quickly, kicking herself for not making a plan beforehand. "If I don't, I signal my person and the *Couronne* goes overboard."

The laughter of the man was not encouraging. "Kensie, you and I both know that you wouldn't leave that particular item in anyone else's possession." Kensie squinted at his remark. *How would you know that?* "But," he continued, "you have kept up your end of the bargain, so I'm willing to accommodate you." There was a snap of fingers, and a second later more footsteps sounded.

This time, however, they did not stop at the border of the minimal illumination. She drew a deep breath upon seeing Catrina, her arms behind her back and a thick cloth wedged between her teeth, being pushed forward by... Van. *I knew I hated that guy!* He held a knife in his other hand, and Kensie noted that he was blocking the way she had entered, and the other man was blocking the only other obvious exit. *Shit.*

She wanted to rush to her friend, but knew that would be a foolish and wasted action. "Cat, are you OK?"

She looked both pissed and scared, emotions with which Kensie identified at the moment. She bit down on the gag fiercely, like she expected to chew through the fabric, and jerked her shoulders as if to pull away from Van, but his grip on her upper arm was firm. Recognizing the futility of her struggles, she settled for nodding.

"She's just fine," Van said with his lip curled in an arrogant sneer. He slid the tip of the knife over Catrina's upper chest and down to her shirt where it covered her breasts. "I was kinda hoping you wouldn't show. We were going to have a little fun later." Catrina's demeanor went from pissed to petrified in an instant, and she froze at the touch of the metal. Van wasn't applying it hard enough to even scratch the skin, but one move or one mistake was all it would take.

"Van, you fucker! Stop!"

He pulled the blade marginally away from Catrina's body. "Such harsh language, Kensie. This is really your fault, you know. All you had to do was not be a bitch to me and this could have all been avoided." Releasing her upper arm with his other hand, he draped it over her shoulder so he could run his fingers over her cleavage. "Of course, if you play your cards right, we might have a real kinky threesome later." Kensie had never wondered what the face of a true sadist looked like, but now she knew. Her blood boiled.

"I swear, if you hurt her, I'll rip your goddamned eyes out." She wasn't kidding in the least. Kensie felt an overwhelming urge to charge Van and doubted the other man would be able to stop her before she succeeded.

"And you still haven't learned any manners," he taunted as his hand continued its obscene caress, moving it down to cup her right breast. With the knife not an immediate danger, Catrina struggled against him once again, her nose crinkled in disgust.

"Knock it off!" the blacked out man commanded without raising his voice, and Van immediately reigned in his twisted enjoyment of the situation. His eyes, though, remained locked on Kensie and easily communicated how much he was enjoying the power he wielded. He not only kept his hand exactly where neither woman wanted it, he flexed his fingers slightly in a perverted caress of the area.

Kensie wanted to get a read on who else might be around. "Where's your little friend? Brian, is it?"

"Brian has no idea that any of this is going on. I invited him along on this cruise so I wouldn't stand out like a sore thumb, and he fell all over himself agreeing because he thought he'd get laid, probably for the first time." Van rolled his eyes and scoffed. "All the women he approaches see him as nothing more than a free drink. Catrina thought it too. I could see it in her eyes." He leaned in and kissed her neck – for the sole purpose of pissing Kensie off, she was sure.

Shadow Man interrupted, a hint of impatience coming through in his otherwise imperturbable voice. "I think that's about enough catching up. Now, you can see that your friend is fine, so let's make our exchange quickly and quietly and be done with all this nastiness." Kensie couldn't believe how his voice remained measured and polite, while she couldn't keep her hands from shaking. Either he had done things like this before, or he lacked a beating heart. While neither bode well for her safety, she felt there was something else, something that she was missing, something that remained just outside of her comprehension. She needed to play for time.

"I told you, I don't have it on me. Bringing it here alone would be kind of stupid of me, don't you think?"

"Yes, it would be" he agreed, "but I don't think you have any other options. You wouldn't dare hide it in your cabin after seeing what my associate –" he nodded in Van's direction "– did to it, and the only other person on this ship that you might trust with it is not in a position to carry much of anything."

Of course he was right. She started to think that her only hope of getting her and Catrina out of this situation unharmed rested entirely on the morality of these two men, but then inspiration struck Kensie. She liked her idea so much that she didn't have to fake the smile that suggested she could play her own devious little games. "True, but you forgot one person."

"Did I now?" His tone suggested he had forgotten nothing, which was distantly troubling. "Whom did I neglect to consider?"

*Perfect English.* Another clue that tickled her mind, but she pushed that aside to play her hand. "The captain of the boat I chartered, Burke. I trusted him to find it with me, so you'd think I could trust him to hold onto it."

"Ahh, yes. Captain Julian Burke." *Wait. How does he know his first name?* Panic spread through her like wildfire. "That would have been a wise choice and a fair consideration, but there is a small problem." Alarm bells went off in her head, but the man remained silent for a couple of beats, drawing out the tension until Kensie almost yelled at him.

"Captain Burke, would you mind joining us?"

A shock that felt like ice water flowed through Kensie as the rugged features of Julian Burke emerged from behind a large control panel.

***

Burke stood behind a panel of electrical breakers as the scene played out. He watched Van get his perverse jollies feeling up Catrina, and a part of him longed to leap on the asshole and beat the living shit out of him.

His stomach churned with the knowledge of what he had to do. Necessary, maybe, but it wasn't something he looked forward to. Hated was more like it. Were the next few minutes going to cost him something he hadn't known he'd needed until a couple of days ago? Was what he was about to do right?

*If you have to ask that question, maybe you shouldn't be doing it, dickhead.* He knew it was far too late for such philosophical concerns – both women were in real danger and he was their only chance, even if they didn't know it. No matter what it cost him.

He heard his introduction and, surprised at the Herculean effort required just to take the necessary steps forward, abandoned the comforting cloak of darkness and made himself visible.

The color ran out of Kensie's already pale face, giving her a spectral appearance in the dim light and making Burke wonder if she was going to pass out on the spot. He felt close to doing the same as he forced himself to face her directly, steeling himself for the rage, the vitriol, the pure hatred that would emanate from her.

But that did not happen. After a few seconds and a few blinks, her lively green eyes changed dramatically. All that made Kensie such a unique person – all the mirth, the intelligence, the mischief, the intensity, even the fear of the moment – drained away like someone had pulled the plug on the pool of emotions in her soul.

He'd seen that look before. As a teenager, he'd had to put his 14 year old Golden Retriever Misty to sleep. He'd sat next to him, petting his loyal friend and companion, and had seen the life leave his eyes and his body. Kensie's eyes died in almost exactly the same way, except that they did not close gently like Misty's. She continued to stare at him, and that look and the agony it represented reached into him far more acutely than any curses or threats ever could.

"Kensie..." he started, but the sentence died on his tongue. What could he possibly say that would make this all right? Words were not adequate to soothe the ache that her countenance suggested. Instead, he broke their shared gaze like a coward, knowing he would never reclaim the right to enjoy her achingly perfect face again.

***

For several seconds, Kensie's mind argued with her eyes. Sure, she saw Burke's handsome face, his slightly unkempt hair, and those broad shoulders, but all she could think was that this was somehow wrong, that there had to be an explanation. It couldn't be that Burke was standing in front of her, on the side of the dirtbags that had kidnapped her friend, threatening to take the *Couronne* from her.

But his face told a different story. Shame and regret clouded the expression that, only a few hours ago, had been joyful and relaxed in her presence. He had the look of a man who regretted what he was doing even as he did it. It was the look of a man who, having been betrayed once before, now knew the other side of the coin.

He'd used her. Burke had made her feel desired and beautiful, spoken to her with such heartfelt passion, touched her with a tenderness she'd never known, taken possession of everything she was – and it was all fake. All bullshit. It had been an act for his financial gain. She'd been had. Suddenly, nothing mattered to her; not the *Couronne*, not her dreams of the future, not even her own safety. Only the image of Catrina struggling in her peripheral vision kept her from just giving up.

Kensie wanted to hate him, but she couldn't muster the energy. She couldn't even make an angry face in his direction. He'd sucked every bit of energy from her, and she was forced to lean back against the dirty tank behind her to stay on her feet. She stared in disbelief.

Then he spoke – just a single word. "Kensie..." But nothing followed. Instead, he looked away, and she felt an acute pain in her chest.

Shadow Man's voice barely penetrated the despondent cloak that enveloped her. "Captain Burke was practical enough to accept my offer of a financial reward for his assistance in this matter. As I was saying, I've neglected nothing. Despite your infantile attempts at subterfuge, I'm sure a woman of your intelligence can see that you are limited to the one course of action I intended. So why don't we just make the exchange so we can put this unpleasantness behind us?"

With what felt like the last drop of energy she had, she lifted the side of her shirt and unzipped the satchel. She felt the heavy treasure wrapped in the soft rag and pulled it free, holding it out in Shadow Man's direction. She never took her eyes off Burke, even though he seemed more interested in her feet than her face.

"Please show it to me. That could be anything in there."

*Take it. Just fucking take it.* She pulled back the folds of fabric until the dim light revealed the silvery glint of metal and the kaleidoscope of jewels. She only saw it out of the corner of her eyes. If she was to be denied the *Couronne*, she didn't care to look directly at it ever again. Her pursuit of it had cost her far more than she'd ever wagered. It had killed her spirit, and now she considered it nothing but pure evil.

She heard the mystery man draw in a breath. "It is quite beautiful, Kensie. I can see why you've been obsessed with it for so many years."

Despite her mournful despair, the statement caught her attention. "How would you know anything about how long I've been interested in it?" she asked, turning her head toward him but keeping Burke fixed squarely in her gaze.

"I know a great many things, Miss Prescott, but they are of no importance. However, one thing I do know is that, unless you wish your friend to have an unfortunate accident right in front of you, you'll surrender the *Couronne* to Captain Burke right now."

"To him?" She couldn't bring herself to say his name, and was loathe to even have his hand touch hers.

"Yes. It's in my best interests to remain anonymous."

"Fine," she spat. It didn't matter anymore. He was already dead to her. Kensie held the treasure out in his direction. Burke would have to come within arms length of her, giving her an opportunity to... *what?* Kensie had no thoughts of attacking him, but she wanted him to see, up close, what he had done to her.

Burke took a slow step forward, as if she was a vicious dog and he was alerting her of his approach so as not to alarm her. Kensie just waited, making him traverse the distance to her, hoping every footfall felt to him like a death march. His body language showed defeat and self loathing, and that pleased her. She wanted him to suffer and wondered if that desire would ever fade.

He met her gaze once more when he got to her, and it was clear he wanted to speak to her. *To say what? To apologize? To explain? To beg forgiveness?* She didn't want to hear it – whatever it was, she no longer cared. Burke started to reach out to take the *Couronne*, but his hand shook as he hesitated.

*Fucking coward.* Kensie pushed it toward him, daring him to so he could see the barren emptiness of her soul. She knew damn well he could physically feel exactly what she was thinking.

"Today, Captain," Shadow Man said, a threatening edge to his voice.

With a jerky, awkward motion, he seized the *Couronne* and pulled it back to his body. Kensie discarded the rag, letting it flutter to the deck. Her hand was only a few pounds lighter, but it felt as desolate as her heart. She wondered if Burke's conscious would be able to withstand the crushing weight of what he had just taken from her. He stepped back to his original position.

Her silent stream of nothingness was interrupted by Shadow Man's voice. "Thank you for cooperating, Kensie. To do otherwise would have been a rather injudicious course of action."

With her focus entirely on Burke, the unique phrase caught her unawares. *An injudicious course...* She'd heard that exact phrase not too long ago, on the phone, in her office, talking to – *holy shit.*

"Dean Talbot?" She could not keep the incredulity out of her voice.

Shadow Man sighed, deep and heavy. "It is rather unfortunate that you made the connection." He stepped forward into the light, leaving no question as to his identity.

"What the hell are you doing here?" Kensie demanded.

"Come now, Miss Prescott. I have many negative traits, but stupidity is not one of them. I knew the second you told me you were going on this cruise what you were going to do. You are a fine scientist, but you are not good at prevarication. However, with your tenacity, intelligence, and voluminous knowledge of Buckwell and the *Couronne*, it occurred to me that you might very well recover it. So I thought I would keep an eye on your activities."

"'Keep an eye on my activities?!' You almost got me killed! I could have brought it right back to the school!"

"There was never any intention to kill you. That aspect of things got a bit out of hand. But, Miss Prescott, I just told you that you aren't a good liar. You were not under the auspices of the university, so you would have been free to do with this treasure as you wished, and I truly doubt you would have turned the *Couronne* over to the university out of an overwhelming sense of philanthropy."

"Then you should have funded me to come here and find it!"

"Perhaps. However, you, better than anyone, know exactly how much it's worth, and I've discovered a few individuals who also know that value. They are willing to pay me far more than I could earn in 100 lifetimes at a state university to own it."

It occurred to Kensie that she was far angrier at Talbot than at Burke, but the reason escaped her in favor of another thought. "What, you think I'll just forget this ever happened?!"

Talbot shook his head. "No, I don't. And that is why this is so unfortunate. I had hoped to leave you on the ship with nothing more than a bruised ego and a sense of loss. But now I am forced to make a most lamentable change of plans." He stepped toward her, fishing a length of rope from his pocket.

Kensie looked to her right. Van's expression suggested he was enjoying the unfolding scenario as he pressed the knife against the side of Catrina's throat hard enough to make the skin around it go white. The only other escape route was forward, but that meant running toward Burke, and even her survival instinct was not as strong as her desire to be nowhere near him, let alone hope for his protection. She would fight it out on her own before accepting any help from him.

"Before Van gets a bit carried away," Talbot said, "please turn around and cross your wrists behind you." Kensie didn't want to resist him with that knife right next to her friend's jugular vein, but if he tied her up as well, they were both as good as dead.

"Leave her alone," Burke grumbled.

"Captain," Talbot responded as he continued to advance, "please don't interfere."

"If you want this goddamned thing, they both walk away," he said in that low growl that had so impressed and aroused Kensie two days ago. Now, it made her skin crawl.

"Go to hell, Burke," Kensie told him. "I don't want your help."

Burke ignored her words, responding to Talbot. "I mean it. Back the fuck up or you'll never see this thing again, trust me."

"I doubt you are ready to watch Van cut lovely Catrina from ear to ear and know it was your fault, so I consider your threat rather empty." He reached Kensie and held the rope up. "And I'm sure the same goes for you, Miss Prescott, so if you'll kindly put your arms behind you, we can avoid any bloodshed."

Kensie tried to play for time. "What are you going to do with us?" she asked, knowing full well the true answer.

"Not that it matters, but I'm only securing some time for us to get away. You'll be released in a few days."

*Bullshit.* She brought her arms up to a defensive posture. "You can't lie either. Fuck off."

Talbot gritted his teeth. "We are NOT going to go through this false bravado. I'll give you one second to acquiesce or I'll let Van indulge his more barbarous side."

"Oh yeah," Van added with a twisted, gruesome smile that told Kensie he'd not hesitate. Catrina's eyes were as wide as dinner plates; she knew her life was in the balance. With no options, Kensie lowered her arms and turned to face away from Talbot. She closed her eyes at the first scratch of the rope against her wrists but opened them at the unmistakable sound of a pistol's action being racked. She snapped around to see Burke with a black gun in his hands, pointed directly at Talbot.

"I said let her go, you son of a bitch."

Talbot paused, but only for a second before he continued binding Kensie. "Impressive, Captain. They must not have used the metal detector at the gangway because of all the tools and machinery being brought on board. However, Van can slide that knife into Catrina far faster than you can aim and shoot, so I suggest you put it down." Van, for all his threatened cruelty, appeared a little frightened. He moved his knife hand away from Catrina's neck just a bit. Kensie felt Talbot's hands shake as he finished tying the knot.

"You'd think that," Burke said, "but you'd be wrong." With a movement almost too fast to track, he pivoted to his left and pulled the trigger in one quick motion.

The sound was amazingly loud in the small compartment but, before Kensie had time to even wince, she saw a tiny dark hole appear on Van's forehead just above his right eye. In the next instant, his body crumpled to the ground. Catrina staggered backward and fell to the deck.

Her ears ringing, Kensie tried to gather her senses, but before a single thought transited her brain, Talbot yanked her back against his body and wrapped his arm tightly around her neck. She felt him duck down behind her, and then she realized why. Burke stood in front of her, the gun pointed in their direction. "I warned you. Let her go. It's over."

Kensie felt him moving his other arm, putting his palm against the base of her skull just above her neck and applying pressure. She recognized it as a *Krav Maga* technique, one that would sever her cervical spine if enough force was applied.

"I don't think so, Captain. Unless you want to hear Kensie's neck snap, you'll put the gun and the *Couronne* down on the deck and leave the area immediately. I'm not as primal as Van, but I'll choose my life over Miss Prescott's every time." He increased the pressure until Kensie grunted. "I mean it – right now."

Kensie's mind raced. Out of the corner of her eye, she saw Catrina struggling to get to her knees without the use of her hands, but her movements appeared spastic. Burke kept the gun pointed at them, his face a fascinating mix of anger and fear. Kensie didn't know if he'd suddenly found his conscious, nor did she know if his actions had made things better or worse, but neither was important. She had to get herself out of this situation.

But how? With her hands tied, she couldn't elbow him in the ribs to break his grip, which was her first instinct. She tried to wriggle free, but he was far too strong to overpower.

"Let her go now!" Burke screamed frantically. Without no good options, he seemed to be losing his cool.

"No, you drop the gun. Right now, Burke!" Talbot ordered. "Her neck is about to give!" That was an exaggeration, but only until he pushed another fraction of an inch. Things popped and cracked in her spine, causing pain all along her back and tingling in her extremities. She began to panic at the possibility of having her life ended in such a vicious manner.

Acting on instinct, she put all of her weight on her left leg and picked the other one up off the floor. She raised her knee and struck back and up with every ounce of strength she could muster. Gaining power from the windup, her heel struck sharply between his legs.

She heard an "*oof!*" and was wrenched backward violently as Talbot maintained his hold while collapsing from her strike, releasing her only when he hit the deck. Kensie turned a clumsy somersault, ending up face down behind some sort of piping. Her neck ached from the hold, and for an instant she feared he had paralyzed her, but a quick movement of her legs proved that incorrect. "Shoot him!" she screamed, petrified that Talbot would get up and carry through with his task, but got no response from Burke, only the pounding of footsteps on metal.

She managed to get to her feet 'and stepped past Talbot, who was writhing on the floor, to take stock of the situation. Catrina was just now kneeling, giving her a fleeting but profound sense of relief. But no Burke. Nowhere. She stepped into the open, her head swiveling back and forth, but not only did she not see Burke, she didn't see the *Couronne*. He might have assuaged his guilt by saving her ass, but he'd taken off with the prize. *Son of a bitch.*

Four men burst into the room wearing bright yellow **Security** shirts. Two of them stopped at Catrina and started removing her restraints. "We heard a gunshot! Is everyone –" The last word died on his lips as he caught sight of Van's form lying on the floor. "Oh shit."

One of the men came over to her and started untying her wrists. "Are you injured, Miss?"

*What? Oh yeah.* "No, I'm fine. Arrest that guy! He kidnapped my friend!"

"What guy?"

"Him!" she shrieked, tilting her head toward Talbot.

The man made no move in that direction, instead continuing to work on her wrists. "There's no one there!"

Kensie twisted her body hard enough to wrench her hands away from the guard trying to untie them, only to find that Talbot wasn't where he'd been a few seconds ago. "Shit! He took off! Find him!"

"Wait a minute!" the man yelled. "Let me finish!" He grabbed at her wrists once more.

She was about to ask if they had seen Burke, but realized if he had the *Couronne*, she'd likely never see it again even if they did catch up with him. She had to find him herself. "Hurry the hell up!" she yelled, pulling at the ropes violently.

"I'm trying!" her liberator yelled in a shaky voice.

She saw Catrina spit a wad of cloth from her mouth. "Kens, you OK?"

"Yeah! You?"

"I might never stop shaking, but yeah. What the hell is going on?"

Kensie was finally able to pull her arms free of the coarse ropes. "I'll tell you later! Stay with these guys and tell Reid you're OK!"

She burst toward the door, easily avoiding the men who were not expecting the move. Racing out of the compartment, she lunged up the stairs as fast as her body would carry her. Shouts from the security guards faded below her as she tried to figure out where Burke would go.

He'd want to get off the ship, and there was only one safe way to do that – the gangway where the passengers normally boarded and disembarked during more normal times. It took her a second to orient herself, but when she burst from the door leading back to the regular passenger hallways, she knew to turn right.

Running at her top speed, it took her only a few seconds to approach the portal and see the door to the compartment swinging violently back and forth – like someone had just gone through it in a hurry. Over her heavy breathing she heard a commotion and shouting on the other side. When she burst through the door she had a fleeting glimpse of the back of a husky man with a red shirt and light brown hair turning onto and racing down the gangway at full speed. Burke. Two of the guards were on their backs, ostensibly having been knocked down by him during his escape.

She did not break stride, but the other two guards were still standing and appeared dead set on not letting anyone else abandon ship. While they may have had their hands full stopping Burke's bulk, the one nearest to Kensie had little trouble catching her lithe body and lifting her off her feet to keep her onboard.

"NO! No, goddammit, let me go!" She struggled violently, pounding on the back and shoulders of the guard, kicking at him violently. "He's getting away! Let me fucking go!" A savage elbow to the man's neck forced him to drop her, but even though she remained on her feet, the other guards had gotten up and were blocking the opening. Kensie wouldn't stand a chance of bursting through them.

"Son of a bitch!" Turning on her heel, she raced back out and toward the stern of the ship. She ignored the sounds of pursuit behind her and alternated between going up staircases and racing further aft, slowing as her body tired. She'd not run this fast nor this far since lettering in the 4 x 100 in high school, and it showed.

Finally, nearing the end of her endurance, she blasted through a door to find herself on deck at the very stern of the ship. In desperation, she went to the railing and leaned over to look down at the concrete pier. At the late hour and with the unscheduled stop, there was very little activity, so she scanned the area, looking for anything that moved very quickly. In a complete disregard for reality, she hoped against hope that she would spot Burke and... what? Call to him? She had no idea, but she still looked down. She wasn't *that* high up – maybe she could jump.

Not surprisingly, she saw nothing that resembled Burke racing around the island. The only activity was at the end of the gangway to which she'd just been denied access, and she realized it was the repair crew leaving the *Amore.* There were enough dim lights on that she could tell Burke was not among them.

After a few minutes of searching and trying to figure out what to do next, she jumped in surprise as the boat horn sounded. She didn't know what that meant but figured it was probably bad, and in a minute she realized just how correct she was. Although it was hard to tell at first in the darkness, the gap between the ship and the wharf was widening. They were getting underway, and that meant she wasn't getting off at all. There was no way she would be able to find him now.

She lowered her head to the railing, too drained to cry, but without the energy to move. Heavy footsteps of people who were probably searching for her rushed by on the decks above and below her. She sat there long enough for the ship to accelerate through the breakwater and turn north toward Puerto Rico.

A noise reached her ears. It was annoying but familiar, and it grew steadily louder until she recognized it as not just a boat engine, but the very distinct engine of *Julian's Empire II*. Kensie tracked the sound until she saw a small shape a little darker than the water with a line of white foam behind it heading out of the harbor and turning on a course that was the exact opposite direction of the *Amore of the Seas*. She watched the red, green, and white navigation lights of the little boat as it got smaller and smaller until they disappeared behind the island.

# Chapter 17 – Changing Priorities

**University of Delaware Lewes Campus Docks, onboard the *R/V Joanne Daiber*, mid-February**

Kensie's bulky coat got snagged on the door handle as she brought another heavy case of sensitive tracking equipment into the cabin of the research vessel *Joanne Daiber*. With a curse, she tugged her arm free and slid the blue plastic box containing scientific equipment under the bench that ran along the portside bulkhead.

It was cold, even for February and even for southern Delaware, with a brisk wind blowing from the northwest. Kensie embraced the discomfort. She should be in her office doing research or planning one of her lessons for her Spring classes, but ever since getting back from Puerto Rico and answering hundreds of questions from the ship's security and the police in San Juan, she had volunteered to do a lot of the grunt work that she usually foisted on her grad students. The physical effort was taxing, but sore muscles and an aching back were negligible compared to the soul crushing anguish that flooded her chest when she thought back on recent events. Plus, she had energy to burn. She'd spent the first two weeks back home moving very gingerly due to the neck brace she wore to recover from the badly sprained upper back that Dean Talbot's cruel hold had caused. She probably shouldn't have been in the office at all, but Kensie was not about to sit around and dwell on her troubles.

***

The questions, both on the ship and in Puerto Rico, had been endless. Although no one ever told her she was considered a suspect or threatened with any sort of charges, her obfuscation had frustrated the officers. She wasn't sure what had been going on or why Talbot had affected Catrina's abduction. His demands had been vague and confusing to Kensie, and she could only offer that maybe he'd thought Catrina to be someone else, someone of means, and planned to exploit his relationship with Kensie to take advantage of her. It had to be, she'd argued, because neither Kensie nor Catrina, nor their families, were in any position to pay even a modest ransom. A quick look into their finances had proven that.

Catrina professed no knowledge of anything beyond stepping into her cabin to find Van trashing her room, and for the most part she hadn't lied. Completely shocked, she'd frozen in place when he'd pulled a knife on her, tying her up and hustling her to the lower decks. Subsequent reviews of security cameras from that area showed them walking down a couple of passageways. Only by carefully scrutinizing the video could one see that the shorter of the two had her arms pulled tightly behind her back.

Of course, they had Van's body and the bullet that Burke had fired into it, but they didn't have a murder weapon, and ballistics tests on the bullet did not match any known guns. Catrina had also truthfully stated that his actions had been justifiable and necessary to save her life.

Still, the police wanted to know who had shot him. Kensie, who was the only person with any real information, had professed ignorance, claiming it was dark and she was far too worried about her friend to remember details about his appearance with any clarity. She gave up what she knew of Van, and in the investigation that followed, the police discovered that he was wanted for several rapes and even a couple of murders out in California. That fact certainly cooled the ardor of the police.

Reid and Catrina offered a few more tidbits about the situation, but Catrina had taken Kensie's request of willful ignorance from earlier that night seriously, and Reid indicated only that Kensie had stubbornly and stupidly handled things herself. They ended up giving very little of value to the police. Kensie was especially appreciative of Reid's responses; even though he hadn't been in his jurisdiction at the time, his actions as an off duty police officer were ethically shaky. Kensie had already thanked him profusely.

Of course, Talbot had disappeared. Kensie had been "asked" to stand at the top of the gangway and scour the crowd for Talbot when the *Amore* docked, no small order when 5,400 passengers and 1,900 crew were on board. It had taken almost five and a half hours, but Talbot had either snuck off, jumped off, or disguised himself, because she did not see him. She understood why more than a few people gave her looks of disdain for holding up their disembarkation.

The officials in Puerto Rico told Kensie that Talbot had sent an email resigning from the university before the ship departed and that his current whereabouts were unknown. Neither detail surprised her. Either he had the *Couronne* and was currently being fawned over by one of his rich contacts in remote parts of the world, or he didn't and was scrambling to survive. She sincerely hoped he hadn't gotten his hands on it, but there was very little that could be done about that now.

Stuck with vague answers and pressured by the cruise line to resolve the situation quickly and quietly, the police, having only dead ends and theories and the body of a scumbag, closed the case. Once she'd been officially cleared of any wrongdoing, Kensie had been eager to get home and begin putting this whole disaster behind her, but being back at school hadn't been much better.

Of course, word got out – not just at the university, but throughout the scientific community, so everyone walked on eggshells around her. One of the senior professors had taken over as interim dean and, now that Kensie could definitively prove where the *Aberaeron Fortune* had met its end, it would be much easier to convince the NAS to justify an expedition to recover the numerous artifacts. It felt like a victory to Kensie, but she had no interest in celebrating. She even declined to lead the expedition, citing stress and her injured neck. In truth, she wasn't ready to be anywhere near the site of such emotion and loss, and doubted she ever would be.

Alone with Catrina back in Kensie's apartment in the following days, she'd detailed the entire story, explaining what had gone down and, to the best of her knowledge, why. To her unfathomable relief, Catrina held no ill will toward her friend for anything despite the danger, and in fact empathized with her loss – more accurately, with her losses.

"I can't believe he took it and ran," Catrina commented upon finally hearing the full story. "That unimaginable bastard." Kensie nodded in agreement. Her chest and throat were so choked with emotion after relaying the story that she could barely breathe, let alone speak. Tears that she had not been able to produce during the remainder of the cruise nor the days in Puerto Rico were finally, mercifully beginning to flow. "I know how much it meant to you. And it's pretty clear how much he meant to you."

Kensie took a deep breath. As much as Catrina understood, she didn't. "Yeah, but no," she said, her voice thick and gravelly. Catrina handed her a tissue and poured another glass of wine for them both. Kensie had pain meds, but this night alcohol was her medication of choice. "I know you're used to being desired and fawned over. I'm not, but that's how I felt, how he made me feel. It was so nice to believe that a guy looking so good could... want me that way." She let out a shuttering sigh. "I can't believe it. I'm such an idiot."

"No," Catrina said. "You're not an idiot for being human and wanting love. He's the asshole."

"The funny part is that I can't get angry. It's just too hard, too much effort." Kensie took a sip of wine and shook her head. "That, and... well..."

Catrina tilted her head at her friend. "And what?"

Kensie debated the wisdom of vocalizing the thought, but realized she couldn't be any more embarrassed by the situation than she already was, and if she couldn't tell Catrina, who could she tell? "It's just that, no matter how I think about it, I really believe that Burke didn't screw me over. There's something going on that will explain it all, something I don't know, but there is no way he wanted to hurt me."

"Kensie..."

"I know, I know. You told me then and you're telling me now."

"I don't mean it that way. But the longer you keep trying to turn this into something it's not, the longer you're gonna be miserable."

"Yeah, I hear you." A sip of wine. "But have you ever been totally certain of something that you have no business being certain about? I know, that makes no sense coming from Miss Rational, but now it does to me. I just don't think he could fake that. I don't think anyone could fake what we shared." She winced as pain from her neck shot up and down her back. "No, you know what? I'm *sure* he didn't fake it. I'm *absolutely certain*. I looked into his eyes down in that ship, and he *hated* what he was doing. I don't know why, but until he stands in front of me and tells me that what we shared wasn't real, that he did what he did for greed and I was too stupid to see it, I know I'm right. Period."

Kensie saw Catrina staring, her brow furrowed in what looked like concern and confusion. She waited for the lecture, the one about facing reality, about not believing what you wanted over what was true. The funny part was that Kensie was usually the one giving such advice, with Catrina fighting her every step of the way.

Finally, Catrina broke the silence. "Well, then, I believe you."

"You do?" Despite her unwavering certainty, she hadn't expected anyone to buy into her insane delusion.

"Yes," Catrina answered firmly. "Every time you've set your mind to something and made those kinds of statements, you've always been proven right eventually. You swore you would get into the doctorate program at Princeton even when no one thought you could do it. You got into an exceptional oceanographic school when everyone said you didn't have a chance because there were more qualified applicants. You told everyone where to find this *Couronne* thing, and even after the best minds in marine archeology told you that you were crazy, you found a way to pull it from the muck right at the 'X' that marked the spot.

"I don't know if I ever said this, but I'm in awe of how you do that. You've talked about how amazed and impressed you are that I'm always chased by guys, but that doesn't really mean so much when you think about it. I'd give that up in a second to have your drive and your smarts. I know this sucks and it feels like you just had the rug pulled out from under you, but you're going to get past this and go on to do amazing, world-changing things. And you know it as well as I do."

Kensie blinked hard at that. Catrina had never done anything to disparage Kensie's academic pursuits and had never denigrated her successes, but it amazed her to think that their admiration was mutual.

"Thanks for that, Catrina. It does feel good to hear it, especially from you."

"It's overdue, and I'm sorry I never said it, but it's the absolute truth. So, if you say that he'll come back to you, that he really didn't fuck you over and that he feels the same way about you that you feel about him, then that's the way it's going to happen. Guaranteed."

***

There was little activity on the wooden dock on the cold and gloomy day, nor did she expect any. The loading of provisions on the *Daiber*, the real heavy lifting with which she was ill equipped to assist, would be done tomorrow in preparation for departure to somewhere off the coast of Georgia. That's when the chaos of loading and reviewing manifests would happen, with the crew and her colleagues hauling their personal gear on board and boyfriends or girlfriends seeing their significant others off. She wanted no part of that and planned to lock herself in her office tomorrow.

She was going to stop by Catrina's on the way home tonight with some take out. Despite her usual confidence and refusal to be treated like a victim, Kensie's friend had started having bad nightmares about her abduction a little over two weeks ago, and they had morphed into an extreme fear of being by herself anywhere in public. It got worse by the day until Catrina flatly refused to leave her house for any reason.

Kensie had collaborated with Reid to come up with a plan to get her help and, much to their amazement, Catrina had acquiesced. She was not a person that would normally tolerate being handled, but Reid seemed to have a way with her, using a combination of guile, orders, and humor to get her to talk to a psychiatrist to deal with what everyone could see was PTSD. After just a few days she was already doing much better, and Kensie took solace that her burgeoning relationship with Reid seemed to be aiding her recovery. It was one good thing about that cruise. She and Reid had agreed upon a schedule, and tonight it was her turn to visit. She would be done here in about an hour. *Maybe Chinese food tonight?*

"Hello!"

The shout from the dock startled her as she organized the equipment in the cabin. Rising quickly, she saw someone she could not identify standing near the stern of the ship, hopping up and down in what appeared to be an attempt to keep warm. He wore a red coat that looked like an arctic snow parka and had the fur lined hood pulled up around his face, reminding her of Kenny McCormick from *South Park*. The irrelevant digression pulled a tiny smile from her face, which was rare enough anymore that she took notice before stepping out on the exposed deck.

"Can I help you?"

The person turned toward her, but she could see very little detail through the hood. He made no effort to show his face, instead standing completely still as if he'd turned to stone. Kensie narrowed her eyes and felt her shoulders tense up; was she in danger? This was not Talbot – this person was too tall and too broad of shoulder – but was this someone he hired to exact revenge? That didn't make any sense, but recent events had taught her caution and a healthy fear of the unknown. Even though it would be stupid for someone to attack her here, she now knew from experience that people didn't always make the best decisions – herself included.

These thoughts flickered around while the standoff continued. After a few seconds that felt like a few years, her well insulated adversary grasped the flaps of the hood and pulled it away. Kensie first noticed a hint of light brown hair peeking from under the *faux* fur before he yanked it all the way off, revealing Julian Burke.

Kensie stared and blinked, unsure of how to react or even how she felt. A thousand questions and scenarios bombarded her from all sides:

> *What does he want?*
> *How did he get here?*
> *Is he here to apologize?*
> *Is he here to kill me?*
> *Is this some sort of trick?*
> *What the fuck do I do?*

Finally, through all the noise and calamity banging around her skull, one emotion exerted control over everything; anger. For the first time since he'd stepped forward in the dingy belly of the cruise ship, rage and fury replaced sadness and emptiness. She felt her face twisting with weeks of pent up animosity, and the subtle change in Burke's expression told her how very ugly she must have appeared. He actually feared her.

*God damn right you should fear me.*

Despite his obvious dread, he did not look away. "Hi, Kensie."

Kensie continued to glare. She wasn't sure what might come out of her mouth, so she didn't bother to try to speak.

"OK, no surprise there," he replied.

"What the hell could you possibly want?" she finally asked. She pronounced *you* so viciously that it sounded like poison to her ear.

Burke took a deep breath. "A couple of things. First of all, I'm glad you and Catrina are OK."

"No thanks to you!" she snapped. "You fucking shot a bullet six inches from her head! She's having a hard time dealing with that in case you're worried!"

Burke took the rebuke stoically, as if he expected it. "I'm not surprised, but I'm sorry to hear that. I wouldn't have taken that shot if I wasn't sure I could make it. I don't know if you saw what I saw, but that guy was aching to kill her, and I know he would have. He was a psycho."

Kensie softened her disposition just a bit. "Yeah, I know. They found out he was wanted for a lot of really bad sex crimes and murders in California."

Burke nodded as if happy to receive confirmation of his diagnosis. "I hope she has some good doctors."

"She does." She offered nothing further. His concern was nice, but it got her no closer to discovering why he was here.

"Good." In the extended silence that followed his answer, he looked down at the dock and then up at the leaden clouds, then toward Roosevelt Inlet where it opened up to the bay. Everywhere but at her.

"That's it?" Kensie demanded. "You came a couple thousand miles to ask me how Catrina was?"

"No, there's more. Sorry, this isn't easy for me." He scratched the back of his head and bit his upper lip. Kensie had never seen him so nervous, but she could not find any empathy for him. If he was here to apologize as a means of gaining absolution, he was going to be disappointed.

"It's not exactly easy for me either, but you better get to the point fast or you can take a long walk that way," she said acidly, pointing to the end of the dock that ended in the canal.

He nodded. "OK, here's the thing. I know what you must think of me, and –"

"You do, huh?" Kensie was yelling now, and she didn't care who might hear her. "You don't really want to know exactly what I think about you, what I've been thinking about doing to you for seven weeks. You fucked me over two different ways, and I can't even decide which one hurts more!"

Burke accepted the rebuke without flinching. "Maybe I don't know. But I probably have a good idea. Will you hear me out?"

Kensie rolled her eyes and threw her hands in the air. "Oh sure. Go ahead. This oughta be a good one."

"I did what I did because I knew that you were in danger from people that were on the ship. You know that now, of course. I was following the ship to surprise you in Puerto Rico, and they called me on my satellite phone just before they killed the power on the ship. They were close to you and I wasn't, and that petrified me."

"Wait," she interrupted. "You were going to follow me all the way to Puerto Rico in *Empire*? Why?"

The vaguest hint of a smile flashed across his face. "Well, that was the plan. I told myself it was because I wanted to protect you, but honestly it was because I just couldn't wait to see you again. Letting you get on that ship without me was the hardest thing I've ever done."

"I'd love to believe that, but I can't. It's just too perfect of a story. You used me, Burke! You saw an opportunity and you took it, and you didn't care how badly it would hurt me!"

He shook his head adamantly. "I *never* used you. The only way I could have a chance of helping you was to get on that ship, and the only way to do that was to go along with Talbot's idea. So, yeah, I saw an opportunity, but it was to help, not use you or hurt you."

That made sense. Neither of them had even given a thought that the danger lay on the ship rather than the island, but that was how it worked out. *Don't believe him, Kensie. He played you once – don't let him do it again.*

"Help me? Right. Where'd you get the gun? You expect me to believe you just 'happened' to find a handgun before you got on board at a moment's notice?"

"No. I figured there might be way more trouble than I was expecting, so I made a quick stop and got it from Navia."

Kensie let out a little *harrumph*. "That I believe. She seems like the kind of person who can get whatever you need."

"Like you don't know."

She was silent for a second, her mind a jumble of anger, hope, desire, and weakness. She couldn't let go of how much she hated him, but neither could she let go of how... completely wonderful he'd made her feel. *Is this just another line of bullshit? Can I possibly trust him?* She probed further.

"So what was the little 'financial reward' that Talbot mentioned?"

"Yeah, he offered me a nice piece of change to help him get the *Couronne*."

"I'll bet he did. And you took it."

"Well, I said I would."

"What a shocker." *See? It's about the money, not you.*

Burke rolled his eyes. "Come on! You think I could've said, 'No thanks, I'll betray this person just for the fun of it?' Think it through. I had to accept his offer."

"How convenient. You had to say OK, so of course you took the money," she said, dousing the tiny ember of optimism she harbored with a bucket of water far colder than any in the frigid bay.

"No." Burke shook his head like he was making his point to a person who'd never heard a word of English. "I didn't take one nickel from that son of a bitch."

*That* threw Kensie for a loop. She'd just assumed that Burke had taken whatever payout Talbot had offered and was now standing in front of her to try and justify it. But hearing him deny it so forcefully, like he was stating a physical law, caused a crack in the wall that she'd built around her feelings for this man. With emotion making her voice break, she asked the most important question of her life.

"Really?"

"Really. No amount of money is worth betraying you."

*Oh my god. Is he actually saying this?* Bewildered didn't begin to describe her mental state. She felt like she couldn't trust anything or anyone – even herself – right now, and being lost in a sea of turbulent and contrasting ideas scared her as much as she'd ever been. She didn't know what to think.

"Kensie, I get that you're epically pissed at me right now. If things were reversed, I'd feel the same way. I can swear up and down that I was doing what I thought was best for you – for us – until next week's Sunday brunch, but it's not what matters."

"What does matter?"

Burke's face took on the appearance of a man jumping out of a plane without a parachute. "What matters is what you truly believe about me. I can use every fancy word in the dictionary, vow that I'm telling the truth, have it written in the sky, but that won't ever change what you really feel." His eyes bored in on hers, and she felt the fervor behind his words. "If you really hate me and can't trust me anymore, then I'll leave and never come back.

"But I know what we shared, and I've never felt anything like it. Nothing even comes close. We made one of those connections that you dream of, that people way more eloquent than me write poems about. You turned my world upside down in three short days. I'd give anything, risk anything, lose everything in a second to be back with you and feel what I felt then."

He took a deep breath, and from five feet away she heard how it quavered. "So, Miss Kensington Prescott, with that brilliant mind, those entrancing eyes, that angelic smile, and that unquenchable spirit, I'm standing in front of you with nothing to hide and everything to gain, but also everything to lose, telling you that I love you, every part of you, and that will never change no matter what you think of me. I'm completely yours if you'll still have me."

Kensie stared at him, her lower lip trembling, her skin tingling. Her head was spinning and her chest hurt with the pounding of her heart. She was too overwhelmed to even get angry at him for using her full name. Suddenly her vision became blurry, and she tried to refocus only to realize that the problem was the tears that filled her eyes.

*You hate him so much because you love him so much. It hurt that much more.* She couldn't fully comprehend her emotions right now, but they ran through her so deeply and powerfully that she trusted them implicitly, and right now they ordered her to believe every word he spoke. There came a time to stop thinking and start believing, and that time was now. What had she said to Catrina back on the ship? She was willing to play the fool for love?

*Well, call me a fool.*

"Burke, dammit, if you're screwing with me right now... " she managed to squeak out between the sobs that started racking her body.

He sucked in air like he'd been holding his breath for an hour. "No, never. I meant every word. Can I come on board without you killing me now?" His awkward smile nearly broke her heart with its sincerity and longing.

"Yes, you jerk! Permission granted!" Burke fairly leaped over the gunwale and in a second they were holding each other with a force driven solely by passion, sharing a kiss that was all the sweeter for the time that had passed since the last one. She couldn't stop laughing and crying while she kissed him, but he seemed not to care. "I love you so much," she exclaimed over and over, breaking their lip lock for just a second to profess her affection before going in for another bite. She hated the bulky coats that kept her from melting into his skin, but Burke's magnificent taste, the way his perpetually unshaven jaw scraped her cheeks, and his powerful grip were enough to satiate her.

For now, anyway.

Kensie felt like she was drunk on the rum she'd consumed on vacation. It was 25 degrees out, but she basked in the heat generated by their embrace, reminding her of the tropical clime under which their relationship had begun.

She pulled back, drinking in his face while she ran her hand through his hair, hoping to hell that she was awake and this was really happening. For his part, Burke looked similarly unsure of the situation, so for a moment they just lounged in the sensation of being with each other.

Finally, convinced of her corporealness, he broke the silence. "I thought I'd lose you, that you wouldn't believe me," he said.

"Something kept telling me that you were the man I thought you were. Our time together was... well, I couldn't force myself to believe that we wouldn't be together."

"Every day that I couldn't get to you killed me," he agreed. "It was worse because I was pretty sure of what you were thinking of me."

That raised a question. "So why did it take you so long to get in touch with me?"

"I kinda had to disappear for a while, especially after the *Empire* sunk in Guadeloupe."

Kensie's eyes widened. "What happened?!"

Burke shook his head. "Not sure. I was heading out in the morning and all the sudden my bilge alarm went off. I looked below and there was a foot of water in the V-berth, and my pumps got overwhelmed. I put out a distress call and tried to gather my stuff, but she was taking too much water, so when a local fishing charter boat came over, I had to get on board with what was in my bare hands. She sunk in like 300 feet of water."

"Did someone sabotage the boat?"

He shrugged. "Not sure, but maybe. She was too solid to go down so fast otherwise."

"You lost everything?"

"Just about," he said, his face dropping. "I liked that boat. She wasn't the sexiest thing and she wasn't the fastest, but she was a good craft. I'll miss her." Kensie kind of understood – the captains she worked with doing her research cursed their boats and railed about their flaws, but every one of them doted on their ship like it was their own child.

Burke shook off the melancholy. "So I hope you understand that it took me a little while to island hop to Florida and then get here with only the few bucks in my pocket."

"I'm so sorry." Kensie felt horrible; even though she'd had no way of knowing, she'd been sitting up here wallowing in self pity and thoughts of revenge while her man was struggling to get to her, probably freezing, maybe hungry.

"Eh – it worked out in the end," he said with a very casual shrug.

"But it's like you're starting over from scratch! How is that OK?"

"Been there, done that. But, on that topic, I have a question for you." He was trying to suppress a smile and doing a lousy job of it, which was so out of place with the topic of conversation that she wondered if he had taken leave of his senses. "Why didn't you ask what happened to the *Couronne*?"

Kensie paused, wondering why it hadn't occurred to her to ask. Listening to him, all thoughts of the treasure that she had lusted after for more than half her life disappeared under the far weightier worry of what he had come to tell her. People, not artifacts, mattered more. She'd had to have her safety put in jeopardy and think she'd lost the love of her life to learn that, and it was a lesson she wasn't about to forget.

"The *Couronne* was a thing. A very important thing, but only a thing. You are someone that I hope and plan to enjoy for some time to come," she arched her eyebrows, "in many different ways."

"Still, I could understand if you blamed me for costing you your holy grail."

"You also made it possible for me to find it, so there was that. Maybe I don't have it now, but I had it for a while, and Shakespeare tells us that's good. I was angry because I thought you took it for selfish reasons. I didn't really understand the situation. I know better now. But it's gone and I have to let it go."

"Really?" Burke asked, his eyebrows raised in surprise. "Goal obsessed Kensie is willing to just give up on such a big deal?"

"No, not really," she admitted. "But I have no way of knowing where Talbot took it. It's one thing to track down a lead – it's quite another to just go off half cocked."

"Wow. I have to say I'm surprised – and a little flattered."

"I understand surprised, but flattered?"

His smile became more serious. "Yeah. While I was trying to see where we stood, you never once asked about the *Couronne*. You put me above it, considered me more important."

Kensie cocked an eyebrow. "That's a bit arrogant of you, considering yourself the most important part of this thing." She was grinning when she said it.

Burke shook his head, enjoying whatever game he was playing. "I'm not the most important thing. We are. And I appreciate you holding us in such high regard."

"You're welcome. There will be other treasures and other goals, but I'm guessing there's only one of you." She slid her hand over his cheek. "And you have been quite a find."

"Thank you. Still, knowing that you prioritized our relationship tells me a lot about you, and us." He shifted in her arms. "It makes me a lot more comfortable with this next part. Can I tell you a secret?"

Kensie narrowed her eyes at him. "I... guess so."

"You 'guess so'? It's a big secret – you should be a little more enthused."

She sighed. "Fine. I can't wait to hear it."

"So, like I said, pretty much every single thing I owned went down on *Empire*. But I did keep a few very precious items on my person, and they abandoned ship with me."

"Yeah, OK. So?"

Burke looked over at the dock and the other two boats moored to it, prompting Kensie to do the same. She didn't see a soul. "Is there a security camera or anything like that in the cabin?"

"Not in the cabin, no. Why?"

"Let's go in there." Without waiting for an answer, Burke turned her body and guided her through the doorway, pulling it shut behind him before getting down on one knee. She nearly panicked until he motioned to her to do the same. *He's not proposing, he's ducking down.* Relieved, she followed his lead.

"Burke, who are we hiding from? What's the big secret?"

He unzipped his jacket and held it open. "Check the right pocket."

"Check it for what?"

He just stared at her.

"All right, I'll check." Reaching for the zipper, she noticed that the pocket sagged dramatically, as if it had something heavy in it. Now more curious than confused, she reached in. She felt cool metal, but it wasn't solid. It was... mesh. It came to her in a blinding flash.

Kensie's hand froze in place. She looked up at Burke to see a very self satisfied smirk on that roguishly handsome face. *This makes no sense!* "But... but you gave it to Talbot!"

"I never said that. You assumed it."

"So you didn't give it to him?"

He turned his palms up and shrugged his shoulders. "If you reach a little further, you'll know the answer to that question."

Kensie hesitated. For some reason, she was convinced that he was kidding or mistaken, that her fingers were touching anything else. Taking a deep breath to insulate herself from the raw emotions that were about to assault her no matter what she discovered, she emptied Burke's pocket and was impossibly, ridiculously, truthfully staring at and holding the *Couronne Ornèe de Joyaux des Anges* in her hands once again.

Somehow, rediscovering the treasure was even more emotionally draining than finding it the first time. Perhaps, knowing the exultation of finding it once as well as the wretched despair of losing it, she more fully understood what it meant to get it back. Perhaps it was because she had the same exact feelings about the man right in front of her.

Burke's sheepish grin shone to her just like the sapphires, emeralds, rubies, and diamonds that sparkled in the cabin, as they both took the dim, depressing light of the day and transmogrified it into the glorious dawn of a new era for her. *No, for us.*

"You saved it," she whispered reverently. "You really saved it."

"Of course I did. You found it, so I made sure I saved it for you." He sounded like he was explaining obvious concepts to an especially backward toddler.

"Yeah, but... You could have done anything with it. You could have claimed the salvage yourself."

Burke shook his head. "Kensie, I already told you I'd never betray you, not for any amount of money. This thing is only important to me because it's important to you. I'd do anything for you, and I honestly don't care about money or even if anyone knows if I was involved in finding it. You never lost this – you just didn't realize you had it the whole time, that's all."

She shook her head to clear the latest tidal wave of emotion that had inundated her. "Wow. You're something else." *Wasn't that the understatement of the year?* "I might have to take back some of the bad things I said about you."

"Hey, don't go out of your way or anything."

"This," she held up the *Couronne*, "is our prize, yours and mine. We share it – all of it. I'd never have found it without you, and that's the truth."

"I'm glad to hear that," Burke told her. "I do need a new boat. I have to do something up here in the cold."

"I'm sure we can figure that out right after we call the British embassy and book a flight to England," Kensie said. She giggled as the trip she'd dreamed of for years loomed as not only possible, but almost a certainty.

"Excellent, but there's one thing we need to do first."

"As unromantic as it sounds, we need to get a safety deposit box in a very secure bank. You think you can get the rest of the day off?"

"Oh, I guarantee it – especially now."

"Great. Let's go." Taking the *Couronne* back from her, Burke returned it to the same inside pocket. He zipped his coat and they rose to exit the *Joanne Daiber*.

"Oh, one more thing," Kensie said.

"What's that?"

She punched him playfully right in the middle of his chest, being careful to aim above the pocket in question. "No one gets to use my real first name, not even you, and not even when you're telling me you love me." She was serious, but not exactly angry. "Next time you call me 'Kensington' you better not be within an arm's length of me if you know what's good for you."

"That's a problem. I was going to name my next boat *Kensington's Empire*."

"You were?" The quaint gesture had a pronounced impact on her. *I'm going to have a boat named after me?*

"Absolutely. I don't ever want to be too far from you, and if I name the boat after you, I'll never have to be. But I can't do it if you, as the namesake, don't consent to it."

Kensie thought for a second. "That's not a rule!" she protested.

He looked up in feigned frustration. "You aren't making this any easier."

Kensie just laughed. She'd not had much time to explore his humorous side, but it seemed just as attractive as the tough side. There was a lot more to learn about this handsome captain, and she couldn't wait to get started.

"OK, then. *Kensington's Empire* it is." She ran it through her mind a few times. "I kind of like that name."

THE END

# Epilogue

*Arnhim's* **Pub, St. Vincent Island, early April**

Navia ran a damp cloth over the bar. It was still a little sticky from her patrons spilling sweet rum on it the previous evening, enough so that she could still see the rings from the glasses that had been stuck to it. Last night had been one of those nights, where the full moon and the trade winds and the ghost of St. Vincent himself had conspired to add another level of enthusiasm to the evening's merriment. It hadn't happened in a while, but she was used to it and decided the benefit of the extra cash in the register compensated for the mess and additional work. She considered getting a more potent cleaning agent, but decided it just needed a little elbow grease, so she dipped the rag in the pail of water once more and set to pushing it down harder.

It was still about an hour before she opened for the lunch crowd, so she was a little surprised to hear the chime on the front door as someone entered. Deliveries usually came in through the back, but maybe this person was new; Navia would have to tell him how to get to the loading doors and that she would meet him there.

She realized her little script was ill prepared for the situation as three men appeared, each wearing a black baseball cap and a yellow polo shirt with a company label on the breast pocket. The man in the middle carried a leather duffel bag and, while he was solidly built, the two men that flanked him had arms as thick as legs. All three had holstered handguns on their hips. They looked fairly non threatening, but Navia stepped to the left and slid her right hand down so it was nearer the .357 revolver that she kept behind the bar at all times.

"Can I help ya' boys?"

"Are you Navia Chatoyer?" the man on the left asked, horrendously butchering the pronunciation of Navia's last name.

"Who be askin' now?"

"Ma'am, we are from ValPro Secure Couriers. We have a delivery for Miss Navia Chatoyer, with instructions to deliver it to her in person only after she provides identification and signs for it." He raised the duffel bag to indicate that it was the delivery.

"Well, OK den. Ya 'scuse me one second." Navia went back to her office, where she retrieved her St. Vincentian driver's license and handed it to him. He gave it more than a cursory glance, looking at it and then at her several times before nodding. He did not return the license.

"Thank you, Miss Chatoyer. Please sign where I've marked."

Navia took the proffered pen and clipboard and signed on the appropriate line. "Wha' I be gettin'?"

The man ignored her inquiry, taking the pad back and comparing her fresh signature with the one on the license. When he was satisfied that they matched, he handed it back to her, and only then did the man holding the bag respond. "We have no idea, Miss Chatoyer. Our instructions are to give you this duffel bag," which he set on the bar, "and this envelope," which he pulled from his pocket. It was about four by five inches and had a wax seal on the flap, ensuring that it had not been opened.

Navia took the envelope and the duffel bag, and only then did she notice that there was a combination lock keeping it closed. "How ya be 'spectin' me to open da lock? Wit ma' teeth?"

"Ma'am, that was not part of our instructions. We've completed the delivery as ordered and provided all the information we were instructed to give, so you have a good day."

By this point Navia was very confused, but these men obviously would be of no additional help. "Then ya gents be havin' the finest o' days as well."

"Thank you." Like soldiers marching in formation, they pivoted on their heels as one and left, leaving Navia holding the envelope and looking at the duffel bag. She wasn't about to get anywhere with the locked bag, so she used a knife to slit open the seal of the envelope and pull out a letter. She recognized the handwriting before she read the first word.

*Navia,*

*I can't tell you how much your friendship and support have meant to me over the last eight years. You've been my confidant, my shoulder to cry on, my bartender (which you know means a lot to me!), my doctor, and my partner in crime. You were a source of comfort when I was sure that I didn't offer any worth to anyone, and I can never quite put how much I value that into words.*

*The trouble that I talked about the last time we were together worked out very well. Possibly even better than I could have expected. A certain 'young lady' that you are quite fond of seems to agree with me, although she remains insistent that you secretly planned to kill her with some grain alcohol one night. And, whether you realize it or not, your help that night was key to how the whole situation came together.*

*I won't be around for a while – there's a lot going on – but I promise I'll visit sometime in the future. In the meantime, here's a small down payment on my bar tab.*

*With all my gratitude and all my love,*

*Your broken down friend.*

It wasn't signed, but Burke's words made her smile. Always a solid judge of character, she'd seen the goodness in Burke even through the dejection that he thought he was hiding from everyone else. She knew just how to handle him, and she also knew that he appreciated her hands off, no pressure approach, even though he would never expose his heart and say it in such direct terms.

At the bottom of the note was a series of four numbers arranged in a square. It wasn't hard to figure out that these were the digits to the combination for the lock on the duffel bag, but it did not indicate the order. She'd have to enter them randomly and hope that one would work.

She started flipping the dials on the lock, and her fifth combination did the trick. She pulled the lock from the case and opened it, peering inside, and the warm grin that came from Burke's note fell away as her jaw nearly landed on the bar. Inside the case were bundles of $100 bills. Not one or two, but dozens. Maybe a hundred. Maybe more. She was far too stunned to do the math, but it had to be well over a million dollars.

"Dat crafty son of a bitch," she said to herself. Things must have worked out "very well" indeed. She put the duffel bag down behind the bar – being sure to close it first – and took a moment to imagine Burke with enough money that he could afford to send her such an enormous chunk. He'd have a couple of boats – one sailboat and one motor yacht – and she could see him on the bridge of one of them, bare chested in the breeze, enjoying the sea air as it flowed through his sandy colored hair. He'd have one hand on the wheel and one hand around Kensie.

Strong, smart, determined Kensie. Navia had realized her strength even before Burke had, and she had been proven correct yet again. She'd made everything right in his world, and suspected that he had done the same for her.

There was only one way to properly salute her absent friend and send him on his way into the next stage of his life. She reached behind the bar and pulled out a box that was coated with dust. It contained an ornate bottle that was still mostly full of a 30 year old *Havana Club Maximo Extra Anejo*, one of the most delicious and valuable rums available, and one for which she charged $125 – per shot. Early on in their relationship, she'd allowed Burke to sample some under the condition that he'd pay her for the drink when he got back on his feet. That had been over six years ago.

She filled two shot glasses with the amber liquor, leaving the bottle out on the bar. "Good on ya, Burke," she said, knowing that her friend could hear her somehow. She raised both drinks, downing the one closest to her first, allowing the rich flavors of caramel, coconut, vanilla, and a hint of oak to majestically dance across her tongue. Then she repeated the procedure with "Burke's" drink, placing both glasses upside down on the bar.

"Paid in full, mah friend. Paid in full."

www.ingramcontent.com/pod-product-compliance
Lightning Source LLC
Chambersburg PA
CBHW071303140726
47996CB00005B/1606